Heartbreak U:

Summer Vacation

Heartbreak U:

Summer Vacation

Johnni Sherri

www.urbanbooks.net

Urban Books, LLC
300 Farmingdale Road, N.Y.-Route 109
Farmingdale, NY 11735

Heartbreak U: Summer Vacation
Copyright © 2024 Johnni Sherri

ISBN 13: 978-1-64556-632-8

First Trade Paperback Printing October 2024
Printed in the United States of America

10 9 8 7 6 5 4 3 2 1

This is a work of fiction. Any references or similarities to actual events, real people, living or dead, or to real locales are intended to give the novel a sense of reality. Any similarity in other names, characters, places, and incidents is entirely coincidental.

Distributed by Kensington Publishing Corp.
Submit Orders to:
Customer Service
400 Hahn Road
Westminster, MD 21157-4627
Phone: 1-800-733-3000
Fax: 1-800-659-2436

Where things left off...

Paris

Four days had passed since we left Cancún and were back in Greensboro. After dropping Franki off at the dorms, Malachi and I headed across town to his place. I didn't have class the next day and was desperate to spend more time tucked underneath him. However, we weren't even there for a good hour before Reese showed up with the kids. Thankfully, she didn't come in. She just dropped them off at the door. After eating dinner and getting the kids down for bed, Malachi and I made love in the shower. Ever since that first night we had sex in Cancún, only so many minutes could pass by before I yearned for his touch.

It was now morning, and we were driving his children to day care. It was the first time I'd ever been on the other side of town. We cut through a fancy neighborhood with homes almost as large as the one I grew up in. When we pulled up, I noticed that the day care was fancy too. It was a newly built, all-pink brick building with a freshly sodded lawn. It even had what appeared to be a state-of-the-art playground on the side—New Primrose Private Academy.

Malachi parked the car and killed the engine. "I'll be right back," he said.

With a closed-lip smile, I nodded before glancing in the backseat.

"You guys have a good day at school, okay?" I told Maevyn and Mekhai.

"Bye, Miss Paris. I'ma miss you," Maevyn said with a smile.

An instant warmth spread throughout my chest as I watched her unlatch her own seat belt. "I'm gonna miss you too, ladybug," I said, giving her the first nickname that came to mind.

Mekhai was two years older than his sister but wasn't much of a talker. I simply kept waving at him until he finally gave in and wiggled his fingers back. When Malachi opened the back door to get them out, I gave him a quick wink. He threw one right back at me before scooping Mekhai up in his arms. Although I'd never pictured this for myself, especially not my college life, watching the three of them walk away, hand in hand, made me love him more. That thug of a man, my man, was truly a good father—something I'd never expected.

Five minutes later, Malachi exited the building and hopped into the car. He reached over the center console and grabbed my hand, bringing it to his lips for a kiss—something he did often. "IHOP or Cracker Barrel?" he asked.

"Definitely IHOP," I said.

He pulled off, driving back through the impressive neighborhood when suddenly, a police siren sounded in our rear. I looked through the passenger-side mirror and saw flashing lights.

"Fuck," Malachi barked, slamming his fist down on the steering wheel. He looked over at me with concern in his eyes. "Just be cool, a'ight?"

"Just be cool? What did you even do?" I asked.

He didn't say anything. He just continued to pull over to the side of the road. "Just be quiet. Don't say shit," he said.

"Malachi, you're scaring me," I whispered.

The first thought that came to mind was if Malachi had drugs or guns in the car. Surely, he wouldn't be so stupid, especially not with his children in the vehicle.

Suddenly, two white police officers in uniforms walked up to our windows. One was on his side, the other on mine. One hand was already at their waists, with their fingers nervously strumming the pistols. My mouth abruptly went dry, and my hands began to sweat.

"Malachi," I whispered with a shaky breath.

"Don't say shit. Just let me handle it," he said.

Upon hearing the billy club tap against the glass, Malachi rolled down both of our windows, allowing the cool morning air to drift in.

"License and registration," the officer on his side said.

Reaching up to his sun visor, Malachi retrieved both items and handed them over. The entire time, the officer next to me inspected the inside of the car with his eyes. In high school, I remember being pulled over for speeding with Brad behind the wheel, but I swear it didn't feel anything like this.

Scanning Malachi's documents thoroughly, the officer asked, "You know why we pulled you over?"

"Nah," was all Malachi said.

"This car was spotted at a recent crime scene. A murder." His eyes quickly lifted, locking in with Malachi's like he was trying to read him.

I gasped out loud. "Malachi," I said, instinctively grabbing his arm. Immediately, I could feel the tension throughout his body.

"Nah, you got the wrong car. Wrong person," he casually told the officer.

"*You got any drugs or weapons in the car?*" *the officer asked.*

Malachi shook his head. "*Nah.*"

"*All right, I'm gonna have to ask you to step out.*"

Flexing his jaw, Malachi clenched down on his back teeth. It was evident that he was seething inside. Reluctantly, he stepped out of the car, leaving me scared shitless inside.

"*This can't be right. He didn't kill anyone,*" *I told the officer on my side.*

"*Miss Paris, be quiet and let a nigga handle it,*" *Malachi fumed, walking to the front of the vehicle with his hands raised above his head.*

The officer grabbed him by the arm and roughly slammed him down on the hood of the car. Instantly, I shrieked, every nerve ending inside of me shaking to the core. As the cop took Malachi's hands behind his back, the police officer at my window moved and cocked his gun, aiming it in Malachi's direction. Without even thinking, I jumped out of the car.

"*Put the gun down. He didn't do anything!*" *I screamed out in a cry, my arms raised in the air as I trembled with fear.*

"*Get back in the car. Now!*" *the officer yelled.*

"*Paris, shut the fuck up,*" *Malachi warned.*

Seeing the cuffs being placed on his wrists as the officer read his Miranda rights, I couldn't keep the tears at bay. Brutally, the cop jerked him up to his feet by force, causing Malachi to flinch in pain. His winced expression and rigid movements were a dead giveaway to his discomfort. He was having difficulty walking at the officer's desired pace.

"*Let's go, boy. Move,*" *the officer ordered.*

Just that quick, I could see Malachi's whole being filled with fury. He pushed back hard, causing the officer to lose his footing instantly. Quickly, the cop recovered and grabbed Malachi that much harder by the wrists. Through the clench of his jaw and the strain of his neck, I could see Malachi trying his best to absorb the pain. Then without warning, the officer reached down, clutched his billy club in his hand, and struck him hard across the leg.

"*Aah, fuck!*" *Malachi screamed out in agony.*

"*Don't hurt him! Please,*" *I cried.*

The officer beside me still had his gun trained in Malachi's direction. "*Ma'am, you need to get back in the car now,*" *he ordered.*

As Malachi continued being shoved in the direction of the police car, he took a quick second to look back at me. "*Call Reese from my phone. Tell her to get in touch with my lawyer.*"

"*Call Reese?*" *I asked. I understood that this was the mother of his children, but I hadn't expected her to be the first person he wanted me to call. If it were about getting a good attorney, my father's old connections alone would do the trick. Hell, as far as I was concerned, we didn't need Reese or any two-bit lawyer she could provide.*

"*Do as I say, Paris,*" *he said firmly from a distance.*

"*I'm not calling Reese.*" *I shook my head stubbornly, sniveling back uncontrollable tears.*

"*You gotta call her,*" *he shouted, resisting the officer who was practically pushing him into the car by his head.*

"*Why?*"

"*Because, Miss Paris, she's my wife.*"

Chapter 1

Paris—The Right to Know

"You doing all right over there, sis?" Bull asked.

I stared out of the passenger window through blurred vision, silently nodding. I couldn't speak—wouldn't dare because I knew it would only come out as a cry, not to mention the tears that clung to my lower lids. I just kept telling myself that I needed to keep it together, if only 'til my head hit the pillow at the end of the night.

As I sat there with a tear-stained face, watching the highway signs whoosh by, I kept hearing Malachi's frantic voice in my head. "*. . . She's my wife.*" Even with all the cops, the guns, and Malachi's arrest, I still couldn't get over the fact that he was married.

"How long have they been married?" I finally asked Bull in a whisper, my eyes still pulled away.

With his free hand, he turned down the radio. "What? What you say?"

I cleared my throat and shifted my eyes in his direction. "I said, how long have they been married? Malachi and Reese?" I knew I was only being a glutton for punishment, but I needed to know. I desperately desired the answers that Malachi wasn't there to give.

Bull shrugged his shoulders. "Since they were like 18," he said and then paused. "I guess that makes what? Five years now? But . . . They ain't even together no more."

I didn't respond. For the remainder of the ride, I just kept quiet, wondering if there had been any signs. There was no tan line on his ring finger, no throwing of the word "wife" in my face, and no trace of her in his home. Hell, not even Reese had mentioned their marriage during our infrequent encounters. I just couldn't understand how I'd missed it.

"I hope Reese's ass is home. Ain't got time to be chasing after her today," Bull griped, cutting the steering wheel hard to the left.

After the cops confiscated Malachi's car, Bull had to pick me up from the police station. We tried calling Reese shortly after, but it just kept going straight to voicemail. So here we were, just shy of noon, en route to her home. Apparently, she lived in a gated community called Lake Jeannette. As we pulled in, I had to admit that the neighborhood was breathtakingly beautiful. Every lawn was an identical shade of green, upholding massive brick houses two and three stories high. The luxury cars sitting in each cobblestoned driveway reminded me of back home.

How can Reese afford all of this? I wondered. Malachi's place was barely furnished and modest at best, but this . . .

When we finally entered one side of the circular driveway, a car was pulling out of the other. Bull must have instantly recognized the vehicle because he sucked his teeth and shook his head. After putting the car in park, he swiped his big hand over his face, then glanced in my direction.

"You getting out?" he asked.

I was just about to say no when I thought otherwise. More than likely, this was the place that Reese and Malachi had once shared—the place he used to call home. There was no way I would miss this opportunity.

"Y-yes. I'm coming," I told him.

My eyes wandered around the property as we ambled up to the ornate wrought iron and tempered glass door. The landscape had been perfectly tended to, from the crisped borders of the grass to the hedges that had all been pruned with care—things my father routinely paid to have maintained back when he was alive.

Bull exhaled a deep breath before reaching out to ring the doorbell. Sheepishly, I stood off to the side. After waiting a few seconds, I could make out someone advancing through the door's frosted glass. I swallowed anxiously, feeling my heart accelerate inside my chest. When the door finally opened, Reese appeared, and my eyes fell guiltily to my feet.

"Bull? What're you doing here?" she asked in surprise. Then her regard shifted to me. "And . . . Where's Malachi?"

I lifted my eyes to see Bull subtly scratching beneath his ear. "He got arrested," he told her with a slow shake of his head. "This morning after dropping off the kids."

"Arrested?" Her eyes ballooned briefly right before she let them close, releasing a deep sigh. "Well, y'all come on in here," she said, tying her silk robe a little tighter around her waist.

After the shock of hearing her use of the word *y'all* wore off, I followed Bull inside. My first impression of the home was that everything appeared to be grand. From the double set of winding staircases to the view of the rippling lake out back. On our way to the kitchen, I observed school pictures of the kids sitting above the fireplace and a few of their scattered toys across the hardwood floors. When we reached the kitchen, Bull immediately pulled up a stool and sat at the bar. It didn't take a genius to figure out that he felt right at home here.

As I sat beside him, I noticed the children's artwork hanging on the stainless steel fridge, drawings of the four of them together as a family. My stomach lurched when my eyes fell on the small, framed portrait sitting to the right of the stove. It was another picture of them together, all dressed in white, with Malachi wearing the hugest smile on his face. Undoubtedly, this was Malachi's home. Not that cold, empty town house he'd taken me to. Although I didn't have a right, I felt slighted and jealous by it all.

Reese walked over to the counter and rose up on the balls of her feet, grabbing an empty mug from the cabinet. "You guys want coffee?" she asked.

Surprised by her composure, I looked at Bull and stretched my eyes slightly. He simply shrugged in response. "Nah, we good," he told her for both of us.

After pouring herself a cup, she turned around to face us. "So, what did he get arrested for this time?" she asked.

I swallowed hard before turning to Bull again. I hadn't realized that this was a reoccurring thing for Malachi, but judging by Reese's pursed lips and her left eyebrow that was practically hiked to her scalp, apparently, it was.

"Said his car was supposedly tied to some murder. I don't know." Bull shrugged as if it were no big deal.

"Murder?" she repeated.

"It's a bunch of bullshit, Reese, so don't even get all upset," he said, trying to smooth it over. "He just needs you to get in touch with Troy. He's gon' need to make bail."

Malachi's arraignment was already scheduled for Wednesday, and just the mere thought of him behind bars made me sick. Yes, I was angry at him for not telling me that he was married, for not letting me choose if I even *wanted* to be a part of this, but now, what could I do? The deed to my heart had already been signed, and the love I now had for this man ran deep.

"All right, well, let me get him on the line now," she said, grabbing her cell phone off the counter. "Where's he at? Guildford County?" she asked, making eye contact with Bull.

Bull simply nodded.

When she finally got this Troy fellow on the line, she began frantically explaining how Malachi had been arrested. She kept looking at Bull for all the answers, except when it got down to the details. Bull shook his head and had no choice but to point to me. "Reese, he gon' need to talk to Paris. She was there," Bull explained.

Reese pressed her lips into a straight line before reluctantly passing me the phone. Up to this point, I hadn't even said two words. I cleared my throat and placed the phone up to my ear.

"Hello," I said softly.

"Mrs. Montgomery," Troy's voice unexpectedly cut through the room. I hadn't realized that Reese had put him on speaker. I frowned when he mistakenly called me Mrs. Montgomery, referring to Reese.

"No, this is, um, Paris Young, Malachi's f-friend," I stammered, feeling like a complete fool as I locked eyes with Reese, seeing the faintest smirk play on her lips.

"Now, I need you to tell me everything that happened," he said.

For the next ten minutes or so, I gave Troy the play-by-play of our run-in with the cops. I told him everything, from the guns that were pointed in our faces to the billy club that was repeatedly struck against the backs of Malachi's legs. I did not leave out a single detail of the horrendous event. Once I'd answered all his questions and he fully understood, I handed the phone back to Reese.

When Bull and I finally began going out the front door, he turned back and stared at her. He lifted his chin and looked down at her curiously.

"I thought you said you was leaving that alone?" he said. Reese's eyes briefly narrowed, then bloomed in recognition. "It wasn't like that," she said, almost defensively shaking her head.

"Yeah, whatever," was Bull's response.

I had no clue what they were talking about. I just wanted to get out of there and return to my dorm. Right when my foot hit the second step, Reese called my name. I looked back, seeing her standing in the doorway. Her eyes glared into mine.

"Malachi loves *me,* Paris. He has since he was 15 years old," she said evenly, batting her eyelashes between each word. "So, whatever you think is going on between the two of you, *don't.* 'Cause I can promise you, it won't last."

Although I wanted to say something—anything to rebuke her words—I couldn't. She was his *wife,* and I was merely an 18-year-old girl hoping this man loved me just as much as I loved him. We stared at each other silently, allowing the reality of it all to sink in. Then suddenly, I felt a light tap on my shoulder.

"Come on," Bull said, nodding toward the driveway. With my shoulders collapsed and my emotions wholly on high, I followed him down the steps of the home.

When we were back in his car, he cranked the engine and shot his eyes in my direction. "Aye, just let that shit she said up there roll off your back, a'ight?"

Even though I softly nodded my head, I knew it wouldn't be that easy for me. Reese was right. He'd chosen her to be his wife for a reason, and, more than likely, for him, I was just some piece of college ass. On the ride to the dorm, I remained quiet, keeping my feelings in check as promised. When we finally pulled up to Holland Hall, I thanked Bull for the ride and practically darted out the door. As soon as those elevator doors closed, I broke down and cried into the palms of my hands. Other than the death of my father, I couldn't remember a time when I'd felt so hurt.

Sniveling back tears and wiping my face with my hands, I walked down the corridor to our suite. That's when I saw Hope banging on our door.

"Hey, girl," I sniveled, giving my best attempt at a normal face. "What are you doing here?"

Without her glasses, she peered at me with a weary expression resembling my own. Her long, black hair was in a thick plait down her back, and her bangs nearly covered her gloom-filled eyes. "Um, I need to talk to you," she said through a shaky breath.

"Is everything all right?"

After a quick glance down at the other end of the hall, she shook her head. "Let's just go inside so we can talk."

"Where's your key?" I asked, placing my key into the lock.

"I left it at my aunt's house," she said.

As soon as we entered the suite, I pulled her into my room.

"Are you okay?" she asked. "You look like you've been crying."

I sniffed a little, then forced my lips into a half smile. "I'm fine. Nothing I can't handle anyway," I told her. "So, what's going on with you? What Asha said isn't true, is it?"

"Asha?" she asked right before her eyes went wide.

"She said you're pregnant, Hope. You aren't pregnant, are you?" I couldn't even imagine Hope having sex, let alone carrying a child.

A lone tear slid down her cheek when she parted her quivering lips to speak. "That's what I needed to talk to you about. I . . . um . . ."

I could tell she was reluctant to say whatever was on her mind, so I gently took her by the hand. "Just tell me," I pressed.

"I-I'm pregnant," she confessed, quickly wiping the tears from her eyes.

I covered my mouth with my hand, trapping the sound of a loud gasp. Sure, I'd heard when Asha said it back in Cancún, but that didn't mean I believed it. Hope was a good girl—a church girl. She didn't believe in premarital sex and would even cringe at the subject.

"I hate to come to you for this, but . . ." She paused, inhaling a deep breath.

"Whatever you need, just tell me." I gently placed my palm on her back after seeing the disheartened expression on her face.

"I need to borrow money for an abortion," she finally let out in a whisper. Her red, swollen eyes stapled to mine.

"An abortion?" I said a little louder than I intended. "Did Meeko ask you to do that?" I could feel myself getting angry.

"No," she said, shaking her head. "He doesn't even know."

My head reeled back as my eyes fluttered fast, wondering if I'd heard her correctly. "You haven't *told* him?"

She shook her head again, releasing more tears from her eyes.

"You can't just kill his baby without telling him, Hope. Have you even talked to your dad?"

Hope looked at me like I was insane. "I can't tell my deddy. He'd kill me. And if he knew I was even thinking about an abortion, he'd kill me twice," she exclaimed.

Instinctively, I patted her softly on the back, hoping to calm her down. "Well, what if you keep the baby? Is that even an option?"

"I have nothing, Paris. No momma, no job, not even . . ." Her voice floated off into a muted silence as she closed her teary eyes.

Suddenly, I could hear light taps against my bedroom door. My eyes lifted to see Franki in the doorway.

"What's wrong?" she immediately asked, eyes cast at Hope.

I glanced over at Hope, seeing her face now buried in her hands.

"Was it that girl Jazz? 'Cause I swear to God, yo, we can go see this bitch right now," Franki seethed. Her eyes revealed her need to settle the score finally.

"It wasn't Jazz," I told her.

Franki exhaled a breath, allowing her shoulders to drop into their natural position. Then she ambled over to sit on the opposite side of Hope.

"It was a bet," Hope said with a crack of her voice, finally raising her dampened face from her hands. "He had sex with me as a part of a stupid bet."

"Who, Meeko?" I asked, glancing between both Franki and Hope for clarification. Franki's eyes narrowed, indicating she was just as confused as I was.

"He took my virginity for five hundred measly dollars," she cried, her shoulders trembling softly.

Franki jumped up from the bed with rage instantly flickering in her eyes. "Who the fuck does this nigga think he is, yo?"

"Franki, please, calm down," I told her. "Hope's pregnant."

Franki's eyes immediately softened at the acknowledgment of my words. "Damn," she muttered, shaking her head. "What are you gonna do?"

"The only thing I can. I'm getting an abortion," Hope said.

Franki's mouth parted from shock. "Wow," she breathed. "Are you *sure?*"

Hope simply nodded her head.

"Meeko doesn't know, and she doesn't want to tell him," I told Franki, hoping she could talk some sense into her.

"She can do what she wants. It's her body," Franki said matter-of-factly.

"But he still has a right to know."

"Where the hell were *her* rights when he made that dumb-ass bet and broke her fucking heart?" Franki snapped.

My hands shot up in surrender. "You're right. Meeko was completely out of line. I hate him for doing this to her just as much as you do, but an abortion? Come on now, that would destroy her, and you know it."

Franki sighed, then gazed down at Hope. "Whatever you wanna do, I'll support you." She leaned down and wrapped her arms around her, whispering something in her ear. Hope just nodded while releasing more silent tears.

For the rest of the night, I decided to abandon my own need to cry. For once, both Franki and I simply catered to Hope. She was utterly distraught and mystified, so the last thing we needed was for her to feel alone. In fact, that night, we all slept in my bedroom. Franki was on the floor while Hope and I practically snuggled in the twin-sized bed. For now, I would push all thoughts of Malachi Montgomery to the back of my mind and just focus on being there for my friend.

Chapter 2

Asha—The Very Bottom

A sudden creak sounded at my bedroom door in the midst of dark silence. "Baby, are you all right?" I heard my momma ask.

I let out a low groan beneath the covers. "I'm fine, Ma," I mumbled.

However, that was a complete lie. When I returned from Cancún, I went straight to my parents' house. There was no way I could face the embarrassment back on campus. Jaxon had utterly humiliated me in front of everyone. He paraded his Barbie doll of a girlfriend around while I was out, bragging to anyone who would listen, claiming him as my man.

How dare he?

And then there was my brother, Malachi, who just sat back and allowed Meeko to talk to me like I was trash. I mean, yes, I knew he was still angry at me for getting the money from Mark, but at the end of the day, I was his sister—his own flesh and fucking blood. He should have come to my defense no matter what. I mean, he was more than angry. Shit, I get it. After receiving a video via text of your little sister blowing off someone you used to consider a friend, with the caption that read Spring Break Sponsor, who wouldn't be mad? But even still, I thought he would at least have my back.

Needless to say, my entire spring break had been a complete disaster. And now, as I lay here with a banging headache, feverish chills, and sporadic bouts of nausea, I wondered if I too was pregnant. Hell, I was half expecting it since I'd been poking holes in Jaxon's condoms all these months.

Slowly, I could feel the blanket being peeled away from my face, revealing the dimness of the room. "Are you *sure* you're all right?" my mother asked again, placing the back of her cool hand against my forehead. "Asha, you're burning up."

"I'm fine, Ma," I grumbled.

As she continued removing the covers, uncontrollable chills spread all over me. "You're not fine. You're sweating like crazy, Asha. I need to get you to go to the doctor."

Feebly, I sat up on the edge of the bed, feeling my head spin like a windmill. My eyes immediately squinted from the bright light as my mother cut on the lamp.

"I'll make an appointment in the morning," I croaked.

Suddenly, my cell phone vibrated on the nightstand. I glanced over at the glowing screen, seeing Reese's name unexpectedly appear.

"What the hell does she want?" my mother asked.

I shrugged my shoulders and grabbed the phone. "Hello," I answered.

"Hey, girl. Did Bull call you?" Reese asked right away.

I looked up at my mother, who was glaring down at me, not even trying to hide the fact that she was annoyed by the sound of Reese's voice. "Nah, call me for what?" I asked.

She sighed. "Girl, Malachi got arrested."

"Arrested?" my mother and I both yelled out at the same time. "What the fuck he get arrested for?" I asked. My mother promptly smacked me on the shoulder, warning me with her eyes. "My bad, Ma," I mouthed.

"Something about his car being witnessed at the scene of a murder. I don't know," she said.

"Jesus Christ," my mother exhaled, cupping both hands over her mouth.

"But Troy's on it," Reese went on to say. "I called him earlier after Bull brought that little girl over here."

"What girl?"

"That Paris chick or whatever her name is."

"Paris?"

"Girl, yes. Apparently, he had her in the car with him when the police pulled him over this morning." She let out a sarcastic snort. "Had her in the car while dropping off my fucking kids. Can you believe that shit?" she scoffed.

I'm not gonna lie. Malachi and Paris's *sudden* relationship had caught me completely off guard. But considering how bad I was feeling, I couldn't even comment. "When's the bail hearing?" I asked.

"The day after tomorrow."

With disappointment written all over her face, my mother sighed deeply. "Well, tell her if she or the kids need anything, just call me," she said.

"Did you hear my momma?" I asked Reese.

"Yeah, I heard her. Tell Miss Iris I said thanks."

"All right, well, just text me the time, and we'll be there," I told her before ending the call.

"What has your brother gotten himself into now?" my mother fussed, shaking her head.

My shoulders hiked impulsively. "I don't know, but I'm returning to my dorm tonight. Maybe I can find out from Paris."

"Paris? Your roommate?" my mother asked.

"Yes. Apparently, she's been messing around with your son," I said, rolling my eyes. Just as I attempted to stand, my knees buckled beneath me, sending my limp body back down onto the bed.

"Asha," my mother shrieked out in a panic. "You don't look so good. Let me get you over to Cone."

I awoke to the sound of slow, steady beeps. My mouth was parched, and my head throbbed in pain. "What happened?" I rasped. I blinked sluggishly, only to see my mother's face finally appear.

"You passed out in the emergency room," she said, smoothing back my hair with her hand. Then she positioned her palm over my brow. "Fever's finally down," she said, looking back over her shoulder at someone.

I ran my hand down my face and cleared my eyes once more. That's when Mark's girlfriend, Meelah, appeared. She was bent over, removing trash from the can. When she finally stood upright, I noticed her light blue scrubs and the hospital badge suspended from her neck. As soon as we locked eyes, a crafty smile graced her lips. It confused me because, as far as I knew, she had no knowledge of Mark and my previous relationship. After a quick nod to my mother, she shot out the door.

Hmm . . .

I attempted to sit up but instantly felt restricted by the tubes in my arms. "What's wrong with me?" I asked, clearing the dryness in my throat. My heart suddenly beat faster inside my chest. *Must be pretty serious.*

My mother shook her head. "They're still running tests. Could just be a late case of the flu," she said.

The doctor entered the room as soon as my head fell back to the sunken pillow behind me. "Ms. Montgomery, I see you're finally awake. I'm Dr. Ahmed," he said. Instantly, I heard the thick, Arabian accent on his tongue and observed the deep clay color of his skin. His glasses rested at the tip of his cratered nose, and his shiny, bald head peeked through his fine strands of salt-and-pepper hair. With a distressed gaze in his eyes, he released a deep breath. "We just received your results back from the lab. Would you like us to discuss them in private?" he asked, holding an open medical chart.

This is it. I'm pregnant, I thought.

"She doesn't need privacy. *Do* you?" my mother asked, tossing her eyes over at me for confirmation . . . damn near daring me to say yes.

"No, it's fine. Just tell us the results," I said, licking my dry lips.

"Well," he said, clearing his throat as he took his index finger to push his glasses up a bit farther on his nose. "After reading your lab results, it looks like you're in the second stage of—"

"Pregnancy," I said.

The doctor adamantly shook his head. "No, ma'am," he said. "You have syphilis, and you're in the secondary stage of the disease."

"Syphilis?" my mother repeated, clutching her chest as her eyes slowly turned to me.

I immediately shrank under her disappointed gaze. "That can't be right," I whispered. "I-I don't have any of the signs."

"Sometimes, diseases like this can be asymptomatic, but it does appear you've had it for quite some time. I'm sure that caused the fever and the nausea," Dr. Ahmed said. He walked over to me with a pamphlet in his hand. "Here's a little more about the disease if you want to read up on it. Of course, abstaining from all sexual activity is going to be your best means of prevention. We'll also need a list of your sexual partners to report to the CDC," he said. Shamefaced, I took the pamphlet from his hand, refusing to look at him in the eyes or at my mother. "Okay, then. I'll have the nurse get you started on a round of penicillin."

I nodded, feeling a swell of tears coat my eyes.

When the doctor left the room, my mother snatched the pamphlet from my hand. "Syphilis, Asha. *Really?* What the hell am I supposed to tell your father when he gets here?" Her eyes were lit with so much anger.

"Ma, you act like someone didn't give this shit to me. *I'm* the one that's sick here. *I'm* the victim," I said in my defense.

My mother tossed her hand up in the air to stop my rant. "Asha, you think I don't know how you've been out here living? Sleeping with these men just for a few dollars? You don't think I know why Malachi keeps his distance from you?" She sucked her teeth. "I'm your mother, Asha. *I* see you."

My chin finally collapsed to my chest as I broke down and cried. Not only had I lost in love with Jaxon and destroyed the relationship with 'Chi, but I had also now misplaced the trust and respect of my own mother. Here I was thinking that everything I did got past her when, all along, she knew. I could no longer look her in the eye.

Gently, she took my wet face in her hands and tilted it back. "You're lucky you only got something that can be cured, little girl. Next time, it could very well be something that takes your life," she warned. "Now, get yourself in order, Asha. Please. You just don't know how bad it hurts my heart to see you like this."

With a stream of tears finally running down my face, I whimpered, nodding my head in her hands.

This health scare and the disappointed look in my mother's eyes had marked the lowest points in my life. After having to tell my father that evening that I had contracted syphilis, I also had to list all of my sexual partners for the nurse. The saddest part about it was that I didn't even know most of their last names. Hell, I didn't even know the real names of some of them. I'd only known them as "Smoke," "Slim," and "Beetle." After all the filthy things I'd done with men for money over the years, I hadn't recalled ever feeling this ashamed. Not only was I failing in school, but I was also failing in life—big time. I knew I needed to make some drastic changes, or things would only worsen.

Chapter 3

Hope—The Truth

I'd been staying back at my old dorm for the past week. Of course, my father wasn't happy about it, but there was only so much he could do all the way from Texas. After a lot of thought and much-needed prayer, I finally concluded that I was going to get an abortion. While Paris was totally against it, Franki told me she'd support me either way. I honestly couldn't blame Paris for how she felt because I'd probably feel the same way if it were me on the outside looking in. I'd be the one preaching about pro-life, honesty, and even having faith. But as the person standing in my own shoes, the person carrying this child, I was downright scared. I was scared of letting my father down, frightened of raising a child all alone, and even more so, terrified of having to stare into its eyes only to see Meeko in them every day.

Today was finally the day of my appointment at the clinic. Even though Franki borrowed Josh's truck, Paris would have to drive since she was the only one with a license.

"Yo, you 'bout ready?" Franki asked from the door.

I glanced up from tying my shoe and nodded. "Ready," I told her. As I stood up from the bed, I pulled a bottomless breath into my lungs. It was my best attempt at calming my nerves.

"Are you *sure* you wanna go through with this?" she asked with concern.

My tongue was too weighty for words, so I simply nodded again instead.

Out of nowhere, a commotion resounded from the living room, startling both of us. Franki leaned back with her hands on both sides of the door frame. Her eyes instantly flashed wide before darting in my direction.

"What is it?" I asked, suddenly hearing the distant voices becoming clearer from the other room.

"It's Meeko," Franki whispered, eyes alarmed. "I guess Paris let him in."

I took a hard swallow before panic finally settled in. Rushing over, I pushed Franki out of the entryway and slammed the door in her face with all my might. As my trembling fingers turned the lock, I heard Meeko's voice booming from the other side.

"Hope!" he yelled. "We need to talk."

"She doesn't want to talk, Meeko. Just give her some space," I heard Franki say.

"Nah, fuck that, yo. She's carrying my baby," he barked.

Hearing those words—that specific declaration immediately knocked the wind out of me. I could hardly breathe. With my back pressed to the door, I slipped down onto the carpet. My heart thundered inside my chest like a conga, and my eyes were already clouded with tears.

"Hope," he said, his voice closer and down low like he knew exactly where I was. "I'm so sorry for hurting you. If I could take all that shit back, that stupid-ass bet, Jazz . . . all of it, yo, I swear . . ." His voice trailed off into a breath so deep that I could hear it from the other side.

Wiping the lone tear that had slipped down my cheek, I somehow managed to find my voice. "Just leave me alone, Meeko. We're over."

"When were you gonna tell me about the baby, huh?" he asked. With my knees hiked to my chin, one sob gradually rolled into the next. "I knew what I was doing when I got you pregnant," he said. "It was the only thing I could think of to get you to forgive me. The one thing I knew would keep you in my life after all the bullshit came out. 'Cause like my mother always says, even your deepest, darkest secrets eventually come to light. So I knew you were gonna find out about the bet sooner or later. Shit, it was only a matter of time, but with your religion and all, I knew you'd come around. You'd keep the baby, forcing you to be in my life. Forever."

"Meek—" I tried, but he kept going.

"You're the only person I've ever had unprotected sex with, Hope. I knew exactly what I was doing," he confessed. "'Cause I . . . I love you."

I began to bawl so hard that my shoulders shook. I don't know if it was his admission to getting me pregnant on purpose or the declaration of his love, but either way, my emotions were running wild. No matter how hard I tried, I just couldn't get in enough air, and when my chest began to ache inside, I knew it was just a side effect of the little crack further expanding in my heart.

"Open the door, baby, please," he pleaded softly. "Let me in."

I shook my head, trying to regain my breath. "There is no more baby, Meek," I let out a soft cry. My hands instantly flew to my mouth, trying to catch the lie, but it was already too late.

Suddenly, a long silence ensued, creating so much tension that my pulse began to race. Without thought, I muted my sobs, needing to hear his response, but there was no sound. Other than the thud of my own heart racing between my ears, there was no competing noise. Not even from Franki or Paris. It was torturing me.

Out of nowhere, I heard a short exhale of air escaping Meeko's lungs, like he had to recover his breath. "The fuck you just say?" he finally said, his voice completely calm.

I closed my eyes and held my cross pendant closer to my chest. "I said there is no more baby, Meek. It's gone," I lied again.

"Nah, yo," he murmured, almost like he didn't believe me. "Nah."

"I got rid of it."

Then without warning, he started banging and kicking on the door. It was so hard that I could feel his anger against my back. I just sat there and cried, taking his blows.

"Meeko, stop!" I heard Franki scream. "You're gonna break her fucking door, yo."

"Break her fucking door?" he roared. "You think I give a fuck about a door? She *killed* my baby." The violent thrashes behind the door continued as I wept. "Open this fucking door, Hope. Open it," he yelled so loud I jumped in place.

"Look, you need to leave before I call the police," I heard Paris threatened.

"Call them niggas. Call 'em," he barked. "I don't give a fuck." His voice was so loud that the words practically ricocheted off the walls. He kicked the door some more, aggressively trying to turn the knob.

"Come on, man." This time, it was a male's voice cutting in from the other side. "Let's go so you can calm down." It was Ty. I hadn't even realized he was there before now.

"Nah. Hope, open up this door." Meeko banged again. "I need to see your eyes when you tell me you killed my baby. Tell me that shit to my face."

If I wanted this nightmare to end, I knew exactly what I needed to do. Slowly, I stood up from the floor. My legs wobbled like a newborn calf's as I went and turned the lock. Reluctantly, I opened the door, coming face-to-face with the guy who'd seemingly embezzled my heart. The guy I'd already pictured my future with. As his red eyes seared into me, I could almost feel his rage. His chest heaved up and down, and his breathing was erratic, with his fists balled at his sides. He was beyond furious.

My parted lips quivered, dripping with both snot and tears. "It's gone," I let out just above a whisper. My stomach practically turned in knots as I thought about the life I was still carrying inside me.

"It's gone?" he repeated, the look of astonishment played out on his handsome face.

I sucked in a breath, holding it for seconds before I could finally respond. "There is no more baby, Meeko. It's over. Now, please, leave me alone." Another tear escaped my eye as I gently closed the door. My feet led me back to my bed, where I flopped down on the mattress and cried all over again.

"You know you don't have to do this, right?" Franki asked from the backseat, finally breaking the somber silence in the truck.

With my regard cast out of the passenger window, I nodded. "I know," I said.

Our entire ride to the clinic had been a quiet one. Not even music played on the radio as Paris drove behind the wheel.

"No, really. I will help you, Hope. Just call me Baby Momma Number Two," Franki joked. Although I couldn't muster up a laugh, I did crack a small smile.

"No, *I'd* be number two," Paris said, finally breaking her silence. "And she'd call me Auntie Paris or maybe Godmommy Paris. I don't know," she mumbled more to herself than us.

"Well, how you know it ain't gon' be a boy?" Franki asked, tilting her head in Paris's direction.

"I don't know." Paris shrugged one of her shoulders, keeping her hands steady on the wheel. "I just want a little girl."

"I thought you already had one. What's Malachi's little girl's name?" Franki asked, snickering beneath her breath.

I glanced over at Paris, seeing her respond with a simple roll of her eyes. Lately, she'd been tense at the mere mention of Malachi's name. I knew his arrest had been hard for her. And now, with his bail hearing being pushed back another week, she'd been borderline depressed. Feeling a quick tap on my shoulder, I peeked back at Franki, who was now leaning forward between the seats.

"Well, if you did have a little girl, what would you name her?" she asked.

"Hmm." My lips puckered as I gave it some thought. "Maybe Rachel or Mary. I don't know. Or maybe Ivy. I've always liked that one too."

"Her name would definitely be Ivy," Paris cut in and said. "There's no way I'd let you name my goddaughter some friggin' Rachel or Mary. As if—"

"But they're both biblical nam—" Hope tried to say but was cut off by the palm of Paris's hand.

"*Like I said,* her name would be Ivy," Paris stated adamantly. "Ivy Marie."

"Yo, wouldn't it be cute if she had your dimples?" Franki said.

I smiled as the mere image flashed in my mind. "And Meeko's wavy hair," I muttered.

Suddenly, the mood in the truck went somber again, and silence persisted for the remainder of the way. When Paris finally arrived at the clinic and parked the truck, she looked over at me. Her eyes glossed over as though she was on the verge of tears.

"Don't do this, Hope," she said with desperation.

Swallowing back a cry of my own, I gave her a look that told her I had no choice. Then I opened the truck door and let myself out. As I ambled toward the clinic with Franki behind me, I held my head high. My eyes blinked overtime just to keep the waterworks at bay. At that moment, I knew I had to be strong—brave. I couldn't successfully raise a baby on my own. At least not without my father's support. I didn't have a car or job. I had absolutely nothing. Nothing but a meal card and three pairs of worn canvas sneakers.

Paris didn't have the same circumstances as I did. Her trust fund alone could probably support three children for a lifetime. So, after forcing my feet to approach the nurse's station, I reached for a pen and added my name to the sign-in sheet. No matter how much it hurt or how scared I was, I had to do what was best for me.

Chapter 4

Franki—Two Steps Back

It was just shy of May, and the temperature outside had already grown to nearly 90 degrees. As I lay back in bed, feeling the warm breeze flow in from the window, I stared at the lean muscles of Josh's back. He was sitting at my desk, shirtless, studying for his final exams. Although I was supposed to be doing the same, I couldn't stop gawking at his body. Thoughts of his soft lips and hands against my skin occupied my brain.

After admitting our feelings for each other in Cancún, Josh demanded an exclusive relationship. He let it be known up front that he wasn't with the little games I typically play. Either I would be *his,* or we would be nothing at all. I happily conceded to his demands, and from then on, we seemed inseparable.

With each day that passed, I found myself falling more and more in love with Josh. Always discovering little things about him chipped away at the wall around my heart. Like the way his eyes would light up whenever his mother called, or he'd always reference her as "*my ma.*" In the armrest of his car, he kept old receipts that he'd sometimes scribble on. An idea, a scripture, or anything he thought he might need to remember, he would write it down so that he wouldn't forget. Sometimes, his eyes would go distant, and he'd laugh to himself. When I'd ask what's funny, he'd simply shake his head but then allow his eyes to connect with mine. Without words, he could make me feel like I was sharing the joke with him rather than being the butt of it. I know it's mad corny, but Josh was sweet. Everything about him was made to be loved.

The only barrier between us was his wanting to abstain from sex. Even though he was no virgin, he was now hell-bent on waiting for marriage. Six months ago, I would have laughed in his face and probably even called him gay, but today—after getting to know him, I couldn't. Josh was all man, heterosexual, and, based on my "accidental" bumps and grazes against his pelvic area, extremely well endowed. I would have moved on without a second thought if it had been any other man. But for Josh, no matter the torture, it seems I was willing to wait.

"Yo, ma, you done studying me back there?" he asked, head still buried in his book.

I beamed. "So what, you got eyes in the back of your head now?"

He let out a small snort of laughter, craning his neck around as a bright smile immediately opened up on his face. "Nah, I just know you," he said.

I sucked my teeth and playfully rolled my eyes. "Whatever, son-son. You don't know me."

Josh rolled the chair back from the desk and quickly rose. As he began stalking toward me, wetting those dark pink lips with his tongue, I studied the carved muscles of his abs. With each of his strides, my mouth watered a little bit more. And when he finally approached the bed, a single pulse jolted from my clit.

Fuck.

A wicked little grin slowly crept across his face like he knew the effect he was having on me. "What you looking at?" he asked, undoubtedly teasing me with his eyes.

I swallowed hard and shook my head. "Not you, nigga." He leaned down and hovered over me, allowing just his knees to catch the edge of the bed. His diamond cross pendant hung between us, and the scent of his cologne wafted in the air. "Give me a kiss," he ordered.

"No." I shook my head again, practically shooing him away. "I'm not messing with you, Josh." Slowly, his head dipped down into the curve of my neck, and before I knew it, his lips attacked me with feathery kisses. His fingers tickled at my waist. "Stop," I squealed out in laughter, flailing around on the bed.

He lifted his face and stared into my eyes. "Then give me a kiss," he insisted again.

Rising up on my elbows, I allowed our lips to meet finally. And just like every other time we kissed, fireworks, bombs, and explosions erupted all over me. It was crazy how even the most innocent displays of affection between us would have my body calling his name. That sensitive little place right between my thighs thumped and ached without warning.

As his tongue intertwined with mine, his hands roamed my frame, and I released a sensual moan. Pulling back unexpectedly, I shook my head and attempted to catch my breath. "No," I told him, placing my hand on his chest. "How the fuck am I supposed to refrain from sex with you all up on me like this?"

He smirked, raising his hand to swipe the wetness from his lips. "My bad, ma. You right," he agreed. Then he moved to an upright position on the bed. "I want you just as bad as you want me, but I gotta do things in the right order. Nobody ever said it was gon' be easy." He shrugged.

I sat up and leaned back against the headboard. "I know," I sighed. "So, what now? Summer break's only a few weeks away."

I'd never admit this to Josh, but the thought of us being apart all summer terrified me. Over the years, male attention had become a necessity of mine. It's like I almost craved it, and not just the sexual parts. In recent months, Josh had become the keeper of my darkest secrets, my protector, and, most of all, my friend. All remnants of the rape and the issues with my father seemed to dissipate with him around. No more nightmares and night sweats. No more peeing in the bed. Hell, I'd even been back to church. I was actually starting to feel like my old self again, and I didn't want to lose that. I needed reassurance that we, or rather *I*, could survive this time apart.

Josh scratched the side of his face before resting his elbows above his knees. "Come stay with me," he suggested. "I'll have my own little spot in Manhattan for my internship."

My eyes briefly lit up at the thought . . . but then reality hit. There was no way I could spend the summer with Josh. I'd already promised Hope and Paris that I'd stick around instead of returning to New York. I'd even enrolled in summer classes. Besides, Hope needed all the support she could get right now, and this time, I refused to be the one to let her down.

"I can't," I sulked.

"Why? You think your moms might trip?" he asked.

I shook my head. "I'm staying here for the summer. You know I can't leave Hope," I told him, my eyes searching his for understanding. "Plus, we're supposed to be moving off campus together."

Josh heaved a sigh before running his hand down his face. "Off campus where?"

"Somewhere off of Cumberland. Not too far," I said.

A frown etched across his face as he hoisted up from the bed. "Mm-hmm," he muttered.

I watched as he went to grab his tee shirt from the hook behind my door.

"Where you going?" I asked, sitting up, damn near in a panic.

"I gotta get back. We gotta meeting tonight over at the frat house," he explained.

"But we ain't finished talking yet. What are we gonna do about this summer?" My voice had suddenly elevated into a whine.

It was all I could do to cover up the anxiety I was feeling. I was so used to those fly-by-night high school relationships, the ones that were never destined to last, that being without him, my new normal, scared the living shit out of me. More than anything, I needed to know the plan . . . for him to tell me that he was coming back for me and that as soon as the fall semester started, we'd pick up exactly where we'd left off.

"What about it?" he asked with his eyebrow hiked.

"Nothing, yo; just forget it," I said, shuffling off the bed with an attitude. I stomped over to my dresser before yanking open the drawer, frustration silently pouring out of every inch of me.

Within mere seconds, I felt Josh's hands around my waist. "Franki," he said lowly, lips lightly grazing the rim of my ear. "There are two breaks this summer. I'ma send you a train ticket for each one." Then he spun me around, so we stood face-to-face, his hands suddenly holding mine. "You got me, a'ight?" He pulled my hand up to his chest so that it was right above his beating heart, using only his eyes to tell me that I was his and he was mine. That everything I'd been feeling for him, he'd been feeling too. "Now, stop pouting, ma. Me and you, we gon' be just fine." Feeling somewhat relieved, I nodded and lifted on the balls of my feet, tenderly brushing my lips against his. "Now, make sure you call me later," he whispered.

He stepped back and began collecting the rest of his things from around the room. When he started for the door, he chucked up his chin and tossed me a gentle smile. "Be good, baby."

I wiggled my fingers, waving goodbye as I watched him walk out the door. Thinking of how desperate I was acting, I had to laugh at my damn self. A bitch hadn't even gotten the dick, yet I'd already become everything I couldn't stand. Clingy, overwhelming, and frighteningly insecure.

"Hey." The sound of Paris's voice abruptly snapped me out of my thoughts. I looked up to see her peeking her head through the doorway. Her hair was pulled back out of her creamy-colored face, and her brown eyes held a natural smile. "Hope and I are on our way out to get mani-pedis. You wanna come with?" she asked.

I pursed my lips to the side. "Now, you know I ain't got no money."

"I'll cover you. Now, come on," she said.

Quickly, I went to the drawer and scrounged for a pair of shorts. After sliding my feet into a pair of old rubber flip-flops, I marched out the door. As soon as I entered the living room, Asha and Kiki entered. I hadn't seen Asha since she waltzed out of Paris's suite in Cancún, and to be honest, I was perfectly fine with that. I was tired of being nice to someone who constantly had their ass on their shoulder. Not to mention the fact that she told everyone that Hope was pregnant. At the time, I prayed that she was only saying that to get under Meeko's skin, but now, knowing it was all true, I wanted to backhand her.

After a quick roll of my eyes, I turned my attention elsewhere but had to do a double take at the sound of her voice.

"Hey, y'all," she said lowly. Her tone was surprisingly soft and kind. Paris and I immediately locked eyes.

"Hey," I heard Hope respond from the kitchen. I swear she could be just too fucking nice at times.

When Asha started making her way toward her, both Paris and I trailed on her heels.

"H-how is everything?" Asha asked. Then she looked over her shoulder to see if someone was standing there. I was leaning on one side of the door frame while Paris had her back against the other.

When she turned back to Hope, she whispered. "You feeling all right?"

Hope's eyes momentarily narrowed behind her glasses right before they ballooned. "Oh yeah. I'm fine," she said, nodding her head. "We're about to go get our nails done. You guys want to come with us?" Through the little window in the kitchen, she glanced out into the living room area at Kiki.

While I huffed a breath of annoyance and rolled my eyes, Paris was across from me, shaking her head.

"Umm, maybe next time. I was in the hospital for a few days," Asha said. "Getting over a . . . a little bug—"

"Oh, wow," Hope said, surprised. "I hope you're feeling better."

"I am, but if I'm gonna have any chance at passing these finals, I need to get my ass in there and study."

"Well, just let me know if you need help stu—"

"Hope, you 'bout ready?" I asked, obviously annoyed.

Hope tilted her little head to the side to peek around Asha. "Oh yeah, I'm ready." She grabbed the dish towel off the counter and quickly dried her hands.

Asha gently grabbed her by the arm when she began walking out of the kitchen. "I, um . . . I told Meeko about . . . you know."

Hope smiled and placed her hand over hers. "I know. It's . . . It's fine."

"I'm a bitch, Hope," she admitted. "It's just—"

Hope cut her off with a shake of her head. "Really, Asha, it's fine. I gotta run, but maybe you guys can come with us next time."

Hope placed a single finger over her lips as she continued on her path. I guess that was supposed to shut me up. She knew better than anyone that Asha only had one more time to catch me wrong before I flew off the hinges. I had absolutely no problem mopping the floor with her ass. However, at that moment, I decided to keep it cool.

After a quick wave goodbye to Kiki, the three of us skated out the door. Paris had already called an Uber ahead of time, so when we walked outside, all we had to do was slip into the car. Of course, Paris had to sit up front while Hope and I rode in the back. And within fifteen minutes, we were pulling up at Serenity Nails and Spa. I found it funny how Paris initially turned her nose up at the little nail shop, but now, she was a regular customer.

As we made our way to the curb, a familiar voice immediately drew my attention. My feet stopped abruptly in their tracks, and the air stalled in my lungs. I could hardly breathe. Cautiously, I allowed my eyes to dart over in that direction. And there he was, waltzing out of the Mexican restaurant next door. Totally carefree with a smiling Levar trailing behind him.

"Franki," Paris said, taking me out of my trance. "Are you coming or what?" She was already waiting by the door.

I stood frozen in place. Trembling. My vision was hazy from unexpected tears and anger now coursing through my veins.

"What's wrong? Is everything all right?" Hope asked, making her way back over. Her voice was laced with utter concern. "Paris, something's wrong. She's shaking."

Then finally, he spoke to me. "'Sup, Franki," Jamel said, tossing his chin in my direction. A slow, cocky grin broke across his face.

He shot a quick glance over his shoulder at Levar before a deep chuckle released from the back of his throat. It was more than evident that I was their inside joke—the root cause of their now obnoxious laughter. I felt sick inside. My stomach reeled as sweat quickly formed on my brow.

It had been months since I'd seen either of them. It was almost like that painful event had been nothing more than a bad dream, as if that night had never occurred. But now, as I stood there shrinking under their stares, their fingers pointing in both ridicule and shame, reality hit. Memory after memory of that night started coming back in spades. My stomach gurgled until I could no longer hold its contents. And without warning, I curled over, vomiting on the ground.

"Oh my God, Franki!" Hope shrieked.

That only made Jamel and Levar laugh harder. *Heartless fuckers.*

"What the hell are those losers laughing at?" Paris asked, removing the curls that had fallen on my face.

"He," I breathed. "Raped. Me," I finally confessed.

"What?" Paris shouted, confused. "Who?"

My eyes trailed up to where Jamel and Levar had been standing, but they were no longer there. For some reason, that set off my internal alarms. I didn't want to believe on any level that I was going crazy—that the images of the two of them had only been conceived in my mind. I jolted to stand up straight and quickly looked back into the parking lot. And there they were, disappearing into an old car, their muted laughter fading in the distance.

"Jamel? Jamel *raped* you?" Paris asked.

I turned back, feeling a single tear trickle down my cheek. "Yes," I nodded. "That same night Hope got banked."

Chapter 5

Paris—Final Release

"Oh shit, here he comes now," Reese said.

Shielding my eyes from the sun, I watched as she took off running across the parking lot, her sheer kimono flying back in the summer's wind. With my heart battling against my chest, I stood there, eager to see Malachi's face again. After Malachi's bail hearing had gotten pushed back twice, it had been almost three weeks since I'd last laid eyes on him. When he stepped out into the open, I immediately noticed the overgrown hair on his head and the scruffy beard that had now formed haphazardly on his face. With the same clothes from the morning of his arrest, that same gold chain draping from his neck, he grinned. Even from where I stood beside Bull by the car, I could see his bright hazel eyes glittering from the sun.

"Mane, that nigga happy as fuck right now," Bull said to himself. I looked up to see his eyes smiling in Malachi's direction.

When I allowed my eyes to travel the same path, my lips curled on instinct. I'd missed him so much that even though things were still unsettled between us, there wasn't anything I wouldn't have done to ensure he'd walk free. But when my eyes finally focused in, I saw Malachi opening his arms to *her*. His smile was a ruler wide, just like in those family photos. And when they finally embraced, he closed his eyes.

Wow.

I stood there, suddenly breathless, like I'd been running for my life. An unfamiliar burn commenced at the bottom of my lungs. There was no way I could stand there and watch whatever it was unfolding between them. Not if I wanted to protect my heart and my pride. As fast as my feet could spin me around, I turned and began walking away.

"Aye, Paris, hol' up," Bull shouted behind me.

I didn't even bother answering him because the tears were already in my throat. I just kept trekking toward Josh's truck. Thankfully, I borrowed it this morning instead of catching a ride with Bull. I couldn't stay there a moment longer. With each of my strides, I could feel water welling in my eyes. But they didn't fall. At least not until I opened the door.

As soon as I slid in and cranked the engine, I heard a light tapping sound next to me. I glanced over to see Malachi's hazel eyes glaring at me through the window.

"Miss Paris," he said. "Open up."

With a snivel, I quickly wiped the wetness from my face. "Go away, Malachi."

He pulled on the handle and opened the door with ease. *Fuck.*

"Why you leaving?" he asked, cupping my chin to study the tears on my face. "What's wrong? Why you crying?"

I snatched my face back from his hand and released a short sniffle. "I don't even know why I'm here," I muttered.

Narrowing his eyes into tiny slits, he cocked his head to the side. "You don't know why you're here?" he repeated, his voice bordering somewhere between anger, hurt, and confusion. "Paris, what the fuck is that supposed to mean?"

"It means I haven't seen or heard from you in three weeks, Malachi. Three fucking weeks. And your last set of words to me was that *she*—" I screamed, tossing a pointed finger over in Reese's direction, "was your wife. You lied to me, Malachi. This whole time," I cried. *Dammit,* more tears.

"Shawty, I ain't lie to you—"

My eyes bucked so hard that I was surprised I could still see. "Oh, so then, you told me up front that you were married?" I asked sarcastically.

Malachi stepped back from the truck with his hands held up in surrender, shaking his head. "I'm not married, Paris. I'm separated, almost divorced."

Boiling over with anger, I practically jumped out of the truck. "And I don't give a fuck if you're engaged. You should have told me."

Apparently, he found humor in my pain because a slow grin crested upon his face.

"Oh, this is funny to you? The fact that I'm hurting right now?" I pointed to my chest.

He shook his head with the stupid smirk still plastered across his lips. "Nah, mama, not at all."

"Oh, I get it. Is the fact that I had to see you all hugged up with your wife over there somehow hilarious to you? Or the fact that not even a full month ago, I gave myself to you."

"I didn't say that—"

"You didn't call me, Malachi. Not even *one* friggin' time," I yelled, hearing the raw sound of heartbreak in my voice. Then suddenly, something dawned on me. "Did you call *her?*"

His eyes softened, immediately filling with remorse. "Mane . . ." he drawled, shaking his head. "You know I got kids, Paris."

"You're right," I said, inhaling a breath so deep that my chest swelled. "You do have kids, and you *also* have a wife. Stay away from me, Malachi."

"Paris," he sighed, swiping his hand down his face. "Don't do this."

Ignoring the grueling pain in my chest—the part of me that just wanted to collapse in his arms, I begrudgingly turned to Josh's truck. As I slowly pressed on the gas, I could hear the echoes of Malachi shouting out my name. My eyes shot up toward the rearview mirror, only to see him standing there with his hands holding the back of his head.

When my eyes traveled back to the road ahead, I cried to the point of sound. Never in my eighteen years had I experienced even a fraction of this type of pain. Malachi had become my everything. My first thought each morning, and the only person I dreamed about at night. Logically speaking, I knew there was no way I could carry on with a married man, but I'd be lying if I said this was easy. Driving away from the man I loved was no simple feat. My mind was so boggled with despair that I couldn't even see the possibility of tomorrow if Malachi weren't in it.

I sobbed the entire way back to campus with my shaky fingers, barely able to grip the wheel. However, instead of returning to the dorms, I told Josh I'd drop his truck off by the rec center. That's where I knew he'd be playing ball. After putting the car in park, I tugged the sun visor down and looked at my reflection. Like war paint, mascara traced my swollen eyes. My nose was redder than a Burmese ruby. I looked a complete mess. With an old tissue that Josh had crinkled up on the console, I wiped my eyes and blew the snot from my nose. I knew it was disgusting, but I didn't even care. I didn't care about anything other than my bleeding heart.

Stepping out of the truck, I surveyed the area for Josh. I immediately noticed a group of shirtless guys across the street. Each stampeding down the court, trading either a ball or obscenities back and forth. With my head hung low, I walked over, hoping this exchange would be brief. I didn't need Josh in my business any more than Franki already had him in it. He knew just about everything, even Malachi's arrest. But no one, not even the girls, knew about him being married. It was so embarrassing.

When my eyes finally landed on Josh, I shouted his name and waved my hand in the air, trying to gain his attention. Of course, he played so hard that he didn't even notice me. However, Ty and Meeko did. Without delay, Ty began heading over while Meeko just stood there glowering in my direction. I knew he was still angry about Hope, but honestly, I felt he had no one to blame but himself. I mean, this girl loved him with her entire heart, yet all he did was rip it out of her chest and fumble it like a stupid football.

"'Sup, Paris? What you doing out here?" Ty asked. Breathing hard as he wiped the dripping sweat from his face.

Afraid he would see the aftermath of my latest breakdown, I cut my eyes away. "Just needed to drop off Josh's keys," I said.

He glanced over his shoulder toward the rest of the guys playing ball. "Ayo, Josh," he shouted, his voice much larger than mine.

With a basketball in hand, Josh's head whipped in our direction. His eyes briefly narrowed before finally recognizing the two of us. After giving us a chuck of his chin, he passed the ball to one of his frat brothers and jogged toward us. As he came near, I tried my best to avoid eye contact, but it was useless. Josh immediately knew that something was wrong.

"What's wrong, ma?" he came right out and asked. He was so observant, almost intuitive.

"Nothing," I said softly, casting my eyes to the side.

"You sure? Look like you been crying."

For the last three minutes, Ty had been so focused on my bare thighs that he, himself, hadn't even noticed the tears in my eyes. "Somebody fucking with you?" Ty asked, finally looking me in the face.

I shook my head. "No, nothing like that. I just got into an argument with Malachi. I think . . ." I released a shaky breath. "I think we're over," I whispered.

"Damn, sorry to hear that. You gon' be all right?"

I nodded and then passed the keys to him. "Yeah, I'll be fine."

"You sure? You want me to drive you back to the dorms?"

"No, I think I'd rather walk," I told him, knowing that the fresh air and time alone would do me some good.

As I turned away, I felt someone gently grab me by the hand. It was Ty. "I'ma walk with you," he said.

"You don't have to do that, Ty. Really. I'm fine."

"No, you not. Let me go grab my shirt, and I'll be right back."

Watching him run toward the bleachers, I sighed. I knew Ty liked me, but I just wasn't in the mood. I was still hurting inside. Nonetheless, when he returned, we began our journey toward Holland Hall. As the sun beat down on us, we walked in complete silence. I kept replaying that last scene with Malachi in my head while Ty swatted away the presummer bugs.

Then he finally spoke. "So, you really think it's over between you and dude?" he asked.

"Yeah," I told him, letting go of another deep breath. "It's over." As I blinked, I could feel the dried-up tears around my eyes.

"Well, you know everything happens for a reason, right? Maybe moving one man out of your life may make room for another. The right one," he shrugged.

Internally, I cringed hearing him call Malachi the *wrong* man, but then I sighed. "Maybe you're right," I admitted.

"Sure, I am," he said, playfully nudging my arm. "Shorty, you pretty as fuck, and you sweet. Any man would be lucky to have you. That's my word," he said.

Warmth instantly spread throughout my cheeks as I blushed. I didn't want to, but it naturally happened whenever Ty was around.

I cleared my throat and tucked a piece of hair behind my ear. "Well, what about you?" I asked, hoping to change the subject. "Why don't you have a girlfriend?"

"'Cause my baby muva won't let me," he said, releasing a low chuckle.

I looked up at his six-foot frame, noticing the serious look on his face. "I didn't know you had a child, Ty." I swear it seemed like every Black man I encountered these days, at least over the age of 18, already had a kid or *two*.

"Yeah, a little girl," he revealed. "Brielle."

"Wow. That's a beautiful name."

"Yeah, that's my princess. She'll be five by the end of summer."

"So, what happened between you and her mom?" I asked. Then I immediately held up my hand. "Unless that's too private."

"Nah, you good," he said. "You want me to be honest?"

"No," I mocked with a silly face. "I want you to lie."

He let out a light chuckle and shook his head. "I hate to even admit this shit out loud, especially to you, but I'ma keep it a buck. I was never faithful to shorty, not even when I was back home. And when I came out here for school, shit just got worse. I never took our relationship seriously. I should have, but . . ."

"Hmm. So you're one of *those*, huh?" I asked.

"One of what?"

"A-a THOT," I stammered, surprised by my own choice of words.

He looked at me with his eyes bugged before we both doubled over in laughter.

"Shit don't even sound right coming out of your mouth. But yeah, I guess you're right. I'm a whole THOT out here, yo." He laughed again.

"Hey, well, at least you can admit it," I shrugged.

"But I can change . . . for the right person," he said, shifting his eyes down at me.

A nervous giggle escaped me as I rolled my eyes. Sure, Ty was attractive. In fact, he was probably physically more my type than Malachi, with his rich caramel skin and teeth that were as white as the moon. I even thought that his Baltimorean accent was nice. It gave him just enough of a bad-boy edge. But even with all that, he wasn't *my* Malachi.

"Well, whoever she is, I hope you find her," I said, noticing we had finally reached the dorms.

"Aye, um, before you go," he said, taking me by the hand. His fingertips gently held on to mine. "Why don't you let me take you out sometime?"

My lips instantly drew inward for an awkward smile. "Ty, I can't," I told him.

"Why not? Too soon?"

I nodded. "Definitely too soon."

"Well, how 'bout this?" he proposed with a lick of his lips. "Why don't we just be friends?"

"Uh, I thought we already were friends," I said with a little laugh.

He smiled. "Yeah, we are. But not really the kind of friends I wanna be." As I was getting ready to curse him, he spoke again. "And no, I'm not talking about sex. What I mean is, we don't really talk, we don't kick it, none of that shit. But I want to," he explained. "Just let a nigga get to know you, Paris. That's all I'm asking."

I shot him a reluctant look, taking the corner of my lip between my teeth. "I don't know, Ty."

He sucked his teeth until his lips finally formed a smirk. "Just think about it, a'ight?"

I gave a slow nod before thanking him for the walk home. When I finally got upstairs to my room, I thanked God that no one was there. I couldn't handle facing anyone else. Sitting on the edge of my bed, I pulled my cell phone out of my purse. I noticed that I had seven missed calls. One was from Bull, five were from Malachi, and surprisingly, there was even one from my mother. Just as I was about to block Malachi's number for good, I realized that I also had a series of voicemail messages. I placed the phone to my ear and listened.

At 10:57 a.m., minutes after I'd pulled away from the Guilford County Jail, *"Pick up the phone, mama,"* he whispered in an exasperated breath. *"We need to talk ASAP."* Shaking my head, I deleted the message with a forceful finger jab.

The following message was sent at 11:09 a.m. *"Miss Paris, where you at, shawty? Call me,"* he said, a little more urgency in his voice this time. I sighed, once again deleting the message.

Then at 11:18 a.m., *"Look, I know you mad, but it's not what you think. Me and Reese ain't even together like that. Just call me so I can explain,"* he tried again.

Next, at 11:22 a.m., *"Stop ignoring my texts, Paris. What, you think this little game you playing is cute? Shawty, I'm tryin'a spend time with my kids and you . . ."*

he said, letting his voice trail off in a groan. *"Call me back."*
With a hard swallow, I deleted that one too.

At 11:40 a.m., *"Mane, you just want a nigga to chase yo' stuck-up ass. I ain't the fucking one. When you start acting like a grown-ass woman instead of like a fucking kid, you got my number,"* he snapped. Then I heard the suck of his teeth. *"Last time I'm calling yo' ass too,"* he muttered, ending the call.

Instantly, I became unnerved. *Did I really want him to chase me? Was this really going to be the last time I heard his voice?* Before my tears even had a chance to slip from my eyes, I wiped them away and deleted the message. Then, finally, I heard one last message come through.

At 12:01 a.m., *"Miss Paris, please,"* Malachi practically begged through a whisper. His voice was wholly depleted from that former tough guy act. *"You know you my gotdamn heart, mama,"* he said. *"If I don't hear back from you, I'm coming over there. Simple as that. I need to see your face. Make this shit right."* Even though Malachi was this so-called gangster, I could tell that with every minute that passed, he was crumbling apart just as hard and fast as I was.

After clicking the contacts on my screen, I scrolled until my finger hesitantly hovered over his name. It hadn't even been a full two hours since I'd driven away, but I swear I could hardly breathe. I don't know how or when it happened, but Malachi had become my air. Right as I was about to hit the button to dial his number, a hard knock sounded at our door. Thinking it was just Franki, who had probably left her keys, I shot up from the bed and went to let her in. However, when I looked through the peephole, I saw it was Malachi. His head bowed, and his fist pressed against the door, waiting.

Although I was mere seconds away from making the call, I knew I couldn't speak to him in person. That would be too much—staring into his sympathetic eyes, enduring his spellbinding touch. At this point, I had little to no faith in myself when it came to resisting him. Hoping not to make a sound, I held my breath and listened to the fast beat of my heart.

"Paris, you in there?" He banged against the door once more.

As I looked out of the peephole, I noticed his eyes slowly traveling up the length of the door. It was as if he knew I was right there on the other side. An instant arrow of pain shot through my chest as I took in the weary expression on his face, one I'd never witnessed before. Gently, I placed my hand up to the door and willed myself not to open it. I had to remain strong. Although people might have assumed otherwise, I was not this bubblehead from Beverly Hills—some rich, spoiled girl who presumed everything in life was hers for the taking. No, I actually had morals and standards about myself. And no matter which way Malachi tried to spin it, the fact remained that he was a married man. In no shape, form, or fashion did Malachi Montgomery belong to me, and under no circumstances would I have ever tried to take him.

Reluctantly, I rose up on the balls of my feet and stared out one final time. That's when our eyes seemingly met like he was looking directly at me. My lips pressed together into a tight, straight line, somehow barricading the sob rising from my lungs. And then, with an ever so slight nod, he turned and finally walked away.

Chapter 6

Asha—Just That Quick

"No, sir, we close tonight at nine," I said into the phone, following it up with a yawn.

I was working at the front desk of my father's gym, hoping to make some extra cash. After what happened in Cancún with Jaxon, I immediately quit my on-campus work-study job. There was no way I could face him after everything I'd been through. I didn't even know if it was him or Mark who had given me syphilis, but either way, I was entirely too embarrassed to find out. And now I was flat-broke, working here for minimum wage with a bare face, a tired bun, and nails that needed to be refilled.

After ending the call, I heard the bell on the front entrance chime. I looked up to see Malachi swaggering in with a determined look on his face. His hair was freshly cut with expensive threads encasing his athletic frame. As he was about to breeze past me, our eyes momentarily met. Not knowing how to respond, since I hadn't seen him since Spring Break, I offered an awkward wave to say hello. Things had already been tense between us for some time now, but after being hospitalized for an STD, one of which I already knew he'd been made aware of, I almost anticipated this moment being weird.

With his gold fronts slightly on display, he chucked up his chin. "Where Pop's at?" he asked.

"In the back. He just got off from work, so he's tired," I said. My daddy worked for UPS during the day, and at night, he would open his gym up for local fighters in the area. Boxing had always been my daddy's passion, but it seems that delivering packages had been his means of income for the past twenty-some-odd years.

Without another word, Malachi walked off toward our father's office. Releasing a sigh, I watched as he continued to stroll away. Admittedly, it still bothered me how distant we'd become. We were so far apart that even a stranger wouldn't predict that we were siblings. Right when my eyes returned to the computer screen to check the last of my emails, I caught bare, sweat-covered abs in my peripheral. Taking in each of his perfectly carved muscles, I leisurely allowed my eyes to travel up to his not-so-quite six-foot frame.

However, staring back at me was just an average-looking face—a six at best. Everything, from his everyday haircut to his plain-colored brown skin, was basic. No waves, smooth, dark melanin, or even a perfect set of white teeth adorned this guy. He had a noticeable chip in his smile, and his eyes were low, almost appearing chinked. Inwardly, I groaned at what a waste of an impeccable body he was.

"What'chu need?" I asked with an attitude.

"We need more towels in the back," he said. "They told me to come up here."

"And exactly who is 'they'?"

He let out a snort and shook his head. "Ya pops, mane. Dang," he said.

With a quick roll of my eyes, I got up from the desk and pulled my short jean shorts down from where they'd been creeping up my thighs.

"I'll be right back," I told him.

After walking to the back cabinet, where I knew we always kept fresh towels, I grabbed a short stack and headed back. As I rounded my desk, I threw a towel at him, which ended up hitting him in the face.

"Damn, it's like that?" he said with a chuckle.

I shot him a knowing look over my shoulder before continuing on my path. When I got to the back of the gym, the repetitious sound of punching bags being hit by leather gloves overpowered the room. The sole stench of testosterone filled the air.

"Damn, it stinks back here," I fussed, fanning my hand in front of my face. Then finally, I saw my daddy coming toward me. "Where you want me to put these at?" I held out the towels for him to see.

"You gave one to Quick, right?"

"Who?" I asked, feeling my nostrils flare. With a simple nod of his head, my father gestured behind me toward Mr. Basic himself. "Yeah, I gave him one. Don't you see it around his neck?"

"Nigga, who the fuck you think you talking to like that?" I heard Malachi's voice boom from my right. His bright, hazel eyes glared in my direction like fireworks, as if they were about to explode from his head.

"I was just saying—"

"Nah, you wasn't saying shit," he cut me off and said, quickly yanking the towels from my hands. "Now take your li'l ass back up front."

All the guys standing around, including the one I now knew as Quick, erupted in laughter. My cheeks instantly burned from humiliation.

"Better yet . . ." Malachi paused, allowing his eyes to rake over me. "Take yo' ass home. And don't come back up in here 'til you find the rest of your clothes."

The banter around the gym continued until my father finally had to raise his voice. "Enough," he said. "You guys," he said, pointing his finger at Quick and the other boxers who were all standing around, "get back to work. And, Malachi, I need to see you guys in my office."

Feeling every bit like that 13-year-old girl who'd been utterly embarrassed by her big brother in front of all of his friends, I sulked, following behind the two of them. Once we were in my father's old, stuffy office that had painted cinder blocks for walls, he slammed the door shut.

"What the hell was that 'Chi?" he asked.

Malachi shrugged, still wearing a scowl on his face. "Don't ask me; ask her. She's the one with that fly-ass mouth, up in here showing her ass for everybody to see."

I sucked my teeth and rolled my eyes. "Whatever, Malachi. I dress like this all the time."

"Exactly. And that right there is the muhfuckin' problem. Ain't you supposed to be taking a break from hoeing?" My eyes instantly bucked from his words.

"Malachi, that's enough," my father barked, seeing my eyes instantly gloss over with tears. "How do you ever expect to run this place if you can't act right?"

"Run this place?" I asked just above a whisper.

My father's regard shifted in my direction before he nodded his head. "Yeah. I'm gonna let 'Chi run this place for a while. See if he can make some things happen around here. Besides, he needs something to keep him out of trouble 'til his trial."

Releasing a hard huff and puff, I spun around on my heels and stomped out the door. As I trekked back up front, I could hear my father shouting for me to return. But I just wanted to get out of there. I was irritated hearing that Malachi would be the one running the gym. One, because I knew he wouldn't let me slide when it came to strolling in late. And two, because I knew he'd embarrass the fuck out of me every time he'd catch me flirting with the guys. There was no way I could work there with him in charge. He'd be sure to make my life a living hell.

After responding to several more emails, I gathered my things and headed out the front door. Due to the days now running long, the sky was still filled with light, and cars still coursed the street. Using the app on my phone, I checked my bank account to see if I had enough to catch an Uber. And, of course, I didn't because I was beyond broke these days. Just as I considered going in to ask my father for a loan, Quick was walking out. A white tee shirt now covered his muscular chest, and a gym bag was slung over his right arm.

"Aye, you need a ride?" he asked, hitting the key fob to his car.

My eyes followed the sound of his doors unlocking until they stapled upon an old silver Hyundai. One that had been rusted out above the tires.

Without giving it a second thought, I shook my head. "Nah, I'm good."

"A'ight," he said, shrugging his lips.

As he began to walk away, I thought, *Do I really want to go back inside and beg for money?*

"Wait," I said, louder than expected. He raised his hand in the air.

With a short glance over his shoulder, a look of surprise etched across Quick's face. "'Sup?" he said, narrowing his eyes.

"I changed my mind. I'm gonna need that ride."

He let out a light snort of laughter before nodding his head toward his car. "Come on," he said.

I followed him a short way down the sidewalk until we finally reached his car alongside the curb. As soon as I went for the handle and opened the passenger-side door, the smell of pure funk collided with my nose.

"Oh shit," I gagged, instantly pulling my shirt up to cover the lower half of my face.

Already in the driver's chair, Quick chuckled. "My bad, my bad," he said, craning his neck to look in the backseat. "It's those dirty gym clothes from yesterday," he explained.

While he reached into the backseat and gathered up his mildewed clothes, I reluctantly sank into the passenger seat, straightaway noticing the shreds of fabric hanging down from the ceiling and the thin coat of dust spread across the dash. The car looked like it belonged more at the junkyard than on the road. I was beginning to have second thoughts. Riding around in something like this was all foreign to me. I mean, Mark drove a brand-new Range, and even Beetle had owned an old Porsche that he kept nice and clean. Hell, even Kiki had a Camry.

"I'm gon' go put these in the trunk," he said. "Be right back."

Still holding my breath from the horrible stench, I nodded.

It didn't take but a few seconds before he returned. "So, where to?" he asked, reaching down to cut on the air.

"I live off North Cedar. You know where that's at?"

"Yeah," he nodded. "I think so."

He pulled off, and we rode not exchanging any words for a while. I just sat there stewing over the fact that Malachi would soon be running the gym. Knowing I'd have to see his stupid face every day and that he'd make my life miserable angered me inside. I could only hope that his being there was only a temporary situation.

Maybe he's not completely out of the streets. Probably just a bullshit cover-up for his case.

"So," Quick said, taking me out of my thoughts, "you go to A&T?"

"Yeah." I gave a nonchalant shrug as I glanced down at my nails. *God, I need a fill-in.*

"That's what's up. So, what's your major?"

I shook my head. "I don't know yet. Probably General Studies or something like that."

"General Studies?" he questioned with a snort. "What kinda job you plan on getting with that?"

"Well, I don't plan on getting a job at all, if you must know," I said with a cluck of my tongue. "I want to be a housewife, a mother. You know, everyday shit like that, that you don't need a degree for."

He chuckled. "And let me guess. You only marrying a dude with money, right?"

Pointing a finger in his direction, I winked. "Bingo."

He shook his head.

"What?" I asked.

"Nothing," he muttered, keeping his eyes on the road.

"No, what? Just go ahead and say it. Typical gold digger, right?" I rolled my eyes.

He shook his head. "Nah. I'm just wondering why you're wasting your parents' money going to a four-year university if the only thing you intend to do is be a housewife. I mean, just find a rich dick to ride, and your problem is solved."

I let out a little laugh, thinking of how salty he sounded. "So what, you mad now? Mad that your li'l dick ain't rich enough for me to ride?" I mocked, taunting him. "Let me guess. You're probably one of them broke niggas from Smith Homes Projects—"

"Hampton Homes," he corrected, gripping the wheel. His nose flared as his chinky eyes focused ahead.

"Nigga, same fucking difference. You just a project bum that ain't never gon' be shit. Some wannabe boxer that ain't never gon' have shit. Yet, you look down at me and my plan like what you got going on is somehow better. Fuck outta here," I spat with a wave of my hand.

Clearly frustrated, he let out a sarcastic snort of laughter and shook his head.

"What? You thinking this little boxing shit you do at my daddy's gym gon' get you somewhere?" I taunted.

"I never said that," he said.

"So then, what? What's your plan? What kind of job you tryin'a get?"

Finally, he turned and looked at me. His full lips turned into a half smirk, half frown, and his dark brown eyes squinted even further into slits. "Mane, I swear you just ghetto for no fucking reason at all. You know that," he said. I scoffed with another dismissive wave of my hand. "I've known your pops for like eight years now and all he talks about is you. Like you're some kind of royal princess. But the way you carry yourself, I swear you'd never know it."

"The way I *carry* myself?" I scoffed, completely offended, as I brought my hand to my chest.

"Yes," he confirmed. "And to answer your question, I go to school too. Guildford Tech—"

"Oh, community college. Of course," I sneered.

Shifting his eyes back to the road, he shook his head again. "Yes, community college. After graduating with a 3.9 GPA, I got a full scholarship to go there."

"Well, if your GPA was all that, seems like you would've gotten scholarships from all over the place."

"And I did, but most were out of state. I can't leave my little brother and sister behind. I'm all they've got."

For some reason, the words *"I'm all they've got"* sobered me. "You mean . . ." I said softly, letting my voice trail off. "Where's your mother?"

Wearing an unconcerned expression, Quick allowed his right shoulder to hike. "She's around," he said. For some reason, I knew asking anything more would be considered intrusive, so I remained quiet. "But anyway, once I finish getting my accounting degree from there, I'm going to UNC Greensboro."

"Why not A&T?"

"Their accounting program isn't as good as UNC's."

I nodded. "So then you don't have some fairy-tale dream of becoming a famous boxer one day. Living some flashy Mayweather lifestyle?" I teased.

"Nah. I mean, if it happens, it happens." He smiled. "But I'm actually good at math; always have been. Eventually, I wanna be a CPA." Suddenly, his car slowed, and when I glanced out the passenger window, I realized that we had pulled up in front of Holland Hall. The sky had completely turned gray, indicating that nightfall was approaching. "Well, anyway, I hope everything works out for you. The whole housewife and kids deal," he said.

Somehow, feeling different from when I'd originally stepped foot in this car, I became ashamed. "Thanks," I mumbled. "And thanks for the ride."

Instead of getting out of the car, I sat there momentarily, taking in his overly angular jaw, those tiny little freckles that scattered beneath his slanted eye, ones you didn't often find on men of his complexion. And then that broad, African nose and thick set of lips that brought sliced peaches to mind. *Hmm . . . nah.*

"See you around," I finally said.

Quick chucked up his chin that was lightly sprinkled with hair and smirked. "See ya."

I hopped out of the car, and as I headed inside the dorms, I ran into our resident advisor, Nina. She was sitting out on the front steps eating sunflower seeds.

"New boyfriend?" she asked, nodding toward the road.

I didn't even have to look back to know she was referring to Quick. "Nah," I told her.

"Didn't think so. Definitely not your type."

Not knowing whether to be proud or ashamed of that, I kept making my way through the door. After riding the elevator up, I entered our suite, only to find cardboard boxes stacked in the living room. Words like "Kitchen," "Bathroom," and "Hope's bedroom" were written on each one. Instead of ducking off to my room like usual, I headed to the back, allowing the sounds of music and laughter to lead me toward Franki's room.

Shaking off the twinge of jealousy I felt, I knocked on the open door. "Hey," I said, peeping my head inside.

"Hey," Hope said cheerfully as she sat with her back against the headboard, lying there as if this was her very own room. Bare brown legs hung out of an oversized tee shirt. She stuffed her face from a bag of Lay's potato chips.

I glanced down at Franki, who was sitting Indian-style on the floor. "'Sup?" she said. The flatness in her tone made me wonder if it was more of a question than a greeting.

"Hey," I said again.

"Sorry for all the boxes out there. We'll be out of your hair by Sunday," Paris said with her eyes cast down in a cardboard box.

"You guys moving?" I asked, surprised.

"Yeah, Paris found us a little house to rent nearby," Hope chimed in. "Four bedrooms and two baths."

"Wow," was all I could say.

For the past four weeks, all three of them had been walking past me, barely saying two words. And while I knew I was the one to blame for all of that, I'd be lying if I said my feelings weren't a little hurt that I hadn't been included. I've never had sisters. Hell, I barely even had friends, but something about the bond they shared made me want to fit in and be a part of it. But I just had this wall up. It had been there ever since middle school, where girls would pick on me for one thing or another. If it wasn't my hair that wasn't done right or my clothes that were ill-fitting due to my slim frame, it was my sneakers because they weren't the latest style. *"Just because you're light skinned doesn't mean you're all that,"* they would say.

But once I got to high school and 'Chi started making a little money, I instantly upgraded myself. From my hair and clothes all the way down to my shoes. Instead of becoming a part of the so-called in-crowd—the girls who'd previously made fun of me, I became their bully. I'd let them know off the top that they were beneath me, and I'd make it a point to shit on them every chance I got. While they were still wearing Nikes on their feet, I was sporting Balenciagas. While they were all carpooling in compact cars, I was getting dropped off by a Lexus, Beamer, or a Benz. I rode around town with niggas that damn near dripped in diamonds and gold. My hair and nails got done regularly, and when I'd go shopping, it would look like I'd bought up the entire mall.

For so long, I'd hated girls. Literally, detested what they seemed to represent: cattiness and competitiveness. But after watching the three of them—Paris, Hope, and Franki, all laughing together, supporting one another through real-life shit, somehow, I felt different inside. It was like a sisterhood or some kind of special sorority that, for the first time, I secretly wanted to be a part of.

"Well, if you guys need any help on move-in day, just let me know," I said softly.

Chapter 7

Hope—Stars in the Darkness

"But I don't wanna be here all by myself tonight," I whined.

I sat back on Franki's bed, sulking as I watched her get dressed for the club. She paired a red skintight dress with some leopard print heels. Her hair was pinned to the side, allowing her natural tendrils to fall over her right shoulder. Franki was a total knockout with a shape similar to Betty Boop's and the face of an African queen.

"Sorry, ma," she said, letting her New York accent cut through. "You're gonna have to sit this one out. I can't babysit you tonight."

It was the last party of the year, and everyone was talking like it would be the biggest event in the world. No, I didn't do clubs or dance, but I just didn't want to be here alone. Other than stepping out on campus to take my final exams, I'd been cooped up in the dorms day in and day out. I needed to be 18 for a night. I needed to breathe.

I sucked my teeth. "I'm not a kid, Franki. You don't need to babysit me. Besides, I'm just going to sit there and watch everyone dance. I just want to go out and listen to some music. I need some fresh air. A change of scenery."

"Well, how about we go for a walk tomorrow then?" she proposed.

"A walk? What do I look like, a dog?"

Laughing, she reached for a tube of lipstick on her dresser. "And what about Meeko? You know he's probably gonna be there."

After our big fallout, I didn't want to risk seeing him again. At least not yet. Ever since my trip to the clinic, I'd fallen both physically and emotionally ill. My heart felt like it had been shattered twice. I needed the solitude and seclusion of these past few weeks, giving me time to mend—to process everything that had happened. However, I was far from being completely healed, and I knew seeing him again this soon might've derailed my progress.

"I don't care," I whispered.

"You don't care? What's that supposed to mean?"

"It means if I see him, I see him, and if I don't, I don't." I shrugged, putting on a nonchalant face, although I was still grieving inside.

"Aw, shit," she muttered with a shake of her head. "Paris . . ."

Being only across the hall, Paris walked right on in, wearing a pale pink bodycon dress that exposed the tops of her shoulders adorning her curvy frame. She held her hair up in a ponytail and clenched a black rubber band between her teeth. "Huh?" she mumbled, raising her brows.

"Hope says she's tryin'a go out tonight."

Paris removed the hair tie from her mouth and began wrapping it around her hair. "Go out where?"

"To the club . . . with us."

"Oh, absolutely not," she said.

"Look, I'm not asking permission from either one of you. And as a matter of fact, I believe that I'm the oldest here. If I'm not allowing my deddy to tell me what to do, what makes you two think I'll let either of you?" I was getting angry.

Paris and Franki locked eyes before Franki finally burst into laughter.

"For Christ's sake, Hope, it's not that friggin' serious. Just calm down," Paris said.

"No. Don't tell me to calm down," I said, shooting up from the bed with my fists balled at my sides. "I'm not some little kid that you can just tell what to do. I'm done with that. My deddy's not telling me what to do. Meeko's not telling me what to do, and neither are the two of you."

Franki allowed her head to fall back, roaring in laughter again. "Yo, I swear them balls you got hanging over there been growing by the day," she teased.

"Shut up, Franki," both Paris and I yelled at the same time.

"It's not funny," Paris said. Then she turned to me, softening her eyes. "Look, realistically speaking, you really don't need to be out in a club right now. You've been through so much, and the last thing we need is for you to run into Meeko. How about we go to the movies tomorrow? Maybe catch a bite to eat?" she tried.

With a hard roll of my eyes, I shook my head and walked past her out the door. "Give me twenty minutes, and I'll be ready," I tossed over my shoulder.

"Oh my God, yo, please tell me she's not about to go in there and throw on that ugly-ass skirt," I heard Franki mutter.

Turning around, I stomped back into her room. I didn't bother acknowledging either of them as I headed straight for Franki's wardrobe, pulling out her black tee shirt dress before carelessly throwing it over my arm. Then I reached down and removed a pair of silver thong-toed sandals from a cardboard box where she'd packed up most of her shoes.

"And I'll be back later for your silver clip-ons," I said, referring to the earrings she'd previously let me borrow since my ears weren't pierced.

After storming out of the door, I headed to my bathroom and jumped in the shower. It didn't take me long at all to complete my so-called look. Once I had on the dress that casually spilled off one of my shoulders and the sandals wrapped around my unpolished toes, I added a thin coat of Carmex to my lips. My long, puffy, black hair hung down my back with little to no style, and my overgrown bangs prickled the tops of my eyes. These days, I no longer wear my hair in a bun. I'd been feeling much too lazy and even more rebellious for that.

With a pair of glasses resting above my nose, I headed into the living room, immediately seeing the girls taking a round of shots.

"I'm ready," I said, stepping into their line of sight.

Franki let out a childish snicker and shook her head. "You cute or whatever," she said. "Earrings are on the table."

Franki and Paris grabbed their purses from the other room as I went over to clip them to my ears. I wasn't a purse kind of girl, so I wore a simple black wallet that dangled from my wrist. After Paris locked the door, we took the elevator to the lobby. Josh and one of his frat brothers, Todd, were waiting in all black.

"Y'all look nice," Josh said, his eyes stapled only to Franki. He hooked an arm around her itty-bitty waist and gently took her by the lips. Before envy could even wash over me, I turned and looked away.

"Come on, Josh. Geez. Let the poor girl up for air, will ya?" Paris complained.

Josh pulled back with a wide grin, thumbing away the wetness from his lips. "Nah, that's not me. That's her," he said, shaking his head. Franki gasped, feigning surprise.

"Oh, I believe you. Miss *'He's not my man. Ain't nobody checking for church boy Josh's pretty ass,'*" Paris mocked dramatically, snaking her neck. Everyone laughed, including me.

"Man, fuck y'all," Franki chuckled, raising her middle finger in the air. Josh quickly tapped her hand down and whispered something in her ear, making her roll her eyes.

Feeling the fun finally commence, we all headed out of the dorm, immediately colliding with the muggy night air. My hair began to swell before I could even enter Josh's truck. Despite my religion, it's one of the top reasons I'd always kept it in a bun. From my experience, natural hair and humidity didn't mix. As Todd and I went to hop in the back, Franki and Paris simultaneously reached for the front door. I couldn't help but giggle.

"Baby, tell her to let me ride up front," Franki told Josh. Her voice was unbelievably sweet.

Paris's mouth dropped open as her eyes stretched wide. "Baby?" she exclaimed. "Oh, so now, you're pulling the girlfriend card?"

"Damn right," Franki muttered.

Paris huffed before finally sliding into the backseat with Todd and me, grumbling something about motion sickness beneath her breath.

Suddenly, I felt Todd lean in toward me. The warmth of his mouth came to my ear. "You look real pretty tonight," he whispered.

I felt my cheeks instantly go warm. I'd been around Todd a time or two before, and from what I could tell, he seemed like a nice guy. He was a tall, lanky guy with a light caramel complexion and small, dark brown eyes. He wore glasses that were a bit more stylish than mine and always kept his hair cut low. He wasn't flashy like the rest of the fraternity guys, constantly stepping on the yard or making some big spectacle in the club. He mostly stood off to the side, observing. Every so often, he threw up a sign or howled some sort of chant but mostly was quiet like me.

It took us about fifteen minutes to get to the clubhouse, and when we pulled up, we saw the line extended well beyond the door.

"Can you get us in?" Franki looked at Josh and asked.

"Yeah, Chevy's got someone at the door," he told her.

As the five of us headed toward the club, I took in all the half-dressed girls standing in line. They all wore high heels and long weaves reaching just beyond their lower backs. My look was completely casual compared to everyone out there, including Franki and Paris. I might as well have been going to the mall rather than the club, but I didn't even care. I'd dressed ordinary my entire life. I wasn't the girl who broke necks or hearts at every turn. I was quiet and demure, attributes that had always gone unnoticed by the opposite sex *until* . . .

When we finally walked through the double doors of the club, the music blared in my ears. Instinctively, I clutched my chest, feeling the loud base rattle inside. As we began weaving through the crowd behind Josh, I held Franki's hand. I was starting to feel antsy for some reason and stopping every few steps just so that Josh could clap hands with this one and that one, which didn't make things any better. *You're popular, we get it,* I thought. I just wanted to get out of the mob, and for some reason, I felt like I shouldn't have come.

Apparently, whatever song the DJ played had Franki's head steadily bopping to the beat. I could tell that she was getting herself hyped for the dance floor. Seconds later, we spotted a couple of empty seats by the bar. Paris all but ordered me to sit.

"We'll be right back. Don't move. Don't talk to anyone. Don't drink anything," she warned.

Feeling belittled, I rolled my eyes. However, I decided to take a seat. While the three of them raced to the dance floor, Todd hopped on a stool next to me.

"You don't dance?" He leaned over, trying to talk over the music.

I shook my head. "No, I don't know how."

His eyes widened in surprise. "You should let me teach you," he said.

"Well, I don't see you out there either. In fact, I don't think I've ever seen you dance."

Todd stood up just as "Wipe Me Down" started to play. His lanky arms went up in a flash and began waving wildly from side to side. When his hands curved at the wrists, resembling the heads of snakes, I knew he was doing his fraternity stroll. I'd seen Josh do it at parties time and time again. When Todd made a silly face and stuck out his tongue, I couldn't help but throw my head back in a laugh.

Suddenly, out of the blue, someone bumped hard into Todd, knocking him off his rhythm. When I looked to see who it was, my eyes locked in with Meeko's cold glare. His face was twisted into a nasty snarl. Just that quick, a lump instantly formed in my throat, and a pang shot through my chest. Sure, I talked tough back at the dorm, but seeing him after all these weeks instantly pained me inside. After letting his eyes sweep me over in disgust one final time, he walked into the crowd.

"You know dude?" Todd asked, pointing his thumb back over his shoulder. I nodded, unable to speak. "Meeko Taylor, right? Football team?" he asked. I simply nodded again.

I thought I'd be okay with seeing him again, but, boy, was I wrong. I needed to get out of there, fast.

"I, um," I let out, taking a hard swallow. "I've got to use the restroom."

Hopping off the stool, I immediately went on the dance floor in search of one of the girls. One swaying body after another knocked into me as I walked through the thick crowd. Finally, I spotted Paris dancing with Ty. Her arms looped around his neck while trying to follow the beat. Then from the corner of my eye, not too far off, I also saw Meeko. The girl dancing before him was bent over with her hands on her knees. She wiggled her jiggly behind all over his groin while swinging her long weave from left to right. His smile was as wide as the Tallahatchie River. *Jerk.*

Without warning, my heart sank to the pit of my stomach, and hot vomit crept to the back of my throat. My hand covered my mouth just in the nick of time before I took off running toward the restrooms. I could hardly see between the tears in my eyes, the clouds of smoke, and the minimal lighting in the club. And before I knew it, I crashed right into someone . . . and vomit shot out of my mouth.

"You bitch!" Jazz screamed. Arms out wide, she looked down at her white outfit, completely covered in puke.

"I'm sorr—"

"It's like you just *want* me to beat your ass," she said, shaking the vomit from her hands. "Learn how to hold your fucking liquor, you drunk bitch."

Before I even realized what was happening, my right fist connected with Jazz's jaw. Everyone that was gathered around gasped in shock. While they continued to taunt her with their laughter, she clutched her face, completely stunned.

"I'm gonna fucking kill you," she screamed.

My mouth opened to respond, but nothing would come out. I couldn't believe I'd actually done something as stupid as that, not with how everything had previously played out in court. My entire case against her had fallen through just because of our stupid fight outside Meeko's dorm room that day. The judge told us that if we ever came back for fighting again, he'd have us both convicted of assault. *And now look what I've done.*

Suddenly, Jazz's eyes darkened as if she were preparing for war. When she drew back an open palm, I instinctively flinched and closed my eyes, expecting her to strike. Oddly enough, it never happened. All of a sudden, people were shoving past me in an uproar, and when I opened my eyes, all I could see was Jazz laid out on the ground with Franki on top of her.

"Not today, bitch," Franki barked, striking her face with one fist after the other.

At this point, blood was spattering from Jazz's nose as she screamed out for help. Two guys standing next to me were also throwing blows, and just a short distance away, I saw random girls pulling at each other's hair. It was like one simple punch to Jazz's face had created pandemonium throughout the entire club. I don't know how to explain it, but adrenaline suddenly coursed through my veins at that moment. I wanted in. Right or wrong, I wanted Jazz to pay. Shoving Franki off of Jazz, I stooped down and sank my knee into her chest. Over and over, I drilled my fists into her face until my arms got tired. I wasn't even sure if I was doing it right, but as her fair skin turned flush, I felt an overwhelming sense of satisfaction.

"Get up, ma. You can't be out here fighting and shit," Franki snapped, gripping my upper arm as she tried to lift me from the ground.

All at once, I felt a strong arm wrap around my waist, hoisting me in the air. Even though my glasses fell to the ground, I couldn't have cared less at that moment. Mentally, I was still immersed in the fight with Jazz, kicking and screaming in rage as I continued swinging my fists midair. It was like I was crazed or something. As

I was being carted out of the club, I saw Paris, Ty, Franki, and Josh also heading for the door. Just as we came in contact with the night air, someone put me down on my feet. When I spun around and saw that it was Meeko, I instantly pushed him hard in the chest.

"Don't touch me. Don't you *ever* touch me!" I yelled.

He locked his hands tightly around my wrists and held me in place. "Fuck you out here fighting for, huh? You acting like a fucking bird now?" he questioned angrily with furrowed brows.

Even though he had my hands bound, I shoved him again, this time much harder than the last. "Get off of me," I screamed.

He instantly rocked back off balance until he had to let go of my wrists. His hands rushed to grab ahold of my waist to keep himself steady.

"The fuck?" he muttered. His eyes doubled in size as his hands slid around to my belly. "You pregnant?" I turned my face away, allowing my gaze to drift somewhere across the street. I wasn't prepared for this. Not now. Snatching me by the chin, Meeko forced me to look him in the eyes. "Nah, answer me, Hope. Are you fucking pregnant?"

I was five and a half months along with a small belly that had grown round and hard. I'd been wearing over-sized clothes these past few weeks to keep it hidden. At the clinic that day, I couldn't go through with the abortion. No matter what I kept telling myself, terminating my pregnancy would go against everything I'd ever been taught—everything I believed in. And every day since, I'd been battling my own fear, wondering how I would do this all alone. Up until now, Paris and Franki were the only ones that knew. I'd even been sending my father's calls to voicemail because I was too afraid that if he'd heard my voice, somehow, he'd know. Most nights, when my head hit the pillow, my mind would race, thinking of the best plan. Should I tell my father and move back home? Should I keep Meeko in the dark and raise my child alone? I'd been so confused. But now, the reality of the situation was staring me right in the face.

"I didn't get the abortion," I said just above a whisper. People were rushing out of the club, and police sirens were getting louder in the distance.

"So you lied to my fucking face." His voice boomed as he nudged my face away.

That's when Franki and everyone else walked outside. "Don't you put your hands on her," Franki warned.

Meeko completely ignored her, keeping his eyes honed in on me. "So, you mean to tell me that you out here in a fucking club, around all this gah-damn smoke with niggas all in yo' face, while you pregnant? That's the type of shit you on now, Hope?" He cocked his head to the side.

"Damn," I heard Ty mutter behind me.

Guiltily, I shook my head. "I was just—"

"Then you got the nerve to be fighting like some . . ." His words trailed off as he gnashed on his back teeth, clearly enraged.

"Meeko, she just wanted to get out. She was only going to sit by the bar," Paris tried to explain.

"You ain't got to explain shit to this nigga. If he hadn't done all the stupid shit he did, she wouldn't be here in the first place," Franki argued.

Meeko looked at Josh, who was standing behind her. "Aye, come get your girl, yo," Meeko warned.

"Nah, son," Franki said, clasping her hands together and wagging her head as she stepped into Meeko's personal space. "He ain't coming to get shit. Like I said, don't put your fucking hands on her." She pointed her finger at me for effect.

With a look of disbelief, Meeko's head reared back. "Man, ain't nobody put their hands on shorty." Sucking his teeth, he shook his head. "You know what, man? Fuck all y'all. Got her out here in a fucking club knowing damn well she's pregnant."

Suddenly, a wave of guilt washed over me because he was absolutely right. Here I was in a smoke-filled club, pregnant with a baby he thought didn't even exist. God, I was wrong on so many levels.

"Meek—"

"Nah," he said, cutting me off as he shook his head. "Don't say shit to me, yo. I'm done."

Before I could say another word, I felt a hand on my shoulder. I looked up to see Todd standing next to me with a look of apprehension in his eyes.

"Everything okay, Hope?" he asked.

Out of nowhere, Meeko stepped forward and crashed a fist into Todd's jaw. The impact of the punch nearly dropped him to the ground.

"Oh my God," I shrieked. "Todd, are you okay?" I rushed to his aid.

"Now, how 'bout you dance on that li'l nigga," Meeko seethed, sending a shot of spit onto the concrete as he pulled up his semisagging jeans.

Josh immediately came to Todd's defense, pushing Meeko back so hard that he stumbled. "What's your problem, B?" Josh snapped.

Ty immediately jumped between the two, his chest puffed out, ready to square up with Josh.

"Guys, stop. Please," Paris shrieked.

Releasing a sardonic laugh, Meeko held both hands in the air. "Ain't no problem, yo, is there?" He looked down at Todd, who was still curled over, checking his mouth for blood. "I bet yo' ass learn not to touch what ain't yours the next time, won't you?" Meeko taunted.

My eyes widened at the audacity. "What *ain't* yours?" I repeated. "I don't belong to anyone. And especially *not* to you."

He stepped into me so close that he towered above my frame. The warm alcohol scent of his breath wafted over me. "You may not, but this right here," he said, slowly placing his palm against my belly. "*That's* mine. And don't you forget that shit." The solemnity in his voice was so intense it sent a shiver down my spine.

"That's Twelve, yo," Ty said. Flashes of red and blue suddenly scanned across his face. "Let's be out."

Franki immediately grabbed me by the hand and began running in the opposite direction, dragging me toward Josh's truck with Paris, Josh, and Todd all following behind us. I kept looking back for Meeko the entire way there, hoping he'd gotten away. Now that he knew about the baby, I couldn't pinpoint exactly how I felt . . . somewhere between sadness and relief. After we all piled into the truck, Josh slammed his foot on the gas. The tires screeched as we weaved through the crowded parking lot. When we hit the road, he started going in on Franki.

"So, now, it's cool for pregnant women to go out to the club? *That's* what we doing now, ma?"

"I'm not that girl's momma. I can't tell her what to do. I can't tell her where not to go."

"Got me out here fighting niggas I'm supposed to be cool with," he muttered, shaking his head.

"Meeko is just an ass," Paris chimed in and said.

"Nah, I would've reacted the exact same way," Josh said, cutting his eyes at Franki with his nose flared. Then he looked at me through the rearview mirror. "You know you gotta take extra precautions now that you're carrying a child, right? Anything could've happened to you. And fighting . . ." His words trailed off as he shook his head in disappointment.

"I told her to stay home, but she wouldn't listen," Franki's voice softened as she tried to explain.

"Well then, you should've told me because I would've left her there. You know damn well I don't condone no mess like that," he scolded.

I didn't even think Josh could get mad, but the tightness in his jaw as he stared at the road ahead had proven otherwise. Suddenly, I felt terrible for being the cause of everyone's drama. I turned and looked at Todd, whose jaw was now swollen and bruised. Like a sad little puppy, he just gazed out the window.

"I'm sorry, Todd," I whispered.

He didn't even respond. In fact, the remainder of the ride was extremely quiet. Paris had fallen asleep against the window while everyone else seemed deep in their thoughts. When we pulled up to Holland Hall, I apologized again to Josh and Todd before finally exiting. As I trekked across the lawn, my arm hooked to Paris's, I could hear the muted sounds of Josh and Franki's argument continuing in the truck. I felt horrible.

When I returned to my room, I jumped in the shower and changed into my pajamas. As I cut off my lamp, my cell phone vibrated on the nightstand next to me. I picked it up, seeing that it was a text from Meeko.

Meeko: You make it home safe?

Me: Yes.

Meeko: When's your next appointment?

Knowing immediately that he was referring to the baby, I returned a quick text.

Me: Next Wednesday at ten.

Meeko: I'll be there to pick you up at nine.

Me: Okay.

At that moment, remorse weighed heavily on my shoulders. Not that I regretted keeping this child, but rather for withholding its existence from Meeko. Though

I tried telling myself otherwise, I knew the only reason I didn't tell him was to punish him. I wanted him to suffer just as bad, if not more, than I'd been hurting these past few months. I'd always been taught that plotting revenge implies weakness, but finding it within ourselves to forgive, that takes strength.

Since the start of my freshman year, I'd been so caught up with trying to live for everyone else that the very core of who I was had somehow gotten lost. I'd been trying to please my father yet still fit in with my girls. I'd been relishing in the depths of being in love yet fearing what the church might have to say. My connection with Meeko had become so powerful and potent that I was essentially fighting over this man, crying over him to the point where I could no longer recognize myself in the mirror. *I've forgotten who I am.*

Me: Can we talk?

I waited an hour that night, hoping Meeko would finally respond. But as the minutes ticked by, I got absolutely nothing. I understood that keeping his baby a secret wouldn't easily be absolved, and neither would me fighting in the club tonight. But with time, I hoped that the two of us could eventually figure things out because, emotionally, I was drowning in having to carry this burden all alone. While Franki promised to help with the baby, Paris offered to pay the rent with her trust. But even with all that, I was still worried. Over and over that night, I prayed that God would dull the aching in my heart. That He would somehow remove the constant troubles scurrying through my mind.

"Have faith, Hope. Hold on. Everything's going to be all right."

Chapter 8

Franki—In This Together

"You want one scrambled egg or two?"

Glancing up from where my head rested on the table, I looked to see Josh standing by the stove. His shirt was off, and his basketball shorts were riding so low that his boxers were on display. Rather than using my voice, I held up two fingers before burying my face back into the crook of my arm. I'd been in a mood since last night, sulking because I knew he'd be leaving today.

"So, you think you're gonna like it here? Being this far away from me?" he said, a hint of a smile in his voice.

The girls and I had been in our new place for three days. Josh was nice enough to help us move in, and he and I have been inseparable ever since. We'd been ordering carryout, watching movies, and damn near smothering each other in this house because we both knew that this day had been right around the corner.

As I lifted my head from the table, I could hear him cracking the egg against the pan. "I'm not that far from campus. Besides, I thought you'd spend most nights here with me."

"You look tired, baby," he said. "Com'ere."

I trudged over, smelling the pork bacon he had sizzling on the stove. After wrapping my arms around his waist, I sighed and pressed my face against his back. "I don't want you to leave," I whined.

He turned around and hurriedly took me in his arms. "I gots to," he said, kissing my forehead. "But I'ma see you in five weeks, remember?" I nodded, thinking about his promise to send for me as soon as the first summer session ended. "But, umm . . ." He lifted his hand to scratch behind his ear, his expression quickly shifting to a more serious one. "I do need to talk to you about something."

I looked up into his dark brown eyes, seeing an unexpected urgency flashing within them. "Yo, you scaring me. What's wrong?" I asked. He cleared his throat before biting down on his inner cheek. "Just tell me," I urged.

"Some of the guys asked me to move into the frat house for senior year," he said.

He didn't have to explain any further. "I see."

"But if you don't want me to move in there, I can just stay in the dorms. Like you said, I'll be over here most of the time anyway."

"Josh, I don't want—"

"Nah, ma, you right. Too much partying and drinking. Girls in and out at all times of the night. I can't be around all that," he said, talking himself out of it before I even got a chance to respond.

"Josh," I said, grabbing ahold of his face so that he'd look me in the eyes. "Just stop."

"Nah. I've made up my mind. I'm good."

"Listen," I said, inhaling deeply. "If you want to move into the frat house, that's fine. I won't be mad."

"I'm not worried about you being mad. I want you to be comfortable wherever I'm at. I don't want you thinking about . . ." His words trailed off as he took his bottom lip between his teeth.

"The rape?"

He slowly nodded. "Yeah, that. I swear I've been looking all over for that nigga . . ." His voice trailed off as he shook his head.

"I saw him," I whispered.

With his eyes suddenly popping wide, Josh's chin jerked back. "You what?"

"I saw him. A few days after we got back from Cancún," I confessed.

"W-where? When?" He was at a loss for words.

"When I went with the girls to get my nails done. He and Levar were coming out of the Mexican place next door."

Tilting his head to the side, he tightened the look in his eyes. "And you ain't say nothing?"

I shrugged, avoiding his eyes. "For what? What good would it do?" I asked, spinning around to walk away.

Josh grabbed my arm but quickly released it. "You know what? You right," he said, letting out a sarcastic snort before pinching the bridge of his nose. Then he turned back to tend to the food.

Occupying the room for the next few moments was an awkward silence with me sitting at the table while he began plating the food. Sure, I had thought about telling Josh, but it had been too much emotionally. I simply wanted to forget it had ever happened. I wanted to start piecing my life back together rather than focus on everything that had caused it to fall apart.

"Food's done," he said, dropping the plate of food on the table before me.

"You're not eating?"

Caressing his inner cheek with his tongue, he shook his head. "Nah, I gotta hit the road," he muttered.

"Josh." Disregarding me altogether, he began walking away. "Josh, wait," I said again, getting up from my seat.

I followed him down the hall to my bedroom, where he began packing the rest of his things. I stood in the entryway watching him angrily tossing clothes into a duffle bag. His face scowled, and his jaw flexed the entire time.

"I'm sorry," I said.

He looked back over his shoulder at me. "Sorry for what? I mean, telling me wouldn't have done no good, right?" he said, cynicism dripping from his tone.

That's when I realized Josh's ego was bruised. He wanted to be my protector—my hero. Yet, here I was, trying to take all that away from him. I walked over and sat next to his bag on the bed. "You're not a fighter, Josh," I sighed, looking up to see the frown still on his face. "I don't expect you to try to fight all my battles for me. That's not why I'm with you."

"Just because I don't fight don't mean I can't, Franki," he snapped. "Here I am thinking we're in this thing together and come to find out, you've been keeping secrets." He was so angry that veins bulged from his neck.

"I just didn't want to drag you down with all my baggage," I tried explaining.

"But I'm your man, ma. *Your* baggage is *my* baggage. Your beef is my beef."

"But you don't fight, Josh. Shit, nigga, you barely even cuss. None of that. What I look like expecting you to track down Jamel and his boys? That ain't you."

Sensing that Josh probably felt his manhood was under attack, I reached for his arm. I didn't want him to feel that I thought any less of him or that I didn't feel safe with him because that was far from the truth. In fact, in Josh's presence is when I felt most at peace. I didn't think about my father like I did when I was back home in New York. Nor did I brood over the rape like I did when a random group of guys would pass me by. Somehow, being around Josh always put me at ease. His entire being personified serenity. But even still, I didn't want him handling this for me. I needed him to let it go.

"You don't need to pretend to be some tough guy just to be with me. I love you just the way you are."

Suddenly, our eyes met as the realization of those little words hit us for the very first time.

He took me by the hand and lifted me from the bed, only to sit down and place me back on his lap. "Ever since that night, I've tried my best to be there for you. Through the nightmares, the breakdowns, everything, I've been there. And here I am thinking that we in this shit together while you out here still thinking you can handle it all on your own."

"Josh, the last person I loved who called themselves trying to defend me is gone. My daddy is locked behind bars 'til God knows when. And after all these years, he still refuses to see me," I cried, shaking my head. "I don't want you in none of my drama, yo. Some days, I feel like I'm fucking cursed, and I just . . . I just can't pull you into that. I love you too much."

He hooked his finger under my chin and gazed into my teary eyes. "Stop saying that. You're not cursed. You're blessed beyond belief, baby. I guarantee that if you start counting your blessings, God will provide everything you desire and more. When things go wrong, just sit back and reflect on all the things that're going right," he said. "And as far as me fighting your battles, you let *me* worry about that." I nodded as he leaned in to peck me gently upon my lips. "The Bible tells us to carry each other's burdens, and in this way, you'll fulfill the law of Christ, right?" He thumbed away a falling tear from my cheek as I nodded again. "Then let me do what I'm supposed to do, baby. Stop making things so damn hard."

Burying my face right beneath his, in the nook of his neck, I put my arms around him and squeezed. "Why you gotta be so perfect, yo?" I whispered.

He released a light snort of laughter. "I'm nowhere near perfect. Now, come on; let's go eat."

I pulled back, wearing a smirk on my face. "Oh, so you eating now?" I asked mockingly.

He twisted his lips to the side and shook his head. "You already knew I was eating," he said, lightly tapping me on the ass. "Now go fix me a plate, ma. I'm hungry."

"Hmm." *I got something you can eat, all right.*

As soon as I stood to my feet, he yanked me back down and kissed me unexpectedly. Our tongues immediately began to dance together so passionately that my lips tingled, and my inner belly started to quake. Somehow, in the back of my mind, I believed that Joshua McDuffey would always have that kind of effect on me. He could shut me right on up and take my breath away all in one little kiss. He peered deep into my eyes when he placed a final peck to my lips, pushing back a wispy curl from my face.

"Oh, and . . . I love you too, Franki."

I didn't expect him to say it back. In fact, a part of me didn't even want him to say it at all. But from the intense glinting in his eyes, I knew he was speaking from his heart. Church boy Josh was definitely in love with the kid.

After sharing another soul-stirring kiss, we finally headed back into the kitchen. Sitting at the table half-dressed, we both ate, talked, and laughed—enjoying the fact that we had the house all to ourselves. When hours and hours had passed to the point of the sun starting to set, Josh decided to stay just one more night. Neither of us wanted to let go, but his internship awaited him back in New York. We had no other choice but to part ways. It almost made me sad knowing I'd wasted over half a year playing games with this man. But now, I had his heart and would be counting down the days until I finally got to see him again.

***

"Uugh," Paris fumed walking through the front door, letting it slam behind her. Her face was bright red, and I could see anger burning in her eyes.

"Shh," Hope said, eyes remaining on the television screen. Still in our pajamas, we sat on the couch watching some off-the-wall show she liked called *Married at First Sight*.

"Don't be coming up in here making all that damn noise," I fussed.

Paris didn't pay either of us any mind. She came in, flopping down on the love seat. "I was at the hair salon, and my friggin' card got declined," she ranted. "Both of them."

"Well, did you call the bank?" I asked.

She ran her fingers through the fine tresses of her hair in angst. "They aren't debit cards. They're my credit cards," she said.

"Well, did you go over the limit?"

She gave me a deadpan expression before ultimately rolling her eyes. "They're Black Cards, Franki. They have no limit." She took her thumb into her mouth and began chewing on her nail as if she were thinking. "It's got to be a mistake," she said. "Let me call the credit card company now."

When she took her cell phone out of her purse, Hope jumped up from the couch and groaned loudly.

"Ugh." With a fuzzy blanket wrapped around her waist, she stomped back to her bedroom, mumbling angrily beneath her breath.

"For Christ's sake, what's gotten into her now?" Paris asked.

I let out a light chuckle and shook my head. "What's gotten into her?" I repeated rhetorically. "Shorty was minding her own business, watching her show, and then you come up in here all loud with your drama. *That's* what's wrong with her."

She pursed her lips to the side as if what I had just said was completely wrong. "You know what I mean. Not just today. For the past few days now, she's been in a mood. A foul one," she said.

"Did you forget about the incident in the club? The fight with Meeko?" I looked at her like she was crazy.

"I just hope he'll man up and at least take care of his kid," she said. "It's a good thing he's got Ty around."

I could feel my nose slightly flare at the mention of Ty's name. I had nothing personal against him, but lately, his name had been rolling off her tongue a little more than I could stand.

"Why?" I asked flat-out.

"Because he has a daughter that he takes care of. He's a good dad." She shrugged. "Maybe he'll be a positive influence on Meeko where that's concerned."

She's so damn delusional. I rolled my eyes. "I think Meeko will be just fine. He's already been checking in with her every day—"

"So they've talked?"

"Nah. Just by text, I think, but he's been asking if she's taking her vitamins like she's supposed to, shit like that. And he's taking her to the doctor tomorrow." Paris rolled her eyes. "Why'd you make that face? What's wrong?"

"Nothing," she said.

"Nah, ma," I laughed. "Spit that shit out."

"I just hope she doesn't fall for his shit again and go running back to him," she said, flipping her hair back off her shoulder.

"Oh, I see what it is," I said, bringing my fist to my mouth for another laugh.

"You see what? What is?"

I simply shook my head, not wanting to call her out. "Nothing."

"No, tell me," she prodded.

I shrugged my lips, indicating that if she wanted the real, I'd give it to her. "You just don't want Hope to forgive Meeko so she can be lonely and miserable like you," I said. "Now, tell me I'm wrong."

"Oh, please," she said, shooting up from the couch with her manicured finger pointed in my direction. "You're just lovesick right now and think everybody's lives should revolve around a man."

I couldn't help but laugh in her face again. Perhaps she was right about me being lovesick, but she knew just like I did that she was still hurting over Malachi. She simply didn't want Hope to be in a relationship because she wasn't in one.

"Whatever, yo," I said with a wave of my hand.

"If I wanted a man, I could have one, Franki. Guys hit on me all the time. Left and right, every day. And well, Ty—"

Suddenly, there was a knock at the door.

"You expecting company?" I asked.

After shaking her head to say no, she made her way over to the window. "Holy shit," she muttered, peeking out of the blinds.

"What? Who is it?" I asked, sitting up in my seat so my feet could hit the floor.

She turned around with a look of distress on her face. "It's my mother."

"Oh," I said. Stretching my lips into an awkward, sympathetic smile as I got up from the couch. "Good luck with that, ma."

As I wandered into the kitchen, I could hear Paris release a loud sigh before opening up the door.

"Mommy, what are you doing here?" was the first thing she asked.

"Well, hello to you too, darling," her mother said.

I glanced out of the kitchen into the living room, seeing the two exchange smooches on their cheeks. Of course, Ms. Rebecca was dressed to the nines. Chanel shades rested upon the blond crown of her head, and she wore white capris with a sleeveless white blouse. Gold accessories gleamed in her ears and around her wrists, pairing nicely with the strappy gold sandals on her feet. She made the simplest of ensembles look like a million bucks.

"So, how've you been?" she asked. She looked around the living room as her finger slid atop the end table as if inspecting for dust.

"I've been well, Mother," Paris said. "When did you get here? Why didn't you call?"

Her mother looked at her and smiled. "Well, I didn't think I had to call before I came," she said. "Besides, I have a surprise for you."

Fireworks instantly went off in Paris's eyes as she gasped. "A surprise?"

"Yes, dear," she nodded. "Look outside."

Paris went to the window and again peeked out of the blinds. "My car," she shrieked excitedly, jumping in place as she clasped her hands.

"Figured I wouldn't need to call for *that*." Her mother winked.

With her arms open wide, Paris ran to her mother and embraced her.

"Franki," Paris called out. "Franki!"

Reentering the living room, I pretended not to know what was going on. "Huh?" I said.

"My mother just brought me my car," she said. "Mom, you remember my roommate Franki?"

This time, her mother held her hand, void of any disgust written on her face. "Yes, I remember. How are you, dear?"

After pushing back the memories of her calling me ghetto trash, I reluctantly shook her hand. "Been doing good. How 'bout you?"

"I've been taking things day by day, dear. Thanks for asking," she replied. Her eyes roamed around the place once more as her lips shrugged semiapprovingly. "This is a nice little place you guys have here," she said.

"Yeah, it's slowly coming along quite nicely," Paris wanted her to know.

"So, where are the other two?" her mother asked.

"Oh, well, Hope's in her bedroom, and, well, Asha . . ." Paris shook her head. "I don't know where she is. She doesn't live with us anymore."

Ms. Rebecca's eyes widened at that a bit. "Oh, I see," she said, adding a phony smile. She reached into her purse and pulled out a set of keys. "Well, here you go. These are the keys to your car." She handed them over to Paris.

"Perfect," Paris said, bouncing on the balls of her feet. "Now, I've just got to call the credit card company."

"The credit card company? What for?" her mother asked.

With a puzzled look etched across her face, Paris shook her head. "Oh, nothing. It's just that my card got declined at the salon earlier. There's no limit, so I don't know why. It's got to be some kind of mistake," she said.

A sudden smile flickered in her mother's eyes. "Oh, about that," she said. "That's no mistake, my dear. I had your cards temporarily cut off."

Paris's eyes nearly doubled in size. "You did *what?*"

"I had your cards cut off," Ms. Rebecca repeated with her chin in the air. "Your spending has gotten out of control, Paris. From now on, I'm putting you on a budget."

"A budg—" Paris could barely say the word. "You can't do that," she exclaimed.

"Oh, but I can, dear," her mother said, raising her finger in the air. "You're blowing through close to five thousand a month." I nearly lost my shit when she shouted out that figure. "If I let you keep that up, by the time you turn 30, your trust will be halfway gone," she said.

"So you're using *my* money to pay the credit card bill?" Paris asked, a look of disbelief playing out on her face.

I took a few steps back, realizing that the tension in the room had suddenly turned thick. This was none of my business.

"Of course, I'm using your money to pay *your* credit card bill. You have got to get your spending under control, Paris," her mother scolded.

Paris's chest heaved up and down as tears filled her eyes. "My spending? Well, what about *you?* You've been gallivanting from continent to continent off of my father's money for years. Now, you're bringing your so-called lover along for the ride. My father left *me* that money." She pointed to her chest.

With her eyes blinking rapidly, a pretentious smile spread across her mother's face. Slowly, she stepped into her, almost closing the gap between them. "I was married to your father for seventeen years. I endured people looking at me as if I were doing something wrong. My own family turned their backs against me for marrying a Black man. They wanted nothing to do with you. But did I care? No. Because I was in love. Your father was the most handsome, successful, powerful man I'd ever met," she said.

"But as the years rolled by, I started spending more and more nights alone. By year five of our marriage, it felt like I was a single woman because your father's work always came first," she said, nodding in recollection. "Hell, if we're being honest, I feel like I practically raised you alone. And over the years, I suffered through two affairs."

All of a sudden, Paris's eyes strained in bewilderment. "That's right, your father cheated, Paris. Not once, but twice." She held up two fingers for emphasis. "So, you see, everything I'm spending, every vacation and every shopping spree, is one I've earned."

Visibly embarrassed, Paris's body went rigid, and her cheeks turned flush. "I've not taken anything that belongs to you, Paris," her mother continued. "The money your father left you in his will is all yours. But anything outside of that, you'll have to earn. You will get twelve hundred dollars a month to pay your bills and to keep your car running. Any other needs you have, the nails, the hair, the shopping . . ." She shook her head. "You'll need to start budgeting for that. There will be no usage of the credit cards."

I could see Paris take a deep swallow. "I can't live off of that. Our rent is nine fifty a month," she cried.

Inwardly, I felt bad because Paris promised to cover all the rent. She was even going to pay the household bills until I found a job.

"Well then, you and your roommates . . ." Ms. Rebecca looked over her shoulder directly at me, "will need to sit down and figure it all out. But that'll be all you get," she said. "Now, when you turn 21, you'll have full access to your trust. But until then, you're gonna have to budget."

"Mommy," Paris whined, "what about for emergencies?"

"You know you *do* have options, Paris."

"Options? What kind of options? You're the one that sent me to school halfway across the country. And now you want me to be all the way out here broke."

"What I mean is, you could always get a job." I knew that Paris's spoiled ass was not expecting her mother to say that. Paris's mouth damn near hit the floor. "Now, I have to run, dear. Enjoy your car and enjoy your new place." Her mother slipped her glasses down over her eyes and proceeded to the front door. Then she quickly turned back with a toss of her hair. "Oh, and if you want to have breakfast before I leave in the morning, just give me a buzz. I'm at the Grandover."

When her mother finally walked out, Paris turned to look at me. "What am I going to do now?" she cried, her face suddenly wet with tears.

She sank down on the couch and cradled her face in her hands. Chewing on the corner of my lip, I sat beside her. "It's gon' be all right, ma. Shit, you getting twelve hundred dollars a month. That's more money than I've ever even seen." I let out a little laugh, hoping to brighten the mood. But when she didn't crack a smile, I put my arm over her shoulders. "But, nah, for real. Everything's gonna be a'ight. I'm just gon' have to get a job. Either way, we in this shit together."

I made sure to send back home just about every penny I had left over from my scholarship to my moms. Although she'd never admit it, I knew my mother depended on that money each semester. My dorm fees would be covered entirely for the next three years, so living off campus wasn't even necessary, but I also knew I couldn't just leave Paris and Hope hanging. Not now, not like this. I'd just have to buckle down and finally get a job because, no matter what, we were in this together.

Chapter 9

Hope—After the Storm

With an open Bible in front of me and half of a banana in my hand, I sat at the kitchen table, scanning the book of Psalms. The morning of my next OB appointment had finally arrived, and I was a heap of nerves over the fact that I'd be seeing Meeko again. Although we texted daily, I hadn't heard his voice or laid eyes on him since that night at the club. Now that everything was out in the open, I didn't know what to expect from him. How would he act? Was he still angry?

"He heals the brokenhearted and binds up their wounds," I whispered just before a knock sounded at the door.

Drawing in a deep breath, I stood up from the table and wobbled my way to the front of the house. With my heart trotting inside my chest, I carefully turned the knob. There, leaning with one arm against the door frame, dressed in all black and with a Baltimore Orioles hat on his head, appeared Meeko. His gaze was pointed toward the ground, allowing the brim of his cap to conceal his eyes.

"Meeko," I said.

Slowly, he lifted his head and sighed as if he were exhausted. He looked first at my face, and then his eyes wandered down to the roundness of my tummy. I wore one of the many sundresses that Paris had given me. It was a soft shade of teal that contrasted nicely against the darkness of my skin. I felt pretty in it. However, when his eyes lingered on my belly for just a second too long, I became self-conscious.

"I've gotten bigger in the last five days, haven't I?" I asked, stating the obvious. After everything had come out in the open about my pregnancy, it seemed that my belly chose to pop even more.

Instead of responding, Meeko stood back and allowed me to exit through the door. I locked up and proceeded down the three short steps of our porch with him straggling behind me. When we reached his car alongside the curb, he kindly opened the passenger door for me. Before getting in, I peered at the steely sky, noticing the dark clouds hovering above us.

"Looks like it's gonna rain," I said, trying to make small talk. But rather than responding, he dipped his head forward, signaling me to get in.

After rounding the car, he hopped in the driver's seat and took off down the street. It seemed like the longest and quietest fifteen-minute ride of my life. Every so often, I kept peeking over at Meeko through my glasses, seeing the same old grimace on his face. Tapping his fingers against the steering wheel at every light was another indication that he was still mad.

"Oh, umm . . . Thanks for dinner last night," I tried.

He released a low snort, then said, "You're welcome."

Yesterday, he'd texted asking if I'd eaten dinner yet. I quickly responded no, thinking he might finally want to get together and talk. But instead of replying, forty minutes later, he had my favorite vegetable Lo Mein from China Grill, being delivered to my door.

When we got to the doctor's office, he pulled directly up to the front so I wouldn't have to walk. Just the simplest touch of his hand as he helped me out of the car made my heart flutter. I loathed the fact that he could still make me feel this way. While he went off to park the car, I checked in at the front desk. After handing over my insurance card to the receptionist, she rapidly clicked away at her mouse. Through her thick bifocal frames, I could see her eyes darting from left to right, perusing the screen.

"Ma'am, it looks like you have a thirty-dollar copay with this plan," she said. Then she put up her hand and shook her head. "I'm sorry, sixty. You didn't have your card last visit, remember?"

Oh, I remember, all right. It wasn't that I didn't have my card. It was that I didn't want my father to get the EOB. I was on his health insurance policy and knew everything would be sent directly to him. As I reached down, fumbling in my purse for money I knew I didn't have, someone walked up behind me. When I glanced back to see who had entered my personal space, Meeko's hand reached across the counter with a crisp one hundred-dollar bill.

"Meeko, you don't have to do that," I whispered. Once again, he ignored me, waiting for his receipt.

Because we were a tad early, we sat nearly twenty minutes in the lobby before finally getting called back. After the nurse checked my blood pressure, she kindly asked me to step on the scale. When I removed my shoes and stepped up on the plate, my jaw instantly collapsed at the digital numbers before me.

"Looks like you've gained six pounds since your last visit," the nurse said with a soft smile.

"Well, is that normal?" Meeko asked, taking me by surprise. "I mean, for her to be gaining so much weight so soon?"

She nodded her head, and her smile broadened at his words. "Oh, absolutely. It's perfectly normal," she confirmed.

She then led us down the hall to a private room, where she asked me to undress. Before slipping out of the door, she handed me a thin, blue hospital gown and white sheet to lay over my legs. Meeko took the lone chair in the corner as I got up on the exam table. I hunched over the curve of my belly, attempting to remove the sandals from my feet. Meeko must have noticed me struggling because he came over and took them off.

"Thanks," I said.

Rather than acknowledging me with words, Meeko subtly chucked up his chin and went to sit down again. Releasing an exaggerated sigh, I rolled my eyes. At this point, his silent treatment was exhausting. Lord, forgive me, but hell, I'd been the one walking around with a broken heart for the past few months. Not only did he put a price tag on my virginity, but he also still fooled around with Jazz after my attack. I was the one whose stomach constantly stayed in knots, just thinking of what my father would say if he were to see me now. Yet, Meeko still had no problem carrying around this enormous chip on his shoulder. If I could get over everything he'd done to me, at least for the well-being of my child, then surely, he could let go of my one little blunder.

I stood up and began removing my clothes. I don't know why, but I turned around, trying to hide myself within the sheet. I hadn't been naked in front of Meeko in months, and since then, my body had drastically changed. Not only had my stomach gotten larger, but also a faint line had developed down the center. My breasts were swollen, and my nipples had turned so dark they were practically a shade away from being black. Throughout Meeko's and my sexual journey, I had begun shaving my hair down there. But now, my bush was as overgrown as the trees in Sequoia National Park. I was way too embarrassed for him to see me naked.

As I struggled to hold up the sheet and unclasp my bra simultaneously, Meeko got up from his chair again. He came over and, from behind, began gently removing my bra. You would have thought his fingers had ice at the tips, the way goose pimples immediately covered the surface of my skin. When he brushed the straps down over each of my shoulders, I naturally closed my eyes, hating the fact that I missed him so much. His fingers traced the contour of my spine until they finally reached the waistband of my panties. I shuddered as he slid them down over my hips. The minute they hit the floor, Meeko scooped them up with his hand and walked back over to his chair. Taking a deep swallow, I gathered my inconsistent emotions and quickly got them in check.

Unexpectedly, there was a double knock at the door. Knowing it was the midwife, I sat on the exam table and yelled, "Come in."

"Ms. Holloway," she said. Greeting me with a warm smile, she walked over with a manila chart in her hand. Then suddenly, her eyes swung over to Meeko in the corner. "Oh, and you are?" she asked.

Standing up from the chair, he extended his hand for her to shake. "I'm Meeko Taylor," he said. "The baby's father."

Just from the way the words "baby's father" poured from his lips, I cringed.

"Well, nice to meet you, Meeko Taylor. I'm Jackie," she said, shaking his hand. She turned back to me and asked that I lie down. "The reason why the nurse had you get undressed today is because you called in last week saying that you were spotting."

"Spotting? What's that?" Meeko didn't hesitate to ask.

"Just a little bit of blood—"

"But I thought you're not supposed to bleed when you pregnant," he said, stepping in closer as his eyes narrowed in confusion.

The midwife shook her head in response. "Typically, no, but it's not uncommon," she explained optimistically. "We'll just have to take a quick look and see what's happening."

As she went to put on her gloves, I discerned the sudden swelling of Meeko's chest. Even his breath, I noticed, had grown ragged. He stepped in even closer so that he was now at my side, gripping the table's edge with his hands. His eyes now unquestionably revealed fear. As she gently reached inside of me, examining the underside of my womb, the room unexpectedly grew still. It was so quiet that I didn't know if it was my heartbeat or Meeko's that I could suddenly hear so plainly between my ears.

"Aha, I see," she said.

"What?" Meeko croaked out, clearing his throat before taking a nervous swallow. "What is it?"

"It appears she has a small polyp on her cervix," she said, now removing her gloves. "That's what's most likely causing the light bleeding."

Lifting up on my elbows, I cast my eyes down at the foot of the table where she was. "What does that mean? Is the baby okay?" I had only heard the term "polyps" last year after Deddy had his colonoscopy. I needed clarification.

"Polyps are most often noncancerous growths. Some can even close up the pathway to your cervix, but it appears yours is sitting just to the right. For now, we'll just continue to monitor it, and after the baby is born, we'll have it removed."

"But her and the baby are fine, right?" Meeko asked.

Another reassuring smile emerged on Midwife Jackie's face. "I don't think there's anything to worry about. Now, would you like to hear the baby's heartbeat?"

Although we both said yes, Meeko did so with much more enthusiasm than me. A mixture of pure anxiety and excitement danced across his face as she rolled up the fabric of my gown. This was his first time actually seeing my pregnancy exposed.

"I know you didn't want to know the sex of the baby last time, but do you think you might be ready now?" she asked, squirting the cool gel on my belly.

When Meeko's imploring eyes immediately fastened on mine, I felt almost obligated to say yes. Slowly, I nodded with ease. I guess I never really wanted to find out without him. It was silly, I know, considering that my previous plan was to keep this baby a secret from him. But I can only explain it by saying that my emotions have been all over the place these past few months. My heart had been downright destroyed and, admittedly, was still in need of repair. Truth be told, lately, decision-making has not been my best skill set.

"Well, okay, then. This is exciting," Midwife Jackie said. After pulling over the ultrasound machine, she spread the gel into a thin layer.

As soon as she placed the transducer on my belly, the fast and steady sound of our baby's heartbeat filled the room. Without even thinking, I glanced up at Meeko and was surprised to see wetness clinging to his eyes. Of course, he was way too macho to let a tear fall, but just witnessing the sentiment caused my heart to skip a beat. Following his line of sight toward the ultrasound machine, I watched in awe as Jackie pointed out all ten fingers and toes.

"Wait, is that . . ." Meeko's voice trailed off as he pointed to the screen.

Midwife Jackie let out a little laugh, then turned to us and said, "Yes. Congratulations to you both. You're having a baby boy."

I knew that Meeko had distanced himself from me after believing I aborted his child, and ever since that night at the club, he'd been ice cold, but without even thinking, I reached out and squeezed his hand. He reciprocated by softly strumming my flesh with his thumb. Gazing into each other's eyes, we shared an amenable smile indicative of the pure joy we both felt. It seemed like, at that moment, nothing else mattered but the sound and sight of the new life we'd created together.

After I dressed again, feeling bits of my heart already restored, the two of us walked back up front to the lobby. Out of the windows, I could see sheets of heavy rain spilling down at an angle outside. As I went to the counter to schedule my next appointment, Meeko asked if I could work around the times he had football practice and weight training. Excited that I was no longer on this journey alone, I quickly agreed.

"I'm gonna go pull the car around," he said.

Once I made my appointment for a day at the end of next month, I waited patiently by the door. Meeko's Honda pulled up within minutes. Before I could even step outside, he rounded the car with a black, oversized umbrella in his hand. As he guided me to the car, resting his hand against the small of my back, I quivered. I could only presume that it was from missing his touch.

But when we returned to the car, the quiet and awkwardness struck again. He was right back to giving me the silent treatment. As we continued driving, the rain beat hard against the windshield, sounding like pebbles plummeting from the sky. Meeko quickly reduced his speed and cut the wipers on high. To cope with the uneasiness of our vibe, I pulled out the ultrasound pictures and began looking at them one by one. Instantly, I beamed. "Looks like he's gonna have your nose," I said lowly, tracing one of the pictures with my finger.

Meeko silently chucked up his chin before reaching over to turn up the radio. I sighed, figuring he was still angry at me—no matter how significant of a moment we had just shared. Halfway back to the house, the rain started falling even harder while lightning bolts twinkled within the clouds.

"Shit," he muttered. "I can't see nothing." Almost every car, including Meeko's, drove at a snail's pace.

"Maybe you should just pull over until the rain stops," I suggested.

Ignoring me once again, Meeko continued the drive along Highway 85. Between him, the blaring radio, and the stormy weather outside, I was beginning to get a headache. I sighed, allowing myself to lazily recline into the seat. Then suddenly, out of nowhere, two cars flew by like a high-speed rail. A surge of water instantly splashed the vehicle, making it harder for us to see. I screamed, immediately seeing all the red lights flashing up ahead. On instinct, Meeko slammed down hard on his brakes, causing my body to soar forward. I was promptly halted by my seat belt, as well as his protective arm.

Meeko cut the wheel hard to the right as the car hydroplaned above the asphalt. We drifted over to the shoulder, barely missing the guard rail. My body trembled, and my heart was hammering away inside my chest. With Meeko's arms still shielding my abdomen, we just sat quietly for a while. Then he leaned forward to cut off the radio.

"What the fuck are we doing?" he asked out of nowhere, swiping his hand down over his face.

"What do you mean?"

He released a deep sigh, and then Meeko's weary eyes swung over and connected with mine. "Shorty, I don't want to be mad wit'chu no more," he said. "I just want us to figure out what the fuck we doing. We need a plan." His hand lightly brushing my belly as he spoke felt natural.

"I don't want to be mad anymore, either," I admitted. "I mean, I'm still not fully over the bet or the whole thing with Jazz, but it's not as important to me anymore." I shrugged, reflecting on my unborn child.

"And, again, I'm sorry for all that bullshit I put you through, Hope. I'm a fucking asshole, I know, but I'm trying to be better," he explained. "I've even got some things lined up to make some decent money. I know I can't work full time because I'll lose my scholarship, but I think I got a plan that'll hold us over for a while."

"I've been looking for a job too—"

"Nah," he said, abruptly cutting me off with a wave of his hand. "You just focus on staying healthy and taking care of my baby. I got the rest."

"Meeko," I tried.

"I'm serious, Hope. All that shit back there at the doctor's office, with you talking 'bout bleeding and shit. And then niggas out here wildin' on the road . . ." He shook his head as if he were at a loss for words. Then suddenly, his eyes hit me with a sober expression. "I want this baby, Hope. Like, I *really* fucking want this." His fingers firmly stretched across my protruding belly once more as if to make sure I fully understood. I nodded, not knowing exactly what else to do. "So what'd your pops say when you told him?" he asked.

Swallowing the lump quickly forming in my throat, I hiked my shoulders like a child.

Meeko's puzzled eyes instantly tapered. "Shorty, what does that even mean?" he asked, shrugging his shoulders to mimic me.

I took in a deep breath and said, "It means he doesn't know, Meeko. Before that night at the club, no one knew except for Franki and Paris. Even Asha thought I'd gone through with the abortion," I explained.

"Damn," he muttered, obviously stunned. "So, when you gon' tell him?"

"I can't," I whispered.

"You gotta tell him. I mean, he gon' be pissed but . . . You still gotta tell him," he pressed. "If you want, we can tell him together." I didn't reply because honestly, I didn't know if that would be a good or bad idea. After a pregnant pause, he said, "I told my muva and sisters this past Sunday."

I sat up in my seat, and my eyes widened at that. "You did?" He nodded and shrugged his lips as if it were no big deal. "Well, what'd they say?"

He released a light snort and allowed the corners of his mouth to turn down. "Wasn't shit they could say," he spoke emphatically. "It is what it is."

Without warning, a loud clap of thunder rumbled above us. It was so loud I jumped in place. Meanwhile, the torrential rain kept coming, so Meeko decided to cut off his car's engine.

"But were they angry?" I asked.

He shook his head. "Nah. Where I come from, niggas start making babies at the age of 13, and by the time they get to my age, they have at least two baby muvas." He laughed. "But they do want to meet you, tho'."

My eyes stretched in surprise. "They do?" Lord only knows what they probably think of me.

"Yeah." He smiled with a faraway gleam in his eyes. "I've been talking to my muva about you for a while now. Figured if you're up for it, we could make a quick trip up there for the Fourth of July."

"Sure." I nodded. "I'd like that."

The rain and thunder suddenly ceased as if God knew there had been some sort of resolve. The clouds opened back up, and although there was no sun, just enough light came through, brightening the atmosphere. Meeko finally cranked his car's engine back up and took off down the highway. We made light conversation on the drive, and in less than fifteen minutes, we were pulling back up to the house. Side by side, we ambled our way up to the front door. When we got to the porch, I pulled out my keys and asked if he wanted to come inside.

"Nah, I got some shit to take care of, but I'ma call you, though," he said.

Just when he turned to walk away, I called out, "Meeko." He glanced back at me over his shoulder with a startled look. "Um, I just wanted to say that I'm sorry."

He turned around to face me fully, narrowing his eyes. "For what?"

I cleared my throat and adjusted the glasses on my face. "I'm sorry for not telling you I decided to keep the baby. You know, I actually did go to get an abortion, but I just couldn't go through with it. I mean, who am I to mess with God's plans, ya know?" I said, slapping my hands down at my side. "And then there was you . . ."

"Me?" he said lowly.

"Yes." I nodded. "My father always says there's no greater honor than being a father. I've seen it my whole life in how he looks at me. He's always made a point to be at every event, every award ceremony, or show I've ever participated in. The way he cried when he had to drop me off last year." I smiled and shook my head at the sentiment. "Even though he can be overbearing sometimes, our connection is pretty special. And no matter how angry I was at you or what you did to me, I just didn't think I could ever live with myself if I stole that kind of joy from you."

Stepping in close, Meeko gently took me by the chin. "And because of that . . . because of this," he said, placing his hand on my belly, "I'm gon' love you forever." He allowed his lips to briefly brush across my brow before turning to walk away.

Feeling my faith somewhat reinstated, I watched as he got in his car and took off. I knew that things still weren't perfect between us, but as I entered the house, I could finally exhale. No longer would I have to bring this baby into the world alone, and I was genuinely grateful for that. *Now, if I could only find the courage to tell my father.*

Chapter 10

Asha—Unlikely Possibility. Destroyed.

"How's the money looking?" my father asked, peering over my shoulder as I sat on the stool.

I opened up the metal container on my lap for him to see. "Not too bad," I said, popping gum as I thumbed through the stack of tens lying in the tray.

We were having a boxing match at the gym that night, and I was in charge of collecting ten dollars a head at the door. Apparently, everyone had come to see Quick fight this new Mexican boxer out of upstate New York. His name was Mateo "The Hitter" Hernandez, and supposedly, he'd won his last six fights. Although it was local, it had turned out to be a big draw. The door had only been open for twenty minutes, and the place was more than halfway packed.

"Looking good, looking good," my father said. I glanced back, seeing him rub his hands together as a wide grin spread across his face. "Now, you just holler if anyone comes up here bothering you. Me and Malachi gon' be in the back," he said just before walking away.

I've worked at the gym under Malachi for the past few weeks. Surprisingly, it hadn't been as bad as I'd initially thought. Occasionally, we'd still butt heads, but for the most part, sharing the same space for hours at a time had proven necessary to restore our relationship. More than anything, we laughed and joked together around here, reminding us of who we used to be to each other. Although my relationship with my brother was still complicated, things seemed to be getting back on the right track.

Just as I turned back, with a toss of my braids, I saw Meeko and Ty swaggering toward the door. One was light and the other just a shade above being dark. Their small gold chains glimmered around their necks as the clean scent of their cologne suddenly drew near. Blowing a great big bubble with my gum, I rolled my eyes at the sight of them. Particularly Meeko after recalling the way he treated me in Cancún.

"Yo, where 'Chi at?" Ty asked, referring to Malachi.

I hunched my shoulders and frowned. "I don't know. He back there somewhere. Why?" I asked, rolling my eyes again with an attitude. They both disregarded me and attempted to cross the threshold of the gym. "Uh-uh. Hol' up," I said, wagging my head. "It's ten dollars to get up in here tonight."

"Ten dollars?" Meeko questioned with a look of disbelief, his nose slightly flaring in disgust. "The fuck for?"

"It's a fight tonight, and ain't nobody getting up in here for free," I snapped, emphasizing it all with a flick of my long, pointed nail and a hard chomp of my gum.

Meeko sucked his teeth and looked over at Ty. "I ain't giving yo shit," he muttered, that same snarl remaining on his face.

With a heavy sigh, Ty reached deep into his pocket and pulled out a folded twenty-dollar bill. "Here, yo, damn," he fussed, practically slapping the money into my hand.

Flashing a facetious smile, I batted my eyes and placed it gently in the money box. "Now, y'all be sure to enjoy the fight tonight, ya hear?" I said sweetly, waving them along.

I heard Meeko mumble what sounded like "stupid bitch" before walking through the door.

"Don't pay yo no mind," Ty hung back and said, letting his Baltimorean accent cut through. "He still pissed that you called him and Hope out in Cancún. I mean," he shrugged with an open palm, "it was fucked up, but—"

"And?" I said, sucking my teeth as my lips pursed to the side. "Ain't nobody thinking 'bout Meeko's trifling ass," I countered.

Releasing a light chuckle, Ty shook his head before following Meeko inside.

After thirty more minutes and another $400, I headed back to my father's safe. On the way to his office, I took in the small crowd and bopped my head to the hip-hop music being played. Carrying the metal box in my hand, I passed the open door of the men's locker room. My eyes immediately zoomed in on Quick. He was sitting down on a stool, getting his hands wrapped. His chiseled upper body was bare and looked to have been lightly coated in oil. He wore silky red and white trunks on his lower half with matching red boxing boots.

When his chinked eyes raised to meet mine, I gasped, almost as if I'd been caught. Blinking rapidly, I turned my eyes away. I firmed my grip on the money box and proceeded down the hall. When I entered the office, Malachi was sitting on the front corner of my father's desk with Meeko and Ty standing before him. The room quieted abruptly, making it obvious they didn't want me to be privy to their conversation.

"What y'all get quiet for?" I asked, making my way over to the safe. "Y'all can keep talking."

Following me with his eyes, Malachi scratched the top of his head. "Anyway, mane," he said, turning back to Meeko. "Get at me by next Friday so we can see what's up."

"No doubt," Meeko said, going in to slap hands.

"Y'all staying for the fight, right?" Malachi asked.

"Might as well," Ty chimed in, his eyes popping wide at me as his lips cynically twisted to the side.

When they left the office, I turned to Malachi with my hand on my hip. "Since when you start hanging with them?" I asked.

"Since I started minding my own business. Stop being nosy, mane," he said, brushing me off. Then he looked at me. "And where the fuck yo' clothes at?"

I peered down at the two-piece biker short set I had on. It was a soft shade of pink, and on my feet were the same colored Chucks to match. I looked good—no, *damn good,* so I sucked my teeth and waved him off. Suddenly, we heard the sound of a bell being struck twice. It was apparent to us that the fight was getting ready to start.

"It's showtime," he said. His bright hazel eyes flickered with excitement as he rubbed his hands together, looking just like my damn daddy.

After spitting my gum into the trash, I followed him down the hall into the crowd. The seating Daddy had set up around the ring was nearly filled. Surprisingly, we found a spot up close to the action. I looked around for my father, then remembered that he was likely still with Quick. Without warning, the emcee cut the music to quiet the crowd. This was just a local, amateur gym, but my daddy always went all out on fight nights. He'd hire a DJ and rent metal bleachers to give it an authentic boxing match feel.

"Coming out from the blue corner, weighing in at 175 pounds, hailing from Rochester, New York, with eight wins, one by way of knockout, and only two defeats is middleweight boxer Mateo 'The Hitter' Hernandez," the emcee announced.

The crowd cheered modestly as the Hispanic boxer entered the ring. With deeply cratered skin, The Hitter wore a nasty mug on his face. Everything from his bold tattoos to the untamed Mohawk on his head made him appear dangerous. For some reason, I instantly grew nervous.

"Now, coming out from the red corner, weighing in at 178 pounds, hailing from right here in Guilford County with seven wins and zero losses is our very own Quincy 'Quick' Anderson," the emcee announced.

Everyone, including me, jumped to their feet as soon as Quick appeared. With a semihump in his back and bold determination in his eyes, I watched as he trekked to the ring, throwing swift jabs in the air. Every inch of him appeared focused and ready. The crowd went wild as he jogged up the stairs and bent down to enter the ring. For some reason, my stomach was now in knots.

"Quick 'bout to take a nigga's head off; watch," Malachi leaned over and said.

Other than the ride he gave me a few weeks back and the occasional hi and bye at the gym, I had no real ties to Quick. But there was something inside of me that really wanted him to win. He's from my hometown, and my father has been training this kid for years, I tried reasoning with myself.

The sound of the bell chimed again, commencing the start of the fight. The first punch was thrown by Hernandez, grazing Quick's chin. The crowd instantly calmed at that. However, Quick simply shook his head, revealing a cocky, chip-toothed grin. Surprisingly, I found that simple act of intimidation to be sexy. After pacing back and forth, they exchanged jabs, sizing up each other. That was until Quick shocked us all by landing a right hook on The Hitter's jaw. The blow immediately stunned him because when Quick went in for a second punch to the gut, he doubled over, appearing to choke on air.

With a sudden rush of adrenaline, I quickly jumped to my feet. As loud as I could, I cheered for Quick to take him out. When The Hitter stumbled back in an attempt to recover, Quick moved in close and followed up with an uppercut. I swear this young man's body was nothing short of pure art, the way the muscular flanks of his back seemed to flex and glisten with his every twist and turn. Taking a deep swallow, I attempted to focus back on the fight. But just as Hernandez fell back against the ropes, he was saved by the sound of the bell. It was the end of the first round, and the entire gym was in an uproar.

My eyes instantly zoomed in on Quick, who was ambling to the corner. As he sat down on the stool, hunched over with his arms resting on his knees, I could see his chest heaving up and down. Daddy immediately got right in his ear. Even from a distance, I could make out my father's words.

"Finish him," he said. He wanted a knockout.

Unfortunately, the second round wasn't as eventful, with Quick and The Hitter only trading a few body shots toward the end. By the time Quick made it back to that corner, my father was yelling so loud that veins bulged from his neck, and spit flew from his lips. However, right at the top of the third, Quick walked into the center of the ring with his eyes stapled to his opponent.

"Chill out. He gon' win," my brother said, grabbing ahold of my knee, which was bouncing uncontrollably.

It was only a half second after the bell chimed when Quick went full throttle, throwing a powerful combination. Every punch had proven to be successful, connecting with Hernandez's head. Again, he was on the ropes, but Quick didn't let up this time. He drilled into his body one fist after the other, rendering him powerless.

"Get his ass!" I shouted. Fist pumping in the air.

Quick pulled back off of him just a hair and struck him again on the right side of his jaw. Upon impact, Hernandez's head flew back, and as if the whole scene was unfolding in slow motion, he collapsed onto the mat. The referee stepped in between the two, waving his hand for Quick to move back. I anxiously held my breath as he began the count.

"One, two, three, four, five, six, seven, eight," he said. When Hernandez couldn't get up, the referee waved his hand again, ultimately deeming it a knockout.

Quick's eyes ballooned, overwhelmed with joy as he stood there in awe. That's when my father quickly jumped inside the ring. He held up Quick's red-gloved hand, instantly declaring victory. Even Stevie Wonder could see just how proud my father was.

"Shit, girl, quit hitting me," Malachi said with a chuckle. I was so excited that I jumped up and down, hitting his arm.

After the emcee officially announced that Quick was the winner, everyone in the stands jumped to their feet. The loud cheers echoed off the painted cinder block walls. With the excitement I felt, you would have thought I had won. It wasn't long after that the crowd slowly started to disperse. As promised, I swept up the remnants of trash on the floor and then headed back up front to my desk.

Amidst a bout of yawns, I closed out a few emails, then decided to call it quits for the night. As I bent down to retrieve my purse from the bottom drawer of my desk, the unexpected scent of Irish Spring collided with my nose. I returned to an upright position and saw Quick standing directly in front of me. He wore a white tee shirt with the sleeves cut off and black basketball shorts that hung low on his tapered waist.

"'Sup, Asha?" he said, licking his lips.

"Heyy," I sang, not quite recognizing my own voice. And just why the hell am I smiling so damn hard?

Not returning the smile, he handed me a folded white sheet of paper. "Ya pops told me to bring this up here to you," he said, subtly scratching behind his ear. "You know, to send to the commission." His head tilted with doubt, uncertain if I understood.

"Oh, right," I said, my eyes instantly widening in recognition. I opened up the paper and quickly skimmed the page. "To report your win, yes." Quick nodded, then slowly turned to walk away. "Aye," I called out.

Spinning back around, he looked at me with his brows pinched together. "What's up?"

"I just wanted to say . . . ummm . . . You looked great out there tonight." *There, you said it.*

His head whipped back, and an astonished look swept across his face. "Wow," he said, his lips easing into a smirk. "Thank you." When he placed his hand over his chest and batted his eyes, I realized he was mocking me.

"Why are you acting so surprised? I'm sure you've been hearing that all night."

"Yeah, I have, but coming from you . . . I'm shocked."

I sucked my teeth and playfully rolled my eyes. "Yeah, right, whatever," I said, flipping back my braids with a flirty laugh.

"Nah, you laughing, but I'm dead-ass serious. Never thought a meaningless dude from Hampton Homes would ever hear such a compliment from the likes of you." He smiled, again revealing that little chip on his front tooth. "I mean, not somebody that just goes to community college and drives around in an old, beat-up Accent and all," he said.

Seeing exactly where he was going with all this, I sighed. "Oh my God. You're never gonna let me live that down, are you?"

Tossing back his head, a deep chuckle released from his lungs. "I'm just messing with you, girl. It's all good."

I shook my head. "No, it's not. Somehow, I've gotten into this bad habit of always judging a book by its cover. And, well, with you, it appears there's more than what meets the eye," I said. "So, basically, I owe you an apology. I came across real—"

"Stuck-up," he said, completing my sentence. We both shared a laugh at that.

"Gee, thanks," I said with another roll of my eyes.

A few moments of awkward silence lingered between us as we stared into each other's eyes like two young kids with a crush who didn't know exactly what to say. Yet, it was almost like we were seeing each other for the very first time. He, this talented boxer who was smart and possibly even attractive, and then me, the girl who had somehow been humbled unpredictably.

A surge of butterflies circled in the pit of my belly just before I heard, "Quincy."

My eyes shifted behind Quick to see a short, brown-skinned girl with platinum blond braids in her hair. She was a bit chubby but undeniably cute in the face. She wore a white, knock-off Versace tee shirt with the word "Versace" boldly written across the chest. And on her lower half, she had short, white jean shorts to match. Quick glanced back at her over his shoulder and immediately beamed.

"You ready?" he asked, throwing his arm around her shoulders.

"Yeah, let's get outta here so we can celebrate your win," she cheesed, staking her claim as she placed her manicured hand on his stomach.

My chest tightened right away, and I recognized that dreadful emotion of jealousy. But for the life of me, I just couldn't understand why. I'd long ago established that Quick was nowhere close to being my type. He wasn't cute enough, flashy enough, and damn sure wasn't rich enough. *So, what's my deal?* Like with Jaxon, I guess Quick had potential, but somehow, this didn't feel the same. Quick had that "it" factor, extending well beyond the powerful punches he threw. He was intelligent and focused, and even with the bread crumbs he'd dropped about taking care of his siblings, I could tell he was kind. *Damn.*

"All right, Asha, I'll catch up with you later," he said.

I peered up into his chinky eyes and forced a smile. "See ya," I let out coolly.

Just as they disappeared through the door, I heard Malachi walking up to my desk. "So, Quick, huh?" he asked, wearing a crafty grin.

"What about him?" I snapped.

He shrugged his lips. "I'on know. You tell me," he said.

I flipped back my long braids and secured my purse on my shoulder. "Ain't nothing there. He ain't my type," I half lied.

He suppressed a chuckle through his nose and shook his head. "You need a ride back to the house, or you just gon' wait on Pops?" he asked.

"Nah, Daddy gon' be here all night. Just drop me off at the house."

After following Malachi to his car, I hopped in and went through my phone. When we hit Benjamin Parkway, Malachi was in a Bluetooth conversation with Bull. I was only halfway listening, but based on my brother's frustration and the periodic mention of my niece and nephew's names, I figured they were most likely talking about Reese.

"So, Big Man saw them out with the kids? *My* fucking kids?" Malachi questioned furiously.

"Yeah, mane, at Daryl's two nights ago," Bull said. "I told him not to call you with this shit. Just let you hear it straight from me, ya feel me?"

"Yeah," Malachi muttered. I glanced over, seeing that he was deep in thought. A vein bulged from his forehead as his hazel eyes gazed out at the dark road ahead.

"So, what you gon' do? Clearly, the nigga is in violation," Bull seethed.

Malachi released an exasperated breath. "I've been trying to play nice because I know this shit with her is a dead end anyway, but—"

"859 needs to handle that shit, breh," Bull cut him off and said, referring to their gang.

Malachi's head slowly nodded in agreement, but he said, "Let me get back to you on that, mane. I gotta figure that other shit out first." He was obviously speaking in code. "In the meantime, I'ma have to handle her."

"You got it, breh. Just say the word."

After tapping the screen to end the call, Malachi gaped over at me. "What you looking at?" he asked.

Glancing back down at my lap, I took in the picture of Quincy that appeared on the screen of my cell. I had been stalking his Instagram page @Quick_Quincyoo almost daily since that night he'd dropped me off at the dorm. Tonight, however, I'd been particularly curious, wanting to see if he had any pictures with ol' girl. Surprisingly, there were none. Most of his page was filled with pictures and videos of him boxing. He didn't even have any of his siblings, which I found a little odd.

"Nothing," I said, quickly tapping off the screen.

"I thought he wasn't your type," Malachi said.

"He's not."

"So, what the fuck you lurking on IG for?" Feeling embarrassed, I didn't say anything in return. "So, when y'all move back into the dorms?" he asked, thankfully changing the subject. "You heard from your roommates?"

Having known Malachi my entire life, I knew that was just his clever way of asking if I'd spoken to Paris.

Although Malachi never confided much about their relationship, I now gathered that whatever it was, was over. He was at the gym early every morning and wouldn't leave until late at night. And on the weekends, he spent most of the day at Momma and Daddy's with the kids. That didn't leave much time for prissy Paris—a young woman who I knew required a whole lot.

"Nah. They all moved out into a house or something."

"A house? All of them?"

I nodded. "Yeah."

"So, that's where you staying when the semester starts back up again?"

"No, they didn't include me." I began playing with my phone to avert my hurt feelings.

"Damn," he muttered softly. "Well, maybe you and Kiki can get a place together."

"Nah. Kiki ain't tryin'a pay no bills. She's too comfortable living at home with her momma," I explained with a shrug. "Ain't no biggie. I'll just be assigned new roommates." Although my nonchalant demeanor probably said otherwise, it still bothered me that they left me behind.

"Hmm. We'll figure out something."

For some reason, hearing him say those words gave me instant comfort. Malachi reached to turn up the radio, and together, bopping our heads, we rapped the lyrics for the rest of the ride home. When I could finally lie in bed that night, I returned to Quick's Instagram page. I studied his most recent posted picture, an action shot of his final punch against Hernandez tonight. Between the grit of Quick's teeth, the beads of sweat on his brows, and his lean muscles that were all well-defined, it was a powerful scene. Instinctively, my finger moved to tap the little heart beneath it.

Chapter 11

Paris—Love Is Like a Battle

"So then, her girlfriend pulls up at my house in the middle of the night and starts banging on my door. Shit straight scared the fuck outta me," Nya said, shaking her head. "We both in there asleep, and ain't neither one of us got a stitch of clothes on because, well . . . You know," she said with a smile, sticking out her pierced tongue as she arrogantly stroked her cornrows back with her hand. I could only see her upper half from where she sat across the table, but I swear it took everything out of me to keep my eyes trained on her face. Without a bra, she wore a man's tank top undershirt. Her hardened nipples were pierced and seemed to keep peeping out at me.

"And so, did you get up and beat that bitch's ass or nah?" Tee Tee asked impatiently, rolling her eyes as she took the straw into her mouth for a sip. She was sitting there with her hair pulled up in a white scarf, a twisted knot resting at the top.

"Nah, I just let her ass keep knocking and making all that damn noise until the neighbors called the cops."

I diverted my eyes up to her face and cleared my throat. "So, now, what's up with you and the girl? Like, are you guys an item or what?" I asked.

She and Tee Tee looked at each other and tittered. "Hell nah. I've been kicking it with dude from around the way named Mike."

"Oh God," I let out, palming my forehead. "I swear you and your love affairs make me dizzy, Ny."

Nya, Tee Tee, and I were having dinner at a restaurant called Village Tavern. I was initially hesitant when Nya called asking if I wanted to hang out, but she quickly assured me that Malachi wouldn't be around. Although our lifestyles and upbringings were worlds apart, the three of us had somehow formed a bond. I considered them friends and had missed the two of them dearly.

"So, what about you?" Tee Tee looked across the table at me and asked. "You talk to 'Chi lately?"

Shaking my head, I allowed my eyes to drift out the window. Although it was eight o'clock at night, the summer's sun was still out, shining bright. As I pretended to be engrossed in the patrons walking by, thoughts of Malachi ran through my mind. I hadn't seen or heard from him since that day at the dorm. And even though each day had gotten easier, I still felt utterly lost without him.

"Why don't you just call him?" Tee Tee said, perhaps sensing the sadness behind my eyes.

I shifted my regard back to her and frowned. "For what? He's a liar."

"I know he didn't tell you about Reese, but Malachi really cares about you. I ain't neva seen him like the way he was with you. Mane, that nigga was in love," Nya said, adding her two cents.

I cocked my head to the side and gave her a deadpan expression. "He never loved me, Nya," I declared.

"How you know?"

"Because he never said it. And even if he had, he never showed it. You don't lie to someone you supposedly care about, much less love," I explained.

"But everybody makes mistakes, right?" Tee Tee tried reasoning.

I raised my hand to get the waiter's attention. "Yeah, but being married is far too big of a mistake."

Suddenly, the two of them glanced at each other, speaking silently with their eyes. I knew then that it was time to get out of there. They were up to something. As soon as the waiter came over to retrieve my debit card, I sucked down the last of my sweet tea.

"You leaving?" Nya asked.

"Yeah, I've got to get back," I said.

Tee Tee didn't say anything. She just peered down beneath the table, where I could tell she was playing on her phone.

"You coming out to Bull and Rita's for the Fourth?" Nya asked, popping a last-minute french fry into her mouth. "You know they have a big cookout with fireworks every year."

"I doubt it, Ny. Malachi will be there, and—"

"Ma'am, I'm sorry, but your card was declined," the waiter cut me off and said. "We tried it twice." He handed me back my card and then stood there, waiting.

As I dug into my purse, searching for cash I knew I didn't have, I saw Tee Tee typing away on her phone. *Gee, thanks.*

Nya, on the other hand, said, "Oh, Paris, don't worry about it. I was gonna treat everybody anyway." She pulled her Visa from her purse and handed it to the waiter.

By the heat I felt instantly rushing to my cheeks, I knew my face was undoubtedly some hue of red. I was mortified. "I've gotta get out of here. I-I'll call you," I stammered, quickly sliding out of the booth without giving her a chance to respond.

My feet traveled so fast to the car, you would've thought the ground was scorching hot. When I finally got behind the wheel, I felt like an out-of-breath child who'd surprisingly made it back to base during a game of tag. When I mashed on the brakes and pressed the start button, my engine stalled. I tried cranking it a second time but was unsuccessful again.

"Shit," I shouted, slamming my fist down on the wheel. My car wasn't even two years old. I couldn't believe this shit was happening to me right now. After releasing a few huffs and puffs, I got out of the car and returned to the restaurant. Nya and Tee Tee were already heading out.

"Nya, do you mind giving me a ride home?" I asked with a sigh. "My car broke down, and well, obviously, I don't have the money to get it towed right now."

Running her hand down her mouth like a dude, she shook her head. "Nah, I ain't drive." I knew Tee Tee didn't have a car, so it was apparent that they'd bummed a ride.

"Come on, you can ride with us," Tee said.

As soon as we got back outside, I noticed Malachi's Benz pulling up in front of the restaurant. I could not make out his face from the dark tint of the window, but I knew that was him. "Thanks, but no thanks," rushed from my lips. I spun around on my heels as fast as possible, making a U-turn toward my car.

"Miss Paris." Instantly, I froze in place at the deep sound of his voice. "Get in the car, shawty," he demanded.

"I-I've got a ride, thanks," I tossed over my shoulder. With my heart thrashing inside my chest, I kept a steady pace toward my car. Once tucked safely in the driver's seat, I pulled out my cell. *Who can I call? Who can I call?*

Suddenly, a hard knock sounded against the window, causing me to flinch. "Ahh," I shrieked, nearly jumping out of my skin. I turned to see Malachi's golden gaze searing into me. His head was cocked to the side as the tip of his tongue wet his bottom lip.

"Let me take you home," he said.

I shook my head. "My ride is already on the way," I lied.

Taking me by surprise, he reached down and opened my door. My eyes immediately took inventory of the tattoos scattered across his bare chest, slithering all the way down to his abs until they got lost in soft curls of hair descending into the rim of his jeans.

"Mama, you know I'm not leaving you out here stranded, right?" he asked, peering down at me. When he dipped his head into my car, the familiar scent of his cologne triggered my breath to falter. My chest slowly heaved up and down from our close proximity alone. "Come on," he gently commanded.

Then without warning, he reached across my body to grab my keys and cell from the console. He strode away without waiting for me to respond or even get out of the car. From the rearview mirror, I watched as he swaggered back toward his Benz. The brawny flanks of his back contracted with every stride. *Fuck.* An unexpected tingle zipped from my core. I didn't want to get into his car, and not just because of his marital status. It was the mere fact that my body still reacted to him. Within sixty seconds of being in his presence, I was physically in need of this man . . . literally yearning for him like a menstruating woman hankering for chocolate.

After remaining there in my car for a few minutes to calm my sexual urges, I thought of who else I could call. My buddy Josh was in New York, and right now, Meeko still hated the world. All the other friends I'd made during the school year had returned home for the summer. Since I was flat broke and without money for an Uber, I was completely stuck and at Malachi's mercy.

Sucking in a restorative breath, I grabbed my purse and exited from the car. I heard my car doors lock as soon as I shut the door. I quickly looked over in the direction of his Benz. Through the crack of the window, I could view him sitting in the driver's seat, holding my key fob in his hand.

As I walked over, I discovered Malachi's hazel eyes raking over my body. I'd lost a few pounds over the last few weeks and had been showing a bit more skin. I had on a floral Valentino romper that cut well above midthigh, and due to my entire back being exposed, I didn't wear a bra. My hair was swept up in a messy bun, accentuating the length of my neck, and garnished by a pair of pink diamond drop earrings that dangled just above my collarbone. Immediately, I went for the back door of his car but discovered that it was locked. *Of course.*

"Shawty, you up front," he said through the window. "I'm dropping them off first."

Releasing a minor groan and a roll of my eyes, I opened the front door and dropped into the passenger seat. I purposely angled my body opposite of his and gazed out the window.

As I reached up to yank the seat belt down, Malachi pulled out of the parking lot. He turned up his trap music so loud that it blared from the speakers. Although it was less than a ten-minute drive to Tee Tee's place, there was little to no conversation during the ride. Faintly, I could hear whispers and laughter between them in the back, but that was about it. When we finally drove up into her yard, I was surprised to see Nya scooting toward the door.

"You're leaving too?" I asked, craning my neck around to the backseat.

"Yeah, I've been staying with Tee Tee all week," she said. "Just call us when you get in."

I nodded and waved my fingers at them as they withdrew from the car. Suddenly, my stomach felt uneasy. Malachi and I were alone in the car. He leaned forward and cut the music down really low.

"Miss Paris." He called out my name so smoothly that my body quivered from the sound. For the first time since getting into the car, I turned and looked him in the eyes. Taking a deep swallow, I attempted to resist the beautiful hazel irises staring back at me. "Where we going?" he asked.

"Uh . . . J-just take me back to the dorms," I croaked, feeling my mouth go dry as I folded my arms across my chest.

Then I heard him release a snort of laughter. "So, you just gon' lie to my face, shawty?" he asked. My head whipped back in his direction, with my eyes practically popping out of my skull. *The friggin' audacity,* I thought to myself. "I know you don't live on campus no more," he said.

Dammit, Asha. "But I'm meeting friends there," I stated matter-of-factly.

Shaking his head, Malachi thumbed the side of his nose. "Cut the shit, Paris. Where you living at now?"

I blew out a frustrated breath before giving him my address. "But this does not, by any means, give you permission to come to my home."

"Whatever, shawty," he mumbled, plugging the information into his GPS.

As we drove through downtown Greensboro, I sat back and watched the orange glow of the sun disappear beneath the horizon. Malachi was on his phone for most of the way, which somehow allowed my nerves to dissolve. When we arrived at the house, I noticed Meeko's car in the driveway. I rolled my eyes at the thought of him possibly weaseling his way back into Hope's heart.

"Thanks for the ride," I said lowly, not making eye contact. However, as soon as I opened the door, I could also hear Malachi getting out on his side. I hopped out and looked at him like he was crazy. "Malachi, what are you doing?"

With blatant disregard for the sound of my voice, he kept trekking toward the house. If I hadn't known any better, I would've thought he'd been here before. Through the overgrown grass of our yard, I traipsed behind him until we landed on the front porch. Without hesitation, he went straight for the storm door, which happened to be unlocked.

As he crossed the threshold, my hand hooked around his waist to yank him back. "Where the hell are you going, mister?" I snapped. However, Malachi never broke his stride. He interlaced his fingers with mine and pulled me closer to him. When my face collided against his brawny back, I instinctively closed my eyes. "Malachi, stop," I whined again, but this time, much less convincing.

With his legs out wide, he waddled with me into the house, holding my hand against his abs to keep me close. "Wassup, mane?" he said, looking down at Meeko on the living room floor. He was putting something together. Hope sat on the couch behind him, eating from a bowl of cereal resting atop her round belly.

"'Sup?" was Meeko's short response as he continued to work away.

"Malachi, let go of me." This time, I screamed. And with a hard jerk, I was able to pry myself away from him.

Releasing a deep chuckle, he walked farther into the house. As he toured the place with his eyes, mapping out its layout, I remained on his heels. But that's when Hope stood up from the couch and came to me with an envelope in her hand.

"Here. This came today," she said. "It says 'Urgent.'"

As I grabbed it from her hand, my eyes discretely traveled back to a shirtless Malachi. He was going from door to door, stealing glimpses of every room. Unbelievable. Mumbling sarcastically beneath my breath, I ripped the envelope open haphazardly. "What's this?" I muttered to myself, pulling out a yellow sheet of paper. My eyes quickly skimmed the page, noting just a few pertinent words. "Oh no," I cried, bringing my hand up to cover my mouth.

"What is it?" Hope asked, peering over my shoulder. After a few beats, to which I knew she was reading, she exclaimed, "It says your rent check bounced." *No shit.*

I was humiliated beyond measure. My eyes inadvertently darted around the space in search of Malachi. However, he was nowhere to be found. Apparently, he'd disappeared into one of the rooms. Then I glanced down to the floor at Meeko, who I now realized had been putting together a crib.

"Yo, the rent check bounced? For this place?" he asked, clarifying with a hike of his brow.

I gripped the back of my neck and released a deep sigh. "Well, that's what it says," I shrugged.

Allowing the tools in his hands to drop to the carpeted floor, he stood up with a look of concern. "How much?" he asked.

"Nine fifty," I said. When his eyes ballooned, I put my hand up to calm him and shook my head. "But it has to be some kind of mistake," I assured him. The way the words rushed from my lips, you would've thought it was the truth. But given the fact that my debit card had just been declined, I knew it was an outright lie.

"Shit," he muttered, swiping his hand down his face. "Give me a day or two. Let me see what I can do."

I folded the piece of paper and stuffed it back into the envelope. "No, really, it's a mistake, Meeko," I tried convincing him again. "Let me go call the bank."

Without waiting for his response, I scurried down the short hall to my bedroom. Trying to budget money had been more difficult than I initially thought. I needed my mother on the phone ASAP. As soon as I approached the doorway, I saw Malachi sitting on the edge of the bed. Just that quick, it had gotten dark outside, so his eyes sparkled back at me like a set of fireflies glowing in the night.

"Malachi, this was cute at first, but really . . ." I sighed. "You have to go." Purposely, I planted myself by the door to maintain distance between us.

"Miss Paris," he said, his deep southern tone rolling off his tongue quickly. "Why the fuck you acting like you don't miss me?"

Ignoring the minor ache in my chest, I swallowed hard and pulled back my shoulders. "I don't," I lied, lifting my chin with conviction.

Slowly, his black silhouette lifted from the bed and began stalking toward me. Little by little, from the bright light in the hall, I could make out the masculine features of his face. By the time he was within arm's length, my heart rate had tripled in speed. I could hardly breathe. When he finally came near so we were standing chest to chest, he took the envelope from my hand.

"I miss the fuck outta you, Miss Paris," he whispered, bringing his lips in close to my ear. My body instantly shivered from the warmth of his breath brushing across my skin.

I needed to put an end to this and fast. "Malachi," I breathed, placing my palms against his chest. But before I could even make out my following words, he leaned in with parted lips.

On instinct, my eyes closed, and I allowed free entry of his tongue. Right there in the entryway, as if we'd been standing under mistletoe, we engaged in the most passion-filled kiss. Sparks immediately flew, and tingles soared from my belly down to my groin. My hands took hold of his globelike shoulders as I rose on the balls of my feet. Deepening the kiss, we exchanged moan after moan, and I could feel the tips of his fingers tease the ruffled hem of my garb. It all caused my heart to flutter and a warm throbbing between my thighs. Without warning, Malachi's hands slid around to my ample behind and gently squeezed.

"I want you so fucking bad, shawty," he groaned lowly, pressing his erection into me. My mouth was so in need of his that I couldn't respond verbally. I grabbed his face and hungrily kissed him again.

With my ass still cupped in his hands like playdough, Malachi lifted me from the floor and swathed my thick legs around his waist. After kicking the door closed, he carried me over to the bed. I cradled him between my limbs and relished the sweetness of his tongue as he laid me back with care. It was like I was so caught up at that moment that all worries about the car and rent had been temporarily shelved. I was officially entranced.

As his lips feathered down my neck and shoulder, an impatient moan floated from my lips. My body was now hot to the touch, and just like a bottle of wine left in the freezer, I was ready to explode. I longed to feel his girth inside of me. Suddenly, he lifted his body from mine and reached over to cut on the lamp. When he gazed down at me with that bright set of hazel irises, my heart skipped not one but *two* beats.

"I just wanna look at you, Miss Paris," he said, wetting his bottom lip with his tongue before taking it between his teeth.

I placed my hands firmly against his abs and slid them down to his pants. "I miss you too," I finally confessed through a whisper.

His beautiful eyes seemed to light up even more upon hearing those words as they raked over me. As I unbuckled the Gucci belt on his jeans, my back unconsciously arched from the bed. I could hear myself panting in want.

Malachi was just as excited. Before I could get his pants even halfway down, his lengthy shaft suddenly sprang out like a water hose filled with gushing water. *Oh my.* My mouth instantly watered at the sight of his smooth chocolate rod.

"You can taste it if you want," he proposed knowingly, winking his eye as he traced my puckered lips with his thumb.

Feeling my cheeks go warm, I peered up at him and softly wagged my head. Although I was curious about oral pleasure, I knew I couldn't do it with him—not even in this lust-hazed state. After releasing a slight chuckle, he reached down to undress me. I shuddered as his prudent fingers slid across the peaks of my shoulders, taking down my straps. When the top of my romper fell to my waist, freeing my breasts to the air, he greedily took my nipple into his mouth. Another moan involuntarily escaped me. His tongue assertively went for the other as I reached out to stroke his length. *God, I'm so ready.*

His hand slid down between us and grazed my lower lips. "This still mine?" he muttered.

With my chest now heaving up and down, I nodded.

"Nah, mama, I got to hear you say that shit," he urged, continuing to suckle on my breast softly.

"It's yours," I murmured, my mind completely gone.

He resumed sliding my romper and underwear down until they were somewhere puddled on the floor. As I lay there beneath him, my body wholly bare, I watched his eyes drink in the sight of me. Even without words, Malachi always made me feel beautiful.

"Yo' pretty white ass got me going fucking crazy," he admitted.

I playfully slapped his chest. "I'm *not* white, Malachi," I let out with a giggle. "But I'm crazy about you too."

After kicking off his pants and shoes, he nestled his frame between my thighs. Diligently, he kissed my lips. Extending his hand down between us, he grabbed his erection and ran its tip down the length of my lower lips. "Wet as fuck," he hissed. "You still on the pill?"

"I am, but we still need some protection."

A look of shock zipped through his eyes before he asked, "Shawty, you been fucking?"

Just by the curt tone of his voice, I knew he was on the verge of anger. I placed a calming hand on his cheek and shook my head. "No, Malachi, but I want to protect myself."

Hearing myself say out loud the words "protect myself" somehow pulled me out of that all-consuming, lust-filled state I was in. As he leaned down, grabbing a condom from his jeans, his cell phone vibrated on the nightstand. I looked over to see a cheek-to-cheek picture of Reese and Maevyn flashing across his screen, and my body immediately went cold.

"It's your *wife*," I said, propping myself up on my elbows to look at Malachi, who now had a wrapped condom between his teeth.

His eyes immediately darted over to his phone. "Mane," he drawled. "Shawty, don't start that shit again. Me and her ain't even like that. We ain't been together in damn near a year."

Suddenly, I felt sick to my stomach. "Get off of me," I screamed, pushing him away. Malachi sucked his teeth but didn't budge. "Get. Off. Of. Me," I yelled louder this time.

Finally, he lifted from the bed with his long, thick dick suspended in the air. "Paris, you trippin', mane," he insisted. "Shit ain't what it seems."

Feeling the tears build in my eyes, I pulled the covers up over my breasts. "Just get out," I cried, dramatically pointing to the door. "I don't ever want to see your stupid face again."

He groaned and cussed under his breath as he gathered his clothes from the floor. Finally, when he was fully dressed, he walked back over to the bed and towered over me. "You sure this is what you want?" he asked, his intense gaze shooting into me.

"Definitely."

Exhaling a snort through his nose, he shook his head and collected his things off the nightstand. Then without uttering a goodbye, he disappeared from the room. Like so many other nights, I ended up crying myself to sleep. My heart and mind were battling. On one hand, I knew that being with Malachi was downright wrong. He was married with kids and, let's not forget, a criminal of sorts, but my heart still ached for him. All these weeks, I'd been just pretending to get over Malachi. Flirting with other guys, hanging out with Ty—it was all a lie. I was so in love with this man that most days, I felt sick. That's how I'd lost the weight. He was unknowingly obliterating me inside.

The following day, I woke to the sound of someone banging on our front door. I groaned and begrudgingly opened my eyes. As I looked over at the clock on my nightstand, I saw that it was just after eight. Hearing the pounding persist, I shot up from the bed and went to my dresser. After finding a large T-shirt to throw over my naked frame, I stepped out into the hallway. Franki was already at the door when I finally reached the living room. Her feet were bare, and her curly hair was wild and sprawled out all over her head. Even from behind, as she stood there in one of Josh's frat shirts and her hand on her hip, I could tell she had an attitude.

"Yo, who the fu . . ." she grumbled, letting her voice trail off with a subtle snake of her neck. Suddenly, she yanked the door open wide. That's when I saw Bull and Asha standing out on the porch. Franki glanced back at me with a roll of her eyes before letting them inside. Visibly annoyed, she stomped back to her room.

"What are you two doing here? Is Malachi all right?" I asked, still feeling slightly foggy and confused.

"'Chi straight," Bull said, handing me a small stack of papers.

"What's this?" My eyes shifted from the papers to Asha, who I'd just now noticed was carrying a large box in her hands.

"Your car's been fixed," Bull said, handing me a spare key.

"Oh," I let out, raking my fingers back through my hair. "Thanks." I was befuddled.

"And there's another piece of paper there about your rent," he let me know.

Confused, I tilted my head to the side. "My rent?" I asked.

Asha dropped her heavy box to the floor and nodded. "Yeah, girl. Malachi paid our rent up for the rest of the year."

My head jerked back. "*Our* rent?"

"Yeah," her eyes narrowed, creating a muddled expression. "He said y'all didn't mind me moving back in." When I looked at her like she was crazy, she hunched her shoulders and whispered to Bull. "He said I could move my stuff in today."

Not understanding, I looked at Bull for help. "Bull, what the hell is going on here? What is she talking about?"

"Shawty, I can't call it," he said, holding up both of his hands in surrender. "You gon' have to take this shit up with 'Chi."

In complete bewilderment, I watched as he turned and exited through the front door.

Chapter 12

Franki—Summer Tease

"Where you at, baby?" Josh asked on the phone.

I was standing in the center aisle of the train with a carry-on bag in my hand, an earbud in one ear, and my cell nuzzled between my shoulder and the other. "I'm about to pull into Grand Central now. Where you at?" I asked.

"I'm circling the block. Just look for a white Audi S5 when you come out."

"A white Audi?"

"Yeah, ma, I'll tell you about it when I see you," he said.

After ending the call, I smiled to myself. Just the thought of seeing Josh's pretty face again thrilled me on the inside. Although we communicated every day, I still missed him like crazy. Not only that, but I was also eager to be back home in New York. I wanted to smell the smog in the air, hear the city's clamor, and feel the hot pavement beneath my feet. I'd also been dying to see this little place Josh was temporarily calling home. Given the cost of living in Manhattan, I imagined it to be some squatty little hole-in-the-wall, but it didn't matter to me either way. As long as Josh and I were together, I'd be content.

Against my better judgment, I broke down and told my mother about my visit. I anticipated a lecture, but her response was just the opposite. She told me that she was glad I'd be able to spend some time with Josh and that I couldn't have timed the trip any better. She needed him to bring me across the bridge so that she could speak with me about something important while I was here. Although I hadn't told Josh yet, I even promised to spend a day or two with her. He already had my week mapped out with after-hours work events, concerts in Central Park, and a fireworks show on the Fourth of July, so we'd just have to readjust.

Finally, the train came to a halt, and after firming my grip on my bag, I paced toward the exit. As I entered the station, the first thing I saw was a homeless man lying on a bench. I dropped a few quarters into his cup before continuing to go outside. As soon as I swung open the door, my free hand shaded my eyes from the sun. After fighting through the sea of people on the sidewalk, I reached the taxi-lined curb. Horns were honking as hordes of people rushed in chaos up and down the street. Suddenly, I spotted a white Audi parked just at the end of the block. Josh.

As I weaved through the overcrowded sidewalk, his handsome face suddenly appeared. My lips nearly burst at the seam and spread into a wide smile. My feet sped up on their own, and they stopped just a yard short of the car. I dropped my bag to the ground and dramatically ran into his arms. He squeezed me back so tightly that all the air pressed from my lungs as I lifted from the ground. To anyone watching, I'm sure it was just another corny scene from a movie, but in that moment, everything I felt was real. The warmth of his touch, the scent of his cologne, and even the beat of his heart against mine—all melted me.

He placed me back on the ground and used his finger to sweep away a wispy curl that had fallen into my face.

"'Bout time," he said, gazing down at me with dark, penetrating eyes.

I wrapped my arms around his neck and softly pecked his lips. "We got hung up in D.C.," I said, stepping back from his embrace. As my eyes did a full sweep of his frame, I instinctively licked my lips. "Damn, yo. You look good," I flattered, taking in the cobalt-blue slacks and heather-gray dress shirt he wore. He looked expensive and even more mature than the last time I'd seen him, even down to the flashy wristwatch. My baby looked fly.

Meanwhile, I stood there with my curly black hair wild. My jean shorts were so small that the pockets hung from the bottom. I also wore a pink Good Vibes tee. Trying to hide his smile, Josh moved around me and retrieved my duffle bag off the ground. When he popped the trunk, my eyes immediately went back to the white Audi parked on the street.

"So, whose car is this?"

"It's a company car," he said. "Gotta give it back at the end of summer."

"Damn," I muttered, taking in its spotless paint and shiny metallic rims. Every inch of the car sparkled as if it were brand new.

When he opened the passenger door for me to get in, I immediately sank into the tan leather seat and relished the cool air. As he rounded the car, I instantly reached over and changed his AM radio station from progressive political talk to Hot 97 FM. By the time he opened the door, I was already twerking in place to "Act Up" by City Girls.

"Why you always changing my radio, girl?" he chuckled, dipping down to slide behind the wheel. I stuck out my tongue and turned the music up a little louder. "You wildin', ma. Put your seat belt on," he said, shaking his head.

After securing my seat belt, I pulled out my cell to shoot my mother a quick text. I just needed to let her know that I'd safely made it to the city and that Josh had come to pick me up. "Why'd you drive anyway? We could've just caught the train," I said with my eyes down as I typed away at the screen.

"Well, my spot is right around the corner. Besides, you've been on the train all day. I just wanted you to be comfortable," he explained, reaching over to take my hand. "You hungry?"

"Hell yea."

"What you got a taste for? Let me guess, pizza?"

As if New York pizza wasn't my favorite, I pursed my lips and playfully rolled my eyes. "You think you know me, don't you?" I asked.

Instead of responding, Josh shook his head and eased his way into traffic. For the next thirty minutes or so, we moved at a snail's pace just to get around the corner. Finally, we pulled up to a parking garage just off Forty-Sixth Street.

"Where we going?" I asked, looking over at Josh, who was now leaning out of the window and punching in a four-digit code.

Just as the gate opened, granting us access to the garage, he reached over and gently tapped me on the chin. "My place," he said.

Damn, I thought to myself. This was definitely prime real estate because every condo in this area ran in the million-dollar range. And I only knew that because my mother used to keep house for people in this part of the city. Although I was stunned, I decided to sit back and play it cool. He pulled into the garage and rode the deck up three stories high until he finally found a park. After retrieving my bag from the trunk, he took my hand and led me toward the elevators. We headed up to the fourteenth level, where the floor carpet looked just as exquisite as the sconces on the corridor walls. When we finally reached his door, number 1438, he pulled out his key and let us inside.

"Shit," I let out as my eyes immediately scanned the quaint space. I stepped in, further assessing the mahogany wood floors and ceilings that seemed to soar at least twelve feet high. The place was observably expensive, from the eclectic artwork on the vintage brick-and-mortar walls to the adjacent white leather sofas that stood in the small living room. From where I stood, I could also make out the galley kitchen in the back and the open loft-style bedroom that was just up a short flight of stairs.

Josh kept close behind as I made my way over to the sliding glass doors. I stepped onto the terrace and inhaled a deep breath before peering down at the city below. With the direct view of the East River, I could only imagine what this would look like at night. It was all breathtaking, even in the light of day.

"This is gorgeous, yo," I said softly, nodding. The warm air gently caressed my cheeks as I leaned over the rail.

"Yeah, I'm definitely gonna hate giving this place up at the end of the summer," he said, standing directly behind me as his hands grabbed the rails to trap me in place. "Hopefully, they'll let me intern again next summer, right before law school."

The reminder of him going away to law school next year slightly sullied my mood. Spinning around to face him, I leaned back and looked up into his eyes. "You know I get sad when you talk about leaving me," I told him truthfully.

"I'm not leaving you, baby. I'm just going to law school. But either way, when the time comes, we'll work it out, a'ight?" He gently hooked me by the chin when I cut my eyes away and began nodding in vain. "Nah, look at me," he said. "We'll work it out, a'ight?"

"Okay."

He leaned down and softly pecked me on the lips. "Now, come on. Let's go order the food."

We both headed back inside, and while Josh went to call in the pizza, I jogged up the five short steps to his bedroom. His bed was neatly made with soft burgundy sheets and a simple gray comforter. A flat screen hung high, catty-cornered, between two of the three walls of his room. And in the corner was his laptop sitting on a paper-filled desk, giving way to the fact that he often worked from home. After checking out his tiny closet packed with suits and ties, I entered his adjoining bath. It was a small white space with just a simple shower and pedestal sink. It was nothing fancy but more than what I had growing up.

When I came out, Josh was sitting on his bed, smiling. "You like it?" he asked.

I nodded. "Love it," I said. From his clothes to the expensive apartment, it was all a reminder of Josh's future—the very successful one he was destined to have.

As he hunched over to slip off his shoes, I noticed his back muscles protruding from beneath his shirt. "You've been working out?"

"Yeah, they've got a gym at the office. So, I like to get in there early before work. Why?" he asked, looking up as he licked his dark pink lips.

God, I'm horny. There was no other way to describe how I felt seeing the pink flesh of his tongue run across his bottom lip. I sauntered toward him, grabbed his shoulders, and gingerly straddled his lap. As he circled his arms around my waist, I gazed into his dark brown eyes.

"I missed you," I purred.

His eyes momentarily softened as he studied my face. "I missed you too, baby," he said lowly.

With our eyes still connected, I moved in slowly and slipped my tongue between his lips. The vast spread of his hands descended my back in a gentle caress before he brought them down to my ass. Within mere seconds, we were kissing like crazed lovers, and I could feel his manhood mounting from down below. As my body began to heat and ache, I unraveled in his arms. My hips gyrated back and forth as my nipples turned to stone. And when I felt his fingertips slither beneath the tiny shorts I wore, a soft moan eased from my lungs.

He suddenly stood up from the bed with my legs still cloaked around his waist. Our mouths still took each other's with so much passion that the sound in the room was just short of making love. As he laid me back on the bed, the tips of my fingers aggressively grazed his ears, desperately trying to deepen our kiss. I was overflowing with desire, wanting nothing more than to feel him inside of me. When he went to unbutton my shorts, my hands anxiously clawed at the hem of his shirt.

"Take it off," I panted. "Please."

He lifted his shirt over his head, revealing the curves of muscles that lay beneath his smooth caramel skin. And around his neck was his signature cross pendant in gold. I couldn't wait any longer, so I shimmied out of my shorts and kicked off my shoes. When I was completely naked from the waist down, Josh's eyes seductively drank me in.

He bit down on his bottom lip and softly shook his head. "You so beautiful, ma. I swear I could stare at you all day," he said sincerely.

God, this is it. My heart throbbed inside my chest as my pussy got even wetter. It was finally going down, and I couldn't wait a second more. I sat upright in the bed and came face-to-face with the bulge in his slacks. I placed my lips right there, over the fabric, making his erection twitch.

"I need you, Josh," I murmured to him, my hands holding his waist.

"Shhh . . ." He hissed, raking his fingers through my hair.

I pulled back and began unbuckling his pants. Before I could even get them down, he said, "Wait, ma, I can't do this."

"But, baby—"

He took a step back and shook his head. "Nah. This ain't right," he said.

"You've got to be fucking kidding me," I let out, planting my feet on the floor. After fastening his pants, he went over to sit by his desk. With his legs cocked wide, he dropped his head between his shoulders and let out an exasperated sigh.

"Yo, Josh, man, stop fucking ignoring me," I called out to him again. Lifting his head, he allowed his eyes to staple on to me before grabbing the back of his neck. "So, you just gon' sit there? You get a bitch all riled up, half-naked with her hopes up high, and you not even gon' say shit?" I was furious and horny.

"Baby," he tried, wiping his hand down his jaw.

"Nah, fuck that. Just because you're celibate doesn't mean I am. I need sex, Josh," I said, looking at him for a response. However, after a few beats of silence, I picked up my clothes and stomped into the bathroom.

Not even a minute later, I heard him on the other side. "I just wanna honor my commitment, Franki," he said. "I know you have sexual desires, and, I mean . . . I do too, but I can't give in to them because I've already surrendered to God." He let out a deep sigh. "It kills me that I'm not able to give you what you need, baby, that I can't fulfill you. But I have to remain focused. I gotta stand in my faith."

After rolling my eyes, I went over to flush the toilet, hoping he'd take the hint. I didn't want to talk about God, nor did I want to hear about his abundance of faith. I wanted him to take me like a savage and fuck me so hard that afterward, I could barely stand. I was ready to take our relationship to the next level, but it was evident that Josh wasn't on board. In fact, it didn't seem like he'd ever be.

Almost thirty minutes later, I decided to come out of the bathroom. As soon as I opened the door, the smell of pepperoni pizza infiltrated my nose. I began walking down the stairs, and before I could reach the bottom step, I saw him eating alone at the table.

He lifted his head from his plate and looked at me with those dark brown eyes. "Want me to fix you a plate?" he asked.

"Nah, I got it."

I grabbed two slices of pizza from the kitchen and sat across from him at the table. Although he tried making small talk here and there, the stubborn part of me persisted. I ate quietly, and when I was done, I went upstairs and got a towel and washcloth from his linen closet. After taking a hot shower, I left the bathroom and could hear him downstairs on a call. I listened in for a few, hearing him make plans for after work tomorrow before finally deciding to tuck myself into his bed for the night.

I don't know precisely when I drifted off to sleep, but the room was completely dark when I felt Josh's arm drape across me. He drew me back into his bare chest and whispered in my ear. "Just be patient with me, ma," he said. After feeling him kissing the nape of my neck, I closed my eyes and fell back into a deep slumber.

I reached for him the following day, but he wasn't there. Letting out a little yawn, I sat up and stretched. Like any other morning, I grabbed my cell off the nightstand. I had a missed call from my mother and a text from Josh.

Josh: I tried waking you before I left for work, but you were knocked out cold. Call me as soon as you get up.

After dialing my mother and telling her I'd be over on Saturday, I called Josh.

"Joshua McDuffey," he answered in a very businesslike voice.

"Hey," I said softly, still slightly in a mood from yesterday.

"You still mad at me?"

I didn't answer right away. Instead, I twisted my lips back and forth, thinking of the best response. Finally, I exhaled and said, "We straight, Josh."

"You sure? 'Cause I don't want to be at odds with you all week, ma."

"Yeah, I'm sure. I just want us to enjoy each other while we can," I told him truthfully.

"A'ight, well, check it. I'm meeting a few of my coworkers tonight after work out for drinks. I want you to come with me."

"Okay," I said, thinking how Josh sounded so grown up. *Coworkers?* "What time should I be ready?"

"I get off at four, so I should be home no later than five," he said.

After we hung up, I got up and fixed myself a small breakfast that I ate out on the terrace. Once that was done, I cleaned up my mess and decided to veg out on the couch a bit. Suddenly, my cell phone vibrated beside me. I looked to see Hope's name flashing across the screen.

I swiped my finger across the screen and answered, "Hello."

"Hey, um, w-when are you coming back?" she asked. Given her desolate tenor, I knew that something was wrong.

"Sunday. Why?" I asked.

She released a sigh so deep that I felt her anxiety through the phone. "My deddy's coming."

"Oh shit," I muttered. "When?"

"He just called and told me he's gonna be here Sunday. He said that he hadn't laid eyes on me in a while and felt something was wrong. I tried telling him that I was fine and that he didn't need to come all the way out here, but he wasn't trying to hear it. Aunt Marlene even told him that she rarely sees me now and thinks something's wrong too."

"Damn," I sighed, shaking my head. "Well, maybe it's a good thing. You can finally get everything out in the open."

"He's gonna kill me, Franki," she cried.

I let out a light snort of laughter at her dramatics. "Ya pops is definitely gonna be angry, but he ain't gon' kill you."

"Well, I just called to see when you were coming back. I don't want to have to face him alone."

My eyebrows instantly hiked. "Well, where the fuck is Meeko?" I asked angrily. "I mean, shouldn't *he* be the one standing next to you since it was his ass that got you pregnant in the first place?"

Hope just groaned. "You know my deddy hates him. I'm afraid that having him there will only make matters worse."

"Nah, yo. Confronting your pops eight months pregnant without the nigga that did it—*that's* the shit that's gonna make it worse. Trust me," I told her. "Look, just talk to Meeko and hit me back. If I need to catch an earlier train, I will, but talk to Meeko first."

"All right," she said softly. "I'll talk to him."

After we hung up, I watched TV for a bit, then drifted off into a nap. By the time I woke up, it was a little after four. I laid the shorts and tank top I planned on wearing that night across the bed, then jumped in the shower. As I was stepping out, I heard Josh coming through the door.

"Baby," he yelled. "Where you at, ma?"

Since his bedroom was loft-style, I hollered back, "I'm up here."

Sitting on the edge of his unmade bed with a towel wrapped around me, I could hear his heavy feet jogging up the wooden stairs. "You 'bout ready?" I heard him ask.

As soon as I lifted my eyes, he stood on the top step, entering the room. A royal blue, two-piece suit adorned his lanky frame. "Almost," I said breathily, taking my bottom lip between my teeth. With an extra sway in my hips, I got up and sauntered over to greet him. I loosely draped my arms around his neck before meeting his soft lips with my own. "I'm sorry about last night, babe."

"Me too," he said just beyond a whisper. His eyes peered back at me with so much intensity as he firmed his fingers around my waist. He leaned in and inhaled deeply just before kissing me on the neck. "Now, hurry up. We gotta get going," he said, gently tapping me on the ass.

I felt so much better now that we'd put last night behind us. The entire time I was getting dressed, I hummed the previous love song I'd heard on the radio. Don't get me wrong. I was still as horny as a prisoner that had just been released from a ten-year bid. But even more than that, I was happy that Josh and I had finally made amends. Truth be told, we'd more than likely face other arguments of this nature in the future, but for this week, at least, I was going to ensure things between us remained copasetic.

Josh's eyes raked me over when I was fully dressed before his head jerked back. "*That's* what you're wearing?" he asked, curiously chucking up his chin.

"Yeah, why? What are you wearing?"

He gripped the back of his neck with his hand. "I mean, I was gonna keep on what I'm wearing now. Just lose the jacket."

"Well, I only brought one dress, and that's for when we see Miguel perform at the park," I told him. He nodded in understanding. "I mean, we're only going out for drinks, right?"

"Yeah. I think I'm just gonna throw on some shorts and a tee shirt then," he said.

After Josh changed into a pair of cargo shorts and a navy Polo, we headed out of the apartment. We walked just a few blocks down before we finally reached St. Pat's Bar & Grill. It was an Irish-themed pub with stained-glass windows and vintage porcelain tiles on the floor. Shortly after we'd entered, I watched Josh's eyes scan over the crowd. He lifted his chin when he finally spotted his people in the back.

"There they are," he said. He took me by the hand and led me down to the far end of the bar. As we neared, I could make out three young Black men. Two were still in their suit jackets with loosened ties, and the other with the white sleeves of his dress shirt rolled up just above his wrists. A young lady was with them. She was laughing so hard her head fell back as she loosely clutched her chest. She had a light, buttery complexion with long, wavy black hair that cascaded to the middle of her back. Even from a distance, I could tell that her figure was a killer in her red sheath dress. Suddenly, I felt underdressed and anxious.

"What's up, y'all?" Josh greeted, slapping hands with one of the guys. "Baby, this here is Kevin," he said, pointing to the light-skinned one with the glasses. "And that's Duke," he said, nodding toward the dark-skinned guy whose slick bald head looked like an Easter egg. "And right here is my man, Will."

As the guys all shook my hand, I heard the girl suddenly pop her lips. "Really, Joshua?" she said, causing me to look in her direction. "You're not gonna introduce me to your girlfriend?"

I don't think anyone else noticed, but I saw a brief tightening of Josh's jaw. "Franki, this here is Summer. And, Summer, this is my lady, Franki," he said.

While the other guys snickered beneath their breaths, she extended her manicured hand. "Nice to finally meet you, Franki. Josh talks about you all the time."

I shook her hand and smiled. "It's nice to meet you too," I said. Then I glanced back at the guys. "So, are you all interns at the firm, or do you guys actually work there?" I asked.

"Both," Duke said with a chuckle. "We're all interns, but we definitely work while we're there."

"So then, everyone here is a senior in college?" They all nodded their heads. "What school do you go to?" I turned to ask the light-skinned guy named Kevin.

"Howard. The real HU," he said, flashing a bright smile. Instead of his glasses making him look geeky, he looked sophisticated. Sexy even.

"And you?" I asked, eyeing Mr. Milk Dud sitting there.

"I'm a Morehouse man," he said, swiping back his bald head as he licked his lips.

Josh scoffed and shook his head.

"Well, Will and I both go to Grambling State. Josh would've gone there too if he hadn't gotten that full ride at A&T," Summer said with a pout. I looked over at Josh, seeing him subtly shrug his shoulders. "Aye, remember that time Duckey tried to cheat off your test during the PSAT?" she asked with a little laugh, turning to Josh as she placed her hand on his shoulder.

Suddenly, I was confused. *Do these two know each other outside of work?* "Wait," I said, glancing back and forth between the two of them. "You two know each other?"

"Oh, you didn't tell her?" Summer asked, looking at Josh.

"Um, yeah," he said, scratching behind his ear. "We went to high school together."

Her nose scrunched as she twisted her lips to the side. "Elementary and middle too," she let it be known with a flip of her long hair.

"Oh" was all I could say. Being blindsided, I wasn't exactly sure how to feel.

"Actually, Josh was my very first boyfriend. My first love," she went on to say, her eyes gazing at the side of Josh's face. Duke let out a palpable cough, attempting to ease the sudden awkwardness. Summer looked at him with wide eyes. "What?" she asked, feigning oblivion.

Suddenly, the small group fell into an uncomfortable silence, each taking sips of their beer and wine. Meanwhile, I just stood there, waiting for Josh to acknowledge what Summer had just revealed. However, he never did. Instead, he leaned over and whispered in my ear.

"What you want to drink, ma?" he asked. I shot him the nastiest look I could muster before ultimately shaking my head.

For the next few hours, things returned somewhat back to normal. My conversation with the guys began to flow quite well. They wanted to know all about me: where I was from, my major, and even my roommates' names. From them, I'd learned that Michaels, Starks, and Lochearn was an all-Black law firm that targeted high-performing students across the country attending HBCUs. Each of them were handpicked for this internship, and with hard work and conceivably a little bit of luck, they'd each been promised a job after law school. Thankfully, Summer didn't attempt to take any more trips down memory lane with Josh. Because if she had, I already had it set in my mind to check the bitch's chin.

After allowing Josh to finish the last of his beer, I finally decided it was time for us to call it quits for the night. "You ready?" I asked lowly, placing my lips up to his ear.

"Yeah. It's getting late, and I've gotta get up early in the morning," he said. I nodded in agreement. And not because I actually gave a shit about him having to get up early the next day. Instead, because I knew that if I sat there any longer, all of his friends would hear me cuss him out. It was bad enough that I'd walked in wearing jean shorts and a tank top while everyone else still wore their work attire. I didn't want to cause any more embarrassment for him.

After saying our goodbyes, even to Summer, we exited the bar. We didn't talk for quite awhile during our walk back home. Then out of nowhere, I felt I couldn't take it anymore.

"Why didn't you tell me you were working with your ex?" abruptly spewed from my lips.

Josh raked his palm over his face and sighed. "I'on know. I guess I just didn't want you to feel some type of way when it don't really mean nothing," he said. "And then she showed up to the bar tonight unexpectedly . . ." he said, letting his voice trail off as he shook his head.

"Did you fuck her?" I came right out and asked.

Josh's head whipped in my direction so fast I thought I'd heard the bones of his neck crack. "Yo, ma, you buggin'," he said, altogether avoiding the question.

"Just tell me, Josh. Did. Y'all. Fuck?" I asked loudly, feeling my temper on the brink of explosion.

He let out another deep sigh and slowly wagged his head. "Let's just talk about it when we get home," he said.

Although it was mighty hard, I followed Josh's lead and momentarily dropped the subject. We hiked down the sidewalk, going in and out of sporadic clouds of cigarette smoke, hearing horns honk and loud music base from the passing cars. By the time we reached the lobby door of his apartment, my face was sticky, and my wild, curly hair had further expanded from the humidity. I exhaled in relief when I finally made contact with the cool air.

On our way up to his apartment, I kept looking at Josh, wondering how he could've withheld such vital information from me. To be honest, Josh was damn near perfect in my eyes. Every seed of doubt the men from my past had planted inside of me had all been excavated and restored by him. And the thought of him having sex with another woman, yet denying me, hurt. Not only was my ego bruised, but it also made me believe that perhaps my feelings for him were a lot stronger than what he felt for me.

As soon as we entered his apartment, I said, "Just tell me."

With his back facing me, he turned the double locks and secured the chain on the door. "She was my first," he finally let out. After a few beats, he finally turned around to confront me as if he were giving me a moment to compose a rational response.

"So, you didn't think telling me you'd be working with the broad was important? The bitch that took yo' virginity?" He opened his mouth to answer, but I quickly cut him off. "Have you fucked her since you've been up here? Is that why you won't have sex with me?"

"No," he answered right away, disbelief showing in his eyes. "I haven't touched that girl in almost three years. She has nothing to do with my celibacy."

"But you chose to give her a piece of you that you refuse to give me."

"It's not even like that, and you know it," he said. "That was before I got saved. Before I got serious about my relationship with God."

Not wanting to hear another quote from the Bible, I rolled my eyes and stomped up the stairs to his room. The sound of his footsteps shadowed closely behind me until he'd finally reached the landing. Irritated, I began removing my clothes. I even thought about staying with my moms for a brief moment, but I wasn't too keen on that idea either. Over and over, she'd been saying that we needed to talk. My gut told me that whatever it was wasn't good. And with everything bad that had occurred this past year, I didn't know if I could take another L.

As I tucked myself in bed, Josh jumped in the shower. I scrolled Instagram, catching up on the latest, until I finally heard the water stop. Quickly, I reached over and cut off the lamp. When Josh made his way to the bed, I was turned over, facing the wall. I stiffened when he snuggled up close behind me, placing his hand atop my hip.

"Damn, it's like that?" he said lowly, his warm breath tickling the rear of my neck.

"Do you still love her?" I asked out of nowhere.

I knew I'd caught him off guard from the sudden silence in the room. "Nah," he admitted. "I don't think I ever did."

Finally, I turned around, seeing only a dark silhouette of his face. "But somehow you love me?" I asked softly, feeling my heartbeat accelerate inside my chest.

This was uncharted territory for us and our relationship, a topic we had yet to breach. I mean, sure, he had told me once before that he loved me. But for the life of me, I just couldn't understand why. Most days, I didn't even feel worthy of his love. He was so patient and kind, while I could be overbearing and tactless. Yet, at this very moment, no matter how scared I was, I desperately needed to know how he felt about me. How could someone like Joshua McDuffey love someone like me?

"Franki, I don't love you for any reason other than the fact that I just do. There's nothing about you that anyone could tell me now or ever, for that matter, that would change that. Please know that, ma. I can sit here all day long and tell you that I love you, but the truth is, even that wouldn't measure up to how I truly feel. Because honest to God, I love you way more than that. You got me, ma. In here." He placed his hand over his chest. "I promise, I don't want nobody else but you."

Chapter 13

Hope—Just Maybe

After an hour of tossing and turning in my bed, I finally got up and caught an Uber to Pride Hall. I only had four more days until my father arrived, and I was nervous to the point of being sick. Until now, I hadn't decided if I wanted Meeko there with me. From months past, I already knew that just the mere mention of his name would infuriate my father. They'd only met once, but it was no secret that Deddy detested him. Still, I needed someone there by my side.

As the Uber driver pulled up to the dorms, I noticed a lot of traffic coming in and out of the building. Given the fact it was summer, this was somewhat odd. Most students had returned home, and the campus had been dead for the past month. Nonetheless, I got out, and with my left hand supporting my lower back and a duffel bag over my right arm, I wobbled to the front door. I wore a long, blue maxi dress that stretched just enough to fit my belly and a pair of rubber flip-flops on my feet. Instead of going for the elevator, I regrettably took the stairs. The stench of marijuana and smoke filled the stairwell as music and banter echoed off the walls. Through the thick lenses of my glasses, it appeared to be a small party happening in Pride Hall tonight.

When I finally got to the fourth floor, passing through small crowds gathered along the way, I continued to Meeko's room. The music was a bit louder now, and I could spot more people hanging out in the hallway. As I neared his open door, billows of smoke rolled out of his room. It was evident that he was having a party.

Finally, I reached his door and peeped my head inside. Through the blue lighting of his lava lamp and the thick clouds of smoke, I could make out people partying in the small room. I immediately spotted Big Mo talking to a girl in the back corner and Ty, sitting at Meeko's desk with a red cup in his hand. With a protective arm wrapped around my belly and the other securing the bag on my shoulder, I wobbled farther inside. That's when my eyes landed on a shirtless Meeko. A lit blunt dangled from his lips as a girl I'd never seen before danced in his lap.

A lump instantly formed in my throat, and I felt nauseated. Although Meeko and I were now on speaking terms, we were no longer in a committed relationship. I never pushed the issue because a huge part of me wasn't entirely over the whole bet thing. And given the fact that Meeko hadn't asked for us to be together again, I quickly deduced that he just couldn't get over me keeping the baby a secret. But now, looking at him with another girl, tears welled in my eyes.

As I spun around to rush out the door, I heard, "Dimples."

I peered back just in time to see Big Mo's ginormous frame stalking toward me. "H-hey, Big Mo," I stammered.

With open arms, he leaned down and pulled me into a bear hug. When he pulled back, his eyes immediately fell to my pregnant belly. "What you doing out? Meeko know you here?" he asked.

"N—"

Before I could tell him no, he hollered over his shoulder. "Aye, yo, Meeko. Hope's here."

My regard instantly shifted to Meeko, seeing him gently remove the girl from his lap. He stood up, lifting his jeans to his waist before gaiting over. Although I wanted to run, I stood frozen in place. Wrinkles formed across his brow as he came near.

"I thought I was picking you up in the morning," he said, looking confused.

"Sorry, I just couldn't sleep and wanted to talk," I shouted, competing with the music. "You didn't pick up your phone when I called so . . ." My voice trailed off as I realized how stalker-ish I was beginning to sound. "Just call me when you're on your way tomorrow," I said, shaking my head in an attempt to combat the embarrassment I suddenly felt.

Just as I turned to walk away, he gently grabbed the back of my arm. "Aye, yo," he yelled over the music. "Everybody, get the fuck out!"

"Meeko, this isn't necessary. Really," I tried.

Ignoring me, Meeko slapped hands with a few of his friends, saying goodbye as they exited one by one. When the girl who was previously sitting on his lap finally reached the door, she boldly stopped in front of us. Her glowing skin was like copper, and her hair draped down her back in long locs. I took in the small piercing in her nose as well as the bar she had in her left brow. Her eyelashes were so long that I secretly wished they were fake. She was earthy and naturally pretty.

"Call you tomorrow?" she asked boldly, looking Meeko in the eyes.

"Uh, yeah. I'll just hit you tomorrow," he said, releasing a sigh as he gripped the back of his neck.

She gave my body a full sweep with her eyes before letting her lips turn up into a smile. And not in a bitchy way either, but rather an "Aw, you look so cute pregnant" kind of way. Having seen that expression so much, I recognized it right away.

"See ya," she said, glancing at Meeko again before exiting through the door.

Of course, the last to leave were Big Mo and Ty. "Damn. Hope just rolled in here with that big-ass belly of hers and shut our shit all the way down," Big Mo teased with a chuckle.

"No, I didn't mean—"

"I'm just fucking with you, Dimples. You straight," he said, tossing me a little wink. He gave me another hug before finally heading out of the door. Ty followed suit, giving me a one-armed hug before following behind him.

After Meeko closed the door, he took the bag from my arm and walked over to the window. Raising it as high as it could go, he attempted to let out the smoke. Then he went over to cut off the music. I did not want to sit on the bed that he and the girl had just been on, so I sat in the lone chair in the corner.

"Shorty, what you doing out this time of night?" he asked, shuffling around his room to pick up red cups and beer cans from the floor. "How you get here?"

I let out a deep breath. "I caught an Uber because I couldn't sleep. My father is coming this Sunday. He'll be here when we get back."

Still lowered to his haunches, he turned back to look at me. "You still ain't told him you pregnant?" he asked.

I shook my head and allowed my chin to drop to my chest. "I'm scared, Meek," I admitted softly.

Meeko dragged his hand over his jaw before sitting on the edge of his bed. "You want me just to tell him?" he proposed, lifting his brow. "'Cause I ain't scared of your pops."

"No," I let out. "Well, not by yourself, at least. Can you just come with me to my aunt Marlene's house this Sunday? And we tell him together? Please."

"Sure." He nodded, shrugging his lips. "Whatever you need."

I timidly cut my eyes away after trading gazes with Meeko for a spell. "Well, that was all I wanted," I said, hiking one shoulder to my ear. "I didn't mean to stop all your fun. You can call your friends back over if you want."

When I stood up to leave, Meeko abruptly sprang from the bed. "Don't leave," he said, his voice bordering a plea. I lifted my eyes to meet his again, instantly seeing them soften. "It's mad late, yo. Just . . . Stay here tonight. Besides, I was gonna have to pick you up for the train tomorrow anyway, right? Ain't that why you brought your bag?" he asked, dipping his head toward my duffle bag on the floor as he released a light laugh.

My cheeks instantly warmed from embarrassment. "Oh. Right," I said, not knowing what else to say.

He went over to his dresser drawer, pulling out an old tee shirt for me to wear. It reminded me of the first time he'd invited me to his room. The shame I felt that day, having to walk through the yard in bloodstained clothes was a feeling I'd never forget. Then out of nowhere, Meeko came and rescued me, making me feel safe and befriended. *Or so I thought.*

As I went into the adjoining bath, I could hear him scuffling around on the other side of the door. After setting my glasses on the side of his sink, I washed my face and quickly brushed my teeth. Once I had his tee shirt draped over me, I smoothed back my puffy hair and exhaled a deep breath. When I walked back into his room, I first noticed his newly made bed. It was evident that he'd changed the sheets. Instead of feeling appreciative, I felt jealous and repulsed. I guess I presumed his only reason for changing them was due to having sexed other women in his bed—the very same bed I'd given him my virginity.

I surprised myself when I came right out and asked, "Was that your girlfriend?"

His eyes briefly flashed a bewildered expression. Then he took a deep swallow and shook his head. "Nah," he said. "Midge is just a friend."

Ah. Midge. With my eyes cast to the floor, I twiddled my thumbs. Suddenly, words I could have sworn were only in my head came out in a whisper. "Well, do all of your friends sit on your lap?"

He scoffed a laugh, swiping his hand down the front of his head. "Shorty and I kick it occasionally," he admitted. "But it's not that deep."

Oh. Internally, I shrank on my way over to the bed. When my knee hit the mattress, I felt a slight tug of my tee shirt, pulling in the opposite direction. I glanced over my shoulder, seeing Meeko standing right behind me. He licked his full brown lips before oddly taking a nervous swallow.

"I just wanted to say good night," he said.

I could feel my brows pinch in confusion just before my eyes darted down to the floor. Neatly arranged was a comforter and a pillow that he'd obviously laid out for himself. He's not sleeping in the bed with me? For the life of me I couldn't understand why that stung so badly.

However, Meeko's fingers suddenly creeping beneath my shirt shifted my train of thought. When he reached for my belly, my chest swelled with a big breath. We hadn't touched like this, flesh to flesh, in months. My breathing came to a passing halt as a slow ache started between my thighs. As he moved to sit on the edge of his bed, his eyes slowly lifted to my face, asking for permission. The rise and fall of my swollen breasts was my only response.

Suddenly, I felt my tee shirt hike a bit more, exposing my cotton panties underneath. The tiny hairs on my arms stood erect as my pulse raced beneath my skin. It had been so long since I'd last had sex, and from the sudden thumping between my thighs, I knew my body was long overdue. Then with his hands spread out like an eagle's wings, Meeko leaned forward and gently kissed my belly. All lips, no tongue, but it seemed I shuddered just the same.

"Good night," he whispered against my skin.

I don't know if it was the baby kicking or butterflies, but I felt a strong flutter inside me. Good night.

As I tucked myself in bed, he got up and flipped off the lights. Darkness instantly overtook the room, but I could still hear distant cars and night bugs chirping from the open window. I could hear him fluffing his pillow as I lay there staring at the ceiling. "You can sleep up here, if you want," I offered, sliding over until I felt my back hit the wall.

"Nah, it's all good," he said. "You look like you're about to pop, and I want you to be comfortable."

After another short stretch of silence, I said, "Meek."

"Yeah."

"You asleep?"

"Nah." He let out a yawn. "What's up?"

"What are we gonna do when the baby comes?"

He blew out a deep breath, and from the little light shining through the window, I could see him rolling over on his back. "I've been saving money. Enough for us to get a place and send the baby to day care when we have class. We'll be straight," he said. His voice was low but reassuring.

My body instantly stilled hearing that Meeko had somewhat of a plan. But there was one little thing that still confused me. Formulating my next set of words, I took a deep swallow. "So you're getting a place for us?"

"I mean, yeah. Even though we're not together, I'd still like us all to be under the same roof. At least until we figure out our next move."

And there it is. Meeko had no intention of us getting back together. In fact, it seemed his only hope was for an ideal coparenting arrangement. And while that was commendable and all, given our ages and the circumstances, I couldn't help but feel slighted. He was closing himself off to me when, in fact, he'd been the one to do me wrong. Why was my heart suddenly on the opposite end? I guess if I were to be completely honest with myself, I'd have to admit that with every passing day of this baby growing inside me, I desired the fairy tale. The loving marriage, the big house on the hill with a white picket fence just as Big Mo described.

"Right," I let out, barely above a whisper, no longer understanding what I was even agreeing to. That night, I slept no better in his bed than I would've in my own bed. I kept trying to picture what our future would look like but kept drawing a blank.

The next morning, we got up and ate breakfast in the cafe using his student card to cover the cost. While at the table, he tried his best to maintain a conversation, but everything from the night before kept playing in the background of my mind. I was utterly stuck in my own head. Even the train ride to Penn Station was a quiet one. While I mostly just sat there reading my book, Meeko drifted off to sleep. The little time he was awake, he spent it on his phone, texting. Of course, my eyes glanced down a time or two, noticing threads from Midge. My chest tightened at the sight. Other messages were from his family and friends asking when he'd make it back home.

When we got off the train, Meeko refused to let me carry my own bag. "You don't need to be lifting nothing right now," he said. "'Cause all I need is for you to go into labor while we're up here." He shook his head adamantly.

Although I was positive that toting a small duffle wouldn't be the cause of me going into premature labor, I was too emotionally exhausted to argue the point. I followed behind him until we were in front of the station, overlooking a one-way circular lane. Yellow taxis were parked out front as people came and went, rushing by. Finally, we heard the double honk of a horn. My eyes immediately followed the sound, and there, down at the other end of the street, was a tall, heavyset woman flailing her arms.

"Come on. That's my muva," he said, taking me by the hand. Short of dragging me through the crowd, Meeko swiftly guided me toward his mother's car. It was an old Toyota Camry the color of New Year's Eve champagne. The paint job had faded on the hood, one hub cap was missing from the front tire, and a black bungee cord held down the trunk in the back.

"There she is," she squealed, beaming with a gapped-tooth smile. "Meeko, you didn't tell me this child was so pretty."

Seldom hearing that description of myself, I inadvertently gasped. But before the air could enter my lungs, she wrapped her heavy arms around me. She had to have been close to six feet tall from how she towered over my little frame. And if I had to guess, she peaked right around the 300-pound mark. But, boy, was she beautiful, with her hair pulled back tightly off her face. Her dark brown skin was smooth and seemed to glow naturally under the summer's sun. And when I withdrew from her snug embrace, I could make out Meeko's low-set eyes. They didn't exactly look alike, but I could see the subtle traces of his features.

With her hands on the sides of my protruding belly, she said, "I'm Kelsey, Meeko's muva." Her Baltimorean accent was just as thick as Meeko's, if not more.

"Dang, Ma. Can I get a hug, yo?" Meeko teased, twisting his fitted cap to the back as he strutted over with his legs out wide.

Her eyes traveled behind me as she balled her lips into a tight smile. "Get your butt over here, boy. Get bigger every time I see you." And that he had. Meeko had packed on at least ten more pounds of muscle this past year alone. It looked damn good on him too. She reached her meaty arms out for a squeeze, and after they hugged and rocked from side to side, she told us to hop in the car.

"Help her get in the front, Meeko. You sit in the back."

Meeko sucked his teeth and rolled his eyes as he threw our luggage in the backseat. "Ma, you act like I'on know that."

"Hey, I'm just making sure." She cracked a smile.

No longer able to balance my weight with my thighs, I plopped down in the seat when Meeko opened the door. Ms. Kelsey was already behind the wheel, staring at me with wonder; well, mostly my belly. I countered with a small smile.

"Lord Jesus, my grandbaby's gonna have chocolate skin and dimples," she said, letting her eyes roam to my face. "We gon' have to beat the girls off of this boy."

It wasn't easy to take in the city with Ms. Kelsey talking nonstop along the way, but I didn't mind. The two of us seem to mesh right away. She began telling me about each of Meeko's sisters and her three grandchildren, who apparently were all awaiting our arrival. She even gave me a rundown of the Fourth of July cookout she had planned. Every now and then, I'd take a glimpse out of the window or glance in the backseat. But each time, it never failed. Meeko was on his phone, his fingers tapping at the screen as a playful smirk teased the corners of his lips.

After riding down Park Heights Avenue and hooking a left on Rogers, we turned down a narrow road. Most of the houses were brick row homes attached by the main walls, but Ms. Kelsey parallel parked in front of a gray, single-family home. My eyes traveled up, first to the damaged blinds in the windows, then to the large front porch carpeted in faux grass. The front door was wide open, making the rips in the screen more apparent. And bordering the tiny front yard beyond the cracked sidewalk was an old chain-link fence. *Hmm.* I'd never seen that before—a fence in the front yard.

"Keisha's still here with the kids. Got my door wide open," Ms. Kelsey mumbled as she cut off the engine. "Come on." She nodded toward the house.

I turned back to see Meeko stepping out of the car. He immediately looked from left to right, allowing his eyes to scan the block. After throwing our bags over his shoulder, he helped me out of the car. Everything about Meeko was strong, from his muscular build down to how he talked, but whenever he touched me, it was always gentle. He took my hand and carefully lifted me from the seat. Following his mother through the gate, I felt his hand guiding me by the small of my back. A shiver journeyed down my spine. As we climbed each cement step leading to the porch, Meeko took a protective hold of my waist, saying he didn't want me to fall.

"Keisha, Kadia," his mother hollered from the front door.

As soon as we crossed the threshold, I could smell the strong scent of a home-cooked meal behind her. A loud rumble ripped from my belly right away. My head fell from embarrassment.

"Damn. You hungry?" Meeko asked. Not wanting to wear out my welcome before it even began, I stubbornly shook my head and shushed him with my eyes. Meeko sucked his teeth. "Man," he drawled. "Shorty, you better stop acting shy and feed my baby."

Ms. Kelsey turned back with her eyes stretched wide. "What? You hungry, baby?"

"No," I told the truth. *I'm not hungry. I'm starving.* "I-I'm fine."

Sure, I had a sandwich on the train, but at that moment, it felt like I hadn't eaten in years. Instead, I allowed my eyes to rove the front room of the house as a distraction, taking in the old wooden floors partially covered by a frayed oriental rug. The living room was made up of a three-piece sofa set. Faux green suede, where the love seat had a streak of silver duct tape, giving away its wear and tear. The wooden coffee tables were all mismatched but properly arranged, holding up a collection of picture frames. To my right, I could see a narrow wooden staircase leading to the second story of their home. And just beyond the front door was a straight path that led to the long galley kitchen. Just as I went to take another step, two little girls in matching pink sundresses and beaded braids came flying down the stairs. "Uncle Meeko!" they screamed, leaping on him one after the other.

He dropped our bags from the force and picked up the littlest one in his arms. "There goes Unc's babies," he said, kissing her on the cheek and patting the other on the head. Then he turned and looked at me. "You remember Unc told y'all I was having a baby, right?" he asked. I scoffed lowly at the claim. "Well, this is my baby's mom, Hope."

Ugh, baby's mom. I swallowed before offering a closed-lip smile. "Hey," I said, wiggling my fingers at the taller one, who instantly clung to her uncle's leg. "What's your name?"

"Destiny," she whispered.

"Destiny," I repeated, my smile slightly broader than before. "Well, that's a pretty name for a pretty little girl." I looked up to the smaller one, who now had her face buried in Meeko's neck, being coy. "And what's your name?"

She never lifted her head, but her long lashes swept up as she peered at me. "Desiree." Her voice was so low—softer than a lullaby being sung in the quiet of night. She was precious.

Meeko instantly tickled her rib cage, making her body squirm against him as she squealed. "Desi, you ain't shy, yo. What you acting shy for, huh?" he asked, his smile bigger than I think I'd ever seen it. "Where yo' momma at?"

"She upstairs," Destiny answered for her, pointing her little finger toward the staircase.

Then suddenly, I heard, "Hope, come on in here and feed my grandbaby, girl."

I could hear Meeko chuckling beneath his breath as my eyes shifted toward the kitchen. Ms. Kelsey stood in front of the stove, stirring something in a large silver pot. Then I looked down at Destiny.

"You wanna go with me? See what there is to eat?" I asked, hiking my shoulder. It was a brave move, considering she didn't know me from a can of paint. But I held out my hand, anyway, hoping she'd latch on. Her dark brown eyes remained fixed on my belly until Meeko gave her a little nudge with his leg. Slowly, she walked over, timid as all get-out, before holding my hand. Together, we walked into the kitchen, and my nose instantly detected collard greens and cinnamon-candied yams.

"You like turkey wings?" Ms. Kelsey asked over her shoulder.

"Yes, ma'am."

"I like turkey wings too, Grandma," Destiny said, surprising me. I looked down at her pretty bronze-colored face and snorted a laugh.

"Ain't nobody ask you, little girl. You gon' eat what I fix ya," Ms. Kelsey responded with a wink of her eye.

Just as my belly growled again, I felt Meeko walk up behind me. I glanced back, seeing he still had little Desi in his arms. "You gon' fix my plate while I take our stuff upstairs?" he asked his mother.

"Ain't nobody up in here eating until I feed that baby," she said, pointing the wooden spoon in her hand at me.

"Dang, Ma." Meeko chuckled. "That's how you treat your only son? The one you ain't seen since Christmas?"

"Hey, you did this, remember? Not me," she shrugged.

With that, I found my head dropping back in laughter. As the amusement subsided, my gaze swung over to Meeko, and we locked eyes immediately. It was only for a few seconds, but warmth spread throughout my chest as we traded smiles. It was a small act, but I felt like I belonged in that moment.

"Desi, you gon' keep Hope company while I take our bags upstairs?" Meeko asked the little one in his arms. She was so shy that when I went to look at her, she quickly turned her head away. Meeko released a chuckle and shook his head. "A'ight, come on," he told her.

While the two of them went upstairs, Destiny and I sat at the dining room table right off the kitchen. She sat beside me with half of her little body hanging off her chair. After silently studying my extended belly, her curious eyes finally wandered up to meet my face. I laughed nervously, pushing my glasses up farther on my nose.

"Why's your hair like that?" she asked out of nowhere.

Flabbergasted, I patted the side of the big puff ball that sat on top of my head. "Uh. Umm, I don't know," I said.

"You need to let my mommy fix your hair. You can't go out looking like that," she told me, her face utterly inexpressive. I scoffed as my mouth slightly parted from shock. "See, look at my hair," she said, swinging her head from side to side, making the beads clack. "It's pretty, ain't it? But it's gon' take awhile for her to do yourns 'cause you got a lot of hair."

Nodding, I softly laughed. It was true, and I didn't put chemicals in my hair. And in addition to my tresses being long, they were also thick. Usually, I'd allow Franki to put a flat iron to it, but since she'd been gone to New York, I'd been wearing a kinky ball on the top of my head.

"You in here talking Hope's head off, girl?" Ms. Kelsey walked in and said. After placing a delicious plate of food in front of me, she asked, "What you want to drink?"

"Coca-Cola if you have it," I said.

"Yeah, fucking right." I heard Meeko scoff behind me. I turned to see him entering the dining room with Desiree now down at his side. "Don't let her trick you into giving her no soda, Ma. The doctor already told her ass to lay off that shit."

It was true. Sodas were on the doctor's *do-not-consume* list, but I also knew an occasional Coca-Cola wouldn't hurt.

"Thank God I didn't have their worrisome-ass daddies around when I was carrying mine," Ms. Kelsey muttered. Then she looked at me and placed a sympathetic hand on my shoulder. "I'll bring you some Kool-Aid, baby."

"Kool-Aid," Meeko repeated incredulously. "We ain't got no juice?"

Ms. Kelsey's neck whipped back as her eyes bugged from her head. "A li'l Kool-Aid ain't gon' hurt that baby." Meeko gave her a deadpan expression, letting her know that he wouldn't budge on the topic. This was no surprise. Over the past couple of months, he let it be known to any and everyone, including me, that there would be no compromising on the health and well-being of our unborn child. Ms. Kelsey sucked her teeth. "Well, let me go see if we got some apple juice. Shit." Then she glanced down at me again and shook her head. I could tell she wasn't used to holding her tongue. "Excuse me, baby."

When Meeko sat down next to me, I wagged my head. "What?" he asked.

"You know one little soda isn't gonna hurt the baby, right?"

"Maybe not one soda, but all the ones you be drinking will."

"All what sodas?" I was confused.

"Shorty, I be seeing all them sodas in your fridge. You ain't hiding shit from me."

"But those are Franki's."

"Oh, so you don't drink her shit?" he asked, extending his neck forward as though he was waiting for me to lie. My shoulders dropped in defeat. "Exactly." He snorted with a shake of his head.

Ms. Kelsey returned a glass of apple juice and Meeko's plate. We both dug right in, with Destiny and Desiree's eyes searing into us from across the table. They were adorable with the same brown-sugar complexion and dark, low-set eyes. One might have even mistaken them for twins if it hadn't been for their size difference. That's how much they looked alike.

"Is it good?" Little Desi whispered to Meeko.

Meeko released a light laughter of air through his nose before pulling a piece of turkey off the bone. "Here, yo," he said, passing it to her. And just as he went to tug off another portion for Destiny, I passed her a piece from my plate. He looked at me with one end of his mouth curved up into a smile. "Thanks," he said.

Before I knew it, everyone, including Ms. Kelsey, ate their meal at the table. As the minutes rolled by, the girls began warming up to me. I learned they were ages 4 and 6 and their favorite colors were pink and purple. While Desi was headed to Pre-K, Destiny would start the first grade in the fall. They both liked playing with dolls and enjoyed watching Princess movies on Disney.

"All right, now, y'all, that's enough. Eat your food," Ms. Kelsey scolded the girls, whose talking had begun to amplify.

Then I heard someone entering the dining room. I looked back to see a pretty, brown-skinned girl walking in with her cell phone up to her ear. She was just as tall as Meeko's mother and wore a long, pink maxi dress on her slender frame. Her black hair was up in a tight, slicked bun with baby hairs swirled around the edges of her face. She looked at me and smiled.

"Girl, let me call you back. My brother just got home," she said. After a few beats, she let go of a hearty laugh. "Yes, his baby muva here too." She shook her head, widening her eyes as she looked at Meeko. "All right, I'll tell him. Let me call you back."

"Who was that?" Meeko asked when she hung up the phone.

"Monie, nigga, who else?" She twisted her lips to the side. "Talm 'bout, tell your fine-ass brother to call me before he go back. I'm like, heffa . . . Didn't I just tell you he was here with his baby's muva." She shook her head as she walked over toward me. "Hey, girl, I'm Keisha. Meeko's big sister," she said, leaning down to where I was still sitting at the table and giving me a one-armed hug.

"Hi," I said. "I'm Hope."

"Girl," she fanned her hand, "I know your name. Meeko gave us a whole rundown on you. Talking 'bout she got this pretty, dark chocolate skin and dimples. All this long-ass hair. But she nerdy as fuck, yo," she said, mimicking his masculine voice. My eyes immediately flew in Meeko's direction, widening with surprise.

With an embarrassed smirk on his lips, Meeko dropped his head and gripped the back of his neck. "Fuck you, yo," he said with a light chuckle. "She ain't need to know all that."

"And stop all that cussing in front of these girls, Meeko," his mother warned.

"My bad, Ma."

"Mommy, you need to do Hope's hair so it can be pretty like yourns," Destiny said out of nowhere.

Once again, feeling self-conscious, my hand traveled up to pat the back of my head.

"I can do your hair for you," Keisha offered, gently tugging the ends of the puff ball on my head. "I mean, if you want me to."

I looked over at Meeko and shrugged my shoulders. "Keisha works in a hair shop downtown," he said, chewing a mouthful of food in between. "You should let her hook you up."

Glancing back at Keisha, I nodded. "Okay, sure." I slid back from the table and quickly stood to gather the empty dishes in front of me. Before I could head into the kitchen, I heard a quick round of knocks coming from the front door.

"Yo, yo, yo," I heard someone shout.

Meeko halfway stood from his chair, leaning forward on the table to see into the living room. "Oh, it's just Mookie and them," he said, looking back at his mother.

Seconds later, three guys appeared in the entryway of the dining room—one light-skinned and the other two just a shade lighter than me.

"Hey, Ma," the lightest one said as he bent down to kiss Ms. Kelsey on her cheek.

"Don't you 'Hey, Ma,' me," she shot back. "Only time you come around is when Meeko comes home."

He put his hand up over his chest as if she'd just wounded his heart. "Now, Ma, you know I be mad busy, working and shit. I still love you, though," he said, winking his eye.

"Uh-huh. That's what they all say." She finally cracked a smile.

Meeko stood and pulled him in for a brotherly hug before doing the same with the other two behind him. Then he pointed his thumb back at me. "Mook, this my baby's muva, Hope," he said. Then he turned around and looked at me. "Hope, this is Mookie. And that's Ant and De'ron." He pointed to the other two in the back.

"Hello," I said softly.

"Yo, she sound all sweet and shit," Mookie laughed, cutting his eyes at Meeko, then back to me. "How in the world did you end up with this crazy-ass nigga?" Before I could respond, Mookie's gaze shot past me with a twinkle of lust in his eye. "How you doin', Keisha?" he asked, dropping the tenor of his voice.

"I'm a'ight," she said noncommittally. Although I couldn't see her, I imagined her rolling her eyes. "Come on, girl, I need to get started on your hair." I glanced back, realizing that she was talking to me. "Y'all stay down here with your uncle," she told Destiny and Desiree.

I hurried to the kitchen, attempting to wash the few dishes left in the sink, and suddenly, I heard Ms. Kelsey come up behind me. "Girl, if you don't get out of my kitchen," she fussed.

"It's really no problem at all, Ms. Kel—"

"Just call me Ma. Please. You're about to have my grandson, which makes us family now," she cut me off and said. "And about these dishes, don't you lift another damn finger. I'm not about to have you standing on your swollen feet, knowing several able bodies in this house can do the job. Matter fact . . ." She glanced over her shoulder and shouted into the dining room. "Meeko, get in here."

Seconds later, Meeko strolled into the kitchen. "What's up? What's wrong?" he asked.

"Tell Hope to go get her hair done. This child up in here trying to clean my kitchen."

"Oh nah," he said, his eyebrows suddenly knitting together. "Go let Keisha do your hair. I'll clean this up."

"Y-you're gonna clean it up?" I asked, stammering with disbelief as my eyes stretched wide.

Ms. Kelsey laughed so hard her belly jiggled. "He sure is. Now, you go ahead. Keisha's waiting on you."

I dried my hands on a dish towel she had hanging on the stove, then peered back over my shoulder and said, "Thanks, Ma."

Meeko's eyes flew in my direction before narrowing with amusement. Then a faint yet fleeting smile graced the corners of his lips.

"We gon' burn one or nah, yo?" Mookie interrupted, stretching his neck into the kitchen.

"Yeah, I'll be out back in a minute," Meeko said. As soon as he broke our gaze, I went for the stairs, searching for Keisha.

The first room I stumbled upon had to have been Meeko's because our luggage was sitting in the middle of the floor. His queen-sized bed was cornered by powder blue walls and was sheathed in a navy blue, timeworn comforter. Suspended from one end of the headboard was an Orioles baseball cap, while gold and silver medals dangled from the other. My eyes traveled over to his wooden dresser, which was lined with football trophies of every size.

Wow. I smiled.

"You ready?" I heard from behind me.

I glanced back and saw Keisha standing in the hallway with a bottle of shampoo in her hands. "Ready," I told her. I followed her into the lone hallway bath, where she ran water in the tub.

She folded a thick towel and laid it above the bathmat. "You think you can get down here on your knees, big momma?"

I nodded and removed the glasses from my face. As I hunched over and dipped my head under the spigot, I could feel her fingers gently dipping into my scalp. "Too hot?" she asked.

I shook my head. "No. Feels good."

After she washed my hair, she placed a dry towel over my head and asked me to follow her to the bedroom. I wasn't sure how much older Keisha was than Meeko, but I knew she had two kids and found it odd that she was still living at home. But when I stepped inside, I noticed a beauty salon station complete with a professional chair. The room was painted a powder pink, reminiscent of her childhood.

"This isn't your bedroom?" I asked, surprised.

"Girl, no. My sisters and I all shared this one room when we were kids. Since Meeko was the only boy, he got his own room," she said, motioning for me to get in the chair. "When I started doing hair in high school, my muva converted this room into a little salon. She moved me and my sisters downstairs in the basement." I watched through the mirror as she gently began combing the ends of my hair. "It was three times the size of this little room, so we didn't mind. Plus, we could sneak boys in from the back of the house."

I snickered to myself. "So, where are your sisters? I thought Meeko said they'd be here today."

"Oh, they're coming. Kadia works late tonight, and Kim should be on her way."

"Kimberlyn, right?" I asked, recalling that Meeko had mentioned her name.

"Yeah, but don't call her that. She goes by Kim. He's the only one that calls her that, and that's just to piss her off," she laughed.

"So, you all live here?" Meeko's sister was so easy to talk to that the questions literally rolled off my tongue.

"Girl, no. Kadia lives with her baby's father in Annapolis, and Kim stays alone just two blocks down."

"And you live with Destiny and Desiree's dad?" I whispered that last part.

She let out a snort. "Fuck no. His crazy ass is in jail."

"Oh, wow." I swallowed. "I'm sorry to hear that."

"It's all good. Nigga ain't 'bout shit. Got caught up on some robbery charges two years ago, and we haven't heard from the nigga since. He was my high school sweetheart, but trust and believe, that ship has been sailed."

"So, what about the guy downstairs? Mookie?" I looked back at her and asked. "I saw the way he was looking at you."

She rolled her eyes and smiled. "Girl, Mookie plays too many games. I'm raising two little girls, and I don't have time for that."

Gently, she tugged my head back, then forward, and began blow-drying my hair. The warm air, combined with the tender touch of her hands, caused my eyes to collapse. Before long, she was using the flat iron to form long ringlets that outlined the sides of my face. When she was all done, she swiveled the chair around so I could see my reflection in the mirror. Without the help of my glasses, I stretched my eyes to see better.

"Wow," was all I could muster. She had done a wonderful job. My hair looked so silky that it almost looked fake.

"You like it?" she asked with a knowing smile.

"I love it. How much do I owe you?"

"Girl, I do my family's hair for free," she said, waving me off like it was no big deal. "Now, let's go downstairs and see if your man likes it."

My neck immediately whipped back in her direction. "Meeko's not my man. We aren't together anymore," I told her.

"Oh, right, 'cause of that little stunt you pulled." She smirked knowingly.

I stood from the chair, suddenly feeling a surge of resentment. "No, you mean the stunt *he* pulled," I corrected with a flick of my brow, fists instantly balled at my sides.

"Yeah, he told us about the bet. But he also called home crying when he thought you aborted his baby."

Shocked, I sucked in a deep breath of air. "He cried?" That didn't sound like Meeko at all.

"Don't tell him I told you that shit, or he'll kill my ass. Let's just say that, that baby," she pointed to my belly, "means everything to him. And mostly because it's connected to you." The tension in my muscles slowly eased as I lowered my eyes, deep in thought. "I've never seen my brother this way about any girl. Like ever." I peered just as she said, "He loves you."

I opened my mouth to speak but didn't know the right words to say. Suddenly, Destiny appeared in the doorway. Her dark brown eyes ballooned with admiration.

"I like your hair," she said softly.

I sucked my lips inward, trying to conceal my blushing smile. "Thanks," I said, having no idea why it pleased me so much to have this little 6-year-old's approval.

She walked over and took me by the hand. "Let's go show Uncle Meeko," she said.

Together, the three of us walked back downstairs, and after getting Ms. Kelsey and little Desi's endorsement, we headed out to the back porch. It was right around ten o'clock. Other than the bright crescent moon, darkness had completely seized the sky. Although the smoke itself had dissipated, the potent scent of marijuana somehow still lingered in the air.

Ant and De'ron were now gone, leaving only Mookie and Meeko behind. They both peered back at the sound of the screen door slamming shut behind us. Meeko's eyes momentarily studied my hair before they finally fell to my face. I would've missed his stifled smile if I hadn't committed his every facial feature and mannerism to memory.

"Uncle Meeko, doesn't she look pretty?" Destiny asked, rushing over to hug his leg.

"Yeah, Keish hooked you up," he said, beckoning me with a chuck of his chin. He licked his lips and tightened his eyes.

I ambled over with my right hand splayed across my lower back. I needed to sit down but didn't want to complain. As I came closer, Mookie found his way over to Keisha, who'd already claimed herself a chair.

"Your back hurt?" Meeko asked.

I shrugged one shoulder. "A little, but I'll be fine."

"Destiny, go back in the house with Grandma and Desi," he said, looking down at her by his side.

"Awww, man," she whined, marching back into the house.

Meeko stepped behind me and eased his hands down to my lower back. Gently, he began massaging the area, kneading it with his thumbs. My eyes closed on instinct, and a soft purr poured from my lips.

He snorted a laugh and said, "You do look beautiful, though." My eyes immediately flew open as I craned my neck back to look at him. His dark, piercing eyes were burning with such deep affection that it warmed my insides. Then his hand rounded my swollen belly so that I was nuzzled against his chest, and he pressed his lips into my temple. "Let's go inside so you can put your feet up," he said against my skin.

"Okay," I muttered, completely surprised.

After taking me by the hand, Meeko led me inside. Along the way, Keisha and I seemingly locked eyes. A teasing grin stretched across her lips before she mouthed, "I told you."

Chapter 14

Asha—To the Rescue

"These are cute. I wonder if they have them in my size," Kiki said, holding a five-inch heel sandal in her hand.

We were at the Four Seasons Mall on a Saturday, doing something I hadn't done in years. Window shopping. Since I was at home bored when she called asking if I wanted to tag along, I said, "Sure, why not?" Not that I desired anything from this basic-ass mall, but even if I did, I couldn't afford it right now. I'd been saving every penny I earned from the gym in hopes of finally being able to purchase my first car. My parents said they would match whatever I banked by the end of summer, and then Malachi promised to double that. They just wanted to see me try for once.

"Since when can you walk in heels that high, Kiki?" I gave her a deadpan expression, tired and irritated since we'd been there for hours.

"Well, I can wear them on date nights. You know, sit down and eat," she quickly explained with a shrug.

"Don't you think you'd at least need a date first?" I knew it had come off as sarcasm, but I was being serious. I couldn't remember the last time Kiki went out with a guy. She was so focused on getting her hair license that she rarely ever made time for socializing anymore.

Rolling her eyes, she placed the high-heeled shoe back on the rack and sighed. "You wanna get something to eat now? I'm getting hungry," she said.

Fortunately, that was one thing my little allowance could afford—food. "Yeah, I'm hungry too."

Together, we strolled to the overly crowded food court, even for a Saturday afternoon. Indecisively, my eyes arced, scanning each restaurant before finally settling on a familiar frame. From behind, he was tall, with the lean muscles of his back visibly bulging through a white tee. He stood with a wide bowlegged, cocky stance. His thick neck and strong, broad shoulders led down to a narrow, sexy waist. My pulse instantly accelerated beneath my skin. Kiki was midsentence when I unintentionally left her standing there. As if my feet had a mind of their own, I ambled toward him.

Why I am so fucking nervous?

"H-hey," I stammered, reaching for the back of his arm.

Quick twisted around, doing a double take before his chinked eyes finally lowered to find me. "Oh, hey, Asha. What's up?" He turned to face me, allowing his eyes to travel down my physique.

Why do I suddenly want him to smile?

"I saw you standing in line and just thought I'd come over and say . . . hi." I anxiously took my bottom lip between my teeth as I fiddled with my thumbs.

Finally, his eyes lifted, reuniting with mine. "That's what's up." His regard shifted down again to my fidgety hands. "I thought your hands would be full of shopping bags. You just now getting here?" he asked.

"No, actually, after I eat, I'm gonna leave. There's nothing for me here," I told him with a shrug of my lips. I wouldn't dare say to him that I couldn't afford anything, especially with all the shit I'd talked about that day in his car.

Then suddenly, his gaze looped behind me as if he were looking for someone. "You here by yourself?" he asked.

I nodded, then quickly remembered Kiki. With a flip of my long braids, I glanced over my shoulder. "I mean, no. I'm here with my girl, Kiki."

Finally, his lips parted into a smile, revealing that tiny chip on his front tooth. "Oh, a'ight," he said.

"Do you wanna sit with us?" The question sailed out so fast I didn't even recognize the sound of my own voice. My shoulders tensed as I held my breath, waiting for an answer.

With his hand swiping over his freshly cut head, he nodded. "A'ight."

I looked back at Kiki and gave her a subtle wink of my eye. Then I gestured with a tip of my head toward Chick-fil-A, letting her know that I'd be getting food from there. After cutting in line with Quick, we proceeded to the register, where I ordered an eight-count nugget with a cookies and cream shake.

"Damn, girl, you ain't hungry, is you?" he teased.

Craning my neck around, I peeked back at my booty, then looked up into his eyes. "Oh, you thought I got all this ass by not eating?"

His eyes trailed my figure before a lopsided grin appeared on his face. He bit down on his bottom lip and shook his head. "You crazy," he muttered lazily.

I knew I looked damn good in my white biker shorts with the crop top to match. It might not have been Versace or Gucci, but I didn't look like no broke bitch, either. Not only did I have style, but also the shape of my body was something most women would pay for. I had a small waist, wide hips, and a plump, shapely ass.

After we got our food, we joined Kiki at a nearby table. She'd ordered some Chinese food and was already stuffing her face. "Dang, you couldn't wait for us?" I asked with a whip of my neck, feigning annoyance.

She covered her chomping mouth with a white napkin and held up one finger. "Sorry, I was hungry," she finally let out.

When Quick set his tray on the table, I realized the two had never met. "Oh, my bad," I said. "Kiki, this is Quick. Quick, this is Kiki." I gave as informal an introduction as I possibly could. For some reason, I didn't want to get them too acquainted.

I dug into my food right away, making small talk with Quick in between. As soon as Kiki finished her food, she left us, saying that she wanted to visit a few more stores. I told her to meet me back at the food court once she was done. As I scrapped my nugget around the barbecue sauce container, realizing there wasn't any left, I huffed.

"I'll be right back," I told Quick.

I got up and walked back to Chick-fil-A, adding an extra sway in my hips. As I secretly wished his eyes were stapled to my behind, I forged in front of the line again. Waving my arm, I leaned over the counter to gain the cashier's attention. "Um, excuse me," I said.

"Yes, ma'am. May I help you?" the petite, blue-eyed brunette asked.

"I need more barbecue sauce. Y'all only gave me one," I told her. She reached under the counter and pulled out three more packs of sauce before handing them over. "Thanks," I said.

When I turned around, my face unexpectedly collided with a hard body. With flittering eyelids, I clutched my chest and took a step back. As soon as I looked up, I was caught off guard by the emotionless glare of Jaxon Brown. Immediately, I gasped, and my jaw collapsed. *Shit.* I hadn't seen Jaxon since the start of summer when I ended my work-study job at Corbett. And to clarify, it was more of me hiding from him each time I feared our paths would cross. Ever since he played the fuck out of me in Cancún, embarrassment would consume me in his presence.

"Uh, h-hey," I stuttered, wondering if he'd received his letter from the CDC.

He squinted his eyes briefly as if he were trying to recognize me from a previous lifetime. *Oh, so you don't know me now?* I cocked my head to the side and folded my arms across my breasts, narrowing my eyes right back.

"'Sup," he said coolly, chucking up his chin.

I rolled my eyes and attempted to step around him, but a pale blonde's delicate frame instantly blocked my path. It was Brittany, his girlfriend.

"Oh, hey," she trilled, eyes blossoming at seeing me. "It's . . ." She looked up at Jaxon who just gave her a dismissive shrug of his shoulders. "You remember? Your friend from Cancún," she tried. She shook her head and rolled her eyes, embarrassed by his lack of response. "I'm sorry, hun. What's your name again?'"

I glowered at Jaxon again, but this time with my fists clenched at my sides. I was seconds away from putting his fraudulent ass on blast. He wanted to act like he didn't know me after fucking me senseless for most of the school year? *Fine.* I was ready to act like a drunk bitch on homecoming night, vomiting up every last detail for Brittany.

But that's when I heard, "Baby."

My eyes followed the sound of his voice until they eventually landed on Quick. He was standing behind Jaxon with his eyes asking me to play along.

"Oh, hey, babe." I smiled, finally sliding around Brittany. "You remember Jaxon, right?" I asked. Hooking my arm around his tapered waist as I nestled myself beneath his arm. *Damn, he smells good.*

Jaxon and Brittany both turned around to see who had suddenly gained my attention.

"Nah," Quick said. Tilting his head as he tapered even more his already chinked eyes. "I'on think." He scratched behind his ear before looking back at me. "This ain't the goofy nigga taking steroids you was just telling me about?" He dipped his head down, trying to whisper, but was still loud enough for everyone to hear.

Oh, he's petty. I love it, I sniggered, seeing Brittany's jaw instantly drop. However, the poker-faced scowl on Jaxon's face remained intact.

"Anyway, babe," I said with a wry smile, "this here is his girlfriend, and they were just saying hey."

"Oh, a'ight. Wassup?" Quick held his hand out, but Jaxon didn't even give the courtesy of looking at it. Quick let out a light snort, then tightened his arm around my shoulders. "Come on, baby."

After waving goodbye to Brittany, we returned to our table, laughing along the way. "Thanks for that," I said.

"Oh, it's all good." He smiled, releasing me from his hold. As soon as we pulled out our chairs to sit, he asked, "So tell me, what's up with you and dude?"

"Hmm . . ." My voice trailed off as I decided how to describe Jaxon and my former relationship. "Well," I said, licking my lips, "I thought him and I were dating last school year. Turns out he already had a girlfriend who doesn't attend our school." That was the nice and abbreviated version.

"So, basically, dude played you?" he asked flat-out.

I nodded, shrugging my lips as I went to dip another nugget. "Pretty much."

"Pshhh, chump," Quick muttered, snorting a laugh. "What did you see in him anyway? He got money or something?"

"No money, but a lot of potential," I admitted boldly. "He's gonna enter the NBA draft next year." He scoffed and shook his head in what I could easily recognize as disapproval. "I'm saving for a car," I told him out of nowhere.

After shoving a waffle fry into his mouth, he peered from across the table. "Oh yeah?"

I nodded. "That's why I don't have any shopping bags. I can't afford shit these days," I laughed.

"Well, it's good for you . . . paying your own way."

"How so?" I cocked my brow. "'Cause it damn sure don't so feel good."

"You'll appreciate things more," he said with a wink of his eye.

When did this chipped-tooth nigga get to be so fine? Adjusting to the moisture in my panties, I shifted in my seat. After taking a deep swallow to gather myself, I rested my elbow on the table and gripped the side of my neck.

"Did you buy your own car? Or did your family help you?" I asked, trying to remove the sudden, lust-filled thoughts from my mind.

Although not on his lips, Quick's eyes smiled at me in jest as if he could hear my innermost thoughts. "Nah," he said, licking his full brown lips. "I worked for everything I got. My first job was at McDonald's. Then I worked at the Foot Locker here in the mall."

"So, you don't work there anymore?"

"Nah. Not no more." He shook his head, placing the straw in his cup between his lips.

"What do you do for money now?"

"Well, the fights your Pops be putting together for me pay cash. It's not much, but it's been getting us by from month to month. Plus, I start my job back at the bookstore next month."

"Wow, I didn't know that," I said, feeling my eyes expand. "So, you said 'us.' You're referring to your siblings, right?"

"Yeah, you remember my sister, Queen, from the gym? The night I fought Hernandez?"

"Sister?" I asked, my eyebrows bunching together.

He smirked. "Yeah, that was my sister."

Oh, good.

"Why? Who'd you think she was?" he asked. Squinting his eyes as a half smirk played out on his face.

It was all I could do to suppress my embarrassment as I lifted my right shoulder to my ear. "I'on know," I said lowly. "I mean, I guess I just assumed she was your girl."

He shook his head and released a light chuckle. "Nah, I'm single. Girls ain't nothing but drama, no way."

My neck jerked back as I palmed my chest. "Drama?" I asked, pretending to be insulted. "You just had the wrong girlfriends, that's all."

With his eyes cast down on the remains of his food, he asked, "So, if you were my girl, you'd be drama-free, right?" The air dithered in my lungs when his dark, slanted eyes deliberately rolled up to meet mine for an answer.

"U-uh," was all I could get out before a wave of heat spread throughout my face. After Quick let out an abrupt chuckle, I knew my yellow ass had turned red. "Shut up," I said with a roll of my eyes. When he continued laughing at my expense, I hurled a waffle fry across the table, striking him right between the eyes. His hooting only got louder.

Dickhead, I thought just before laughing myself.

After eating in partial silence, with him chuckling to himself every now and then, we headed out of the food court. When Kiki sent a text saying that she'd meet me at the car, Quick offered to walk with me. As we headed out, I noticed a jewelry kiosk coming up in the center aisle. It wasn't anything pricy, just some costume jewelry that was pretty enough to catch my eye.

You have no money. You have no money. You have no money was the mantra I silently kept on repeat in my head.

"You wanna stop here?" Quick asked, pointing to the jewelry. He must've noticed me eyeing the sparkling pieces from afar.

With downturned lips, I waved my hand dismissively. "Nah. I've done enough window shopping for one day," I told him.

"You sure?" He waltzed over to the kiosk, pointing at the ugliest pair of earrings I think I've ever seen—green and gold cluster stones with a stud-backing. "I can see you rocking these," he cheesed.

"My grandmother wouldn't even wear no ugly shit like that. Now, these . . ." I said, pointing to a pair of gold Bohemian earrings with white tassels that hung like silk. "These are my type." I lifted the earrings from the display and turned them over to see the price.

Thirty-five fucking dollars. Shiiid.

"May I help you?" a heavyset white lady suddenly asked. She'd been sitting on a stool on the other side of the kiosk.

"No, I'm just looking," I told her, forcing a smile.

When I returned the earrings to the stand, Quick said, "You sure? If you like them, you should get 'em."

"No," I said, as I sliced my hands in front of me, my long nails now gone. "I'm saving for a car. If it's anything outside of that, I don't need it." I gave a subtle nod of my head in closing. I guess it was more of a confirmation for myself than for him.

"Willpower," he muttered. "That's what's up."

The two of us continued on our path until we finally ended up in the parking lot next to Kiki's car. She was already in the driver's seat with her cell phone up to her ear when I pressed my back against the passenger window. The sky, already swathed in deep hues of gray, told of nightfall.

"Well . . ." I released a deep sigh, looking down to brush imaginary crumbs off of my bare thighs . . . anything for me not to have to look him in the eyes. "Thanks for rescuing me in there," I said. *Why am I so nervous?*

Quick's hands slipped into the pockets of his jeans before he rocked back on his heels. "No biggie," he said. *Shit, don't tell me he's nervous too.*

"Look, I know we didn't get off to a very good start, but—"

When Quick released a teasing snort of amusement, I rolled my eyes.

"Your eyes too pretty to get stuck in yo' head," he said with a hike of his chin. His chinked eyes were even smaller, and his lips parted just enough for me to see that little chip in his tooth.

My cheeks warmed again, suddenly, I felt a flutter of sorts in the pit of my stomach. It was a sensation I hadn't often experienced with men. I took a hard swallow, regaining my composure.

"What I was trying to say was . . . I-I apologize for how I came off that day when we first met. I'm trying to . . ." I closed my eyes and shook my head at a complete loss for words.

"No need to apologize for being who you are, right?"

"But still, I shouldn't have judged you. I shouldn't have ever said shit about what you have or don't have. And now that I've been able to sit through a whole meal with you . . . I think I'd like to get to know you better. Like . . ." Shit. Never had I attempted to approach a man like this before. At least not sincerely and without ulterior motives. Men always asked me for *my* number. They always called *me* to go out on dates. *They* were the ones who'd apologize. But yet and still, here I was with my heart thumping loud between my ears, palms wet with anxiety, trying to ask this man to see me again. "Can I get your number?"

Quick's Asian-like eyes instantly mushroomed with surprise. Although he covered his jaw with his hands, I could tell by the lift in his cheeks that he was smiling. "I'm shocked," he finally let out.

"Why? You seem like a good dude. My father likes you. Malachi likes you. Why are you so surprised?"

"Because I'm not your type," he said flat-out. "My pockets not long enough, remember? I don't drive no flashy car, and dudes like me, coming from where I come from, probably won't ever be rich and famous. I can't do nothing for you." His eyebrow hiked as if to question me.

"Friendship," I let out anxiously. "Maybe we could be friends. I'on know," I said with a shrug of my shoulders, trying to play it cool.

"Friendship, huh?" he asked, staring sternly into my eyes. Just as I felt the sting of rejection beginning to burn, he fished his cell phone out of his pocket. "Give me your number," he ordered. The numbers rattled off my tongue so quickly that I had to take a deep breath once I got through. "A'ight, I'ma call you," he said.

After dipping down to the window and putting his hand up to say goodbye to Kiki, he strolled off into the dimly lit parking lot. I stood there, taking in the way each of the muscles in his back bounced with every stride. Just as he got a few yards away, he glanced over his shoulder.

"Pick up when I call you, Asha," he said with a smirk.

Just those few little words had me cheesing from ear to ear. By the time I got in the car, Kiki was looking at me like I was crazy. "What?" I said, smiling.

"So, you really like him, huh?" she asked.

"Maybe," I shrugged, a smile still on my face. "Why? You don't think he's cute?" I'd never asked for Kiki's opinion before because, more often than not, I didn't care. The men I traditionally ran with had money, so it didn't matter what the fuck they looked like. But now, for some reason, with Quick, I wanted to know her take.

"Oh, hunni, that nigga is foine," she let out dramatically, pursing her lips.

"Really?" My neck jerked back. "You think?"

"Definitely. I mean, I'd fuck him."

My eyes instantly ballooned. "Kiki," I laughed. She didn't even talk like that, so it took me by surprise.

"What? I would," she shrugged her shoulders with a straight face.

My eyes doubled back, and I saw there wasn't a trace of a smile on her lips. "Don't get hurt, bitch," I warned.

Finally, she broke out in laughter, holding up both her hands in surrender. "You know I would never entertain a guy you obviously like," she assured, playfully rolling her eyes.

"I know," I sighed. Then I glanced back over at her again, seeing her pull the seat belt strap across her chest. "I know I don't tell you this a lot, Keeks . . . but . . . You're my girl. The only one that seems to tolerate my bullshit and has been by my side since day one." I nodded, reflecting on the undeserving loyalty I'd received from her over the years. "You mean a lot to me."

"Aww," she cooed, fanning her face before reaching over the console for a hug.

I put up my hand to stop her. "Uht," I said. "Did I say I needed all that? Just wanted to let you know. That's it. That's all."

She knew I was a hard ass, so she just rolled her eyes and shook her head.

The sky suddenly darkened as we finally pulled out of the parking lot. I felt my cell phone vibrate against my thigh. I lifted it to see Paris's name appear on the glowing screen.

"Hello," I answered, a natural attitude already projected.

"Asha, please come get your brother. He's got a friggin' gun!"

Chapter 15

Paris—Distorted Perceptions

"I was starting to think you weren't going to show," I said, standing there with the door partly opened, peering out at Ty on the porch as the hissing sound of night bugs flowed in from the yard.

He quickly wiped his forehead with a minor lift of his Orioles baseball cap, only to drop it back down to his head. "My bad, yo. Got caught up," he said, slightly straining his neck and eyes to look into the house behind me. "Can I still come in?" he asked.

The place was unusually quiet, with Hope in Baltimore and Franki visiting Josh in New York. I wasn't exactly sure where Asha was, but I remembered her leaving with Kiki several hours ago. Communication between her and us still wasn't the greatest, but the past few weeks had shown she'd been trying, softening her approach and minimizing the number of times she'd roll her eyes. It wasn't an extreme amount of effort, but even a one-eyed man could see she'd been trying.

I received a call from Ty this morning while on his way to the rec asking if he could come over for what he called a "Netflix and chill" kind of night. Of course, I was hesitant at first, but not having much else to do on a Saturday night, I ultimately agreed. He was supposed to be here by seven. Yet, it was now approaching ten as I stood there staring back at him in my pj's.

I glanced back into the dark living room, seeing nothing but the glow of the television screen behind me. "Sure," I said. "Come on in."

I stepped back, allowing him inside before locking the door. He slipped off his shoes by the door as if it were second nature before padding over to the couch. When I flipped the switch on the wall, he squinted, instantly shielding his eyes from the bright light.

"Damn, shorty," he muttered.

"So, like, what do you wanna watch?" I asked, grabbing the remote control as I plopped down on the cheap sofa.

Of course, the tiny cotton shorts I had on rose even more around my thick thighs. I glanced over at Ty, seeing his tongue practically flapping out of his mouth, and he looked just like a thirsty dog. I reached over and quickly grabbed my throw blanket from the armrest. Once it covered my lap, I tucked my feet beneath me and booted up Netflix on the TV.

"So, what are we watching?" I asked again, looking at him once more. That's when I noticed the red rimming his eyes. "Are you high?" I asked, suddenly annoyed.

His dark pink lips spread into a lazy grin as he scratched behind his ear. "Huh?" he let out, a goofy, faraway expression slowly taking over his face.

"Wow, I swear, you and Meeko are the only athletes I know that seem to get high every day." I shook my head.

"Before you cut on the movie, what you gon' fix for us to eat?" he asked.

"Eat?" I repeated. My eyes stretched wide as I sat up to glare at him. "Ty, it's ten o'clock at night."

"But I'm hungry," he all but whined. "And I know you not gon' let me eat what I want to so . . ." He smirked flirtatiously, then licked his lips. "What you gon' fix me?"

I rolled my eyes and couldn't help but laugh at his attempt at seducing me. "Fine," I said. "We've got pizza left over in the fridge."

When I hopped up from the couch and went toward the kitchen, I could feel Ty's eyes on my ass. I adjusted the thin straps of the tank before pulling down my shorts, already knowing they'd eventually ride back up.

As I began heating his food, he called out to me. "Shorty, it's hot in here. Y'all got the air on?"

I stuck my head out of the kitchen, only to see him removing the gray tee shirt from over his head. Smooth, honey-colored pecks now stared back at me as they sat above his perfectly carved abs.

I took a deep swallow, tucking my hair behind my ear. "Y-you can cut the air down if you want." I pointed to the thermostat on the living room wall before stepping back into the kitchen. I covered my heated face with my palms and sighed softly. Yes, Ty was handsome, so attractive that the sight of his bare chest and arms seemingly made my body warm all over. But if he thought he'd be getting anywhere with me sexually, especially anytime soon, he was sorely mistaken.

Once his pizza was warmed, I poured him a large cup of red juice that Franki made from Kool-Aid. I'd never had it before, but it was pretty good. Just as I was carrying it all out to him in the living room, I saw him with his muscular arms stretched out across the back of the couch. He cocked his legs out wide in his basketball shorts as he sat back like a king.

"Comfortable, are we?" I teased.

"Hell yeah. It's not every day a nigga like me gets to be served by a beautiful-ass woman like yourself," he said, laying it on thick with a quick wink of his eye.

Just as I bent down, placing everything on the coffee table in front of him, I could hear the lock rattling on the door.

Asha, I immediately thought.

But to my surprise, as soon as the door swung open, Malachi appeared, his tattoo-covered chest just as bare as Ty's, and his jeans hanging on so low that the top of his Armani boxer briefs were full-on display. His bright, hazel eyes landed on Ty first, then immediately flew over to me.

"Malachi?"

"The fuck?" he muttered, stepping farther in. His face immediately twisted into a scowl as his hand motioned toward a shirtless Ty. "The fuck is this, Paris?" he spat.

Already recognizing the jealous rage in his eyes, I rushed up and placed my palms against his chest. I tried pushing him back, but he was too strong. "Malachi, what are you doing here? H-how did you get in?"

"Fuck you mean, how did I get in? I pay the bills in this muthafucka, don't I?" he asked, his voice booming as he glared at me. His heart beat so fast against my hand that I thought it would literally burst from his chest. "So, you fucking this nigga now?"

I looked back at Ty, seeing him suddenly stand from the couch. "Aye, man, I'on want no trouble, yo," he said.

That only seemed to infuriate Malachi more because he charged farther into the house, pushing me along with him. "Nigga, did I ask for you to fucking speak?" He reached behind him, tugging at the waistband of his jeans before finally pulling out a gun.

"Please!" I screamed. However, the sound of my voice went ignored as he pushed me aside, charging directly at Ty. Before I could even regain my footing, Malachi cracked him over the head with the butt of his gun. Instantly, Ty dropped to his knees, blood emerging from his temple. "Malachi, please. Nothing is going on between us," I cried. My entire body was now trembling in fear as streams of water poured from my eyes.

"Nah, fuck that," Malachi said, pressing the gun harder into Ty's skull. His chest heaved with full-on rage.

Ty was still in a kneeling position, scared shitless with water now pooled in his eyes. "Ain't shit going on between us, yo. We was just chillin', yo, I swear." Ty held both of his hands up, pleading for his life.

"Nigga, you work for me and got the fucking nerve . . ." Malachi's words trailed off as he clenched down on his teeth. He shook his head as if he were in the most unbearable pain. My heart bottomed out when I heard the sound of his gun cock. I did the only thing I could think of at the moment. I ran off to grab my cell phone from the other room.

"You calling the cops on a nigga, Paris? That's how you gon' do me?" I heard Malachi yell from the other room. My shaky fingers rushed to dial Asha's number. Thankfully, she answered on the second ring. "Hello."

"Asha, please, come get your brother. He's got a friggin' gun!"

"A gun?" she shrieked.

"Yes. He's gonna kill Ty. I just know it," I bawled, my face completely wet with tears.

"Aw, hell," she mumbled. "I'm on my way."

As I tiptoed back into the living room, a sense of terror washed over me from the sudden silence. When I entered, Malachi was pacing back and forth with his hands resting atop his head, his right hand still gripping his gun.

"Malachi," I whispered cautiously. He looked at me with weary eyes that were now trimmed in red. "What did you do?" I asked, looking around and seeing that Ty was no longer present.

"I let the little nigga go. Ain't that what you wanted?" I gulped, seeing the injured look in his eyes. After releasing a deep breath, he dropped both his hands down by his sides. "You called the cops on me?" he asked lowly.

I shook my head. "No. You know I'd never—"

"I don't know what the fuck you would do no more," he roared, cutting me off.

"I called Asha."

Malachi's eyes narrowed before they began wandering my body. He started at my breasts, then traveled down to my toes. "Yeah, you fucking that nigga," he nodded.

"I am not," I protested with a sniff of my tears. "We haven't even kissed." As I stepped in to close the gap between us, I sensed that he was now somewhat calm.

He sucked his teeth. "You must take me fo' a fucking fool, mane. Both y'all sitting here half-naked, ten o'clock at fucking night, and I'm supposed to believe what? That y'all just friends? Fuck outta here with that bullshit, mane." He waved me off with a suck of his teeth.

Malachi and I weren't even a couple, but I desperately wanted him to believe me for some reason. I needed him to know that Ty and I were nothing more than mere friends—at least for me. I wanted him to know I had compared every man I'd encountered to him since that day outside the jailhouse. Yet, none seem to compare to him at all. But as I opened my mouth to speak, no words would escape me.

He stepped close so that the heat emitting from his body immediately latched on to mine. Gently, his hands gripped the backs of my arms, sending a shiver down my spine. "I told you once before that you were mine, Paris. Didn't I?" he asked. "But now you done went and fucked that nigga." He closed his eyes, gripping my arms a bit tighter as he clenched his jaw once more.

"But that's just it, Malachi. I'm not yours. You're married. Remember?" I knew it was poor timing, but it was the truth. I couldn't keep going 'round and 'round with him about this.

He reached into his back pocket and pulled out a folded stack of papers before tossing them to the floor. "Shawty, when I told you that you were mine, I meant that shit." His hazel eyes hit mine, penetrating me with a deep gaze. "Now, look what the fuck you just did. You just killed that li'l nigga."

As he backed away, I looked down and saw the words *Divorce Decree* boldly stamped on one of the sheets. Two signatures were already inked on the dotted lines. A lump instantly formed in my throat as I bent down to pick up the scattered papers from the floor. By the time I stood back up, he was already gone. I rushed over to look out the window, seeing the headlights of his car already beaming through the darkness. I burst through the screen door, screaming his name from the top of my lungs.

"Malachi!" But his taillights just faded in the distance as he drove off into the night. At that moment, it felt like all the air in my lungs had vanished. I couldn't do anything but drop to my knees and cry.

Malachi was divorced. *He didn't lie.*

About twenty minutes after I'd made my way back inside, Asha burst through the door. "Where he at?" she asked, completely out of breath and in full-on panic. Her wide eyes searched around the front room.

I looked up at her from where I'd curled myself on the floor. "He's gone," I croaked.

As I lay in bed that night, I texted Malachi over twenty messages. Even if it was just for him to curse me out again, I desperately needed him to respond. However, he never texted back. It left me crying a river into my pillow that night. The very next morning, with swollen eyes and my hair sprawled all over my head, I found myself banging on his front door. After knocking for five minutes straight with no answer, something told me to look in the window. I cut through the bushes and pressed my nose against the dewy glass, peeking through the partially opened blinds. Everything in his living room was gone—only blank walls surrounded by the shine of hardwood floors remained. A pang shot instantly through my chest as my heart rate sped up.

Just as I reached into my purse to grab my cell, attempting to call Malachi again, I heard a nearby car door slam. I looked over to see his neighbor on the other side of the yard stepping out of her blue Honda. "You looking for Malachi?" she asked. She was slightly older, in her midforties, if I had to guess. Her pale white face was decorated with dark brown eyes and thin pink lips that spread into an uneven smile. Her chestnut-colored hair fell just to her collarbone, and although she appeared to be around my height, she was much thinner than me.

"Yes, do you know where he's at?" I asked with tremors in my voice.

"He moved out a few days ago. From what he told me, the 'For Sale' sign should be going up any day now," she said.

My heart instantly sank. *No. No. No.*

"Well, do you know where he went?" I asked, hardly able to speak.

"H-he didn't say."

Nodding, I stepped out of the bushes and returned to my car. Like a zombie, I drove around for hours until I finally ended up at Lake Jeannette. I'd only been to this place once, but somehow, I'd committed it to memory. Slowly, I pulled around the circular driveway in front of Reese's massive home, seeing again that same manicured lawn. When I parked the car, I noticed her standing by her truck, bent over, buckling little Mekhi in his car seat. Maevyn stood next to her, twisting from side to side as if waiting to get in.

As soon as I stepped out of my car and slammed the door, both Maevyn and Reese turned around. Maevyn's eyes mushroomed before she ran over to me with her pink poufy dress blowing back in the wind, the sound of her jelly sandals clacking on the concrete as she smiled. "Miss Paris," she sang, wrapping her tiny arms around my waist. I hadn't seen her in months, yet she somehow remembered me. I bent down and hugged her, whispering in her ear just how beautiful she looked. Her hair was twisted into two pigtails with pink ribbons tied on the ends. Tiny diamonds shone brightly in her ears as a silver bracelet gleamed around her wrist.

"Maevyn," Reese called out to her. "Getcho behind ova' here, li'l girl," she yelled. I looked up at the grimace on her face as she looked at Maevyn with discontent in her eyes.

"Bye, Miss Paris," Maevyn whispered before running back to the truck.

After she hopped inside, Reese made her way over to me. Her eyes were full of attitude as she twisted her lips to the side. "What do you want?" she asked, folding her arms across her chest.

"I-I . . ." *Shit.* "I'm looking for Malachi. Is he here?"

"You've got some nerve coming here to look for my husband."

Husband?

"Oh, cut the shit, Reese. The two of you are divorced. Malachi already showed me the papers," I told her, popping my hand on my hip. She rolled her eyes but never parted her lips to refute the claim. *Thank God.* "So? Is he here or not?"

"Look, I don't have time to deal with one of Malachi's teenage groupies this morning," she scoffed. "I've got to get my kids over to my momma's for church."

"Groupie?"

"Yes, *groupie*. You're no different than the rest."

I took a few steps forward and boldly looked her directly in the eyes. "Actually, Reese, I beg to differ. I think you know that I'm much more than that. That's why I bother you so much. Malachi loves me."

She gave me a deadpan expression. "He told you that?"

Unfortunately, Malachi had never used those exact words, but still, I maintained confidence. "What Malachi and I share is none of your concern. When him and I first . . ." Unsure of the right words to use, I took a deep swallow and tucked a lock of hair behind my ear. "When we first started seeing each other, I had no idea he was still married. So, for that, I want to apologize because I'm not a homewrecker, nor do I condone that type of behavior," I said with a hike of my chin. "However, moving forward, I will not tolerate your bullying, the sly remarks, or any disrespect."

Reese's head dropped forward in disbelief. Then she snaked her neck and stepped into me. "*Tolerate?* Bitch, you must be out of your fucking mind," she spat. "I may not have been Malachi's stay-at-home wife, raising his two kids, but at the end of the day, I'm still 859." She tapped her fist hard against her chest twice and looked me dead in the eyes. "Don't you *ever* forget that shit."

"I'm not scared of you, Reese," I lied. She intimidated me with all her "gang talk," but I knew I had to hold my ground.

Then suddenly, we heard Maevyn call out. "Mommy, let's go. Grandma's calling your phone," she said. I looked up to see her little body halfway hanging out of the truck.

"Don't bring your ass here no more. Malachi hasn't lived here for well over a year. So if he's your so-called man, I'm sure it won't be too hard for you to track him down. But you won't find him here."

With a final roll of her eyes, she waltzed back to her truck, hopped in, and quickly drove off. I got back into my car and tried calling Malachi once more. When I got his voicemail, I hung up and sent him another text.

Me: I promise nothing happened between me and Ty. Not even a kiss. I've been crying all night. Please call me back. I love you.

Chapter 16

Franki—Always and Forever

"I'm so proud of you, baby," Josh whispered in my ear. The warmth of his breath tickled my skin.

With his chin hooked over my shoulder, I sat back securely between his thighs. Both of us were sitting on a soft blanket in the dead center of Central Park. It was the Fourth of July, and the sun was out of the clouds. Live music was flowing from the stage above, and a warm body seemed to cover every blade of grass on the lawn.

"Thanks, I guess," I shrugged.

"What you mean, you guess?"

"I mean, it's just Burger King, yo. Ain't no biggie," I told him.

Earlier that morning, I received a call from the head manager at Burger King. He told me I had gotten the cashier job I'd applied for a few weeks back. Although Josh was delighted by the news, I was no longer feeling it. I mean, he was living in a million-dollar apartment on Forty-Sixth Street, wearing tailored suits to work while I was offered a greasy job at a fast-food restaurant. I didn't feel proud at all.

"Aye, you gotta start somewhere, right? They paying money, ain't they?"

"Yes," I sighed.

"All right then." He gently took my chin with his fingers and turned my face around. "Smile," he said. I furnished a quick, fake, close-lipped smile before rolling my eyes. "You buggin', ma," he said with a shake of his head. I returned to my position and snuggled back against his chest.

The next few hours were filled with me wrapped in his arms, swaying from side to side as he sang the lyrics to every one of the songs performed. His melodic voice was just as good, if not better, than the performers that graced the stage that night—Miguel, Queen Naija, H.E.R., Ro James, and Lucky Daye. By the time nightfall hit, we were eating hot dogs and sipping beer while watching kids run across the commons with sparklers in their hands.

"They about to start the fireworks," he said excitedly, nuzzling me tighter from behind.

Suddenly, bright rainbows began shooting through the pitch-black sky, firing off, one by one, with booms so loud the earth nearly trembled beneath us. Although I'd been born and raised in New York, I had never witnessed the fireworks in Central Park. They were terrifyingly beautiful. Josh pointed up at each one as I sat back, watching in awe.

When the show was over, Josh got up and helped me stand. After he brushed off my backside, we folded up the blanket and gathered up the rest of our things. Hand in hand, we walked to catch the bus back home. During the ride, I lay my head on his shoulder and closed my eyes.

"That was so dope. Thanks for taking me," I told him.

"You ain't got to thank me for treating you like a man should treat his woman. That's what I'm here for."

"I know, but . . ."

"But what?" I opened my mouth to speak but hesitated. "Talk to me, ma. What's up?" he urged.

"I've just never been in a relationship like this before. I never wanted to be around anyone for more than a few hours at a time. Now, here you come with all this Prince Charming shit—" He laughed, I didn't. "And I just don't know what to do with myself. Like, I'm a damn mess whenever we're apart, crying over you and all." My nose flared in disgust. I couldn't believe that I was now that girl.

"Pshhh. Whatever. You don't be doing no crying."

"I do." He twisted his lips to the side, giving me a knowing look. "Okay, maybe not crying, but I be sulking, babe. Like, for real. I hate that I'm leaving you tomorrow." I wrapped my arm around his waist and cuddled him tighter.

"It's just one more month, Franki. We'll survive."

"You know most niggas would be out here fuc—I mean screwing any and everything moving. But you, you out here doing real boss shit while staying true to me. I can't do nothing but respect it."

Josh leaned down and tenderly pressed his lips into my forehead. "You ain't never gotta worry about me doing you wrong like that, ma. I love you too much."

The following day, Josh drove me to my mother's apartment across the city. She and I were supposed to spend this past Thursday together, but she ended up catching some kind of bug. I was more than prepared to come and take care of her, but she asked me to give her a few days instead because she didn't want me to catch it. So, now, here it was, four hours until my train was to depart, and I was about to see my mother for the first time since setting foot in New York City.

"Just call me when you're ready," Josh said, leaning over the console with his lips already puckered.

After giving him a quick peck, I hopped out of the car and headed for the brownstone en route to see my mother. When I let myself inside, I expected to see her sitting in the living room or smell food cooking on the stove. Her body was programmed to get up early, and since it was Sunday, dinner was automatic. However, the apartment was unusually still and quiet.

"Ma," I yelled. I dropped my keys on the coffee table before walking back to her room. When I peeked my head inside, I saw her sleeping in the bed. I walked over and gently nudged her arm. "Ma."

Her eyelids fluttered open and slowly widened before she took me in. "What time is it?" she croaked.

"It's after eight. You still don't feel good?" I asked, examining the dark circles around her eyes.

"I'm getting there." As soon as she sat up in bed, she began coughing repeatedly. She leaned over to clutch her chest in obvious discomfort.

The painful sound alone made me wince. "Have you been to the doctor yet?"

She cleared her throat and shook her head. "I go tomorrow," she rasped. "Probably ain't nothing but the flu."

"In July, Ma?" I asked rhetorically. "That don't sound like no flu."

She shrugged and held up her hand. "Just reach over there on my dresser and hand me that envelope," she said.

I walked over and grabbed the white envelope just as she had asked, immediately realizing it was another letter from my father. "What's this?" I said.

"Just open it up and read it," she instructed weakly.

The envelope had been pried open, so I knew she'd already read it. Still, I pulled it out slowly and unfolded the white sheet of paper before sitting down on the edge of her bed.

My darling Francesca,
Every night this past month, I've received these mystifying messages in my dreams. Some I can make out, while others I'm still slowly trying to piece together. But there are two things I'm sure of: these are direct words from God, and they are strictly meant for you. It's been eight, almost nine years, but I would love for you and your mother to visit me. Something deep in my spirit is telling me it's time. I need to lay eyes on my baby girl. I hope you still have an inkling of trust in your old man and know I'll always have your best interest at heart.
Never forget that I love you, Franki.
Forever and Always.
Your father,
Pastor Wright

"So? That's exciting, right?" my mother asked.

"Why now? He ain't been wanting to see us." I tossed the letter on her nightstand. "Nigga practically left us for dead and—"

"Now, you shut your mouth, little girl. Your father may not be perfect, but he loves us. And he must've had good reason for not wanting to see us all these years."

I sucked my teeth. My mother had no idea how I'd been suffering in silence all these years. All she knew was that he'd murdered a man with his bare hands and had no real clue about why. The load of our heavy secret seemed to be lifted whenever I was around Josh, but now that I was back home, reading a letter my father personally penned, I could feel the weight of everything pressing down on me again.

With my head spinning, I got up from the bed and started for the door. "Franki," my mother called out to me. Before she could get out another word, she started another round of coughing.

"I'll call you when I get back to school, Ma," I told her, looking back over my shoulder and smiling halfheartedly. "Just let me know what the doctor says."

When I got back up to the front of the apartment, I called Josh.

"Hey, baby," he answered on the first ring.

"Where are you? Can you come back and pick me up?"

"I hadn't even made it around the block good. You ready to leave already?" he asked.

"Yeah. She's still sick and . . ." My voice trailed off as I thought about the letter from my dad.

"And what? What's wrong?"

"Nothing," I sighed. "I just need you to hurry back."

"A'ight. Give me like five or ten minutes."

I left my mother's apartment and sat on the front stoop while waiting for Josh. I couldn't believe that after all these years, my father finally wanted to see us. What would he say? Would he want to talk about everything that happened all those years ago? The thought of confronting it all over again frightened the shit out of me. It's like every day I was fighting to bury the pain deeper and deeper, but now the thought of seeing him again was bringing everything back to the surface.

Five minutes later, I saw Josh's car rounding the block. I jogged down the steps and quickly climbed inside. "Everything a'ight?" he asked, putting the car in park.

"No," I let out with a shaky breath. "It's my dad. He wants to see me and my moms."

"Is that a bad thing?"

"I don't know," I sighed, gripping my forehead out of frustration. "We haven't seen him in almost nine years. I've done my best to put the shit behind me, but now he . . ."

"Now he what?"

I shrugged. "I guess he wants to get it all out in the open. I don't know."

"And how does that make you feel?"

"Fucking scared," I told him honestly.

"Baby, can I tell you something you may not want to hear?"

I looked at him, seeing the sincerity behind his eyes. "Okay, I guess."

"Being able to finally talk about it with the people you're most afraid to talk to it about is the only thing that's ever gonna heal you. Yeah, I drag you to church and force you to open up with me, but that's because I know it'll help. But when you open up your mouth to tell your truth, that's gonna be the thing to set you free, finally, ma. That's the only way you'll put all this behind you for good. Don't be scared." He reached over and gently grabbed my hand, interlacing his fingers with mine. "I'll be right there if you need me."

"You mean it? You'll go?"

"I won't go inside because it's a private moment that the three of you need to have, but I'll be waiting for you outside if you want me to."

I nodded. "I want you to."

He pulled my hand to his lips and kissed it so tenderly that a tingle shot down my spine. "I'll be there, ma. Now, come on. Let's go get you something to eat before it's time to get you on that train."

Chapter 17

Hope—Surprise!

As I stood on Aunt Marlene's front porch, my legs trembling with my organs all jittery inside, I inhaled a bottomless breath. Upon seeing my father's truck in the driveway, I was a complete ball of nerves. It hadn't been but two hours since Meeko and I had gotten off the train, and now here we were, ready to finally reveal my pregnancy. Everything was moving in slow motion like a horrible dream, and my breaths had turned shallow because I could hardly breathe.

"Shorty, you ready?" Meeko asked, gripping each of my shoulders from behind.

I sighed and shook my head. "I'm scared. Maybe I should tell him over the phone."

"Nah, we here now. It's time to get this shit out in the open," he said.

After sucking in a deep breath of his own, he stepped in front of me and tentatively rang the bell. He shot a quick glance over his shoulder at me before slipping his hands down into his pockets.

"I think I'm gonna throw up," I said.

He chuckled softly through his nose. "Shorty, calm down. You gon' be a'ight. Just take a deep breath. Relax."

Although it was less than a minute, it felt like an eternity before I finally heard someone come to the door.

"Oh God, oh God," I breathed out in a panic, shaking my hands out in front of me. This is the end.

When the door finally cracked open, Aunt Marlene's slender frame suddenly appeared in the entryway. Although I could see her, it was apparent that she hadn't yet noticed me behind Meeko's tall stature.

"C-can I help you?" she asked with one of her eyebrows raised. She was more than familiar with Meeko's name but had only physically seen him once. The sound of recognition was completely absent from her voice.

"U-uh . . ." Meeko stammered for a bit until he finally just stepped aside.

Aunt Marlene's eyes immediately fell on my bulging belly before they bloomed in utter shock. "Hope, no," she whispered, pulling her fingers up to her open mouth.

My chin instantly fell to my chest—my head collapsing in shame.

"Can we come inside?" Meeko spoke for me.

Aunt Marlene let out a shaky breath and widened the door to let us in finally. When I felt my knees buckle beneath me, Meeko reached back and swiftly grabbed my hand. It was instinctual like he knew my legs and feet wouldn't move to take this journey alone. I wobbled behind him as he led the way inside, tightly squeezing his hand. My stomach was bubbling with anxiety, and my head was swimming with doubt. I was so unprepared for Deddy's wrath.

As soon as we entered the living room, the familiar scent of Aunt Marlene's pot roast inundated my nose. My stomach growled loud enough for both my aunt and Meeko to hear.

"You gotta eat something soon," he said.

"I'll be fine," I muttered. There was no way I could eat at a time like this.

Without warning, my father emerged from the back of the house wearing both an Aggie Pride tee shirt and the biggest smile on his face . . . that was . . . until his eyes finally landed on me.

"Please tell me . . ." His words drifted off as his jaw suddenly dropped. "You're pregnant?"

Clearing the nerves from my throat, I blinked back fresh tears from my eyes. "Yes, sir," I whispered.

I looked up to see that his irises had glossed over too. "Dear God," he gasped, cupping his hands over his mouth. As if he'd just gotten the wind knocked out of him, he dropped down to the couch and buried his face in his palms. He was utterly stunned to silence. I don't ever recall a time when I'd felt this low. Even when my mother died, it was an altogether different kind of pain.

"Deddy," I tried softly.

"Give him a minute, Hope," Aunt Marlene said, holding up her finger.

Meeko and I stood there in awkward silence with our sweaty hands intertwined, waiting for my father's following words. My heart raced inside of me, thumping so loudly I could hear it clear between my ears. "Deddy," I tried again. I was a real daddy's girl at heart, so the quiet was almost unbearable. I needed him to say something.

Finally, my father's head rose from his hands, and his red, puffy eyes rolled up to Meeko. "You got my daughter pregnant?" he asked in a deep, calm voice.

Meeko's chest swelled in a deep breath as he chucked up his chin. "Yes, sir," he answered.

I was immediately taken aback. Meeko was far from the respectable "yes, sir, no, ma'am" kind of guy. In fact, he was the complete opposite. He was a filthy-mouthed slang user who, as he would put it, "just didn't give a fuck." But as I stood there watching his head held high, his Polo shirt buttoned all the way to the top, I felt a passing sense of relief. At that moment, I could only fathom that his level of respect toward my father was out of his devotion to me. And I appreciated it.

Slowly, my father stood from the couch, and within the blink of an eye, he charged directly at Meeko, sending him back against the wall.

"Deddy," I screamed. "Stop!"

"You low-life thug, you. Got my daughter pregnant. I should break your goddamn neck," he roared, gripping the collar of Meeko's shirt as he roughly jacked him up against the wall. My 50-year-old father was no match for Meeko's muscular build, but Meeko didn't fight back. Not once. Instead, he held up his hands in surrender and kept his head lifted in the air.

When Deddy moved to wrap his hands around Meeko's throat, I immediately rushed over to separate the two. "Deddy, please," I cried out again, trying to pull back his arms. Aunt Marlene tried from the other side, but Deddy held on tight.

"I should kill you!" my father screamed, tightening his grasp.

"Stop. Please!" I tried harder to pry him away, but Deddy's grip was so tight that he was now shaking. I didn't know what to do, so I dug my fingernails deep into his flesh, making him recoil instantaneously.

"Get off of me, goddammit!" His hand mechanically flew back and flung me off him until my bottom struck the floor.

"The fuck, yo!" I heard Meeko say, shoving my father back. Within a matter of seconds, he was down by my side. One hand splayed across my belly, and the other pressed tenderly against my upper back. "You a'ight?" he asked, his voice trembling with concern. "Do I need to call an ambulance? Talk to me, shorty. You gon' be a'ight?"

Truthfully, the fall's impact hadn't hurt one bit. It was my heart that was in so much pain. As I sat there whimpering, my shoulders jumping in despair, I somehow found a way to nod my head. It seemed that gesture was all Meeko needed to take me by the hand and lift me to my feet.

"Hope, are you all right?" Aunt Marlene rushed over and asked.

Meeko didn't even give me a chance to respond. He threw his hands up, blocking any chances she had to get next to me. "She's fine, yo. Just back up," he told her with a grimace. He was livid.

With his arm swathed around my shoulders, we headed back for the door. The sounds of my father's deep sobs as he repeatedly asked God "why" played out in the background. When we got to the car, Meeko carefully tucked me inside and strapped me in. During the entire ride home, I cried, thinking my life would never be the same. I had just broken my daddy's heart. Meeko didn't try to console me—didn't even say that everything would be all right. Instead, he just let me cry out loud.

When we finally walked through my front door, Franki and Paris were sitting in the living room with the TV on. Of course, they immediately asked what was wrong because the devastation was still evident on my tear-stained face. I didn't even have enough strength to answer them. Instead, I just kept walking with Meeko to my room until he closed the door behind us.

He sat on the edge of my bed and began to slowly undress me, first removing my oversized tee shirt, then sliding down my little cotton shorts. As I stood there between his legs in nothing but my bra and panties, with my belly on the verge of explosion, I felt completely numb.

"Go get in the shower, shorty," he told me.

I got in the shower as he instructed and bawled my eyes out even more beneath the warm water. Almost an hour later, I finally stepped back into the room. He was still there, reclined in bed above the covers with his hands resting behind his head. A bottle of water and a bag from China Grill sat on the nightstand as the smell of my favorite vegetable lo mein lingered in the air. I grabbed a nightshirt from my dresser drawer and quickly slipped it over my head, letting the towel around me hit the floor.

After joining Meeko on the bed, I propped my back against a pillow and pulled out the carton of lo mein. With chopsticks in my hand, I began devouring it like a ravenous dog. I was starving and didn't care that Meeko sat there staring at me. The entire time I ate, he didn't say a word. He just sat there and watched. After I was finished, I got up and threw my trash away. When I returned to the bed, Meeko was standing with the sheets pulled back for me. I slipped beneath the covers, and like a father to a child, he hovered over to tuck me in good night.

When he reached up to cut off the lamp, I whispered, "Stay. Please don't leave me."

And he didn't. He kicked off his shoes and climbed right in on the other side with his clothes still on. As he cuddled me close from behind and draped his arm around me, I exhaled deeply. Although I was still shaken from the day's events, I felt safe in his arms. I closed my eyes and allowed him to rub my belly until I eventually fell asleep.

It wasn't until about four in the morning that soft raps against our front door woke me from a deep sleep. Startled, I hastily sat up in the bed, but Meeko told me to lie back down and go to sleep. He got up and went to answer the door. As I shifted the pillow beneath my head, trying to get comfortable again, I was halted by the sound of Deddy's voice. I couldn't make out exactly what he was saying, but I immediately recognized that tone.

Oh God. What's he doing here? With my heart beating out of control, I got up and crept to my bedroom door for a better listen.

"I need to talk to my daughter," my deddy said.

"She's asleep right now. Maybe you should try again later this morning," Meeko told him.

There was silence before I heard my father let out a profound sigh. *God.* He was still hurting. "I promised her mother I'd do better than this," he finally said. At the mere mention of my mother, emotions took over me, and tears sprang into my eyes. "Just tell me this. Why *her?* Of all the young girls you could have preyed on and ruined, why my child?" he asked.

"Sir, I know I'm not worthy—shit, never even said I was, but . . . What I can tell you is that I've never been more drawn to anyone in my life. Your daughter is perfection. When people talk about 'beauty from the inside out' and all that other shit, I swear to God that's her. She's the type of girl whose eyes shine brighter, and her skin glows just from all that fucking light she has inside. Her life may not be by the book or to your liking, but she's the best damn person I know. Straight up. And if by some chance God has mercy on me for the fucked-up shit I've done . . ." His voice trailed off just before I heard him inhale a sharp breath. "My son will be just like her."

The tears formed in my eyes slowly began to roll down my cheeks, and my heart swelled inside my chest. The only time I'd ever heard Meeko talk like that was when we were making love. And not to say that he was being disingenuous, but hearing him say those things about me to my father at four in the morning, no less, definitely shed some light. Perhaps he really did love me.

After my father told him he'd try again a little later, Meeko closed the door and returned to the room. I wobbled back to bed as fast as possible and returned beneath the warm sheets. By the time he crossed the entryway, my eyes were already closed. I lay there as still as a single footprint on a bed of snow, pretending to be asleep. He got back in bed, where his arms resumed their rightful place around me, and it wasn't long before we both fell back into slumber. When I woke up hours later, my room was full of sunlight. With a morning yawn, I stretched my arm over to feel for Meeko, but he was no longer there.

After going into the bathroom for a quick brush of my teeth, I headed out into the living room. I was surprised to see Franki, Paris, and Asha sitting around watching TV. At first, I thought it would be weird for Asha to move in, but most of the time, it felt like she belonged.

"Good morning," I said.

"How you feeling, mama?" Franki asked, genuinely concerned.

I shrugged my shoulders on the way to the kitchen. "Okay, I guess."

As I was fixing myself a bowl of cereal, Paris walked in and stroked my puffy hair. "You wanna talk about it, babe?" she asked.

I shook my head and sighed. "Not really."

Franki walked through the entryway just as I put the spoon up to my mouth for a bite. "So, what happened?"

I blew out a frustrated breath, recalling everything that had happened. "Deddy was so mad when he saw me that he actually tried choking Meeko to death. And when he wouldn't let go of him, I jumped in. My deddy accidentally knocked me to the floor and—"

"Jesus," Paris said in concern. "Are you all right?"

"I'm fine. Meeko was so mad, but I think he calmed down once he realized I was okay."

"So, what's your pops saying now? He gon' help support you and the baby?" Franki asked.

I shook my head. "The conversation never even got that far."

"Damn," she muttered.

Paris put her arm around me and lay her head on my shoulder. "Everything is gonna be all right, friend," she said.

Suddenly, Asha appeared, and instead of the three of us, it was now four bodies crammed into the small galley kitchen. All of us were still in our nightclothes, and Franki and Asha were wearing silk scarves wrapped around their heads.

"Have you heard anything from him yet?" Paris asked her. The sadness in her voice caused me to look at her.

"Nah, don't nobody know where that nigga at," Asha replied.

"Who?" I asked, taking another spoonful of Cinnamon Toast Crunch into my mouth.

Huffing a frustrated breath, Paris threw herself back against the counter. "Malachi," she said, folding her arms across her chest. "I've been calling and texting him like crazy, and he won't pick up the damn phone."

"I thought you weren't dealing with that nigga no more," Franki said.

Paris hiked her shoulders in a partial shrug. "Things change," she said softly.

"I'm surprised you even care, considering he just pulled a gun out on Ty the other night," Asha said, holding the refrigerator door open to look inside.

"He *what?*" Franki's eyes ballooned as she pulled her fist up to her mouth, laughing like a dude. "That nigga's wild, yo."

"He pulled a gun out on Ty? Why?" I asked.

"It was just a big misunderstanding. Ty was over here to watch a movie one night—"

"At ten o'clock at night," Asha emphasized with a cluck of her tongue. "Shit, if you gon' tell the story, tell it right."

"Yes, fine. It was at ten o'clock at night. I was already in my pajamas, and it got hot in here, so Ty decided to take off his shirt. Well, in walks Malachi . . ." She stopped mid-sentence as if suddenly, another thought had occurred. "Wait. Did you guys know that Malachi has a key?"

"He has a key?" I repeated. "To our place?"

"Yes." She flew her arms in the air dramatically. I could only assume that Asha knew since she just laughed. "Well, anyway, he comes through the door and spots Ty half-naked on the couch. You already know where his mind went. Of course, he thinks we've been screwing around. But I swear nothing happened between us. Like, absolutely nothing."

Asha pursed her lips to the side as her light brown eyes danced with amusement. "You sure?"

"Positive," Paris exclaimed.

"So, when did he pull out the gun?" Franki was eager to hear the rest of the story.

"It all happened so fast. As soon as he saw Ty and me standing there in my pj's, it was like he just went crazy. He walked right over to him and hit him on the head with his gun. Ty started bleeding and everything," Paris said with her palms out flat like she was still trying to understand everything. "Guys, I was so scared. Like, oh my God, I thought he was gonna friggin' kill him."

Asha sniggered. "He prolly was. My brother is crazy over you."

"Well, I just want him to know that nothing happened. I need to tell him that I . . ." Her words floated off as sorrow unexpectedly filled her eyes.

Suddenly, I could hear my cell phone ringing from the other room. I excused myself from the conversation and shuffled back to the bedroom with my hand supporting my lower back. Our place was pretty small, but just that short walk had me completely out of breath when I answered the phone.

"Hello."

"Hope." I immediately went silent upon hearing my father's voice. "Are you there?"

I cleared my throat and sucked in a deep breath of air. "Yes, sir. I'm here."

"I know things got out of hand yesterday, but we really need to talk."

"I know."

"Bring the boy back over again tonight."

Great, I thought. "What time?"

"Aunt Marlene said dinner should be ready by five. I'll see you both then."

As soon as my father hung up, I called Meeko. Like always, he answered on the first ring.

"What's up?"

"Hey, umm . . ." God, I was nervous. "My dad wants us to come back over tonight."

Meeko released a deep sigh into the phone. "Shorty, I'm telling you right now . . . That nigga can put his hands on me again if he want to, but I'm laying his ass the fuck out. The only reason I took that shit last night was because of you, but I'm not doing it no more. So either he can act like he got some fucking sense or—"

"Meeko, he's calmed down now. I think he'll be fine," I said, gripping my forehead.

"Well, I hope so because I'm not taking shit off that nigga no more. Daddy or not," he ranted.

"Meeko," I snapped again. I couldn't take anymore. This supposed war he thought he had with my father was starting to give me a headache. "Can you please just be here by four thirty? Aunt Marlene said dinner would be ready by five."

"I guess."

"Okay. I'll see you then."

It all felt like déjà vu as we stood nervously on the front porch of Aunt Marlene's home. My stomach was twisting, and panic started to settle in. I pushed my glasses farther up my face and clasped my clammy palms over my protruding belly. Again, Meeko stepped up to ring the bell. However, when my aunt opened the door this time, she let us right on in. She even gave me a tight hug when I crossed the threshold. She led us right to the back of the house, where Deddy was setting the dining room table. Tension instantly filled the room when Meeko's and Deddy's met eyes. Thank God Aunt Marlene took him into the kitchen with the excuse of needing his help.

"So, how far along are you?" my father asked me.

"Thirty-six weeks." Not wanting to make eye contact, I placed the silverware on the table.

"Wow," he said with his eyebrows raised. "You're gonna be a mother any day now. What are your plans?"

My dry mouth parted to speak, but words had temporarily escaped me. Thankfully, it wasn't but a second later that Aunt Marlene and Meeko entered the dining room with trays of food in their hands. I was saved by the bell. Once they laid everything out, we all sat down and allowed Deddy to pray over the food. Then we dug right in after that, devouring the smothered pork chops, collard greens, rice, and gravy she had cooked. The food was delicious, but if it hadn't been for Aunt Marlene's small attempts at conversation, the room would have been completely quiet.

Finally, my father decided to speak. "So, when are you moving back home?" he looked at me and asked.

"I'm not moving back home," I told him softly. "Meeko and I are getting a place."

I knew my father well enough to know that the unfazed look on his face was a complete sham. He was fuming on the inside. Although he tried to remain calm, his eyes told a completely different story as he looked at Meeko. "Then I take it the two of you are getting married?"

Meeko immediately started choking on his food. I had to reach over and practically smack him on the back until his coughing finally slowed. "No, we aren't getting married, Deddy," I said.

No longer able to hold it in, my father dropped his dinner napkin on his plate and sat back in his chair. A flabbergasted expression quickly swept across his face. "So, not only are you pregnant, but you're also gonna be living in sin too?"

"I know it's not ideal, but—"

"You're damn right, it's not ideal," my father cut in and said.

"How are you gonna be able to afford a baby, Hope? And what about school?"

"Nah, I've got everything handled from a money perspective," Meeko explained. "She don't have to worry about nothing, and she can still go to school."

"Well, actually . . . I think I'm gonna take the next semester off," I said, pushing my glasses up farther on my face.

Given the tightness of Meeko's jaw and his wide-eyed expression, it was clear that I'd breached our united front. "Shorty, what you mean you not going to school next semester?" he leaned over and whispered.

I cleared my throat and took a deep swallow before I spoke. "I've thought about it and . . . There's no way

I could be both a good mother and a good student one week after giving birth. It doesn't even make sense," I told him. "Plus, I want to be able to bond with the baby. Maybe even try breastfeeding him." I shrugged.

Meeko's jaw remained clenched, but he nodded before returning to his food.

"So you're having a baby, dropping out of school, and shacking up. What else?" my father asked.

"Yo, didn't you just hear her say she wasn't dropping out of school?" Meeko barked with a bang of his fist against the table.

"Meeko," I gasped, placing my hand on his back. It was all I could do to try to calm him down. He was seething inside, and I didn't know how long he could keep his temper at bay. "Well, I'll start school the following semester, and if I have to, I'll get a job."

That's when Meeko completely lost it. He dropped his metal fork down to the ceramic plate, making it rattle. "The *fuck*, yo," he snapped, pushing back from the table. "I told you straight up that you didn't have to get no fucking job, didn't I? I already told you I got it."

"Yes, but—"

Meeko exhaled a sharp breath and shook his head. "Shorty, why you sitting here tryin'a front on me in front of ya pops? Like I'm gon' be some fucking deadbeat dad." Before I could respond, he stood up from the table and walked to the front room.

My father's disappointed regard grew even more. "And you wonder why I'm so worried about you."

"Not now, Deddy," I said.

"If not now, then when?"

"Deddy, you know I love you. And I appreciate everything you've done for me over the years. You raised me without Momma, and I'll always be grateful. But I'm not perfect, Deddy, nor will I ever be. I want you in my life, in my baby's life, but . . ." I swallowed back my emotions, trying to get all this out finally. "But if you don't stop with this, you're gonna push me away. Is *that* what you want?" When he didn't answer, I shot up from the table with tears in my eyes. As fast as my large belly would allow, I went to find Meeko. He wasn't in the living room, so I peeked out on the front porch. He was sitting in Aunt Marlene's rocking chair with his elbows resting on his knees. His head dipped down between his shoulders.

"Meeko," I whispered. He peered up at me and wiped his hand down over his face. "I promise you it wasn't like that. I only said I'd get a job *if* I had to."

"But you don't."

"Meeko, nothing's set in stone between us. We aren't even together anymore." All I knew was that Meeko hadn't touched me sexually in months, and he was now seeing some pretty girl named Midge. I had no idea how things would turn out between us. "How do I know things won't change? That *you* won't change your mind about this whole big plan of yours?"

"'Cause you should fucking know."

Although water quickly pooled in my eyes after crying all night, I declined another tear to fall. "But I don't. I don't know anything anymore."

Meeko's eyes instantly softened, letting me know that he was hurt. And while it wasn't my intention to wound him with my words, it was my truth. I'd been thinking long and hard during our trip to Baltimore, wondering if anyone would ever come into the picture, would he abandon me along with this so-called plan of his. I wanted to believe that Meeko would never do that to me, but I also knew that in life, things change. It was time for me to start thinking like a grown woman and, more importantly, like a mother. I needed a plan A, B, *and* C.

"Let me just say goodbye, and we can leave."

Chapter 18

Asha—So Much for Secrets

"Malachi, please call that girl," I told my brother.

He had just dropped a stack of forms on my desk and had already turned to head back to the rear of the gym.

"Nah. I'm good on that," he tossed over his shoulder.

I got up from my chair and followed close behind him. "Give the girl a damn break. She's not even fucking Ty."

Malachi sucked his teeth while keeping an even stride. "And how you know that?" he asked.

"Because she doesn't even like him. All she can do is talk about your no-good ass."

He chuckled and glanced at me over his shoulder. "Why I gotta be all that?"

"Because, nigga, you ain't shit," I joked. Finally, we reached my father's office, where Malachi immediately claimed a seat behind the desk. I sat down in the chair across from him. "But for whatever reason, she seems to love yo' ass anyway."

"Shawty don't love me," he muttered, his lips pursed to the side.

"Shiid. I know you fucking lying. She ain't been doing all that damn boo-hooing and crying for nothing." When I saw his golden eyes finally contemplating my words, I said, "You know she went over to Reese's house to find you?"

His head reared back in surprise as his eyes bucked wide. "Say word?"

"I'm serious." I laughed. "Of course, Reese told her that you don't live there no more and not to bring her ass back, but that's how desperate Paris was to find you. She's been blowing up Nya and Tee Tee too. Now she wants me to take her to go see Momma and Daddy."

His eyebrows dipped in, and his nose wrinkled with confusion. "Go to see Ma and Pops? For what?"

"I guess she thinks they'll know where to find you. Shit, I feel bad for lying to the girl. I mean, I come in here and see you damn near every day, just to go home and see her crying. Just talk to her, please. You've got this court date coming up, and even though I hate to say it, you never know what the outcome might be."

He released a deep breath of frustration before running his hand over his face. "I know, but—"

"Look, I know Reese damn near broke you when she fucked around with A.B., but honestly, Paris ain't like that. And not that she's my favorite person in the world, but I can tell that you really like her. A lot. I just don't want you to be so stubborn that you'll regret not following your heart one day." Malachi narrowed his eyes while trying to downplay the smirk unfolding on his lips. "And yes, Paris is prissy as fuck," I continued. "Spoiled, bougie . . . Shit, I could go on and on. But beneath all that, she's good peoples, 'Chi. Don't do her like this."

He gave me a single nod after finally allowing his head to collapse against the leather chair. "I hear you."

"That's all I ask." I held my hands up in surrender.

I got up from my chair and started for the door. As I was about to enter the hallway, Malachi shouted out behind me. "Thanks, sis."

I looked back at him and smiled. Every day, it seemed Malachi and I were making massive strides in our relationship. Of course, he still bossed me around at the gym, but things between us were pretty cool for the most part. I guess he could see that I was trying to turn things around in my life. I was no longer sexually involved with any members of his gang, and instead of fucking for money, I was legitimately out here getting it on my own. Sure, it was only a dollar more than minimum wage, but low-key, I could tell that he was proud.

When I returned to the front, I noticed Quick sitting on the edge of the desk with his book bag draped off his arm. Unbeknownst to him, I'd caught him red-handed. He was pulling a piece of peppermint out of my candy dish. As I neared, I could smell fresh soap emanating from his skin, indicating he'd just gotten out of the shower. He wore a simple white tee shirt and black basketball shorts that hung low on his waist. Tall, black socks and Nike slides sheltered his lengthy feet.

"Hey," I said, touching him gently on the arm to gain his attention.

He glanced over his shoulder and smiled, showcasing that slight imperfection in his front tooth. "What's up, Asha?" he said.

I rounded my desk and plopped down in my chair. "You heading out?"

"Yeah, in a minute. But I wanted to ask you something before I left."

"Ookayyy," I let out a laugh.

"Um . . ." He stammered with a scratch behind his ear.

"Oh my God." I laughed, seeing how nervous he was all of a sudden. "Let it out, boy."

"So, um . . ." He stood upright and clasped his hands together at his waist. "Well, my boy is an artist, and he's having one of those sip-and-paint events . . ."

"Okay," I smiled, already knowing where this was headed since we'd been talking on the phone every day since we'd left the mall.

"I was wondering if you wanted to come out with me. Get your paint on," he said, smiling flirtatiously as he licked his thick, brown lips.

"Sure, I'd love to."

"A'ight, cool. Tomorrow around five, I'll come pick you up?"

I nodded. "Sounds good."

"Oh, one more thing before I jet," he said. He reached around and pulled a small gift bag out of his backpack. "I think this is for you."

I could feel the wrinkles on my forehead as I took the bag from his hand. "What's this?" I asked lowly. I saw the earrings I'd wanted from the mall when I opened it. "Oh my . . ." I gasped, covering my mouth with my hand. It wasn't that they were expensive like the jewelry Mark used to buy me, but it was the fact that he remembered and thought enough of me to go back and get them.

"Those were the ones, right?" he asked.

"You didn't have to do this, really."

"I know, but I wanted to. I thought they'd look good on you."

My heart melted a little at that. "Thank you, Quick," I smiled.

He chucked up his chin and started for the door, but Mark's girlfriend, Meelah, came storming inside before I could watch him leave. Her hair was messy, and she looked like she hadn't slept in days.

"Where is he?" she shouted on the last of her breath. Her chest heaved up and down.

"Who?" I asked, coming toward her. "Who are you looking for?"

"I'm looking for your fucking brother, little girl," she snapped, rolling her eyes as the frown she wore etched even deeper on her face.

Judging by the crazed look in her eye and the sick feeling in my gut, I knew she was there for trouble. "He's not here," I lied.

"You lying little bitch," she seethed. "I already seen the nigga's car outside. Tell him to get his ass up here—now!"

Folding my arms across my chest, I gave her a deadpan expression. There was no way I was just going to let her come up in here thinking that she was running shit.

"Yo, what's going on? What's wrong?" Quick tried to intervene.

"I need to see Malachi—*now*," she demanded.

"But she just told you he's not here. Maybe you should try back another time," he tried reasoning. He glanced over his shoulder, noticing how everyone around the gym had begun to look up front. Then he turned back to Meelah with a hike of his left brow. "Baby girl, you making a scene. Just come back later."

"Man, I don't give a fuck about a scene. My boyfriend has been missing for four whole days, and I know he had something to do with it."

"Girl, please. Mark just probably found some new pussy," I told her with a dismissive wave of my hand. "Just give him a few days, and that nigga'll be back."

"Fuck you, bitch," she spat.

She lunged toward me before I knew what was happening, as if she was ready to fight, but Quick swiftly caught her by the waist.

"We not doing all that in here. Calm down," he said.

"Nah, fuck that bitch. She thinks I'm playing with her," she yelled, angry and out of breath.

Clearly, the bitch had me mistaken because I was far from weak. I uncrossed my arms and bucked right back at her. "I ain't scared of you, bitch. You act like I wasn't fucking that nigga anyway." I was so upset that, at this point, any and everything was now flying out of my mouth. All bets were off.

"Yeah, go right ahead and brag. Tell everybody how you was fucking him and every other nigga from here to Charlotte."

"Whatever, bitch. You just mad that I had *yo'* nigga," I spat.

"No, baby," she clapped her hands. "*You* just mad because of that sick-ass pussy between yo' legs." She flicked her pointed fingernail toward the onlookers in the gym but kept her eyes fixed on me. "Bet none of these niggas up in here know how you was sitting up in that hospital bed with syphilis for two days straight, do they?" My cheeks scorched from embarrassment. Everyone's eyes, including Quick's, were now fastened on me. "That's right, look at you," she further tormented me. "Couldn't even deny that shit if you tried. Dirty bitch."

"Aye, that's enough," Quick barked, holding her back by the shoulder. "Like she already said, 'Chi ain't here. Come back another time."

"Yeah, I'll be back all right. And next time, it'll be with the cops because I know Malachi did something to Mark. This just ain't no fucking coincidence. He already told me about their beef because of *that* bitch." She pointed to me. "And now, all y'all want to play stupid. Nah." She shook her head. "Everybody up in here know how that nigga get down. But I'll be back . . . That's for damn sure."

When she stormed out of the gym, I suddenly realized I had tears in my eyes. Her telling everyone that I had contracted syphilis had humiliated the shit out of me. It's not something I wanted anyone to ever find out about me, especially not Quick. Although I still had two hours until the end of my shift, I sniffed back my emotions and went to grab my things. On my way out, Quick grabbed my elbow.

"I thought you didn't get off until five?" he said.

I ran my hand through my shoulder-length hair and sighed. "I just gotta get out here."

"Well, let me give you a ride," he offered.

My eyes slightly twitched from shock. *How can he not think I'm disgusting?* After taking a deep swallow to regain my composure, I nodded and allowed him to lead me out to his car. As he drove down the highway, I sat quietly in the passenger seat, staring out the window. I kept wondering if everything I was doing in my life to better myself was making a difference.

"I like your hair like that," Quick said, taking me out of my thoughts.

"Thanks."

He probably didn't know that I'd been wearing my hair like that because I could no longer afford to get it done. After allowing Momma to give me a trim, I'd just been blowing it out every week. I missed my braids and bundles so much, but I would just have to make do for now.

"So, um, what that girl back there said . . ." He started, hesitation completely submerged in his voice.

"Yeah, what about it?" I nonchalantly asked. Too afraid to look him in the eyes, I kept my gaze cast out of the window. I wouldn't dare risk seeing even a hint of repulsion on his face.

"I mean . . . Is it true? You were in the hospital?"

I took a deep swallow and slowly nodded my head. "Yep." For some reason, I was holding my breath and waiting for the ball to drop.

"Damn. That's messed up that someone gave that to you. You gotta protect yourself at all times," he said, surprising me.

Finally, I turned to look at him. He was sitting there, leaning back with one hand controlling the wheel. "I've definitely learned my lesson," I told him honestly.

"I bet. You must've been real sick if they kept you in the hospital."

"Yeah, apparently, you can die from it if it goes untreated. It's not something you often hear about people getting, either. Herpes, Chlamydia, HIV, yeah . . . but syphilis? The shit was crazy. And the hardest part about it all was that my mother was there when the doctor told me. I ain't never felt so ashamed in all my fucking life." As I recalled everything that happened, overwhelming emotions hit me all at once. "How could I be so stupid?" I murmured.

Quick reached over and placed his hand on top of mine. "Don't beat yourself up, baby girl. Just take it as another hard lesson learned. Believe me, you gon' make plenty more mistakes out here. But the key is to just look at them as an opportunity. An opportunity to change yourself into something better than you were before."

I sighed. "I know, I know. I think I'm harder on myself than anyone."

"Most people are," he said.

"It's like I'm trying to change, and I'm trying to do better, but then shit like this happens, and I just want to go right back to being that same person who doesn't give a fuck. Self-protection mode, I guess." I shrugged.

"Exactly what do you want to go back to? If you don't mind me asking."

"What I mean is, if people are still gonna treat me like I'm a ho . . . calling me out on who I fucked and didn't fuck, I might as well still get down like that. At least, then, I was getting money. Now, all I'm doing is working and preparing for school. I haven't had sex all summer, and that sad fact alone is frustrating in itself. I guess I'm just trying to be a better person all around, better to the people around me . . ." My voice trailed off as my shoulders hiked again.

"Then just focus on that."

Suddenly, the car came to a stop, and I realized we were sitting directly in front of my home. Staring deep into my eyes, he leaned over the console and ever so gently pinched me by the chin. As his face neared mine, I gaped down at his parted lips. I could tell they were on standby, preparing to devour me. When he got so close that traces of his scent, soap, and mint, were practically floating up my nose, I froze.

Oh my God. He's gonna kiss me.

That's when his eyes closed, and I panicked, instantly pulling back. "My bad," he said. His eyes fluttered open, only to change into a confused state. "I just thought . . ."

I shook my head and closed my eyes. It wasn't that I didn't want him to kiss me but more so about the fact that I didn't feel worthy of it. Hell, less than an hour ago, he learned I'd recently had syphilis. Yet, somehow, he still wanted to be intimate with me. Not only that, but he was also kind and sweet. His words of encouragement made me feel like perhaps I wasn't the most terrible person in the world. That maybe . . . *Just maybe,* I deserved someone to love me for me.

"I like you. A lot," I confessed, battling against everything inside of me that told me, *"He's not sincere"* or *"You're not worthy."* He looked at me with an even more confused expression on his face. "I just got scared," I whispered.

When he didn't react like I thought he would—returning to my personal space for a kiss, I pulled my feet into the chair and tucked them beneath me. Rising to my knees, I leaned over and delicately placed my unsteady palms against his face. As he peered up at me, my heart began thudding so hard I could feel its vibration in my throat. And my breathing—it was anything but calm. I closed my eyes and tenderly pressed my lips against his, inhaling a deep breath through my nose. When I felt the tip of his tongue pierce the seam of my lips, flutters like I'd never felt before interspersed throughout my entire belly. Gradually, his tongue swept over mine, and like one rolling wave after the other, our mouths began to dance. He kissed me so long and hard that I started to ache between my thighs. I unconsciously moaned.

He pulled back abruptly, brushing the wetness on his lips away with his hand. "My bad," he said.

"No." I shook my head. "Don't apologize. Please."

He stared at me and slowly licked his bottom lip. "A'ight, I won't apologize," he coolly said with a smirk.

Unexpectedly, he reached up and took me by the chin again, only this time with more confidence. When he lifted his back from the driver seat, bringing his face back into mine, I sealed my eyes and allowed him to kiss me on the lips. It wasn't some fast peck either but rather slow and deliberate . . . where every part of his plump mouth pressed flush against mine accurately. He pulled back, licking the taste of my lips off his own once more.

"Call me," he whispered.

Chapter 19

Paris—Now or Never

"All rise," the bailiff said.

I'd been sitting in the very back row of the stuffy courtroom, awaiting the outcome of Malachi's trial. It had been nearly three weeks since I'd last seen his face. Yet, as I sat here today, it was determined that not much would change. The only part of him I could make out was the back of his freshly cut head. Well, that and his broad shoulders that were seemingly cloaked in a gray blazer. Directly behind him sat Asha and who I assumed to be their parents. Tee Tee, Nya, Bull, and Reese were seated just a couple of rows behind them. Although I didn't know them by name, the rest of the seats behind him were filled with people who were there to support him.

Seven months ago, a young man by the name of Hasaun Sharif was brutally attacked and killed in Hester Park. A street camera planted on Groometown Road caught the image of a man getting out of the driver's side of Malachi's car and then returning shortly after. Of course, the timing all lined up with Hasaun's exact time of death. Under the streetlights, the video clearly showed a picture of a man six or more shades lighter than Malachi in complexion. Although the man's arms were exposed in his short-sleeved shirt, the baseball cap on his head completely concealed his face. The angle of the camera would not reveal the man's true identity. But this evidence didn't seem to prove Malachi's innocence. The fact still remained that it was indeed Malachi's car—matching plates and all. And the story he gave of his car being stolen but not reported didn't seem to stick. The prosecutor also highlighted the fact that Hasaun was a member of a rival gang that had beef with the 859 crew. In fact, several witnesses had been called to the stand testifying to just that fact. Allegedly, Hasaun was responsible for attacking a female member of 859 earlier that year. Supposedly, the gang wanted revenge.

It seemed they were also trying to throw the whole book at Malachi and the kitchen sink. Aiding and abetting, along with accessory to murder, were the charges that he was facing. The only thing that gave me hope was his attorney, Troy. He stated that he didn't believe the accessory to murder charges would even stick because the act of murder had yet to be proven. The murderer for the crime wasn't even in police custody.

I quickly rose to my feet and watched the judge enter from a back door. The entire courtroom was muted to the point that you could've heard an ant scuttle across the floor. When he finally sat on the bench, the tension in the air got so thick I could hardly breathe. Everyone in the courtroom quickly took their seats as the jury came out in single file.

"Will the defendant and the defense counsel please stand," the judge said. My heart rate instantly spiked to a new level as I watched Malachi up ahead. "Members of the jury, have you reached a verdict?"

"Yes, Your Honor, we have," one of the jurors said, standing to his feet. He was a tall, slender white man in his midthirties, if I had to guess. He had dirty-blond hair that swept across his forehead, and a pair of old glasses pressed snugly against his face. The skinny blue tie he had paired with a plaid shirt gave him the look of a professor.

"Members of the Jury, in the case *Malachi Montgomery vs. the United States,* on the charge of accessory to murder, what say you?"

The juror brought his fist up to his mouth before clearing his throat. "Your Honor, the members of this jury find the defendant not guilty."

Everyone in the courtroom, including me, instantly erupted in merriment. It got so loud the judge had to bang his gavel several times.

"Order in the court," he yelled with a hard roll of his eyes. When the crowd finally settled back to silence, he gazed over to the jury again and asked, "Members of the Jury, on the charge of aiding and abetting, what say you?"

From the back of the courtroom, my eyes zoomed in on the juror. He cleared his throat again, but this time, he took a noticeable swallow . . . so obvious that it caused me to hold my breath. Instantly, something twisted in my gut. "Your Honor," he said. "The members of this jury find the defendant guilty."

"Malachi, no," I screamed, jolting to my feet as fresh tears spilled from my eyes.

Although I'd shouted to the top of my lungs, the sound only seemed to fade into the background of everyone else's cries. The crowd was in such an uproar that the judge had to bang his gavel several times. I bowed over in my seat with my elbows pressed against my thighs and sobbed uncontrollably.

"Order in the court! Order in the court!"

With my head reeling and my heart nearly splitting in two, everything the judge said after that was fuzzy. The only thing I remembered hearing was that sentencing would be held at a later date. By the time I lifted my wet face from my hands, everyone was preparing to exit the courtroom. As I stood up from my seat, I caught a glimpse of Malachi up front, hugging his mother over the rail. When he pulled back from her shoulder, our eyes momentarily locked. Unlike mine, his expression was indifferent. His hazel eyes were cold and seemingly unaffected. Unexpectedly, his regard and attention shifted toward his attorney. When they began to converse, I broke down and cried even harder. *He still hates me.*

As I trudged out of the courtroom with more tears slipping from my eyes, a gentle hand abruptly tapped me on the shoulder. Sniveling, I looked back and saw Asha standing there behind me. Her glassy eyes were as red as fire, matching the tip of her nose, and her lips were quivering. When she held out her arms for me, I didn't even hesitate. I rushed into them, burying my wet face on her shoulder. At that moment, none of the petty issues we'd had in the past even mattered. We were both hurting over the verdict of Malachi's trial. As I wept, her arms enfolded me like a protective coat, shielding me from an emotional storm.

Suddenly, I felt someone gently tugging us apart. It was Malachi's mother. Her skin was as dark and smooth as Malachi's, and her eyes were like pools of rich chocolate. "Get yourselves together, ladies. Now," she said. Although her tone was calm, her words were unyielding. "My son is strong. He's gonna be just fine. Don't let him see you falling apart like this."

Sniffling back my emotions, I slowly nodded my head. "I'm so sorry, Mrs. Montgomery. I just . . ." I couldn't even get the words out. Just the mere thought of permanently losing Malachi had them lodged in my throat.

When I continued to blubber into the palms of my hands, Mrs. Montgomery reached out and hugged me. I'd never met this woman before, but somehow, her familial touch instantly felt like home. "He's gonna be just fine, baby. Don't let him see you break down like this. We got to remain strong for him," she whispered in my ear. "I'm having dinner at the house this Sunday. I want you to come by and eat with us, okay?"

"Yes, ma'am." I nodded, pulling back from her embrace. I glanced back at Malachi again, where he stood up front with his father and attorney. They were in deep conversation, so I turned back for the door.

"Thanks again, Mrs. Montgomery," I said, looking at Malachi's mother. Then my eyes shifted to Asha. "I guess I'll see you at home?"

"Yeah." She nodded with a sniff. "I'll see you back at the house."

With both heavy heart and feet, I plodded out of the courthouse that day, wondering if things between Malachi and me would ever be the same.

I inhaled a deep breath, sucking in my abdomen before smoothing over the front of my navy blue skater dress. My index finger reached for the doorbell, but Malachi's mother pulled open the door from the other side before I could even press it.

"You made it," she said, beaming, white teeth contrasting against her midnight skin.

"Of course." My heart was beating so hard inside my chest, I silently prayed she couldn't hear it. I stepped over the threshold, passing her the liter of Pepsi I had in my hand.

"Thank you, baby. You definitely know my son," she said, referring to Malachi's love of the soda.

When I entered their home, I immediately drew in the scent of a home cooked meal, something I rarely had since the girls and I couldn't cook. As I followed behind her, I kept trying to calm myself. I still hadn't seen

Malachi since the day of his trial and I was downright nervous to see him again. As we walked into the house, Mrs. Montgomery gave me a quick tour of the place, showing me where the living room, dining room, and bathroom all were. When we finally reached the kitchen, I saw Asha standing by the counter barefoot, sprinkling paprika over the deviled eggs.

"Hey, girl," she greeted me with a smile. Her straightened hair hung down to her shoulders, and her face was free of makeup, giving her a more youthful appearance. She wore frayed jean shorts that she paired with a white tank top that read *Black Queen* on the front.

"Need any help?" I asked right away.

Mrs. Montgomery grabbed my sweaty palm. "Come on, let's go out back first," she said. "Malachi and his daddy are frying fish out on the back porch."

My heart raced even faster at that, and I could feel myself growing hot. "Does he even know I'm here?" I leaned over, whispering to Asha on my way out. Of course, her eyes gave nothing away. She simply pulled her lips into a straight line and shrugged her shoulders.

As I followed behind Mrs. Montgomery, I exchanged my inhales for exhales repeatedly until we finally reached the sliding glass doors. Within mere seconds of me planting my foot out on the back porch, I heard Maevyn screaming my name.

"Miss Paris," she yelled, running up from the yard.

I held my arms open for her, flinching as she ran toward me full speed. The jellies on her feet clacked against the wooden deck. "Hey, Maevyn," I said as she wrapped little arms around my waist.

I gazed down at her, admiring her dark chocolate skin and hazel eyes. As she panted, I noticed the beads of sweat that had formed around her brow and the little stains on her lavender tee shirt. She wore two frizzy pigtails in her hair, and the borders of her mouth were sticky like she'd just finished eating a sweet treat.

"Miss Paris, you wanna come play with us? We playing kickball," she said, pointing out into the yard where Mekhai was now standing by his lonesome.

Then suddenly I felt *his* presence approaching. "Maevyn, go play with your little brother. I'll be out there in a minute," Malachi said.

"But, Daddy—"

Malachi didn't have to say another word. He simply cocked his right eyebrow and pointed his finger toward the yard. Without delay, Maevyn took off running, making a clean jump off the three steps of the deck.

"Now, I know I gave that child a bath this morning," Mrs. Montgomery said, shaking her head. "She looks like she's been working on a farm."

"I guess she's been playing hard," I said with a little laugh, eyeing Maevyn from afar as she did partial cartwheels in the low-cut grass.

"What you doing here, Paris?" Malachi abruptly asked, his voice completely taciturn and unkind.

Mrs. Montgomery tucked her chin-length hair behind her ear and cleared her throat. "Well, let me go see what your daddy's got going over here," she said, excusing herself.

Finally, I cut my eyes over at Malachi, seeing him stand there with a white tank top displaying his tattoo-covered arms. Those hazel eyes and bottom row of gold teeth sparkled in the sun.

"Your mother invited me," I said, with an ever so slight lift of my chin.

"I'on know what the fuck for."

My mouth instantly dropped. "You know what? Fine. I came here to check on you because I care. You've been shutting me out, and it's breaking me because . . ." My voice suddenly vanished into the air as I thought about Malachi's pending imprisonment. "Just forget it. I'll leave," I finally snapped, shaking my head.

As soon I spun on my heels, ready to depart, he reached for my hand. Just that simple gesture, the slightest touch, caused goose bumps to rise across my skin. Because of the hold he had on my heart, I turned back, looking at him through blurred vision, my emotions literally trapped in my throat.

"Did you fuck him?" he asked outright.

For the life of me, I couldn't understand why he was still hung up on this. I exhaled a sharp, shaky breath as my shoulders dropped in defeat. "Malachi, I swear this will be my last time answering this. As I've told you a thousand times before, I've never slept with Ty. We didn't even kiss." With his eyes immediately softening, Malachi inched his way closer to me. "But," I said with my finger pointed up in the air, instantly halting his steps, "*if* I did, I would've been well within my rights because, as far as I knew, you were still married—"

"Listen," he said, cutting me off. "Reese will always be my friend, Paris. Always. I'm not even gon' lie to you about that. I've known her since we were kids, and as the mother of my children, I'm gon' always have love for her. But what I can promise you is that the marriage, that shit is done. I don't love her like that no more. I fucked up by not telling you the deal from the beginning, and for that, I'm sorry." He looped his arm around my waist and pulled me into him with so much authority I gasped from the slight collision of our bodies. With my hands spread against his brawny chest and our pelvises almost connected, I stared up into his eyes. "I'm sorry," he whispered again.

"Did you hurt him?" I asked, referring to Ty.

With a tight jaw, Malachi chucked up his chin and tapered his eyes into slits. Then he sucked his teeth. "Nigga's still breathing," was all he said.

Although I knew I couldn't show it, internally, I felt a major sense of relief. I hadn't seen or heard from Ty since that night, and it'd been weighing on me mentally. While I didn't want to be with him romantically, I honestly didn't know if I could live with myself if he'd been harmed.

"I've been going crazy without you," I softly admitted.

"And I been crazy over you." I snorted a laugh, shifting my eyes away. Gently, he grabbed me by the chin and forced our eyes to meet once more. "I miss yo' white ass."

"Malachi, I'm not whi—"

He abruptly covered my lips with his own, altogether nixing the sound of my whiny voice. Without warning, he buried his eager tongue inside my mouth and slowly slid his hands down to grip the plumpness of my ass. I gasped when I felt his stiff erection stabbing me in the stomach. "I swear fo' God . . ." He groaned against my lips. I'm sure my face was cherry red as I leaned forward, giggling into his chest.

"Ew, 'Chi, get a room," I heard Asha say.

I looked back to see her waltzing out of the house with a tray of deviled eggs. However, Malachi didn't pay her any mind. His lips slowly progressed to the nook of my neck, where more wet kisses were placed against my skin. Being back in Malachi's arms had me feeling as giddy as ever—light-headed to the point where it all felt like a dream. The only problem was that I knew it wasn't meant to last forever.

"Are you gonna introduce me to your friend, son?" Malachi's father suddenly asked.

I glanced up to see his tall, lanky frame gaiting toward us. With a dingy towel in his right hand and sweat stains

in the center of his cotton shirt, he smiled. He had the
same light buttery complexion as Asha, but his golden
eyes matched Malachi's to a tee.

"I'm Paris. It's nice to meet you, Mr. Montgomery," I
said, extending my hand for him to shake.

He sandwiched my hand between his own and smiled.
"Nice to finally meet you too, Paris," he said. Then he cut
his cunning eyes over at Malachi and gave a single wink.
"I see you got taste like your ol' man," he muttered.

Malachi snorted a laugh and shook his head. "Pops,
you crazy, mane."

"Welp, the fish is all done. I guess it's finally time for
us to eat," his father said, rubbing his somewhat bulging
belly.

"Paris, you and Asha come on in here. I need help
bringing out the rest of this food," Mrs. Montgomery said.

Neither of us hesitated as we followed behind her.
Inside, she filled our arms with trays of her home cooking, stacking the serving utensils on top. Malachi came
in after us, forcing the children to wash their hands. We
ended up eating out in the yard, where two picnic tables
stood under an ivy-laced pergola, providing just enough
shade from the August sun. Of course, Maevyn was sure
to sit right next to me, and when we went to say our grace,
she lightly squeezed my hand.

"How are those greens, Mae?" Mrs. Montgomery asked
her.

With her eyes closed, she licked the grease off her little
fingers, then popped them out of her mouth. "They real
good, Grandma," she said, dramatically shaking her head.
"And the fish is outta this world, Pop Pop." We all broke
out in laughter at her remarks. She was the cutest little
thing with such a big personality.

While Malachi sat next to me, checking Mekhai's fish
for bones, I didn't waste any time before digging into

my plate. Everything from the potato salad to the baked macaroni and cheese was cooked to perfection. So good that I caught myself moaning as I chewed. You see, growing up, we always had a chef prepare our meals, and since my mother was constantly dieting, the menu rarely, if ever, included soul food. Needless to say, like a child who'd gotten a hold of her first piece of candy, I sat there taking it all in. Mrs. and Mrs. Montgomery smiled as I went back for more.

"So, tell me something about yourself, li'l lady," Mr. Montgomery said.

In the midst of chomping a mouthful of food, I held up my finger for him to give me a second. "Well," I swallowed, "I'm about to start my sophomore year at A&T this month, and of course, you already know that I'm roommates with Asha," I started.

"So, what are you majoring in?" Mrs. Montgomery asked.

Great. "Um, well, I'm really not sure yet. I was thinking business, perhaps."

Mr. Montgomery nodded his head. "A business degree will take you a long way. That's smart, young lady," he said.

"You think you might want to go into business for yourself one day?" Mrs. Montgomery asked.

"Maybe." I hunched my shoulders, feeling unsure. "I mean, I love clothes and fashion, so I was thinking of owning my own boutique one day. But I'm really not sure just yet."

"Well, you're young; you've got time to decide. But I tell you one thing. There's nothing like working for yourself. If only my gym made a little more money, I wouldn't be working for the man today. Boxing is my passion, you know. It's in our blood."

"I know," I looked over at Malachi and smiled. "Malachi's shared a lot with me about your family's history in boxing. He even said he was good . . . once upon a time."

He placed his hand on my bare knee and grazed his thumb lightly across my skin. "I still am," he said. Then he looked across the table at his father. "But, Pops, I been told you to quit UPS. I got y'all."

"No offense, son, but I'm my own man. I takes care of mine. Plus, you know your momma would never stand for that."

"That's right. We get our money the *right* way. However you get yours is on you, but *we,* us in this house, want no parts of it. That's exactly what's gotten you into this mess now."

And finally, there it was. Not once since I'd walked through the door had Malachi's case been mentioned. While I was half expecting to see them all in a grief-stricken state, they seemingly appeared just the opposite. In fact, their cheery disposition nearly made me forget just how sad I'd been these past few days. From what Asha told me, Malachi was only a few weeks shy of being taken into custody. For how long, we didn't know.

"We not talking about that today," Malachi said.

"Well then, exactly *when* are we gonna talk about it?" Mrs. Montgomery asked with a weary expression on her face.

"Not. Now," he barked through clenched teeth, banging his fist on the table as he abruptly jumped to his feet. "And damn sure not in front of my kids." With a sudden glower covering his face, he snapped his fingers two times. "Mae, come on, let's go," he said, then reached over to pick up Mekhai.

"Where are you going, Malachi? I didn't mean to upset you," his mother said.

"Nah, I gotta take them back over to Reese's anyway, Ma. They got school in the morning," he told her. He was trying to calm himself.

With her lips pursed, she looked over at Maevyn and wriggled her index finger down. "Just sit back down and eat the rest of your food, baby. You ain't going nowhere," she said.

"What?" Malachi asked, his eyebrows knitting together in confusion.

"I've already told their momma I'll take them to school tomorrow. Now, just sit back down and enjoy your dinner, 'Chi."

"Nah," he muttered, shaking his head. "I'm not hungry no more."

I watched as Malachi turned around and trekked back through the grass with little Mekhai in his arms.

His father must have noticed the concern on my face because he said, "Don't worry, Paris. He'll be all right. He's been up and down like this all week."

"Up and down?" I questioned.

"Yes, honey. Sometimes, he's doing just fine, and other times, he just don't want to be bothered. Especially if someone brings up his . . ." Mrs. Montgomery's eyes quickly diverted across the table toward Maevyn, who was still chowing down on her plate. "His legal concerns," she went on to say.

"I see," I sighed, realizing how hard all of this must have been on him. "I think I'm gonna go check on him and then head on home." I stood from the table, preparing to head back for the deck.

"Are you sure?" she asked, rising from the bench. Before I could respond, she said, "Well, at least let me pack you up a plate."

"Just go on in and see about 'Chi. I'll get it for you," Asha chimed in.

I gave her a small smile and nodded my head.

When I entered the house, I didn't know where to find Malachi, but instinctively, I eased my way down the hall leading to the back. All of the doors in the corridor were open—well, all except for one. Slowly, I turned the knob, feeling nervous, like I was an intruder. As soon as the door cracked open, I peeked inside. Malachi's body appeared stretched out in the center of a king-sized bed. He was lying on his back with Mekhai already fast asleep on his chest.

"I guess all that heat out there wore little man out, huh?" I whispered.

Malachi nodded, then mouthed for me to "come here." After quietly shutting the door behind me, I tiptoed inside the bedroom. As I eased down onto the bed, he opened his arm, silently beckoning me to lie beside him.

"Are you okay?" I asked softly, peering up into his eyes as I nestled against his side.

"I will be."

"You wanna talk about it?"

He sighed and softly shook his head. "Not really."

We shared a few moments of silence before I finally said, "I'm scared, Malachi."

He angled his face toward me, squinting his hazel eyes. "Of what, mama?"

"Of losing you forever."

He tilted his head down and pressed a tender kiss into my brow. "Shawty, you ain't never gon' lose me. Never," he said.

"Well, do you know how long of a sentence they're talking?"

He heaved a low, exasperated breath. "My lawyer saying anywhere from thirty-one months to six years," he said, shrugging his shoulders. "Sometimes, I feel like my mama and n'em just don't understand. I know she wants me to be strong, but this shit has been hard as fuck on me. Not knowing how long they plan on keeping my black ass locked up and then not knowing how long I'll have to be away from my kids . . ." His voice trailed off as he rubbed Mekhai's little back with care. "And then there's you . . ."

"Me?" I asked, confused.

"I was so mad about you fucking that nigga Ty—"

"But I didn't—"

"Yeah, I know that now, but I didn't before. It's like, right when a nigga finally got everything in order, thinking shit was finna be sweet between us again, I walk in and see that fuck nigga sitting on your couch. Shawty, I didn't know what to think." He shook his head. "The only thing that kept me from pushing that nigga's wig back that night was you. I thought you were gonna call the cops on me."

"But I would never—"

"And if I'm keeping it all the way real . . ." he said, "if anybody would've asked me just two hours ago, I would've told them that I didn't fuck with yo' ass at all."

"Wow," I let out softly.

"I'm a selfish nigga, Miss Paris. Possessive over any and everything I feel is mine. And for some crazy-ass reason, from the very first time I laid eyes on you, I felt as though you belonged to me. You fucking Ty would have canceled all that shit."

"What you fail to realize is that I was yours, Malachi. You just weren't mine."

Subtly, he nodded his head. "You right, shawty . . . You right. And a nigga is man enough to admit when he's wrong. I should have told you what it was from the jump."

I sucked in a deep breath of air as unexpected tears polished my eyes. "Thank you, Malachi."

"For what?"

"For apologizing. I don't know why, but I really needed to hear you say that." He tilted his head down and kissed my forehead again, causing my eyes to close.

I stayed like that, snuggled against him and Mekhai until I eventually drifted off to sleep. By the time I woke up, the sun had been traded for the moon, and the entire house was without sound. I immediately sat up, noticing right away that Mekhai was positioned between us while Malachi lay on the other side, fast asleep. I glanced over at the nightstand, seeing the glowing numbers of the digital clock read 10:58 p.m. Hurriedly, I reached over Mekhai and gently shook Malachi's arm. He stirred in his sleep but never fully woke up, so I decided to lie back down. I realized my days with Malachi were quickly coming to an end. And while I didn't want to be disrespectful by sleeping over at the Montgomerys' home, I'd risk just about anything to be in his presence just a little while more.

Chapter 20

Franki—The Painful Truth

"Thank you so much for driving us all the way up here," my mother said, glancing over at Josh.

It was early Friday morning, and we had just crossed the bridge to Rikers Island. I had only been back in New York for two days, and we were already on our way. Neither my mother nor I had seen my father in over ten years, so our nerves were completely shot. In fact, the entire ride up here felt somber and tense. As I sat there in the backseat with an uneasy feeling in my gut, I simply stared out of the window.

"You're welcome, Mrs. Wright," he said. Then he craned his neck back and looked at me. "You ready, ma?"

Chewing on the corner of my lip, I softly nodded. "I guess so," I said, hiking my shoulders to my ears.

"Everything's gonna be just fine, baby, you'll see," my mother said with a bit of a cough. "Now, come on. The next shuttle bus is gon' be pulling up soon, and we need to go in for the first security check."

All of us, including Josh, got out of the car and walked over to the Central Visiting Building. But before I could walk in, Josh gently cupped my face in his hands and planted a soft kiss on my lips. "Just breathe, ma. You're shaking," he said, bringing his hands down to rub the sides of my arms. Although it was approaching 90 degrees outside, my limbs trembled like a cold winter's day. I was just that nervous. "You gon' be just fine, baby, a'ight?"

I nodded and pecked his lips again before walking over to join my mother at the entrance. As we waited in a single-file line, taking one small step toward the building after the other, Josh shouted out behind me. "I'ma be right here when you get back, a'ight?"

I smiled. Somehow, those simple parting words gave me just the correct dose of comfort. I was actually able to breathe as I crossed the threshold of the door. However, waiting on the other side were metal detectors and German shepherds with their tongues flapping out of their mouths. Armed officers stood nearby with scowls on their faces, eager to pat us down. Naturally, my panicky state returned. It was worse than getting through TSA when the airport was on high alert. Never in all my life had I experienced anything like it. I even had to lift up my bra just for them to inspect me for drugs and weapons that day.

Needless to say, the entire search took over an hour and concluded just before the bus came to transport us to the prison. As we rode across Rikers Island, seeing the maze of brick buildings lined with barbed wire, my anxiety spiked even more. Wiping my clammy palms down the front of my jeans, I could feel my heartbeat trapped inside my throat.

"You doing all right over there?" my mother asked, placing her hand on mine.

I nodded, but in reality, so much was going through my mind that I couldn't help but feel some kind of way. I kept wondering if he would still recognize me. I mean, hell, let's be real. It had been over a decade since my father last saw me—no pictures, no phone calls—nothing. I was scared he wouldn't know who I was.

"It's okay to be scared, Franki. I'm a little scared too," she said just before coughing into her hand.

"You still got that cough, Ma?" I asked.

"I'm all right," she assured me.

After another hour of waiting, my mother and I, along with other visitors, were finally led into a large, open room. It was nothing to write home about, just four painted cinder block walls surrounding a cold, concrete floor. Suddenly, the correctional officers instructed us to sit at individual tables while they called the inmates out one at a time. My mother and I impatiently waited while holding each other's hand. It seemed every time someone would walk through the door, I'd unconsciously hold my breath. It was a wonder I hadn't passed out, considering my father was the next to last to be called out.

"Warren," my mother shouted, jumping to her feet as her hands cupped her mouth. Other than a few flecks of silver in his hair, my father still looked the same as I'd remembered . . . six feet tall and with a caramel complexion and a thin mustache tracing his upper lip. He was shy of 40 years old and still had his strapping physique. Even in his orange jumpsuit, he looked handsome, and I could see what had kept my mother pining after all these years.

When his eyes finally landed on us, they lit up with instant recognition, and he smiled. His gaze honed in on my mother, and I watched tears suddenly pool in his eyes. Faintly, he shook his head and pressed his hands against his lips in prayer. Somehow, at that moment, I knew he was giving God thanks. Before he could fully reach us, my mother stepped forward and gently placed her shaky hands on his face.

"Warren," she whispered. A single tear slid down his cheek as he took her hand and pulled it to his lips for a kiss. Over the last ten years, she never entertained another man. Not even once. She didn't even have one that she considered a friend. And on her left hand, she wore her wedding ring that had remained fixed, faithful, and true.

Based on the few prison movies I'd seen in the past, I thought the officers would tell them not to touch, but they didn't. They let them embrace each other for what felt like forever. When they finally pulled apart, my father looked at me with a gleam of something peculiar in his eyes. *Pride.*

"Francesca," he said.

I stood up from my seat, timid as all get-out—like meeting a stranger for the first time. Unlike me, my father didn't think twice. He instantly wrapped his arms around me while mine remained immobile at my sides. My mind went completely numb as he hugged and squeezed me to the point where I felt like I could hardly breathe. When he finally released me, we all sat down at the table. My mother was all smiles while I, on the other hand, just sat there trying to untangle my thoughts.

He sucked in a deep breath before taking a deep swallow. "I first want to thank you both for coming here today," he said. "This was never a place I wanted either of you to visit me at, but as you both know, God has been speaking to me more and more these days. I finally feel the need to make things right."

Finally? Make things right?

"Tuh," I scoffed beneath my breath.

"What's wrong, Franki?" my mother asked.

I shook my head with a derisive shrug of my lips. "Nothing. Go 'head," I insisted.

After taking a deep breath, my father turned to me and looked me in the eye. "Ten, almost eleven years ago, I failed you as a father. I never told anyone, not even your mother, what I saw when I walked into the church's basement that day. Not even my own attorney knew the full story." I clenched my jaw in anger as tears began to fill the rims of my eyes. My father sucked another heap of air into his lungs before facing my mother. His shoulders were suddenly hiked, and a look of apprehension was written across his face. "Ten years ago, I caught Deacon Baisworth molesting our daughter," he revealed.

"You *what?*" my mother asked in shock, looking between us as her eyebrows wrinkled in bewilderment. Tears suddenly welled in her eyes.

My father took a deep swallow and nodded his head. "Yes. He was . . . um . . ." His voice floated off as a sudden look of anguish took over his face.

"He was what?" my mother demanded to know.

"He had his hand beneath her dress, coaxing her sexually."

Hearing the actual words come out of his mouth practically knocked the wind out of me. All of a sudden, I felt like I couldn't breathe, and my vision was now blurred from tears.

"Exactly what did he do, Francesa?" my mother asked, looking at me. I unlocked my mouth to speak, but nothing would come out. "Tell me, please," she cried.

"Do you remember when Sister Robin took all the kids down into the basement right at the beginning of service?" I asked. "And then, midway through, Deacon Baisworth would sometimes come down and help her?" My mother nodded her head as wetness continued to coat her cheeks. "He would play games with me, put together big puzzles, anything he knew would take a long time. And when Sister Robin would line up all the kids to go back upstairs, he would tell her that we would finish our game, and then we'd be right up. Well, as soon as everyone would leave, he'd sit me on his lap and play with my hair. He'd tell me just how pretty I looked while his dick poked at me from beneath." I exhaled a shaky breath and looked up at the ceiling in hopes of trapping the tears in my eyes. "And then he'd slide his hand under my skirt and stick his finger in me. Ask me if the shit felt good." I shook my head, snorting a laugh of disgust. "Sometimes, he'd make me touch him and—"

"Enough!" my mother shouted. "That's enough." She slapped her hands over her face and began to bawl her eyes out. While my father placed his hand on her trembling shoulder, trying to comfort her, I just sat there and watched. At that moment, my body felt frozen, and my mind seemed to drift off into a daze. I didn't exactly know how to feel. This was the second time I'd ever told that story. The first time, I relayed it to Josh.

"When I saw him with her down in the church basement that day, I just . . . I snapped," my father said.

"Why didn't you say anything, Warren?" she asked him. Then she looked at me with her eyes softening sympathetically. "You could have told me, baby. It wasn't your fault."

"I was ashamed," I admitted. My chin hiked as I flicked a falling tear from my eye. "Daddy kept it a secret, so . . . I thought I had to too."

"And I was wrong," my father said, his voice loaded with pain. "I was wrong for not telling the police exactly what I saw that day. And for not telling them why I did what I did. If I had, maybe I wouldn't be sitting here today." My father pleaded guilty to a voluntary manslaughter charge and was sentenced to fifteen years in prison. He blew out his breath and shook his head. "But more importantly, I was wrong for not getting you the help I knew you would so desperately need, Francesca. Although we haven't been in contact, I still feel you." He placed his hand over his chest as tears streamed from his eyes. "I feel when you're in pain. Every time you've felt ashamed or unworthy, unloved . . . I swear I've felt it all. That's just how connected we are."

"I've stopped believing," I whispered guiltily, my head dropping in disgrace. "I've stopped praying, and . . . I've sinned."

My father placed his hand on top of mine. "*In Him we have redemption, Franki, through His blood, the forgiveness of our trespasses, according to the riches of His grace,*" he whispered.

I nodded, instantly recognizing that same Bible verse that Josh would sometimes recite to me. It reminded me that any bad situation could be turned around, and any sin could be forgiven. Over the next twenty minutes or so, my mother told my father how I was attending the University of NC at A&T in Greensboro, North Carolina. She told him of my plans to be a doctor, and he told me he was proud. She even mentioned that I had a boyfriend named Josh.

Before the visit finally ended, we all bowed our heads and prayed together as a family—something we hadn't done in years. And just before he walked back into the prison, he told my mother that he wanted her to start visiting him. He even said that he would be sending us both letters. That day, I went into the prison feeling apprehensive, confused, and even angry. But by the time we left, I only felt relieved.

On the drive back, I ended up sitting in the front. I filled Josh in on the whole visit while my mother sat quietly in the back. It seemed the roles had been reversed, and she was now the one trapped in an emotional head-space. When we finally returned home, my mother asked if I would walk her upstairs. Since I was staying the week with Josh, I turned and told him that I'd be right back down.

When we walked into the apartment, my mother dropped her purse on the coffee table and sank on the couch. She let her head fall back as she closed her eyes. I could tell that she was tired.

"All right, Ma, you good? 'Cause I'ma head out," I told her, standing by the door.

Her eyes popped open, and she sat upright in her seat. "Wait just one minute," she said. Then she patted the sofa cushion next to her. "Come sit for a minute, baby. I won't keep Josh out there too long."

I sat beside her as she'd asked and gave her my undivided attention. I assumed she wanted to talk further about me being molested as a child, so I took a deep breath to prepare myself. "So, what's up?" I asked.

"I didn't want to tell you in front of your father but, baby, I'm . . . I'm sick." She placed her hand on my leg and looked at me remorsefully.

"Sick?"

She released a shaky breath and nodded her head. "I have lung cancer, Franki."

"Cancer?" I breathed, feeling like the wind just got knocked out of me. "Are you sure? You don't even smoke." I looked into her eyes, noticing the dark circles around them for the first time since I'd returned home this week. My eyes wandered to her frame, which had suddenly seemed frail.

She gently patted my leg to calm me down. "I don't smoke, but I've been around it for years, Franki. Remember Mrs. Butler's house on Twenty-Third and Mr. and Mrs. Parker's place over there on Shore Road?" she said, reminding me of the houses she used to clean. "They all smoked cigarettes. And to answer your question, yes, this is very real. I've already been to the doctors, who confirmed it."

"So, what now? You gon' leave me too?" I shot up to my feet, feeling a mixture of both hurt and anger at the possible outcomes. I thought I was through with crying for the day, but the tears had suddenly returned.

"It's already progressed to stage three. I'll start chemo next week, and then I'll have to go in for surgery," she said.

"Mommy," I let out in a low whimper, still in a state of disbelief. For the life of me, I couldn't understand how this could be happening to *my* mother, of all people. She was the strongest person I knew.

"Just let me tell your father when the time is right. We just put our family back together today, and I didn't want this news to have it fall apart. He doesn't need to be in there worried about me too." I dropped back down onto the couch and put my arms around her as I sobbed. She patted me on the arm. "Mommy's gonna be just fine, Franki. God's got me, baby," she promised.

By the time I got back into Josh's truck, the tears on my face had dried, but I knew my eyes were still puffy and red. "What's wrong, ma? What happened?" he asked, noticing my demeanor right away.

I wasn't ready to talk about it, so I folded my arms across my chest and shook my head. "Nothing," I murmured.

Surprisingly, Josh didn't push the issue. We drove back to his place in silence while I scrolled through my phone, checking Facebook notifications and my Instagram feed. When I saw that Paris had posted a picture of her and Malachi, I couldn't help but crack a half smile. She was sitting on his lap, smiling and posing for the photo while he had his long tongue stuck out, licking her cheek. She looked happy.

When we finally got back to Josh's loft, I left him standing in the foyer. Although we hadn't eaten dinner, I was too depressed to do anything besides lie down and go to sleep. I plodded up to his room, and just as I began kicking off my shoes, I heard his footsteps coming up the stairs.

"Franki," he said.

I lifted my shirt over my head just before craning my neck around to look at him. He came up, wrapping his arms around me from behind, and kissed the top of my shoulder.

"I think I've been patient enough, ma. Tell me what's wrong," he said.

I shook my head, lying once again. "It's nothing," I whispered, shimming out of my pants.

"Stop telling me it's nothing. You insulting my intelligence," he said. When he spun me around to face him, I could barely look him in the eye. Our connection was so deep that I knew he'd instantly recognize the sadness in them. "You know you can tell me anything, right?"

"I know," I nodded.

He put his index finger beneath my chin and forced our eyes to meet. "Then if you know, tell me what's wrong. I can see it in your eyes."

Silence lingered between us for a few seconds before the words finally rushed from my lips. "My mother has fucking cancer, Josh." The next thing I knew, tears filled my eyes, and my knees grew weak. It seems Josh lifted me in his arms just in the nick of time. "I can't lose her too, Josh," I cried into his chest.

"You won't ever lose her, baby. Ever," he said. "Don't say that, ma." He carried me over to the unmade bed and gently laid me down. With tears sliding from the corners of my eyes down into my curly hair, I watched as he crawled between my legs. He hovered over me and thumbed away my tears. "Shh, don't cry, baby. Everything's going to be okay."

"I can't lose her too, Josh. I just can't. I've already lost my daddy to prison. And I've been mentally preparing myself to lose you too—"

"Lose me?" he asked with his eyebrows drawn together. "I know you said we'd still be together when you go off to law school next year, but I'm just being real with myself. Long-distance relationships don't work, Josh," I told him.

Sure, I had Paris and Hope as my friends, but the only people on this earth I couldn't live without were my mother and now Josh. They were the ones that kept my heart constantly beating.

Just when I thought Josh would try to reassure me with words like he always did, he leaned down and kissed my lips. And it wasn't his usual, sweet little peck, either. It was urgent and unyielding. Resolute with infinite purpose. As he sucked on my lips and tongue, I felt his strong hands gently caress my hips. Everything about his body lying on top of mine at that moment felt different. Josh's body was expressing itself to me like never before—like he was making a statement. There was more desire, more power, and more love.

My heart fluttered inside my chest when his lips traveled to the crook of my neck, peppering it with more kisses. His palms slowly guided themselves up my back, unsnapping my bra with ease. Within seconds, he peeled it off and pitched it across the floor. He flickered his tongue across my hardened nipple before taking it entirely into his mouth.

"Oh," I moaned.

When he began to suckle my breasts, alternating from left to right, I arched my back, presenting more of myself to him. A rush of heat and moisture instantly spread throughout my lower half. He kissed that tender place in the center of my breasts before slithering his tongue down my abdomen. Suddenly, I felt his fingertips prying beneath the waistband of my panties, and before I knew what was happening, he had worked them down over my hips. Without warning, Josh's head dipped between my thighs, causing me to hold my breath. When the tip of his wet tongue contacted my pussy, I closed my eyes.

"Josh," I cried out in a warning, tears trickling from my eyes.

"Ssh. Let me take care of you, ma."

He scooped my legs over his shoulders and commenced teasing my clit, licking, kissing, and sucking me every which way until I was trembling and panting beneath him. My sweaty hands gripped the sheets as I squeezed, holding on to my orgasm that was right on the brink. That's when I felt not one but two of his fingers dip inside of me—pushing and pulling out of my core as his mouth fixedly kept at work.

"Mmm, you taste so good, baby," he muttered. He flicked his tongue over my clit once more, and I fucking lost it. *Shit.* My body tightened around his fingers as I pushed the back of his head farther into me.

"Oh, Josh," I wailed. Tingly fireworks erupted from the very pit of my belly and swelled throughout my groin. My body quaked feverishly, releasing every emotion I had pent up inside—perhaps even a little more.

Josh unapologetically licked his fingers clean as if he'd just devoured the best meal of his life. Then he rose to his knees and removed his shirt from over his head. My eyes immediately drank in his butterscotch skin that cascaded over one lean muscle after the other. It may not have been tatted up with ink, but Josh's body was definitely a work of art. His chest and abs were carved to utter perfection like a true Olympian. When he went to unbutton his shorts, my eyes naturally shifted down toward his pelvis. The mere sight of his erection jutting out—hard, long, and strong, made my entire body ache even more.

He hovered over me and whispered in my ear. "You still on the pill?"

I nodded as more tears slipped from my eyes. "Are you sure you wanna do this, Josh?" I asked. "Because I don't want you to do it out of pity or because—"

Josh didn't respond with words. Instead, he reached down between us and slid the head of his muscle between my slippery folds. I gasped, then let out a low, sensual moan. As his dick sat eagerly at my entrance, torturing me in the most erotic sense, he peered down into my eyes.

"You don't ever have to worry about being in this world all alone, ma, 'cause you got *me*. All of me—mind, body, and soul. Near or far, no matter how many miles apart, my heart's gon' be with you forever."

And with one single thrust of his hips, Josh rocked into me, filling every single inch of my core. "Oh God," I cried, my mouth dropping open from pleasure.

I watched as his long eyelashes fluttered closed, and he bit down on his bottom lip. "Shit," he hissed with a subtle shake of his head. "You feel so perfect, baby. Just like I knew you would." As his body dove in and out of mine, he kissed my lips and thumbed away the remainder of my tears.

"I love you so much," I whimpered. I'd had numerous sex partners in the past—probably more than most girls my age could count but never had I experienced pleasure like this before. Josh was worshiping my body with his own. Partaking in communion with me laid out before him as the holy table. And I surrendered . . . to *everything*. It was passion, purification . . . It was true love.

"I love you too, ma." He continued snaking his hips, plunging in and out of me that night until my cries eventually echoed off the walls.

Chapter 21

Hope—Look at Me

While everyone was out enjoying the first party of the school year, I was thirty-eight weeks pregnant and stuck in the house. Meeko and I had just moved into our new apartment, and it felt like we were finally settled in. Furniture was in every room, and our belongings had all been unpacked. Even the baby's room was complete with a white crib and blue elephant comforter set, courtesy of Deddy. He ended up buying the baby so much stuff that we didn't even need to have a baby shower.

Little by little, he had definitely started to come around. He still wasn't happy about my decision to stay in North Carolina, but he made it clear that no matter what, he would be there for me and my child. And while that brought me some sense of comfort, I still felt alone. At this point, Meeko and I were more roommates than anything else. We slept in separate bedrooms, and the affection between us was minimal at best. When he'd see me uncomfortable or wincing in pain, he'd massage my lower back. He'd occasionally rubbed my swollen feet while I vegged out on the couch. But beyond that, there was nothing—no hugging or kissing, and definitely no sex. I'd been horny my entire pregnancy but had been too scared to do anything about it.

Hmm . . . I thought to myself as I lay back on the couch, contemplating whether I should call and ask him to come home early. I had already stuffed my face for the night, and the only thing occupying my time was the marathon of *Living Single* flickering on the TV screen. Meeko had gone to the Clubhouse with his friends tonight, and although I wasn't big on partying, I couldn't lie and say I wasn't jealous.

Finally, I had gotten over the bet Meeko made with his friends. I'd even gotten over the fact that he was working for Malachi after he assured me that it was only a temporary thing and that it wasn't anything illegal. And though I still wasn't fully convinced, honestly, what could I do? At this point, I was just hoping we could move on. Our baby would be coming any day now, and I'd be lying if I said I wasn't ready for us to be a family. Over the past few months, he'd been swearing that he'd take care of me no matter what, and in *my* mind, that meant my heart too. I was ready for him to make good on his promises. No matter how often I tried convincing myself otherwise, I was still in love with Meeko Taylor.

With a slight strain on my lower back, I lifted myself off the couch and wobbled to my bedroom. It wasn't anything to write home about—just a twelve-by-twelve-foot space with a cherrywood poster bed and dresser. The lavender comforter set with matching curtains was the beginning and end of my décor it seemed. I was just too tired to do anything more to my room than that.

After sifting through my top drawer, I finally located the black nightie Franki bought me a couple of months ago. It was just after Meeko started coming back around again—taking me to my doctor's appointments and bringing me food. It was then that she boldly predicted we'd get back together.

***

"What, you don't like it?" she asked, holding the black nightie up to her chest.

I shrugged. "It's not that. It's just I've never worn lingerie before. Besides, Meeko and I aren't even together anymore."

She sucked her teeth and gave a dismissive wave of her hand. "But y'all still love each other. I peep that shit every time he comes over here, bringing you all kinds of food late at night."

I laughed. "Well, I am pregnant with his baby, Franki. Isn't that what he's supposed to do?"

"If he ain't your man . . . not really. Well, at least where I come from. Shit, you'd be lucky if his ass is in the delivery room."

"Wow," I murmured.

"So, you gon' try this on or not?" she asked with the nightie in her hand.

I shook my head and scrunched up my nose. "For what? Meeko and I aren't gonna have sex. And I'm definitely not sleeping with anyone else." A crafty little smile eased across her lips. "What?" I asked.

"Look, now that you're sexually experienced, I don't have to sugarcoat shit, right?" Something told me not to, but I nodded my head anyway. "I heard that pregnant women stay horny all the time, and their pussies stay wet. Is that true?" she asked.

"Oh my God, Franki," I gasped before covering my face with my hands.

"What?" she laughed. "Don't get all shy now, ma. You wasn't shy when you was popping that pussy," she teased. "But nah, for real. Are you hornier now than you were before?"

Knowing that she wasn't going to let up, I released a deep sigh. "I guess."

"You guess?" She looked at me, confused.

"Well . . . Yes. I-I do have urges. More so now than before," I admitted.

She smiled. "I knew it, yo. I knew it," she practically cheered. "And Meeko ain't tried to fuck yet?"

I don't know if it was her uncouthness or that she was right about that fact, but I rolled my eyes. "No. He hasn't tried to have sex with me," I disclosed.

"But you want to?" she asked, a look of excitement written on her face.

I shrugged. "I mean . . ."

"Here," she said, tossing me the lingerie. "Just put this on before he comes over one night, and that's all you have to do. You won't have to ask for the dick or nothing."

"I'm not doing that," I scoffed, feigning being appalled.

"Hey," she said, holding up both her hands like she'd surrendered. "Suit yourself. I mean, you can always just keep playing with yourself in the shower."

My mouth dropped as she backed out of my room, that cheesy little smile still on her face as she spun around and walked out the door.

I snickered to myself at the memory. After taking the nightie out of the drawer, I went to hop in the shower. I shaved my legs and *down there* as best I could without hurting myself. Once I got out, I lathered my legs with wild berry-scented lotion and let my hair down from its bun. My mane was still partially straightened, and from all the prenatal vitamins I'd been taking over the months, it now hung past my back. My bangs had grown so long they reached my chin and could no longer be considered bangs.

The lingerie Franki had given me was a see-through, baby doll-style nightie that opened in the front. After slipping it on, I added Carmex to my lips and looked myself over in the mirror. Sure, my face was chubby, and my nose had spread, but I didn't think I looked half bad. Even with the dark line going down the center of my beach ball of a belly, I still felt good. I went back into the living room and grabbed my cell phone off the couch. When I dialed him, he answered on the second ring.

I could barely hear him over the music, so I knew he was inside the club. "Shorty, what's wrong? You a'ight?" Meeko asked right away.

Just as I was about to respond, I heard a woman's voice. "Meeko, come on," she whined.

"Aye, gimme a minute," he said.

Then I heard another feminine voice cut in, sounding much different than the first. "He'll come find us, Midge. Now, come on."

That's when I realized he was with *her*. My heart dropped to the pit of my belly, and sadness quickly welled in my throat. I couldn't speak. I hung up and rushed back to my bedroom, feeling downright distraught.

With my heart and love for him aside, I just couldn't understand how Meeko still had time to see Midge. He had football practice five out of seven days a week. He even worked a job that had him gone throughout the wee hours of most nights, and then there was me. No, I hadn't been very demanding of his time, but before we moved into the apartment, Meeko checked in on me two, sometimes three times a day. How on earth did he still have time for *Midge*?

While my heart was slowly breaking and my mind was racing out of control, I flooded my pillow with tears in the dark. Then about an hour or so later, the light suddenly flickered on. I didn't even bother lifting my face because

I knew it was Meeko. I instantly recognized his heavenly vanilla-cedar wood scent.

"Hope." I could hear the panic in his voice before the bed unexpectedly dipped down beside me. Then I felt his hand gently splayed across my back. "Shorty, what's wrong? Is everything all right?" he asked.

I finally turned and looked at him, not caring about red or puffy eyes. "I'm fine," I said.

"Nah, no, you not. You hurt? Is it the baby?" His eyes traveled down the length of my body, inspecting me. I guess he thought my pain was the type that could be seen. But little did he realize my affliction was the kind that could only be felt. It was my heart. "Do I need to call you an ambulance?" he asked.

I sat up in the bed and shook my head. "No. The baby's fine, Meeko. You really didn't have to stop your fun just to come and check on me."

Meeko's eyes slowly wandered down my body again, but this time much slower. For a brief moment, I watched his eyebrows wrinkle as if he were confused. But then his eyes went wild, widening in anger. When he abruptly jumped to his feet, I clutched my chest—alarmed.

"Shorty, you had some nigga in my house?" he questioned, clenching his teeth as his fist balled at his sides.

"What? No."

"Then why the fuck you got that on?" he spat, pointer finger wagging up and down at my lingerie. "You out fucking another nigga with my baby inside you?"

The accusation in itself caused fresh tears to surge in my eyes. "I'm not having sex with anyone, Meeko. I wore this for *you*," I cried.

His eyes immediately softened, and his mouth slightly parted from shock. "Y-you wore this for me?" He stammered over his words.

I averted my eyes and shrugged my shoulders. "Just forget it. I'm embarrassed enough as it is."

Meeko sighed deeply before dragging his hand down over his face. "My bad, shorty. I should've never came at you like that." He came over and reclaimed his seat on the edge of the bed before looking me in the eye. Hesitantly, he reached over to my chest and took the ends of my hair between his fingers. "You look beautiful, Hope. Always do."

I don't know if it was his closeness or how he gazed into my eyes, but my heart began beating faster inside my chest. I swallowed hard and looked away. "Thank you," I said just above a whisper.

Softly, he gripped my chin and turned my face toward him. When our eyes locked, I felt my breath turn ragged, my chest heaving up and down. Slowly, he leaned into me with his eyes open wide. Just when my eyes dropped to his beautiful mouth that was faintly parted, he came in and sucked on my bottom lip. I closed my eyes, enjoying the feel of his lips on me for what had to be the first time in months. Before I knew it, my body was heated all over, flamed in stifled passion, from the top of my head to the very soles of my feet. Although I was still nervous, I boldly grabbed the sides of his face and slipped my tongue into his mouth. As we deepened our kiss, he crawled between my trembling thighs, laying me back on the bed.

"What are we doing?" he whispered between kisses.

I kissed his lips again and said, "You're making me feel good."

"Is it safe for the baby?"

My eyes popped open wide at that. "Yes, of course. Why wouldn't it be?" I sat up on my elbows, looking at him as he hovered over me. He pulled back with a frustrated look and sat down on the bed. "You don't want to? Is it because of *her?*" I asked, letting my insecurities show.

His forehead wrinkled at the speculation. "What? Because of who?" he asked.

"Midge. You were with her tonight."

His eyes expanded in revelation. "Midge ain't my girl if that's what you're thinking," he said.

"Well, if she's not your girl, then who is she?"

"Like I told you before, she's just a friend."

"A friend you've had sex with?"

An awkward silence lingered between us as I held my breath, waiting for an answer.

Then finally, he said, "I don't know where all this is coming from, but me and you ain't been together for quite awhile."

It wasn't what he said but rather what he *didn't* say. His omission was like razor blades to my wrists, a dagger straight to the center of my heart. I was beyond crushed. "Then why am I here?" I croaked, feeling a warm tear trickle down my cheek.

Meeko exhaled a breath before scooting closer to me in the bed. "Because—"

"Because of the *baby*?"

Deep in thought, he paused for a beat, and I could see his mind at work. Then finally, he shook his head. "No, it's not because of the baby," he admitted. "It's because no matter how fucked up shit's been between us, I just can't seem to live without yo' ass. And believe me, a nigga has really tried." He released a faint snort of laughter. "It's like I feel ten times better when I'm around you than I do when we're apart, no matter the circumstance. Shorty, real talk. I'm not even the same person without you in my life. You make me better. And as far as the baby . . ." he said, touching my stomach. "The baby just gave me hope."

"Hope for what?"

"That you'll let me love you again."

"Meek—"

"I'm sorry for the bet, Hope. I wish I could go back in time and change all the fucked-up shit I did, but I can't."

"I know." I nodded softly. "I'm sorry too. I should have told you about the baby."

He shook his head. "Nah, that's on me."

"C-can we please try ag—"

Before I could even ask, Meeko hurriedly covered my mouth with his own. He clutched my arms, holding me steady, just as my body melted into him. Once again, desire had taken over me, sending heated ripples of passion throughout my entire body. When his strong hand journeyed up to the front of my throat, a desire-filled moan rose from the bottom of my lungs. I reached down between us and massaged the firm bulge that tented his sweatpants. Although it was low, he let out an appreciative groan that made me feel sexy. He kissed me on the chin, then sucked on my neck before traveling down to my breasts. Above the sheer fabric, he gently grazed each of my nipples with his teeth, causing me to gasp and shudder all at once. As his mouth roved farther south, placing sweet kisses all over my hardened belly, goose pimples covered my skin.

"I love you, I love you," he whispered repeatedly. I wasn't sure if the sentiment was meant for me or our baby, but either way, it didn't matter. My once hollow heart somehow now felt full.

My eyes fluttered open when he began peeling off my elastic, stringlike thongs.

"Wait," I panicked. Peering down at him over my belly as he nestled amid my dark chocolate thighs. It seemed my pregnancy hormones, accompanied by Meeko's touch, had me a tad gooier down there than usual. Honestly, I was embarrassed.

However, Meeko kept going. He slid my wet panties to the sides and yanked my hips down farther to meet his face. "Shorty, you wet as fuck for me, huh?" When he tongue kissed me *down there,* I could hear the sloshiness of my own sex. I covered my face with my hands.

He reached up and batted my hands away. "Look at me," he demanded.

I propped myself up on my elbows and did as he'd asked. I watched as he flicked his tongue over my sensitive bud, causing me to shiver and moan.

"Oh God," I cried, closing my eyes.

"Open ya eyes, shorty. Look at me," he said.

I opened my eyes and stared down at him once more, only this time, he was staring right back at me, watching me intently as the tip of his tongue led a trail of pleasure all the way down my slit.

"*Ssss,*" I hissed. My muscles tightened just as I clutched the sheets between my fists. "Meeko," I moaned, panting.

Suddenly, his tongue stiffened and dug into me deeper. Plunging in and out of me with such deliberate acts, reminiscent of making love. When I felt his teeth scarcely scrape my clitoris, then on my outer lips, I exploded. Shaking in such a seizurelike frenzy, I lay there, unsure if I could survive another orgasm that powerful.

While my body came down from its high, Meeko kissed the innermost parts of my thighs. I could hear him whispering, *"I love you"* again, but I knew it was specifically meant for me this time. After quickly removing his clothes and cutting off the lights, he spooned me beneath the covers. His hands found my swollen breasts as his hard muscle speared into me ever so gently from behind.

"Shorty, I missed you so fucking much," he whispered in my ear. The warmth of his sweet breath caressed me.

"I missed you too, Meek. Ooh God," I moaned.

His body pumped into mine until another unexpected orgasm ripped through my body like a cyclone. I trembled uncontrollably as words from a foreign language spilled from my lips.

After Meeko released inside of me, I drifted off to sleep in his arms. However, we weren't asleep for very long. His cell phone vibrating on my nightstand woke me from my slumber. I glanced at the glowing screen, seeing Midge's name light up in the dark.

"Meek," I said, nudging him with my elbow. "Meeko, it's your phone."

"Huh?" he said groggily.

"Someone's calling your phone."

He reached over me, grabbed his cell, and turned it off. I don't know why that bothered me, but before I knew it, I sat up in the bed and leaned over to cut on the lamp.

Meeko sucked his teeth and squinted his eyes from the light. "Yo, what you doing, shorty? What's wrong?" he asked.

I gestured toward his cell phone. "You need to tell her, Meeko, because I don't want to play any more games. I no longer want to be hurt. Tell her that you and her . . . whatever it is, whatever it *was*, is now over."

Still in a daze, he stretched his eyes a few more times before running his hand over his face. He was still tired and disoriented, but honestly, I didn't care. I wanted the small problem resolved before it became a bigger issue. After handing him his phone, I got up from the bed, leaving the evidence of our lovemaking behind, smeared on the sheets. As I walked out into the hall to use the bathroom, I stopped just beyond the door.

"Shorty, wassup? You called?" I heard him say.

I couldn't make out her response, but he said, "Nah, shorty, I'm not coming back out tonight. I'm laying up with my baby's mom." Then he cleared his throat. "I mean, my girl." After a few beats, he let out a deep sigh. "I don't know what to tell you, Midge. We're back together." He paused and let out an audible snort through his nose. "But you mad cool, yo. For real, I wish you the best."

She must have hung up on him at that point because he chuckled and then muttered, "Stupid broad."

When I heard him rise from the bed, I waddled faster than a duck being chased by a fox. Once inside the bathroom, I turned on the light and softly closed the door. As I sat on the toilet, I heard him knock on the other side. "Shorty, I already know you was eavesdropping," he chuckled. "You can come out now."

I urinated in the toilet, but when I went to wipe myself, fluid continued to pour out of me like a broken pipe. "Meeko!" I screamed, standing to my feet.

He burst through the door with a panic-stricken face. His eyes blossomed in terror. "What's wrong? What happened?" he asked, looking me up and down. Then finally, he noticed the small puddle on the floor.

"I think it's time, Meek. My water just broke."

Chapter 22

Asha—Nina from Holland Hall

I held tight to Quick's arm as we walked toward Laurel Street. It seemed the sun was fully out just in time for Homecoming as folks tailgated right before the game. We were playing Howard University, so the crowd was thick. As we trekked through the leaf-lined streets, I could smell smoked barbecue permeating the crisp air. The sound of Greeks strolling and the marching band played off in the distance.

I had to admit that it felt good finally to be living carefree. To not be worried about makeup, flashy jewelry, and name brands for once. I wore a navy blue and gold Aggie tee shirt with a simple pair of light blue jeans. Sheltering my feet were the Air Max Malachi had bought for me just last summer. I have only worn them twice. And since I'd already bought my car, a black 2016 Acura RDX, I splurged a little on my hair. I had a fresh set of goddess locs draping down my back with gold hoops dangling from my ears.

The streets were packed with people, young and old. Folks had come from not just our university but from HBCUs nationwide. Between the tailgating, the parties, and the concerts, A&T's Homecoming had always been the place to be, at least as far back as I can remember.

I waved to a few people I knew along the way until I eventually laid eyes on Mama. She sat in an Aggie Pride pop-up chair, sipping from a beer bottle. Her head bobbed as her fingers snapped to one of many beats. My daddy and Malachi were just a yard behind her, manning the grill. And then there was Paris. Fully suited in Aggie pride herself, face paint and all, as she played football with Maevyn in the street. Her nails were freshly manicured, and her ponytail had that particular white-girl swing.

"Hey-hey, y'all," I said, approaching everyone with a smile.

"Hey, baby. Who is this?" Mama asked. A crafty smile was on her lips as she raked her eyes over Quick.

"Quincy," Quick said, extending his hand for my mother to shake.

Her cheeks hiked, broadening her smile as she allowed him to take her hand. "Nice to meet you, Quincy. And you are?" Her wily eyes danced back and forth between us as her eyebrows bounced up and down.

"Ma—"

"I'm her boyfriend," Quick said, speaking over me. My jaw dropped as I cut my eyes toward him. My mind was in a complete state of shock. Sure, Quick and I had been seeing each other for a couple of months now, but never had he referred to me as his girl. Hell, we hadn't even had sex yet, which was something I'd never experienced before. My eyes ballooned as he peered down at me with a lazy grin.

"Relax, Ash. Close your mouth," he teased. I could feel my cheeks heat as I blushed.

"Well, it's nice to meet you finally, Quincy. You fight down there at the gym, right?"

"Yes, ma'am. I've been training under Coach since I was knee-high," he said, gesturing with his hand.

"Auntie Asha," Maevyn screamed. She scurried over and wrapped her arms around my legs.

"What are you doing out here, li'l bit?" I asked, bending down to kiss the top of her head. "And where's Mekhai?"

"Mekhai stayed at home with Momma. But me and Miss Paris was playing football. You wanna play?"

I looked up and saw Paris standing right in front of me. "Oh no. Not Miss Bougie Paris? I know she ain't out here throwing no football around," I joked.

"Well, I tried to teach her some cheers, but she totally got bored." Paris shrugged her shoulders before leaning in to hug me.

She and Malachi had been inseparable since my mother invited her for Sunday dinner. If she wasn't at Mama and Daddy's house, he would be at ours. She'd even thanked me for trying to talk some sense into Malachi that day at the gym. Apparently, he'd told her what I said about her and Ty.

"And I know it wasn't nobody but you who put these girly-ass ribbons in her hair," I told her, sliding the silky blue and gold ribbons in Maevyn's hair between my fingers.

Paris giggled, shrugging her shoulders once more. "Well, she likes them."

From the corner of my eye, I saw Malachi slowly approaching us. Light beads of sweat sprinkled his face as he squinted his hazel eyes from the sun. He wore a white undershirt stained from food and sweat, and a dingy white towel hung out of the pocket of his jeans. He smelled like charcoal as he came up behind Paris, snaking his arms around her waist.

She shrieked out in surprise as he kissed her lovingly on the neck. Never had I witnessed my brother being so in *love and* affectionate—not even with Reese. And the fact that Paris was standing there with all thirty-two teeth on display as he melded his smoky, sweat-covered body on to hers spoke volumes too. She was completely gone over this fool. His final court date was scheduled for next week, and it seemed they were making every single day they had left together count.

"What up, mane?" Malachi said, slapping hands with Quick. "Where y'all parked at?"

"Over there on Boyd Street," Quick said, pointing his thumb back in that direction. "Traffic's crazy out there."

"Yeah, we parked over there too, but we arrived a few hours ago. Had to get this food burning on the grill," Malachi said. "Y'all hungry, though? Y'all tryin'a eat? 'Cause the food's almost done." He glanced back over his shoulder and hollered out to Daddy. "Aye, yo, Pops. How much longer on the food, mane?"

My daddy held up his hand, indicating we had another five minutes.

"Y'all ain't got a hot dog or nothing?" Quick asked, rubbing his belly. "I'm starving, bruh."

"I got you. Come on."

While Malachi and Quick went over to the grill, Maevyn pulled Paris back into the street to play ball.

"You look good, you know that?" my mother said as I flopped into the seat next to her.

"I thought I always look good?"

"Well, you know what I mean. You look happy. Healthy," she said. "I'm glad you're finally getting your life together."

"Did I tell you that I finally decided on a major?" I asked excitedly.

"No. What is it?"

"Family and Consumer Sciences with a concentration in Fashion Merchandising and Design."

"Okayyy, good. Now, exactly what is that?"

"I want to be a high-end fashion retail buyer. You know, the one who decides what kind of clothes, shoes, and jewelry go into the stores? I would get to select everything the store stocks."

She shrugged her lips and smiled. "I can see you doing that. You're smart. You can do anything you want."

I rolled my eyes and laughed. "You sound just like Quick."

"Well then, I like him already."

Just when I turned to look at him, someone caught my eye. "Hope," I shrieked, jumping up from my chair. Paris was already flying past me.

"Oh my God, he's so cute," Paris cooed.

We both stood there admiring baby Matthew strapped to Hope's chest. He had this deep chocolate skin with the silkiest head of black hair I'd ever seen. He wasn't even two months old, but already, he looked just like Meeko. Their full brown lips and dark, low-set eyes were almost identical. The thing that resembled Hope was the deep set of dimples in his cheeks.

"Heyy," Hope sang. "Y'all remember Deddy?" I knew she had issues with her dad in the past, so I was surprised to see him standing behind her.

"Hi." Paris and I both waved.

"How are you young ladies today?"

"Fine," Paris said.

"You taking him to the game with you?" I asked, pointing at baby Matthew as my regard shifted back to Hope.

She gave me a deadpan expression. "Now, you already know. Meeko would have a fit. The temperature is supposed to drop to 38 degrees tonight. Plus, with all that noise and craziness in the stadium, it's not safe. Certainly not a place for a 7-week-old baby. Deddy's gonna take him back to Aunt Marlene's, and I'll pick him up after the game."

"Hi, I'm Asha's mother, Iris," my mother said, butting in. She wedged between Paris and me while extending her hand for Hope's father to shake.

"Nice to meet you. I'm Ron."

"He's so beautiful," my mother said, gazing down at the baby.

"Thank you," both Hope and her father said at the same time.

"Deddy," Hope squealed. We all laughed at how cute they were, both claiming the baby as their own. They had come a long way since this summer, and I was happy for them. This had been his third time coming back from Texas to see Hope and the baby.

"So, how long are you here for?" my mother asked Hope's father.

"I'll be here for the next few days. Been here since Monday," he said.

"Nice. I know exactly how it feels to spend quality time with your grands."

"Iris," Daddy shouted from the grill. "Get over here and stop running yo' flap."

Mama pursed her lips and rolled her eyes right before excusing herself. I knew, just like she did, that Daddy was just jealous because he saw her talking to another man. After we ate and passed baby Matthew around, we sat back and watched the Greeks step along the street. Pink and green, black and gold, red and white, even purple with spots of blue flashed before us, each marching to their own beat, hooting their own unique call. Paris's eyes gleamed wide as she watched in awe with Maevyn sitting on her lap.

Before the sky could turn dark, Mr. Ron packed up the baby and took him home. While we headed to the football game, Mama and Daddy stayed back and cleaned up the grill. We ended up beating the Bison 30–16 that night. Meeko scored three touchdowns for 120 yards. Hope screamed and cheered so loud that by the end of the game, I knew her throat had to be raw. And when everything was finally over, Quick took my hand and led me back down a litter-filled Laurel Street. The moon's light was already flourishing in the sky, and a nippy breeze had begun gusting through the air.

"They're having a party over there at the frat house. You wanna head over to pregame for the club?" I asked as we settled into his car with the heat turned all the way up.

"A'ight. Cool with me," he said. He pushed back in his seat and drove off with one hand on the wheel.

The traffic surrounding the stadium was still crazy, so it took almost thirty minutes just for us to get a few miles down the street. As we sat in a standstill, stuck between the bumpers of two cars, I looked over at him and smiled.

"I meant to ask you, what was all that girlfriend talk from earlier about?"

"You don't wanna be my girlfriend, Asha?" he smirked.

"Of course. I didn't say that I—"

"Well then, stop asking so many questions and kiss your man." We both leaned over the console, meeting halfway before our lips finally touched. Almost instantly, I could feel the butterflies brewing inside me as he greedily sucked on my lips and tongue. I guess our heated kiss lasted just a second too long because the guy behind us eventually blew his horn.

The rest of the way to the frat house, we held hands and talked like we'd been best friends for years. He told me about his mother being in and out of rehab and about his absent father, who his siblings had never met. I'd only met his sister and brother once, but he told me that he really wanted me to get to know them. He said we'd definitely be spending more time together. Although the thought was short-lived, fleeting almost, I couldn't help but think that maybe, *just maybe,* I was falling in love.

I'd never experienced this with Mark, or any other guy, for that matter. Speaking of Mark, I hadn't seen or heard from him in over six months, and ever since Meelah's little outburst at the gym that day, I hadn't heard from her either. It's like they both just magically disappeared. I asked Malachi if he'd hurt Mark, and he came right out and told me no. But I knew my brother. Mark had been violating Malachi and 859 for the longest. It was only a matter of time before he'd be dealt with. If Malachi didn't handle him himself, it would be someone from the crew.

Before we could even make a complete turn down the block, flashes of red and blue lights scanned across our faces. Several police cars were lined up in front of the frat house, the same exact place of Hope's attack. The yard was filled with concerned faces, mostly the kids from my school. We parked just a few houses down and then crept up the street.

When we stepped on the lawn, the officers were dragging Jamel, Twan, and Levar out of the house in cuffs. Standing off to the side was a girl I recognized from my sociology class.

"Hey, girl, what's going on?" I asked.

She shook her head, holding a weary expression on her face. "They're saying they gang-raped that poor girl. You know her, the pretty RA who lived in Holland Hall." Then suddenly, she snapped her fingers like she'd suddenly remembered. "Nina, that's her name. They raped Nina Grimes."

Chapter 23

Paris—Never Say Goodbye

Fourteen hours, thirty-eight minutes, and forty-three seconds.

Forty-two seconds.

Forty-one seconds.

Forty.

"What you got going through that pretty little head of yours, Miss Paris?"

"Nothing," I whispered.

"So you just gon' lie to me?"

I sighed. "I'm not lying, Malachi, I just—"

"Then tell a nigga what's on yo' mind. 'Cause I can't do silence right now, shawty. Not tonight," he said.

Malachi was laid back with his fingers laced behind his head. His eyes closed as the ceiling fan whirled above us. Positioned in the bed beside him, I watched his black-tatted chest rise and fall, unable to get tomorrow off my mind. We'd been together daily for the past fifty-two days, yet tonight felt different. Everything, including the air I breathed, felt sad. This would be my last night with Malachi. My last time, possibly, ever seeing his face.

"I'm just a little down. That's all," I said lowly.

"Yeah," he sighed. "Me too, mama. C'mere." He opened up his arm and allowed me to snuggle against him.

"Tonight, when you hugged and kissed Mekhai, I cried," I snorted, thinking about how much of a lame I was.

"Why were you crying?"

"Because he hugged and squeezed your neck like he knew he wouldn't see you for a while. Like he didn't want to say goodbye. And then Maevyn . . ." I swallowed hard, letting my voice trail off.

"Baby girl wild, ain't she?" he muttered with a throaty chuckle.

"I can't believe Reese just came flat-out and told her you were going to prison."

"Reese is just being honest with her—"

"She's 4 friggin' years old."

"But Mae's smarter than your average 4-year-old little girl, Paris. I would've never lied to her and told her some bullshit story about me going off to college or fighting in some fucking war. That's not me. Besides, I want my kids to come visit me." I could feel him hunch his shoulders beneath me. "She would've found out anyway."

"So, what did you say to her?"

"I told her simple and plain, '*Daddy did some bad things, and now I gotta pay the price. I got to go away for a little while.*' Mae's smart; she understood that. She cried, but . . . She understood." When the water from my eyes hit Malachi's chest, he firmed his grip on my waist. "Shawty, don't tell me you crying again."

"What am I going to do without you?"

"Do what you been doing. Go to school, join that club thing—"

"It's called a sorority," I sniffled a laugh.

"Well then, that. Just have fun and live your life."

"I promise I'll wait for you. I'm gonna come see you every weekend and—"

"Shawty, you don't even know where they gon' send my ass. I could be hours away."

"It doesn't matter how far, I'll drive."

He gently nudged me off of him before sitting upright in the bed. With a stern expression, he glared down into my eyes. "I'm not asking you to come see me, Miss Paris."

"B-but you just said you wanted Maevyn and Mekhai to visit you. And I assume Reese?"

"That's different."

My vision blurred even more as emotions swelled in my throat. "You know what? Just forget it," I let out. Feeling equally hurt and confused, I hopped over his body to leave. But before both feet hit the floor, he hooked his arm around my waist. "Just let me go," I cried, so furious that my hands were shaking when he brought me down into his lap.

"Nah, sit the fuck down," he demanded. "Our last night is not gon' end like this." I could hear the frustration in his voice as the strong beat of his heart thudded against my back.

"I love you, Malachi. I've never felt like this before. I'm scared," I confessed, feeling more vulnerable than I had ever felt before. Then slowly, I craned my neck around and gazed into his eyes. I needed to see his reaction. I needed to know exactly how he felt.

"If I've never told you or haven't told you enough, I love you, Miss Paris. These past couple of months with you have been everything to a nigga. Real talk." He snorted a quick laugh through his nose. "I mean, shit, who knew a bougie white girl from Beverly Hills would end up keeping a nigga's attention for a whole year."

"Malachi," I said, slapping his arm, giggling as I sniffed back tears.

Then suddenly, Malachi's expression turned serious as he looked me square in the eyes. "You know you my heart, Miss Paris. You know that. But I can't ask you to hold me down. I can't put shackles on you too."

I could feel the hot tears as they slipped from my eyes. "So then, this is it? This is it for us?" I asked in a whisper.

He sighed. "I just wanna spend tonight showing you just how beautiful you are. How much you mean to me," he said, turning me around to face him fully.

"How do I know that any of this was ever real?" I asked, searching his eyes.

Malachi's hazel eyes slowly dropped to my lips as if under a spell. "Because of this," he said. He leaned in and pushed his soft mouth against mine, causing my eyes to flutter close. When my lips unlocked, he gently caressed my tongue with his own. His manly hand slid up my spine and cupped the back of my neck, pulling me in closer. He kissed me so passionately that every part of my body tingled with torturous pleasure. I could hardly breathe at that moment, yet I refused to stop.

Minutes flew by like seconds until, finally, he pulled back. "Take this shit off," he demanded, skimming his fingers down the sides of my breasts.

We yanked my tee shirt over my head and aggressively flung it to the floor. I was down to my underwear when I finally straddled his lap . . . Nothing but hard dick covered in sweats, flexing beneath me. His hands gripped the plumpness of my ass as we kissed and grinded our bodies together. We were both panting and clawing at each other like wild animals in heat, wanting our flesh to become one, knowing it would be the last time.

"I love you," I whispered against his lips, my fingers lightly grazing his ears.

He simply grunted in response while his hands stayed persistent, grating my hips back and forth, grinding me over him. The friction on my clit felt amazing yet agonizing all the same. I was palpitating and percolating down there like a hot volcano about to erupt. And when his mouth finally worked its way down my neck and across my collarbone, a shiver eased down my spine.

With one big swoop, Malachi lifted me in the air. Then he turned and laid me down gently on the bed. Just as he lowered his face to my sex, pulling down my panties with his teeth, I said, "Wait."

"What's wrong?"

"I think I want to . . . I want to try that with you."

Malachi's eyebrows wrinkled briefly before he finally understood. "Nah, mama. Tonight is about you."

"I know, but I've never . . ."

I had never given a man oral pleasure before, and I wanted my first time to be with him. I wanted to experience all of him before time escaped us. I could tell by his expression that he didn't fully understand that at first, but he suddenly nodded.

He lifted to his knees and hiked his chin in a backward nod. "C'mere," he said lowly, swiping his tongue across his lower lip. A hint of his gold teeth just barely peeked through.

I sat up in bed and watched as he leisurely lowered his sweats like he was putting on some kind of show. Then, like a caged animal finally being set free, his lengthy dick sprang out—wild, fast, and hard. I swallowed nervously and batted my eyes.

"Don't be scared now," he teased. He took himself in his hands and began stroking it, working the whole muscle from base to tip.

"W-what do I do?" I asked, nervously tucking a piece of hair behind my ear.

"Start by kissing it right here." He pointed to his smooth mushroom head.

With my heart hammering inside my chest, I leaned in and braced myself at his thighs. After closing my eyes, I kissed him with a curious swirl of my tongue, immediately tasting a mix of salty-sweet, like butter praline or caramel popcorn. When a low groan grumbled from his throat, I looked up into his eyes. They'd already narrowed to slits, only showing slivers of hazel. Gently, he moved his fingers through my hair, rounding them to the back of my neck. Then he brushed his thumb back and forth across my jaw.

"You don't have to do this," he said.

For some reason, that only spiked my arousal, inspiring me. I took him back inside my warm mouth, but this time, deeper, pushing well past the head. I watched his jaw drop in utter pleasure. Just as I began twisting my hand around his pub-covered base, he tightened his fingers in my hair.

"Grip it tighter," he coached. "Damn." His eyes were hooded with lust as his abdomen hallowed like he was holding in a deep breath of air.

I felt so sexually empowered, so in control for once at that moment. I loved it. I dipped over him repeatedly, each time taking it a little bit farther than before. His hand screwed just a little tighter, faster, until finally, his body clenched. I peered up at him again, noticing the strain in his eyes.

"That's enough," he said, his voice jagged and breathy like he couldn't bear it anymore.

I flattened my tongue and eagerly took him to the back of my throat once more, but this time, he pushed me off. "I said that's enough," he barked.

"But, Malachi—"

"That's not what I'm trying to do tonight, Miss Paris." He laid me back on the bed and kissed my lips. "Tonight, I need to make sure you'll always remember me. That you'll never forget how a nigga made you feel."

"I could never forget," I assured him, my head shaking from side to side as tears welled in my eyes. When his fingers peeled off my panties, I ran my hands down his chest and abs. "I love you."

"I love you too," he said.

He pushed his pants down the rest of the way and finally settled between my thighs. As his fingers brushed wispy pieces of hair out of my face, we held an unwavering gaze. "Will you at least write to me?" I asked.

"Shh," he said, gently placing his thumb over my lips. "You're beautiful, you know that? You deserve the best this world has to give. Promise me you won't ever settle for less." I nodded as my eyes blinked overtime, struggling to keep the tears at bay.

Then without warning, the tip of his dick plunged into me so deeply that I released an audible breath. My eyes squeezed shut, and all I could do was hold on to his brawny shoulders in an attempt to relax. Then he kissed me ever so sweetly that my body naturally arched toward him, welcoming him inch by inch.

"Say you'll always be mine," he said, slowly working his hips.

"I'll always be yours," I cried into his mouth, tears running from the corner of my eyes.

Little by little, Malachi's gentle strokes began to turn hard, pounding into me with so much passion that it felt like I was being both punished and pleased all at once. I swear the music of our bodies clapping together was the most powerful sound I'd ever heard. Like our own special language, one that only he and I would ever share.

"Ungh . . . ungh . . . ungh . . ." I moaned over and over again, almost in a timed rhythm that matched each of his thrusts. His body was traveling into me so deeply that I could practically feel him inside my chest. Like he was trying to get lost in me—burying himself inside my soul. As the muscles of his back worked and toiled beneath my fingers, I held on for dear life.

Then finally, he gripped my thighs and crashed into me once more. "Fuck," he growled against my ear. It seems that was all it took to send my body over the cliff. Tremors crept up from my core, and my body tightened around him. Without warning, he pulled out of me and dipped down to lick my breasts. He teased my pebbled nipples between his teeth as I moaned.

"Malachi, please," I begged. "Put it back in."

He dipped down and covered my sex with his mouth, his hands sliding under my ass as he delivered more flicks of his tongue. My hips bucked, and my thighs tightened around his face. *Oh my God.* I was ready to friggin' explode.

"Pussy tastes too muhfucking good," he mumbled against me, his head twisting from side to side like he was savoring his last meal.

When he dipped his tongue inside of me, I let out a muted scream. As my body convulsed, Malachi kept licking and sucking, lapping me up as I damn near fell off the bed. It was as if he knew that everything inside me was being released at that moment, and he wanted it all, like he was refusing to leave any parts of me as leftovers for someone else.

"Good girl," he whispered as my heaving body finally stilled.

Then he returned to his position on top of me and slid back in. With our fingers interlaced, he began tunneling in and out of me, much softer than before. It was more deliberate, like he was trying to feel every peak and valley so he'd never forget. And it wasn't long before he had me right there again, ready to blow. After a final swivel of his hips, I watched Malachi's hazel eyes turn white as they rolled to the back of his head. He spilled his soul inside of me that night as our bodies spasmed together.

"Oh my gosh, what are you guys doing here?" I asked, seeing Hope and Franki on the steps of the courthouse.

"What do you mean, what are we doing here? We weren't gonna just let you go through this alone," Hope said with a dimply smile. She looked so pretty in her tight black slacks and fitted sweater as she struggled to stand in three-inch heels. She had parted her long hair down the center, and a new pair of sleek frames rested above her dainty nose.

"Thank you, guys. Especially you, Franki. I know you've really been going through a lot." Unlike Hope, Franki wore an empty expression on her face. Her dark eyes appeared sad.

Not only was her mother terminally ill, but also after finding out that Nina had been raped, Franki grew gravely depressed. In fact, she blamed herself for the entire thing. She said that had she gone on to report her rape to the police last year, Nina would've been spared. Over the past few weeks, I'd worried about her sinking into a dark hole, but Josh assured me she'd be just fine. He said that she just needed time to heal. Hands down, he had been her saving grace, *her sanity*. He'd been taking her to church for counseling twice a week and convinced her to move back home. Franki needed her mother and father more than ever now. After being accepted by NYU, she planned to move back by the end of the semester.

"Of course, ma. You're my sister," she said, leaning in to wrap her arms around me. "Where's Malachi?"

"He went to have breakfast with the kids this morning before riding over with his mom and dad," I sighed.

I guess my face wasn't doing the best job of hiding my pain because they both reached around to rub my back.

"I promise you gon' get through this, yo. Just keep ya head up," Franki said. Unbeknownst to her, her short words of encouragement truly meant a lot. She'd been through so much this past year, yet she somehow found it in her heart to care for me. Although she'd be moving on

next semester, I knew right then that she was someone
I'd never forget.

Mr. and Mrs. Montgomery walked up with Asha as we
headed inside the courthouse. Everyone wore long faces
and had on the all-black funeral attire to match. It was an
awfully sad sight.

"Paris, there you are," Mrs. Montgomery said, coming
over to hug me. She embraced me so tightly, and for so
long, it felt like she didn't want to let me go.

"Where's Malachi?" I asked.

"He's already in the courtroom with his attorney. He
was looking for you," she said, sympathy showing in her
eyes.

In my mind, I was chastising myself for not leaving ten
minutes earlier. I'd gotten stuck in morning traffic, and
now I'd miss my last chance to see him again.

I will not cry, I will not cry, I will not cry.

I released a shaky breath as I quickly tried to get myself
together. I promised Malachi that I would be stronger
today than I had ever been before. That I wouldn't shed
another tear. After all, I wasn't the only one with a broken heart. Malachi and his children were the ones who
would suffer the most. His going to jail wouldn't be the
end of the world for me. It was just the end of our world
together . . . Two unlikely people from two extremely
different realms of society who haphazardly fell in love.

"He told me to give you this," Asha said with teary eyes.
She pecked me on my cheek and encased me in her arms.
"A hug and a kiss."

I hugged her back and nodded my head. "Thank you,"
I whispered.

She winked before discreetly slipping an envelope into
my hand. I was confused but didn't question it. I simply
tucked it into my purse and followed behind Mr. and
Mrs. Montgomery. This time, when we took our seats in

the courtroom, I didn't sit in the back row. I sat directly behind him with his family. Malachi wouldn't even turn around in his seat, but I knew he felt me because we'd grown so close.

After a few more minutes, the judge entered from the back and sat on the bench. "In the case of *Malachi Montgomery vs. the United States,* I will now pass sentencing," he said. "I agree with the jury on the verdict of guilt for the criminal charge of aiding and abetting. For soliciting another person to commit voluntary manslaughter, a class D felony, I hereby sentence Malachi Montgomery to thirty-eight months in jail. Court is adjourned."

He banged his gavel, and that was it. It was over. No crying, no hollering, no big outbursts in the court. Just an eerie silence that covered the room. My stomach churned from the reality of it all. Not even Hope and Franki's hands on my shoulders from behind could comfort me. Suddenly, Malachi stood from his chair and turned to shake his attorney's hand. While his lawyer stood with slumped shoulders, Malachi's were pulled back, showing he was still strong. He was making a statement, telling everyone in the courtroom that when everything was said and done, he would be okay.

When the bailiff came over to take him away, he finally turned around to face us. Tears lingered in my eyes, but I didn't let them fall.

He looked at me and raised his chin. "Be good," he mouthed.

"Always."

He put two fingers over his lips and blew a kiss to his mother just before the bailiff cuffed his wrists. I sat there numb, watching as they led him away until, finally, he disappeared.

Epilogue

Hope

Present day. Three years and two months later . . .

"You ready?" Meeko asked from the door.

I was admiring myself in the long mirror, noticing how the short, black, sequined dress I wore clung to my petite frame. Since giving birth to Matthew, I now have a few more curves. My hips have expanded from my waist, and my breasts sit up like mini-globes stuck to my chest. My eyes traveled down to my legs and landed on my feet. The black, four-inch heels have a way of making my calves appear strong. Pleased with my appearance, I smiled and flipped my long, straightened hair back off my shoulders.

"Damn, shorty, you look good," he said, raking his eyes over me.

I felt an instant rush of heat spread throughout my cheeks. It's odd that he still can make me blush after all this time. "Thanks," I beamed.

As I looked him over, I noticed he was wearing all black too. The only difference is that he has a platinum chain gleaming around his neck and small diamonds in his ears. On his wrist sat a diamond-embezzled watch. His hair was freshly cut but not too low. He knew I loved to see his waves. He looks so delicious that I have to swallow before I speak.

"You too, babe. You look . . . amazing," I said.

When we walked into the living room, Aunt Marlene was putting together a puzzle with Matthew on the floor. He just turned 3 a few months ago and has been more than a handful lately. Thank God for Aunt Marlene. She's the main reason I could finish my degree on time after taking an entire semester off. See, on those late evenings when Meeko was held up in the streets, she would keep Matthew while I went to school—night classes. I am forever indebted to her.

As soon as Matthew noticed me, his entire face lit up. He quickly jumped to his feet. "Mommy, Mommy. You so pretty, Mommy," he said. He came over and hugged my legs. I leaned down and swept my hand across the thick, curly bush on his head. Meeko still isn't ready to cut his hair, and I don't push the issue because it makes Matthew appear more babylike in my eyes. Secretly, I don't want him to grow up.

"Aw, thank you, Matthew." I looked over at Aunt Marlene, whose eyes also observed my attire.

"You look sharp. Both of y'all," she said, noticing Meeko behind me. "I see you don't wear your glasses no more."

"Sometimes I do, but I'm wearing my contacts tonight."

"And where are y'all going again?"

"A friend of ours is having a welcome home party," I told her.

Meeko picked up Matthew and tossed him into the air, causing him to let out a series of giggles. "You ready, man? You gon' be good at the party?" he asked, kissing him on the forehead.

"I'm a good boy, Daddy." Matthew smiled, showcasing his deep dimples.

"Yeah, a'ight, I hear you, man," Meeko said as if he didn't believe him.

Aunt Marlene and I laughed because "good" wouldn't be the best word to describe Matthew. Yes, he's adorable and tremendously sweet, but he's also wild as ever. He has yet to master the skill of listening and thinks he can just do whatever he wants.

On our drive over, Meeko held my hand while Matthew slept peacefully in the back. "How was your day at work?" he asked.

"It was long. I don't think Alicia's getting fed at home again," I say, referring to one of my kindergarten students.

"So, what you gon' do? Call CPS or go there by yourself again?" I know this is a trick question because the last time Alicia came to school hungry, I took a bag of groceries to her home. She lives in the very back of the Smith Housing Projects, and I naively went there at night. Her mother cussed me out, and I almost got robbed on my way back to the car.

I sighed. "I'm gonna call CPS this time."

"Yeah, you better," he warned before kissing the back of my hand.

"Well, how was your day?" I changed the subject.

"Long as fuck," he griped. "The contractor and his guys were late getting over to the house. We lost half a damn day."

After graduating with his degree in business, Meeko began flipping houses with the money he'd saved. He swore he was no longer in the streets, but it's hard to believe some days due to his demanding schedule. Either way, he doesn't work a typical nine-to-five job. At 24 years old, he's self-employed and makes enough money for me to quit my teaching job. However, because we're not married, I refuse. Although he bought us a four-bedroom home in Irving Park last year, and all our debt is paid, I still work. He also begs me to give him another child, yet he hasn't proposed. Currently, these are our only issues as a couple. I love him with all my heart. I'm sure he's my soul mate.

Deddy has completely come around as well. He comes to visit at least four times a year, and, in turn, we take an annual flight out to Alto for his birthday. Meeko and Deddy have actually become quite close. They talk on the phone at least once weekly and share business information. The relationship is odd, considering their past, but I appreciate the sense of peace. I am no longer the monkey in the middle.

"Wow," I said in awe as we pulled into the circular driveway. The Lake Higgins home sitting before my eyes is massive. It's one of the largest I've ever seen—outside of TV. It appears that every light in the house is on, adding to its grandeur, and I can hear music thumping from all the way outside.

"Damn, they doing it big," Meeko said. "You ready?"

"Ready."

Meeko grabbed Matthew from the backseat, and he had to carry him in his arms because he was still asleep. Together, Meeko and I walk up to the house, holding hands.

Franki

"Oh my God, look at her," I said, watching Hope as she entered the house.

She looked like a petite-size model with her flawless dark brown skin. Her long hair was straightened, and her figure was now about a size six. She even wore makeup, which surprised me. The last time I saw her was last year's homecoming, and she was in chill mode: jeans, an Aggie pride tee shirt, and a messy bun. However, tonight, she looked sexy. I stood from sitting in Josh's lap and squeezed through the crowd to go over and greet her.

"Franki," she squealed, wrapping her arms around me. Although we live miles apart, it feels like we haven't missed a beat. I guess it's the fact that we talk on the phone almost daily. I know all the ins and outs of her relationship with Meeko, and she knows mine. I know the exact day Matthew took his first steps and can remember precisely how much he weighed at his last appointment. I know all about her kids at school and even Keisha's new boyfriend, Mookie. And because she's held to secrecy, Meeko still doesn't know that his sister is dating one of his longtime friends.

"You look good, girl. What, you trying to find a man tonight?" I teased.

"Don't get fucked up in here tonight. Med school," Meeko said, coming from behind her with Matthew in his arms.

"Yeah, a'ight," I said, fake punching him in the gut before hugging him.

Over the years, Meeko and I have gotten to be pretty cool too. We all spent Hope's birthday together last year and New Year's Eve the year before that. Even though Hope doesn't fully believe it, I know he's still in the streets. I don't bother to tell her this because I don't want to upset her. I just continue praying for his safety and that he'll get out of the game soon.

"When did you guys get here?" Hope asked.

"Our flight landed this afternoon, and we checked into the hotel at three."

"I told you that you guys coulda just stayed with us," she whined.

"I know, but . . ." I shrugged. I didn't want to come right out and tell her that Josh's nightly dick-downs cause me to scream literally, and I refuse to let our passion disrupt her home.

"Where my boy at?" Meeko asked, referring to Josh.

"He's over there." I pointed, seeing him sit across the room with his legs cocked wide. Typically, Josh dresses in button-up shirts, sweaters, and suits, but today, he's wearing blue jeans and Tims, looking "oh so" New York. I love it. I love him. "Come on," I said, leading the way.

Before we could get halfway across the room, Mrs. Montgomery came over and took a sleeping Matthew out of Meeko's arms. She hugged us and made small talk before whisking him away. As the four of us continued to slide through the sea of people standing in the front room, I noticed that Meeko knew more of them than I did. He stopped and slapped hands with several guys along the way. There's an odd mix in the house. Half I recognize from A&T and most were now Greek. The other half looked hood.

"What up, yo?" Meeko said, slapping hands with Josh before bringing him in for a brotherly hug. After Josh hugged Hope, the four of us entered the kitchen to get drinks. I poured Hope and me some premade margaritas while Josh and Meeko grabbed a beer. Since Paris was nowhere to be found, we sat in the living room area to catch up while we waited.

"Did I tell you that I was thinking about returning to school to become a principal?" Hope turned to me and asked.

I saw Meeko's eyes balloon right before he clenched his jaw. "Shorty, don't start that shit tonight, a'ight? We having a good time," he said.

"What?" She turned to him and asked. "I *am* thinking about going back to school." I knew Meeko wanted to say more, but for the sake of not making a scene, he simply shook his head and took a swig of his beer. Hope then turned around to me and rolled her eyes. They are clearly having some issues, but their love is evident. It's in the way he holds her hand and how she gazes into his eyes . . . The way they waltzed through the door, looking like the perfect little family. "So, how much longer do you have in school?" she asked.

"Well, since this is my first year of med school, I have at least seven more years to go," I sighed. "Josh has just one more year to go before he can sit for the bar. I'm jealous."

Josh and I both attended NYU and shared an apartment in the village. Of course, his parents were disappointed when they found out we were shacking up. But when they found out we'd already eloped over two summers ago, right after my mother passed, they were downright pissed. Thankfully, Mrs. McDuffey got over it quickly and became somewhat of a surrogate mother to me. And to make it up to Pastor McDuffey, I attend service at his church almost every Sunday. So far, things are working out.

My mother fought a good fight—almost two years, but in the end, cancer prevailed. I was thankful the prison let my father out to attend her funeral. He and I both bawled the entire service. She was my biggest supporter, my loudest cheerleader, and now, she was gone. For the first six months after she died, I felt like I couldn't breathe. Like my air supply had been cut in half. But slowly, I'm beginning to heal, taking it one day at a time. I'll never forget her, though. I think about her daily, but rather than dwell on the fact that she's no longer here, I cherish our memories.

As a result of everything, I now get a letter from my father once a week, and I visit him in Rikers twice a month. He and I have grown close again and have already made plans for when he gets out next spring. I have completely forgiven him—more for my own good than his.

"Is Asha coming?" I asked. I haven't seen her since the last homecoming, but she and I keep in touch like the others.

"No, she's still in London doing her internship, remember?" Hope replied. I snapped my fingers and nodded, indicating that I had forgotten. I thought she was coming back this week but then quickly recalled her internship with *Vogue* magazine which will last until the end of next month.

After Quick got his first major fight last year, he moved out to Vegas with his brother and sister. He and Asha tried the long-distance thing for a while, but eventually, they broke up. She was crushed and cried almost every day straight for a week. However, I will say that his coming into Asha's life at the time he did changed her life forever. He aided her in becoming a better person, and if nothing more, I know she's grateful for that.

Suddenly, the music stopped, and I heard a clinking noise. Josh tapped me on my thigh and pointed his finger up. When my eyes followed, I saw Paris standing at the top of the staircase with a champagne flute in her hand. She looked amazing in a pink bandage dress and silver heels. Her curvy figure was Instagram-worthy, and her hair was now cut into a long bob. She was gorgeous.

Paris

"I'd just like to thank everyone for coming," I said, looking out into the small crowd. Although my cheeks hurt, I can't seem to remove the smile on my face. I was just that overjoyed.

I instantly spotted Heather, my BFF from Cali, standing in the corner with her new boyfriend, Sean. Nya, Tee Tee, and Bull all stood at the bottom of the staircase while my sorors were scattered throughout the room. Then suddenly, Franki's beautiful head full of shiny black curls caught my eye. She sat beside Josh in the formal living room with Hope and Meeko across from them. I felt my smile stretching even wider at the sight of them. Although I saw Hope every week, I hadn't seen my girl Franki in quite some time.

As I began to speak, I felt Malachi's strong arms wrap around me from behind. Everyone was cheering so loud that I could barely hear the words he whispered into my ear.

"Send all these muh'fuckas home so I can get in that again," he said.

The vibration of his voice against my ear instantly caused me to get wet. But I shook it off and playfully smacked him on the arm. "Not yet," I said. Then I looked back out into the crowd and smiled. "I've waited exactly 1,165 days for this exact moment, guys. To celebrate my king, my love, finally coming home. Let's make a toast . . ." I said, raising my glass. "To Malachi." Clinks, whistles, and applauses immediately filled the room.

With our hands intertwined, Malachi and I walked down the steps like celebrities. Since the very beginning, Malachi has always been treated like royalty. Women would flirt and drool over him, while men showed fear or respect. But tonight, as his queen, it seemed I was getting just as much love. Everyone wanted to hug both of us as we inched toward the crowd. Everyone kept telling him how much he'd been missed while pointing out that I'd "held it down." Just as I started to make my way over to Franki and Paris, Heather rushed me with a hug.

"Oh. My. God," she loudly squealed in my ear as I hugged her back. "He looks like the friggin' Rock."

It was obvious that she was referring to Malachi, whose arms were twice the size as they were before. His neck was thick and corded like the trunk of a tree, and his abs were rock-hard. I'm in love with his new body and have enjoyed every inch since eight o'clock last night. Although I'm strutting like Beyoncé in these heels, my thighs and everything in between are sore. And by how his hand was gripping my ass, I doubt I'll get relief anytime soon. Just the thought of him delivering my body more pleasurable pain thrilled me.

"How you doin', Heather?" he asked her, reaching for a hug.

She closed her eyes when she embraced him and took a noticeable whiff of his scent. "Don't make me smack you, ho," I whisper in her ear.

"What?" she giggled, then shifted her attention back to Malachi. "I'm doing good. Just super happy you're home. My bestie has really been missing you," she said.

He peered down at me with those hazel eyes of his and smiled right before kissing me on the lips. We continued through the crowd, stopping to talk to Bull, Nya, and Tee Tee. We both promised them a game of spades before the party ended. By the time we made it over to the other side of the room, I was exhausted from talking, hugging, and smiling in everyone's faces. Hope and Franki stood and came to give me a group hug while Malachi slapped hands with the guys. I took a step back to look them over. While Hope was her usual beautiful self—smooth, dark brown skin and dainty facial features surrounded by long, jet-black hair, I was more intrigued by Franki's appearance. I guess it's because, unlike Hope, I don't see her very often.

Of course, I follow her on Instagram, Snapchat, and Facebook, but seeing her in person is different. Her curly hair was a few inches longer, framing her pretty brown face, and her black jumpsuit showed off a body that was even firmer than it was in our freshman year. "You bitch. You've been working out, haven't you?" I asked her, feigning jealousy.

Franki laughed and pointed her thumb back at Josh. "That's him. He gets me up every morning at five to work out." Josh slipped his hands into the pockets of his jeans and shrugged. The corners of his lips curled up into a smile. Although he's not real big like Malachi, I could tell he's been working out too. His muscles were a bit leaner, like a point guard's.

As Franki continued to talk with her hands, I noticed the one-and-a-half-carat diamond ring on her finger. While she blabbed about how hard med school was and gave excuses about why I hadn't heard from her in over two weeks, Josh stared at her the entire time. I recognized the gaze in his eyes because it was the exact same way Malachi looked at me. He was head over heels in love with his wife. She was his everything.

"This house is dope, yo," she said, looking around. "How long you been in here?"

I explained to her that until a week ago, I was still living in the four-bedroom house Malachi purchased for us that summer. Yes, he bought the property from the owner and had us believe he just paid the rent. Little did I know, my name was also on the deed. It was one of the things Asha handed me in that envelope that day. Information on how to access some of his money was also in there. He did all this, thinking he'd never see me again. With that money, I started my online boutique. It took time, but eventually, it turned a profit. It was so successful that I ended up opening three shops—one in Greensboro and two in Charlotte. I even have a few celebrity clients that I style.

With Malachi's money and a little of my own, I had this house built from the ground up. It took two years to complete, but it seemed I'd time it perfectly. It was finished by the time Malachi came home. It was 8,000 square feet, with seven bedrooms, eight baths, a finished basement, a theatre room, an in-ground pool, and basketball and tennis courts, all on a five-acre lot in Lake Higgins. It's better than anything I could ever dream of.

Suddenly, I felt someone tugging on my arm. I turned around and saw my sorority sisters, Courtney and Ceira, standing behind me. They both wore the same shade of pink and based on the bounce in their shoulders and the wiggle in their hips, I knew they wanted me to dance. I smiled when I heard the DJ begin to play our song, "Set It Off." I immediately got in line, and we started to stroll. My shoulders were shimmying, and my feet were stepping in sync as we danced through the crowd, flinging our hair and "skee-weeing" to the beat. When I heard Nya laughing at me, telling me that I still can't dance worth shit, I gave her my middle finger but kept right on stepping along.

The next thing I knew, the DJ switched the music, and the rest of the Greeks joined in. They began calling and strolling too. I could tell Malachi's patience was wearing thin with all this when he pulled me out of line. "Where the kids at?" he asked.

"Downstairs with your mom and Aunt Saavy," I said.

Meeko was right behind him. "Matt's down there too, yo. Let's go check on 'em," he said.

Malachi didn't even respond. Instead, he headed right for the basement. Since he's been released from prison, he hasn't wanted to be separated from the kids. Reluctantly, Reese agreed that we could keep Maevyn and Mekhai for the next three weeks. Over the past few years, Malachi somehow convinced her to let me spend time with them. Although I am still young at 22, I love them as my own. Maevyn's my mini-me, while Mekhai's my little prince.

Of course, it wouldn't be right if Reese and I didn't have our fair share of spats over the years. At first, we argued over silly stuff, like Mae's hair or when I was supposed to bring them home. But now, we're somewhat cool. Since Mae kept me in the loop, I attributed Reese's improved attitude to her new boyfriend, Cliff.

The four of us headed into the basement, leaving Franki and Josh upstairs. Josh was stepping with his frat brothers while Franki sat back enjoying the show. As we descended the stairs, we could feel an instant change of pace. It was much cooler and quieter down here. Mr. Montgomery was playing pool with his brothers while Mrs. Iris and Malachi's aunt Saavy sat with the kids.

Matthew immediately rushed over to Meeko, allowing him to scoop him up in his arms. Matthew kicked and squirmed when Meeko smothered his face with kisses and tickled his sides. His little giggle was so contagious that we all fell out laughing, including the other kids.

"Prince," Malachi called out.

Our son, Prince, ignored his father's voice and continued to pry the tablet out of Mekhai's hands. When he wouldn't let go of it, Prince began to whine. "What you crying for, mane? You can't get everything you want. Yo' momma don spoiled you, didn't she?" Malachi asked, lifting him in the air.

"I haven't spoiled him," I lied. I've never spanked Prince and try my hardest to give him anything and everything he wants. My mother said I've been overcompensating for Malachi's absence.

Speaking of my mother, she and I are now on good terms. Once she found out that I was pregnant, she gave me full access to my trust. She was disappointed at first but quickly got excited about the arrival of her first grandchild. In fact, she and Mrs. Iris were the only ones in the delivery room with me that June when I gave birth. Prince Myron Montgomery was an even seven pounds. He has bright hazel eyes and a head full of silky brown hair. At 2 years old, he looks so much like Maevyn and Mekhai that it's ridiculous.

As I sat there and watched Malachi rock our little guy to sleep, I laughed at how funny life is. Here, I thought I'd never see the love of my life again. Yet, God blessed me with his child. Malachi wouldn't even allow me to visit him at first, but then I got Asha to tell him that I was pregnant. I cried when we finally met face-to-face after four months of being apart. The craziest part of it all was that he cried too. Malachi, the thug—Mr. 859 himself—actually cried. Not boohooed, of course, but noticeable tears were in his eyes. He told me how much he loved me and asked that I keep his child. Of course, I would have never told him no. Prince was an extension of him, something I could have never given up.

"Miss Paris, I'm tired," Malachi said from the couch. Prince lay asleep in his arms. "Kick all these niggas out so I can lay up under you like I want. I just wanna be with you and the kids. Fire up a blunt, fuck, and go to sleep."

"Malachi," his mother hissed as I covered up my face.

"My bad, Ma. My bad."

I laughed. "Okay. I'll go up and tell everyone that the party's over."

"And, Meeko, I'ma get up with you this week, mane," Malachi said, reaching out for Meeko to slap his hand. "We gotta talk." Hope's eyes cut over to Meeko suspiciously, but she didn't utter a word.

After clearing the house, Franki and Hope were the last ones to leave. We hugged and promised to hang out before Franki returned to New York in three more days. When I got back inside the house, I stepped out of my heels and walked up the stairs. Everything was quiet and clean, thanks to Mrs. Iris and Aunt Saavy. When I reached my room, Malachi was on the balcony smoking a blunt. I sat in his lap and took it out of his hand.

"The kids all in bed?" I asked, taking a deep pull. I let my head drop back on his shoulder before allowing the smoke to emit from my lips.

"They're all knocked out."

"Good."

A few moments of silence lingered before he wrapped his arms around my waist and said, "Thank you, Miss Paris."

Confused, I craned my neck around to look him in the eyes. "For what? The party?"

He shook his head. "Nah, mama. For loving me."

At that exact moment, my heart felt overwhelmed with joy, and I instantly knew that out of anywhere in this world I could be, I was in the exact right place. That my attending NC A&T State University, a Historically Black University, was not just some coincidence. It was destiny. The beautiful people I've met, the things I've learned, and the culture I wouldn't have otherwise known are all destiny.

"Thank you, Malachi," I said softly. "Thank you for loving me too."

Dear Readers,

Thank you so much for your patience with this book. The amount of support I received for *Heartbreak U* was so abundant that I wanted to ensure my all went into this finale. I know most of my stories typically end with pregnancies, weddings, and honeymoons, but these characters took a totally different path. Next year, please anticipate individual, interrelated stories from these young ladies where they'll continue their journey. In addition to that, please also be on the lookout for the paperback edition of my series Loving a Borrego Brother. Part 2 will be an extended version compared to the original e-book, where more has been added to the narrative.

I would also like to personally thank Desiree Granger and The Cafeteria Book Club, Genesis Woods and Shantaé and the Literary Rejects Book Club, Nako and Nako's Reading Group, SIRR (Sisters into Reading and Reviewing), The Messiah Wives, as well as Dama Cargle and The Takeover Book Club for their continued support of *Heartbreak U*. Each and every one of you have made writing this finale fun.

To my editor Miss Jay from Jaypen Literary, thanks for always fitting me in and giving me constructive feedback. And to my Miss Tina V., the one that gives every book of mine a thorough examination before it's finally released, I appreciate you. Your proofreading skills are incredible, and I am so grateful that I found you.

As always, thanks to each and every one of you for your continuous love and support.

~Johnni